Praise for Lorrie Thomson's Novels

What's Left

"*What's Left Behind* is an emotionall
hope, and happiness."

—Amy Sue Nathan, autho

"A beautifully written tale of love, loss, and healing . . . that will fuel lively book club discussion!"

—Barbara Claypole White, award-winning author of *The In-Between Hour*

"A phenomenal testament of motherhood at its rawest, most beautiful core. *What's Left Behind* is a tale of love, sacrifice, and family that stayed with me long after the last page was turned."

—Sharla Lovelace, award-winning author of *The Reason Is You*

"Empowering and inspiring."

—*RT Book Reviews*

Equilibrium

"Thomson's first novel treats issues of loss, mental illness, adolescence, and sexuality with great openness and sensitivity. Fans of Kristin Hannah and Holly Chamberlin will similarly appreciate this hopeful, uplifting story about family, friendships, and a second chance at love."

—*Booklist*

"An emotional, complex, and deeply satisfying novel about the power of hope, love, and family. I couldn't put it down!"

—Lisa Verge Higgins

"Riveting . . . Very uplifting . . . Romantic, yet heartbreaking all the way through, this novel is a beautiful take on starting over in life."

—*RT Book Reviews*

"Tender, heartbreaking, and beautifully realistic. Fans of Anita Shreve will be riveted by this intense and compassionate story."

—Hank Phillippi Ryan

"One beautifully written novel . . . A lovely, heartfelt read that I plan on revisiting soon."—Heroes and Heartbreakers

Books by Lorrie Thomson

Equilibrium

What's Left Behind

A Measure of Happiness

Published by Kensington Publishing Corp.

A Measure *of* Happiness

LORRIE THOMSON

KENSINGTON BOOKS
www.kensingtonbooks.com

This book is a work of fiction. Names, characters, places, and incidents either are products of the author's imagination or are used fictitiously. Any resemblance to actual persons, living or dead, events, or locales is entirely coincidental.

KENSINGTON BOOKS are published by

Kensington Publishing Corp.
119 West 40th Street
New York, NY 10018

All Kensington titles, imprints, and distributed lines are available at special quantity discounts for bulk purchases for sales promotion, premiums, fund-raising, educational, or institutional use.

Special book excerpts or customized printings can also be created to fit specific needs. For details, write or phone the office of the Kensington Sales Manager: Kensington Publishing Corp., 119 West 40th Street, New York, NY 10018. Attn. Sales Department. Phone: 1-800-221-2647.

eISBN-13: 978-0-7582-9333-6
eISBN-10: 0-7582-9333-X
First Kensington Electronic Edition: September 2015

ISBN-13: 978-0-7582-9332-9
ISBN-10: 0-7582-9332-1
First Kensington Trade Paperback Printing: September 2015

10 9 8 7 6 5 4 3 2 1

Printed in the United States of America

For my brave niece, Rebecca Thomson

CHAPTER 1

The end of the world came with a sound track.

At four o'clock in the morning, Katherine Lamontagne drove through the darkened streets of Hidden Harbor, Maine, and angled into her spot in front of Lamontagne's Bakery, her pride and joy. She filled her lungs with the familiar sweet brine of the ocean, the scent of hard-earned serenity.

The first smoky hint of changing leaves singed the air. Along Ocean Boulevard, the summer's maple leaves gave way to reveal underlying bursts of warm gold and orange, evidencing the vacation town's reluctant slide into autumn. On the radio, the DJ's voice droned on about the upcoming Y2K and the associated crash of every single computer in the country, as though no one had thought to prepare for a future beyond 1999. In case anyone missed the DJ's dire hyperbole, REM's "It's the End of the World as We Know It (and I Feel Fine)" intoned in the background, driving home the point.

Katherine cut the engine, but the song still hummed through her brain like an auditory afterimage of doom. She leaned across the passenger seat and rolled up the window, savoring the stretch, the elongation of her spine. She flexed her fingers. Then she fashioned her long, dark hair into a work-ready chignon, slid her purse onto her shoulder, and stepped into the darkness.

When she passed beneath the streetlight's soft umbrella of light, an involuntary shiver contracted her shoulders, raising tiny hairs on the back of her neck. She furrowed her brow and glanced in either direction down the empty sidewalk. Silly-me grin on her face, she gave her head a clearing shake and turned her key in the lock. Above Lamontagne's door, the bell jingled its welcome. One hand clasping the door handle, she angled inside the bakery and switched on the lights.

She blinked once, twice. But her sight refused to clear.

Her pinewood tables and chairs lay on their sides, as though an early autumn storm had gathered strength at sea and unleashed its torrent across her café. Beneath the unforgiving lights, shards of jagged glass and hills of sugar glistened and glowed—all that remained of her sugar dispensers. Scattered napkins ringed the floor in front of the coffee station. Gray sneaker tread footprints stomped across their white perfection. Swirls and jabs of spray paint blackened her pale-blue walls and snaked across one of her canary-yellow booth seats, the design as chaotic as her childhood. Trick of memory, in her smoke-free bread- and pastry-redolent café, her father's stale cigarette smoke narrowed her breathing passages. The corners of her eyes stung.

Who would do this to her? Why? What had she done wrong?

Katherine's hand shook the door. The jingle bell dinged, like the wail of a burglar alarm. She pried her fingers from the door handle and wrestled the key from the lock.

For twenty-five years, she'd awoken the citizens of Hidden Harbor with their first cups of freshly brewed coffee. She'd nourished them with daily breads. She'd sweetened their birthdays, anniversaries, weddings, and graduations with made-to-order cakes. Golden yellow or French vanilla? German chocolate or devil's food? Their preferences she knew by heart. Their life events marked her calendar. Their voices she recognized on the phone. Everything in her adult life, good and bad, had started at this bakery. Everything she'd loved and lost. Everything she still hoped to recover.

Celeste.

What if she'd come in early again, determined to wow Katherine with a new recipe? What if Celeste had interrupted the vandal? What if the intruder had found her first? Katherine tried taking a breath, but the inhalation caught in her throat. And an off-beat pulse hammered from within her gut.

"Celeste!" Katherine's voice echoed in her ears half a second before rational thought returned. Dear, sweet, infuriating Celeste had left her employ weeks ago, gone to culinary school in New York to rid herself of Hidden Harbor, Lamontagne's, and Katherine.

Thank God Celeste wasn't here to witness this disaster. Then why did Katherine wish she were?

Don't panic, don't panic, don't panic.

Exactly what you told yourself when you were clearly panicking.

Katherine chewed the inside of her cheek. Her ragged breath sounded in her ears. She tiptoed through the debris. Glass crunched beneath her clogs and ground into the treads. Balled-up napkins covered the coffee station counter, as though a child had pitched a cookie tantrum. Strawberry goo smeared across her checkout counter. A handful of PB&J cookies lay in a crumpled heap, sans the jelly. The trays of leftover black-and-white, M&M, and sugar cookies were empty.

She didn't give a damn about the pastries.

The register sat open and empty, exactly as she'd left it at closing time. Every night, she counted out $150 for her register bag. Profits too late for a bank run went into a larger zipped pouch. She secured both bags in the back in her combination safe.

She didn't give a damn about the money.

In the kitchen, Katherine hit the light switch. The overhead fluorescents flickered to life, illuminating her clean work-tables, her shining stainless steel sinks. Katherine nodded at her ancient Blodgett oven, the kitchen's workhorse. While waiting for her bread dough to rise, she could bake forty-eight pies in the faithful machine, a dozen per rack. Oven trouble meant bakery trouble.

At the moment, Katherine didn't give a damn about the Blodgett.

Katherine tiptoed across her clean floor and into her stock-room. Proof boxes. Rolling ladder and wheeled bins of flour, oats, nuts, and dried fruit. The top shelf displayed a row of mason jars filled with specialty flours. The chest freezer hummed against the left-hand wall. On the right, a paisley skirt hung beneath a narrow marble work counter.

Katherine dropped to her knees and lifted the skirt.

The combination safe was locked. Crazy, irrational, but she had to know for sure. Her palms pulsed with perspiration, and her fingers slid on the wheel. She spun the lock to the right, missed the first number, took a steadying breath, and began anew. Three tries later, the dead bolts gave and she swung the door on its hinges. She pushed aside the register bag, heavy with change. Her earnings pouch? Okay, she cared a little. She checked the bills against the tally sheet. All there. The stack of singles she kept separate from the two bags would've done little to tip a scale, but they weighed heavy on her heart.

At the far end of the safe, a plain white dishcloth secreted her prized possessions. She held the cloth to her nose, inhaled. Her fingers twitched, her cheeks heated, her heart hurt. Time hadn't dulled the power of memory.

"I'm sorry," she said, the same apology she'd offered her ex-husband when she'd failed to provide him with a good-enough reason for wanting a divorce. The empty words that failed to salve Celeste's rage. The brokenhearted send-off for the one person incapable of questioning Katherine's motives.

She unfolded the dishcloth and ran her fingers across the hospital bracelets she kept as reminders, touchstones of all she'd lost.

Not for the first time, Celeste Barnes's mind-body connection failed, a betrayal she took personally.

Celeste sneaked back to her own dorm, washed up in the bathroom, peeled off last night's jeans, and changed into her chef whites. She race-walked across the New York campus of Culinary America, hoping against hope that movement and the nip of autumn air would revive her fogged-in memory. Tuesday's first class, Fillings and Icing, didn't start for another half hour, but Matt had headed out from his dorm room while she was still in his bed, and she was determined to chase him down. She didn't want to make a big deal about last night. But they needed to talk.

High-noon glare highlighted the maple and oak leaves' past peak colors. Last week's gold had turned to brown mustard. Tangerine-orange had, seemingly overnight, darkened to rust. Sun slanted off the redbrick buildings and jabbed a finger into the headache pulsing behind her left brow bone. When she'd first arrived on campus two months ago, she'd worried she'd stand out, starting a degree at twenty-two instead of eighteen. But in the world of baking and pastry arts, she needn't have worried about her age.

Some students had come here straight from high school. Others, like her and Matt, had taken a more circuitous path to pursue their life's dream. She'd survived six years as an assistant baker at Lamontagne's. Six years when she'd worked her ass off to try to please she who could not be pleased. Celeste was better off without her. Culinary America was the best thing that had ever happened to her.

Celeste should really call Katherine to tell her so.

Matt had come from a background in food styling, creating

and photographing treats that delighted the eye but not the palate. Want to make a heavy cake into a lightweight? Create a false bottom. He taught Celeste that the secret to making no-melt ice cream was scooping a well-crafted mixture of frosting and powdered sugar. Not ice cream at all but a clever, convincing imposter. According to Matt, food photography was all about lighting, framing, and exposure.

They both fought to prove their worth. Celeste because she'd never gone to college, never ventured from her tiny hometown, the job she'd worked since high school. Matt was an even easier student target. You had to try that much harder to prove yourself real when your expertise came from faking it.

They commiserated about the other students. Their petty rivalries. Their overblown egos. Their backstabbing backroom wagers. A sidelong glance in Matt's direction or a hand signal under the table conveyed their wordless language. Matt was like a brother to her. The white cotton of her pants swished between her legs, roughing her thighs, and, shit, she was sore.

What the hell had happened?

A chill ran up Celeste's sleeves, the cotton of her chef whites lousy defense against the changing winds. She hunched her shoulders, blew out a breath, and considered taking a nap on a tree-side wrought-iron bench. She really needed a shower.

Less than an hour ago, she'd awoken in Matt's shade-darkened dorm room, the ghost of a forgotten dream slipping from her consciousness as soon as she'd opened her eyes. Matt was sitting in the chair by the window, as though waiting for her to wake up. His forearms leaned on his jostling thighs, and he waved a pencil before him, keeping time to a silent beat. Two hours before their first class, his shoulder-length brown hair was pulled back in a ponytail and he was a vision in chef whites.

She was completely naked.

"What happened?" she'd asked him, hastily covering herself with his thin sheet, as though she were an actress in a romantic comedy, as though she hadn't known the meaning behind the pinched ache between her legs, the strain of an inner thigh stretch. The musty mushroom smell coming from his bedside trash can.

"You're a lightweight, Celeste," Matt had said, regret narrowing his features. "And I'm not much better."

No, she wasn't.

She hadn't been that out of it, had she? She hadn't had that much to drink. She hadn't intended to boink Matt. Her good buddy. Her platonic friend. She'd never felt any attraction toward him, no overblown stirring of the nether regions when she'd caught his wrist to halt him from overmixing a batter, no do-me-now lust when he'd lean close to show her how to frame a stylized puff pastry within her camera's lens. But it had been a long time since she'd had sex. And even though Matt had never inspired her specific lust, she'd admit to a general persistent stirring. Even though her memory refused to surface, she understood the gist of the deed, if none of the details.

Might as well yank up her big-girl panties.

Celeste hoisted her backpack on her shoulder, ducked into the side door of Barnstead Hall, and clomped up the metal stairs leading to the shiny, bright practice kitchen. The front entrance brought you past an ornate reception area with glass and mirrors, and the largest of several demonstration kitchens. The place where they entertained famous chefs, bowed down before their superior white pant legs. But she preferred the older side of the building, the winding hallways, a smaller building within a mammoth structure. You could take the girl out of the small town—

The foreign tone of Matt's voice halted her in the shadowed hallway, seconds before the words hit her. "*Oh, yeah.* She needed it bad, and I was glad to give it to her."

Male laugher carried into the hallway. A deep and guttural whoop echoed off the top-of-the-line stainless steel appliances.

A spoon banged against a stainless steel bowl. Celeste's eyes blinked with every hollow clang. Her hairline prickled with perspiration.

"Details, brother. We need details." Drake's voice now. Last night's party host was the Neanderthal who'd asked her out on the first day of class by telling her she needed to get laid. The joker she and *her* brother Matt had dissed in private, tolerated in class.

The Matt she knew had two sisters he adored. He respected women in general and Celeste in specific. The Matt—

"Nice body," Matt said.

"Tell us something we don't know," Drake said, his voice taking on an angry edge.

"Don't you worry. I'll give you proof," Matt said.

Celeste shook her head. Her hand shook the strap of her pack. The cotton of her chef whites clung to her underarms. She flattened herself against the wall, willed herself to disappear. Hoped against hope she'd somehow misunderstood what she'd heard. The Matt she knew—

"She's got the sweetest birthmark, right about there," Matt said, referring to a heart-shaped mole on a part of Celeste's body she wouldn't have been able to examine unless she'd been standing naked in a house of mirrors and double-jointed.

Please. God. Stop.

"She was an animal. Woke me up twice for more . . . a little of this. A lot of that."

"Three times?" A guy's voice sounded high-pitched, like a grade school boy telling a dirty joke.

Celeste was the joke.

Celeste slapped her hands over her mouth. Bile pressed the back of her throat and her stomach cramped, like the first time she'd gone down on her boyfriend, Justin, in high school. Like the first time she'd discovered he'd, post-breakup, spread rumors about her appetite for sex. Like every single tortuous day she'd endured snide looks from girls, wolf calls and obscene tongue-in-cheek pantomimes from boys.

Celeste imagined walking into the kitchen with her head held high. They were grown-ups, weren't they? Equals, consenting adults. She had nothing to be ashamed of. *Hey, guys. What's so funny? Did I miss anything?* She imagined the guys' cheeks pinking beneath her scrutiny, Matt flushing but feigning ignorance. Then she imagined catching obscene gestures in her peripheral vision, words and phrases whispered behind her back. She imagined those same male classmates standing too close and testing her with their eyes, their gazes stripping her bare, examining and dissecting every inch of her body, and reminding her she was less than the sum of her parts. She was nothing.

Less than nothing.

Because she had the audacity to try to forget.

Celeste drove through the night, fueled by strong coffee, a lead foot, and the blue-hot flames of mortification. The fact she'd misjudged her friendship with Matt was bad enough. The fact she'd misjudged herself far worse.

Less than fifteen hours ago, she'd fled campus after having stopped at her dorm long enough to shove clothes in her bedraggled blue-striped tote and grab a blueberry muffin from the mini-fridge. She'd driven around in a daze, attempting to shore up her battered dignity. Then she'd made her decision and headed for home.

She'd crossed from New York to Connecticut, cut through Massachusetts, caught five hours of Z's at a New Hampshire rest stop, and zigzagged along the Maine coast all the way to Casco Bay's best kept secret: her hometown of Hidden Harbor. Her dignity had degenerated, and the blueberry muffin had long since rolled beneath the passenger seat, road grit overriding sugarcoating.

In all that time, her memory had refused to resurface.

Minutes before three on Wednesday morning, Celeste

parked her trustworthy Cabriolet, Old Yeller, in her parking spot before Lamontagne's, Katherine's bakery. The owner's neighboring spot was vacant.

A week or so ahead of New York foliage, a hint of decaying leaves already mingled with the ocean air. A few solitary leaves rattled across the empty sidewalk, skeletons scratching the concrete. The storefront looked the same as when Katherine had purchased it from the previous owner, 1999 masquerading as 1976, a fact Celeste never hesitated to remind Katherine. The fact Katherine was supposed to have sold the bakery to Celeste months ago, that back in May, Celeste had already mentally cut the time-consuming breads from her menu and planned out October's pumpkin cheesecake, whoopie pies, caramel apples, and apple strudel, had meant nothing to Katherine.

Katherine's reneging on their verbal agreement and the associated meaning—she felt Celeste wasn't ready to run her own shop—meant everything to Celeste.

Yet here she was, in a compromising position, second time in less than twenty-four hours.

Her reflection stared back at her from the bakery's glass front. Even in the streetlamp's low light, the hollows beneath her green eyes appeared bruised, shades of the unintentional Goth look she'd sported six years ago, during her junior year in high school. An unseasonably warm breeze caressed her cheek, like a mother comforting a child, and Celeste shook off the misplaced sensation.

Katherine Lamontagne wasn't her mother.

The fact the baker had acted the part since Celeste's parents had abandoned Hidden Harbor for warmer shores meant nothing. Katherine had reminded—okay, nagged—Celeste into eating three meals and two nutritious snacks a day because passing out behind the counter would've been bad for business. Their arrangement had been purely professional, no blurred lines.

Same as her friendship with Matt.

The coffee in Celeste's stomach churned in revolt, as though a wand were foaming milk for a cappuccino in her belly. She wiped the sour taste in her mouth with the back of her hand and acknowledged the slightly sore sensation between her legs that hadn't lessened. That and a few glimmers of memory evidenced her folly.

She'd downed two screwdrivers. She'd accepted Matt's ride back to the dorms. She'd kissed him good night.

She'd kissed *him*.

Celeste's key fit into the lock, and the glass door gave, opening into the café at the front of the shop. The customer-alert bell jingled. Canary-yellow vinyl booths with light-green trim lined two walls, but the seat farthest from the door appeared lighter than the rest. When Celeste went to take a closer look, even the trim was different. Red instead of green trim proved Katherine still needed Celeste to tell the difference between the two colors, if nothing else. She ran her hand along the cushion, free of the permanent center indentation. Why would Katherine have replaced a lone cushion? Baby-blue paint, Katherine's only other update since her long-ago purchase, made the place look as much a nursery as a bakery. Back of the café, slant-front glass cases housed rows of pastries. The aromas of vanilla, butter, and spun sugar softened the air and wrapped Celeste in a hug she didn't bother resisting. This warmth and sweetness was her home, her siren song calling, her safe haven. Last time she'd spoken to Katherine, Celeste had told her boss she didn't need her, her bakery, or Hidden Harbor.

Not the first time Celeste had spoken her mind and regretted it.

Celeste slipped into the kitchen and found her apron on the hook, same place she'd left it upon storming out months ago but without the fuzz of flour and the scourge of deep-set stains. She held the cotton up to her nose and inhaled the baby powder–scented laundry detergent Katherine used on all the dish towels and oven mitts. The smell rattled Celeste's jaw, rattled her. Celeste's mother had warned her not to burn her bridges, not to bite the hand that fed her. A mixed metaphor Celeste hadn't appreciated until today.

Celeste turned on the industrial Blodgett oven, and the bad old girl's pilot light fired to life. She consulted the master bake sheet, a mammoth blackboard Katherine propped up by the stockroom door. Despite Katherine's best efforts at erasing, smudges from past weeks' orders bled through to the present. Nothing a little baking soda and water wouldn't correct, but Katherine had never been good at taking Celeste's advice.

When Celeste had worked here, Katherine split the master bake sheet into Celeste and Katherine columns. Now the entire gargantuan list fell to Katherine.

A dull headache thrummed behind Celeste's eyes. Hunger pains stabbed her gut, but she knew better than to give in to her body's demands before she'd taken care of today's business. She knew better than anybody that if you wanted to earn your keep, you'd better roll up your sleeves, rewrite the master bake sheet to include a Celeste column, and get to work.

An hour later, when the front door jingled and Katherine Lamontagne breezed into the kitchen, the bread dough was rising, warming the air with the satisfying aroma of yeast and flour. Inside the mammoth oven, apple, peach, and pumpkin pies baked and browned, and Celeste was hand folding wild blueberries into the muffin batter. Celeste raised her gaze to Katherine Lamontagne's dark-brown eyes.

Neither woman blinked.

"You're back from New York," Katherine said.

"Apparently."

Katherine's gaze widened, and her jaw set. "What are you doing here?"

Celeste gave the batter bowl a solitary pat. "Stirring up the blues."

Katherine shook her head. She turned to shed her peacoat and don her apron. She pulled her thick, dark hair into first a ponytail and then a chignon, her fingers working like magic. No matter how many times Celeste had studied Katherine, she'd never been able to replicate her process. Today, the sight of the back of Katherine's neck—pale and vulnerable beneath the harsh lights—made Celeste feel like crying.

Probably just sleep deprivation.

Katherine turned around. The slight imperfection of her cowlick only enhanced the do. Her gaze lighted on Celeste's eyes and softened. "Why'd you come back?"

"Maybe I missed your apple tarts."

"You were supposed to show me how much you didn't need me. You were supposed to finally get a degree and open up a shop in New York," Katherine said, her tone at once accusatory and foot-stomping disappointed.

"I never said New York."

"Anywhere but Hidden Harbor."

"Maybe I like it here."

"You needed to leave."

"Maybe I wasn't ready? Maybe you were right to go back on our deal?" Celeste's cheeks tingled with heat. The sound of her own voice—thin and unsure, every statement a question—made her throat itch. Who was she? She wanted to take inventory, to strip down in front of a full-length mirror and seek the missing smart-ass Celeste. She hadn't felt this way about herself in years, every failure a certainty, every insecurity exposed. She hung her head, and a chunk of hair sprang from her ponytail.

"Oh, Celeste. I never said you weren't ready. I said *I* wasn't ready to retire at forty-six." Katherine sighed. She reached into her pant pocket and took out a handful of hairpins. "How many times have I told you to keep your hair off your face?" Katherine swept Celeste's hair from her throbbing forehead, her hands cool as summer tea. Then she cajoled Celeste's unruly auburn mop into a bun, snug and secure.

Katherine tipped Celeste's chin up. "New York didn't work out?"

A flash of Matt's face streaked across Celeste's vision. The expression she'd previously identified as regret now seemed like what? Embarrassment? He sure hadn't sounded embarrassed when he'd bragged about sleeping with her the way her big brothers used to brag about nailing a bull's-eye during target practice. Who was she to judge character? Any way Celeste looked at it, she was screwed. "Something like that."

"Want to talk about it?" Katherine asked.

Celeste slid the muffins into the convection oven, and her eyes dampened. For a nanosecond, she imagined sobbing on Katherine's shoulder the way she'd cried in her mother's arms after the Jerk Justin high school breakup that had sent her on the Bad Mad spiral that still lurked.

Hold it together, girl.

You didn't bare your soul to your employer. You couldn't get drunk, boink a classmate, have him blab about it to the whole class, and then expect your classmates to take you seriously.

Celeste couldn't admit what had happened and expect Katherine to take her seriously.

Celeste had only seen Katherine drink once. They'd shared a bottle of sparkling wine after hours when Celeste had turned twenty-one. Freixenet, because Katherine insisted it went best with the Black Forest birthday cake she'd baked for Celeste. Celeste had never seen Katherine lose her head, with the exception of Katherine's divorce two years ago. And in the middle of last spring's thaw, her ex-husband, Barry, had started coming in for coffee every morning when the bakery opened at six. Katherine's excuse? She'd never shown him how to use the coffeemaker.

When Celeste turned around, Katherine's hands were planted on her hips, her eyebrows raised, as she awaited an answer to her question.

"Not really." Celeste cleared her throat. "I don't really feel like talking about what happened."

"Okay." Katherine nodded, but her gaze held on to Celeste's, searching for answers. Then Katherine consulted the master bake sheet and ran her finger down the checked items. "Had anything to eat yet?"

"Does coffee count?"

Katherine let out a small laugh, and Celeste's heart fluttered at her collarbone. "Not if you picked it up at a convenience store hours ago," Katherine said.

"Guilty."

Katherine went into the café and returned with an apple tart on a white stoneware dessert plate. "Eat while I get some proper coffee started."

Celeste stared at the tart, perfectly proportioned, with golden-brown crust. Light from the overhead fixture shone off the apples. She inhaled the white chocolate of the glaze, and the tang from the apples puckered the sides of her mouth. But when she lifted the pastry to her lips, her throat tightened. She returned the tart to the plate. Her hands shook. "Too much coffee," Celeste said in deference to the tremble, but they both knew that was a lie.

Ever since the burglary, whenever Katherine was alone at the bakery, she jumped at every sound. The rumble of a truck passing through the center of Hidden Harbor pooled tears at the back of her throat. Errant Dumpster odors slipping beneath the back door had Katherine checking and rechecking the stockroom and restrooms, in case an unhygienic intruder were hiding, biding his time to wield black spray paint against her walls and booth seating. Every morning, she stepped from her car and race-walked beneath the lamppost, blunt-edged key thrust between her pointer and middle fingers like a weapon. *Don't mess with me, or I'll what? Scratch you silly?*

And even though Katherine hated guns, her safe concealed the .22 she'd purchased within hours of the burglary, her biggest concession to newfound fear.

When a stranger broke into your sanctuary, stole, and fouled, nothing was sacred. Everything, no matter how precious, was tentative and up for grabs. And Katherine hadn't needed her ex-husband, Barry Horowitz, to point out the obvious similarities between the crime and the layers of loss that had upended and toppled their marriage. Katherine didn't need Barry to sit Celeste down on his chaise—or whatever furniture currently occupied his therapy office—to confirm the shadow of loss that haunted the young woman. Yet here he stood, front and center and Katherine's first customer of the day.

Barry set his black coffee on the counter, then dug into his snug jeans pocket and produced a crumpled dollar bill. Katherine smoothed and folded the bill and slipped it into her apron on the pretense she'd yet to open the register. Later she'd add the dollar to the envelope of singles in the safe, all from Barry's wallet.

Barry gazed around her, peering over her shoulder and into the kitchen. "Is that Celeste?"

So Katherine caved. God help her, but the man had a gift for drawing people out of their shells and into the open. Usually that gift didn't extend to her. Katherine set her palms atop the bakery case and lowered her voice. "Found her in the kitchen when I opened up. Looked like she'd been here for hours. Something's wrong. She drove all night from New York."

"She misses her mother."

"I'm not her mother," Katherine said. "I'm not anybody's mother," she added, a regret Barry should've known, better than anyone save herself. But when he gave her a sad smile, she shook it off. "Besides, Celeste is a grown woman."

"You're mother enough. And you never outgrow needing your parents, no matter your age." Barry stroked his beardless chin, a cliché shrink joke that hadn't lost its ability to charm Katherine. Worse, the gesture drew attention to a face—boyish looking at fifty—she still adored and those pale-blue eyes. "Hmm. Come to think of it, you never outgrow the need for your long-lost wife, either."

"Ex," Katherine reminded him. "And I'm not long lost, I'm right here."

Barry laid his hand on hers. "You're three miles away," he said, referring to the distance between Barry's house that had always been too big for two and her apartment on the first floor of a Victorian.

Celeste wheeled a speed tray through the kitchen doorway, and Katherine snatched her hand away from Barry.

"Morning, Celeste," Barry said.

Celeste rewarded him with her first genuine smile of the day. "How's my favorite gym rat?"

"Couldn't be better. Bench-pressed two-fifty last night."

"It shows."

Barry had coped with their divorce by losing the weight that had crept up on him over the course of their ten-year marriage, a pound for each year, giving up his Volkswagen Golf in favor of biking to work, and lifting weights as though he were a man half his age. Katherine had coped with their divorce by gaining the weight Barry had lost.

Celeste filled the display case with blueberry muffins and came out from behind the counter. "Well?"

Barry smacked his head with the heel of his hand. "Almost forgot." He shrugged out of his fleece. According to protocol, Celeste ran her hands up and down either biceps. "Nice!" she said. Then, throwing a look over her shoulder to Katherine, "He's going to make some lucky woman a fine husband someday."

"Spare me," Katherine said, although her heart, hard as stale bread, flickered in her chest. At least Celeste overstepping gifted Katherine a glimpse of the girl who'd stormed from the bakery months ago, too fast to let the door hit her.

Then Celeste scurried past Katherine and back into the kitchen, the joie de vivre drained from her face.

Katherine waited until Celeste disappeared into the far end of the kitchen. "Did you see that? Did you see that look on her face?" Katherine tried not to notice the way Barry's button-down gaped, pulled tight across his fit chest. She tried not to wonder whether his chest hair had grayed, along with the hair on his head. She tried not to remember how the curls tickled her lips when she took them between her teeth.

Barry aimed his shrink gaze at Katherine and nodded. "You're worried about your girl."

Katherine aimed her best anti-shrink gaze at her ex. But, heaven help her, she still felt validated. The Stinker. "She drove all night, she barely slept."

"She's passionate, like another woman I know."

"She was passionate about leaving."

"She changed her mind. Got there, and it wasn't what she'd expected. She was disappointed. Sound familiar?"

Katherine had never been disappointed in Barry. When they were married and trying to conceive, he'd been disappointed in her. She ignored the dig. "She's all wound up. Wound into herself." Katherine huffed out a breath, looked to the pressed tin ceiling.

"Oy vay, Katherine. You are such a worrier. You sure you're not Jewish? An honorary Jew?"

"Not anymore."

"Jewish by inoculation." Barry waggled his brows over his coffee.

Heat pulsed from Katherine's cheeks. She hadn't been inoculated in quite some time, and she'd half a mind to tell Barry flu season was upon them. But then she remembered the reason she'd divorced him: to give him a chance for a family with someone else.

Despite showing up at her bakery six mornings a week, he dated most weekend nights. Barry would never say so; he'd never be that cruel. But town gossip wasn't known for its sensitivity.

Barry's playful grin turned serious. "Here's an idea. Have you asked Celeste why she's back?"

"Give me some credit."

"Want me to read her mind?'

Katherine grinned. If Barry possessed that skill, he would've divorced her years before she'd gotten the nerve to do the deed.

"You found her hard at work, first thing this morning? I'd say Celeste must be the mind reader. She must've sensed you've been scrambling without her, searching high and low for a helper or two. She must've read it in the tarot."

"Hush up."

"Never mind. That would be you. So why didn't you sense her returning?"

"I'm sensing you leaving now. Am I right?"

"Got any mundel bread?" he said, referring to the Jewish pastry she made for him. Sad to say, when she'd tried the biscotti-like cookie at Lamontagne's, it didn't sell half as well as actual biscotti, but she hadn't minded the special request at-home cookie order. She hadn't minded any of his requests. With the exception of his determination to start a family, the man was too laid-back, too accommodating, too trusting.

Years ago, with Barry out of the room, Katherine's OB/GYN had asked whether she'd previously given birth. And even though the doctor had seen inside her, even though he was bound to keep her secret, she couldn't coax the truth past her lips.

To what end? What purpose would her admission serve? She'd gotten pregnant when she'd slept with a stranger. She'd gotten pregnant because back in the day, she used to sleep around. A generous serving of cake, a second glass of wine, a few mind-blowing orgasms? Why deny herself any form of pleasure?

And so, she'd lied to the doctor about whether she'd previously given birth. As far as Barry was concerned, the vague stretch marks on her stomach were easily explained, weight gained from donuts, not delivery. Sometimes she wanted to throttle Barry with the truth.

Divorce had been easier.

"Nope, no mundel bread. Care for a biscotti?"

"No thanks, I'm trying to cut down." Barry smoothed a hand down his bulge-free belly, and Katherine imagined another woman cooling the ridges of his appendix scar with her fingers, warming the curved white line with her tongue. The image hurt, made Katherine's center cave in, like a cake at high altitude. She forced herself to hold the thought. Hold tight, so she could do the right thing and let him go.

CHAPTER 2

Three weeks ago, Zach Fitzgerald's mother kicked him out of the house, changed the locks, and told her twenty-three-year-old son to stop acting like a teenager. That made sense, since the last time he'd really belonged anywhere he'd been twelve.

There were signs, of course, that he'd chosen not to notice. His height for one. Nearly five foot seven by the time he'd turned thirteen, he towered over all of the boys in eighth grade, most of the girls, and both of his parents. His younger brothers couldn't really be counted upon to measure up ahead of him, but their fair hair should've provided a clue. Zach's dark hair stood out in family photographs, as though he were destined to become the proverbial black sheep. As though he'd never had a choice. And then there was the singing. His parents had met in the Arlington, Massachusetts, Unitarian church choir, both of them soloists there to this day. Zach's brothers didn't care much for church, but Ryan studied voice at Berklee, and Donovan, now a senior in high school, was the lead singer for a rock band he'd formed freshman year: Prodigal Son. Even Zach had to admit, his brothers' singing didn't suck.

On the other hand, Zach's singing sucked big-time. He'd rather eat glass than attempt to carry a tune.

And after having eaten his way across two dozen Casco

Bay bakeries, he would've rather eaten glass than choke down another once-favorite pastry. Gingersnaps burned his tongue, their bite a battle he waged inside his mouth. Cheesecake, a treat his mother made every Thanksgiving, curdled as soon as it passed through his lips. And he could no longer open his mouth for lemon bars. The slight pucker of sour fruit now bathed and numbed his tongue.

Yet here he was. Quarter past six, most of the sleepy town's storefronts were still dark, and Zach was pulling his dependable Volvo, Matilda, into a vacant spot by Lamontagne's Bakery, in search of an older woman. Weeks of wandering hadn't sated that hunger.

According to nonidentifying information, the woman of his dreams was, or had been, a baker. Twenty-four years ago, she must've lived in or around Brunswick, Maine. Having completed his canvas of coastal towns from Brunswick to Phippsburg, Zach set his sights on Hidden Harbor's only bakery.

The last time Zach had seen this older woman, she'd been younger than he was now. That notion rearranged his insides, like the summer he'd worked as a high-rise window cleaner and his platform outside the John Hancock building's fifteenth floor snapped, leaving him dangling over Clarendon Street.

Not his favorite odd job.

A couple of guys in work pants and construction boots entered Lamontagne's, followed by a woman wearing scrubs. Then a guy around Zach's father's age made his exit. The older guy stood back from the glass window, hand shading his eyes, and stared inside. He claimed a bike propped beneath the awning, took his time fastening a helmet onto his head, and started off slowly down the street. Zach had half a mind to follow the reluctant cycler out of town. Instead, he worried his St. Anthony pocket token and silently recited the prayer asking for the restoration of things lost or stolen. *Dear St. Anthony, please come around, something's lost and can't be found.* "Amen."

Inside the bakery, Zach took a breath and played the guessing game. Fruit pies, he figured. Apple and peach. Something chocolate for sure. He could practically taste the cocoa. Éclairs, he wagered. And definitely biscotti.

One of those tall carts on wheels stood beside the glass bakery case, and a woman with brown hair in an old-fashioned bun crouched behind a case arranging éclairs. *Bingo!* Zach gave himself a point on an imaginary whiteboard, even though no one was playing but him and—let's face it—the stakes weren't all that high for this little game. But the woman—

She stood, and Zach's heart lurched in his chest, thrill overriding disappointment. An older woman's hairdo on a woman his age. The girl wasn't who he was looking for, but maybe he'd been looking for the wrong thing all along.

Nice body. Not too skinny. He liked the boobs pressing the top of the apron. Cute girl-next-door face. Huge eyes looked sad—

Busted.

The girl caught his gaze, caught him staring, and her eyes blinked three rapid-fire times, as though he'd startled her. Adrenaline rushed through Zach, better than a coffee buzz. He sent her a half nod and a full smile. But then she folded her arms beneath her chest and tipped her head. She held his gaze but refused to return the smile. "Looking for anything special?"

Zach came over to the counter, eager to take a closer look. Freckles across the bridge of her nose. Full lips he could make good use of. And he was dying to catch a glimpse of what hid beneath the starched apron. *Focus, Zach.* "What do you recommend? What's good?"

"Everything's good. But I recommend the blueberry muffins. They're special today."

"Oh?"

"My secret recipe."

"What's in them?"

Zach didn't usually shy away from a pretty girl. But he couldn't dodge the feeling this one was shaking him down to see where his character settled, and his gaze slid away, canvassing the shop. The construction guys hunched over steaming coffees. The woman in scrubs headed for the door, nose in her bakery bag.

"If I told you, it wouldn't be much of a secret, would it?" the girl said.

Zach's shoulders twitched, his body adjusting to the bakery's warmth. Nothing to do with the so-called issue he had with secrets.

When your parents sat you down on your thirteenth birthday and told you that you were adopted, everything in your life simultaneously fell into place and broke apart.

The girl tore bakery paper from a dispenser and swiped a blueberry muffin from the case. "You staying?"

"Umm." Zach hadn't thought about whether he'd stay in Hidden Harbor. Didn't usually worry about where he was going to sleep until the sun went down. Even then, car camping—

The girl furrowed her brow. But he liked the way her eyes smirked, as if they were sharing a joke, instead of the joke being on him. "Take-out or eat-in?"

"Eat-in. Definitely," he said. How else could he get her name, her number, and—if he got lucky—a place to stay better than his car?

"Excellent." The girl nodded. But instead of setting the muffin on a plate, she handed it to him. "It's on the house, if you tell me what you think."

Zach never passed up free food, one of the traits he shared with his brothers. And his parents, come to think of it. Fitzgeralds loved to eat.

There he went again, imagining he knew his place.

Zach bit into the muffin. Not too sweet, like the sugar-laden pastries he'd forced himself to eat over the last few weeks. And, yeah, butter made everything better. The blueberries burst in his mouth, sweet and tangy and still warm. If the muffin were a woman, he'd propose.

The girl leaned a hip against the counter. "Well?"

Zach swallowed, ran his tongue over his teeth, and gave her his honest assessment. "I'm in love."

The girl laughed, the sound even better than the muffin. She glanced over her shoulder, raised her voice. "Tell that to my boss," she called into the back room, and then returned her attention to Zach. "She doesn't like when I change a recipe."

"Your boss?" Zach said, and another woman came out from the kitchen.

Zach's shoulders twitched for the second time. Difference was, he didn't bother trying to convince himself the shudder was due to temperature change.

This woman was the right age. No doubt about that. But if age were the only test, Zach would've laid claim to women up and down the rocky coastline. Her height worked. She wasn't that tall, maybe five-six, five-seven. But she wasn't short either. And from what he'd read, you estimated a kid's height by taking the parents' average and subtracting two inches for a girl, adding two for a boy.

But her hair was the clincher. Dark and shiny. Zach's gaze hovered at the woman's hairline, the cowlick Zach had fought for years, until he'd given up and let it do whatever the hell it pleased.

The woman smiled, but it didn't reach her eyes. She ran a hand across her forehead and smoothed the hair that defied smoothing. "I'm Katherine, the owner of Lamontagne's. Something I can help you with?"

Katherine.

The back of Zach's head tingled, as if his brain were firing, searching for a connection to the name. Gut reaction or wishful thinking?

Either way, if Zach had met Katherine ten years ago, he would've asked her about all the stuff he thought made him both special and an oddity. Did she think Christmas decorations looked more monotone than magical? Could she tell who was calling, seconds before the phone even rang? Did her left ankle itch before a storm? He would've wanted to know if cola cramped her stomach and whether hearing the National Anthem made her want to run to her bedroom, cover her head with a pillow, and cry like a baby.

In recent years, when he'd been flitting between college girls and college majors, he would've wanted to know how she'd known she was a baker. How could you decide on one profession, when choosing meant cutting off your options?

Now his options were limited. Now the blueberry muffin spoiled in his belly and threatened to revisit his mouth.

He'd chosen not to alert the Mutual Consent Registry because they would've let his birth mother know he was searching for her. That would've given her the chance to withdraw her consent to contact and to send him away a second time.

If Katherine was his birth mother, what was stopping her from sending him away in person?

He considered the glass cases filled with pastries, cakes, and pies. The rounder stacked high with loaves of bread peeking from open bags—dark ryes, French baguettes, and sourdough. Coffee service took up a side table. Booths lined either wall. The door jingled, and three women pushing strollers rolled into the shop. Place like this, he bet, would be hopping all day until the two weary bakers turned the sign in the door from *Open* to *Closed*.

In terms of odd jobs, he'd done far worse. "The question is," Zach said, "how can I help you?"

★ ★ ★

Katherine made a fool of herself looking for her son.

A few years ago at Shaw's, she'd followed a tall dark-haired man from eggs to paper products, only to have the man turn toward her before the Scott paper towels, revealing his handsome, but Asian, face. She was ashamed to admit, while on a date last year at the Highland Games, she'd caught the eye of another man. Only to discover, upon closer inspection before the whiskey sampling, the man was about ten years too old to be her son. And last summer, a day at Popham Beach had taken an awkward turn when a preschooler on Fox Island had asked why a strange lady was staring at his father.

She should've known better.

Unlike Zach Fitzgerald, none of those young men had eyes like sapphires and moved with the sureness of a man on a mission. None of those young men sent the pulse at her neck quickening as though a stranger had ripped her babe from her arms. None of those young men made her think she was being haunted by a ghost from her past.

The return of none of those young men had been predicted in the tarot by a horseshoe spread and the appearance of the Chariot card, depicting a traveler on a mission.

And she'd bet her life that none of those young men shared a January 1, 1976, birthday with her son.

Zach did.

Zach's job application trembled in Katherine's hand, and Zach followed her through the café. She nodded at her newest regulars, two well-muscled men, sitting at their usual two-top, construction ready and right on schedule. The men pushed back from their seats and got up to refill their carryout coffees. Then they'd head down the street to work on the siding at Suzy Q's Soft Serve.

The Wednesday morning mothers' group occupied the booth on the right—three women who'd taken Katherine's advice regarding lemon bars representing the sweet and sour experience of motherhood and then promptly gotten pregnant within weeks of one another. Despite what Barry called Katherine's woo-woo leanings, she'd lifted that bit of cosmic insight from the air on a day when she'd had too many lemon bars and too little shelf space. Placebo treatment? Did the remedy really matter if you believed?

Zach slid onto the brand spanking new seat cushion, the vandal-inspired speed delivery. Not unlike the three-hour birth of her son that supposedly never happened with first-time moms.

There were exceptions to every rule.

"So . . ." Zach set his hands, palms down, on the tabletop, in the way of a man trying to hasten a decision in his favor.

Katherine tried superimposing Zach's jawline, shadowed by beard stubble, with the faded memory of a tiny, peach-soft face that had fit in the palms of her hands. Delicate nose and pouty lips. Her son's gray eyes had stared so deeply into hers, she was convinced he was taking mental notes and memorizing her features. Worse, she was certain he was gazing straight to her soul. That could describe millions of newborns. Did that describe Zach Fitzgerald on the day he was born?

When Zach caught her staring, tears pressed behind her eyes. "Give me a moment." Katherine dropped her gaze to Zach's job application. She took a slow breath and ran a finger down the page, even though she'd already memorized his most telling details.

His fingers were long, like hers. His muscles moved with the ease of a body accustomed to activity. His list of jobs ranged from chimney sweep to ski instructor. He'd even tried his hand at high-rise window washing, proving himself a thrill-seeking daredevil. Like another man she used to know?

Like a man Katherine was once upon a time acquainted

with, back when her body had moved with ease. Back when she'd mistakenly thought a one-night, or weeklong, fling between consenting adults didn't leave any lasting marks. Before she'd made the biggest mistake of her life.

She'd thought, briefly, that any guy who, like her, lived without ties might've been the one who could tie her down. And the tarot's Wheel of Fortune card had heralded momentous change and confirmed her assumption.

No one came to the tarot without a whole host of assumptions.

The magnetic feeling of being watched raised Katherine's gaze.

"Thanks for giving me a chance," Zach said, as though she'd already hired him for general help, a salesman assuming the sale. Above the table, his body jostled, a side effect of below-the-table leg jiggling.

Twenty-five years ago, a man named Adam had sat in the same seat, unmoving, looked into her eyes, and then, lightning-quick, worked his way into her bed.

Truth be told, it hadn't taken much work. And the bed had been his.

Actually, the bed had been owned by Holiday Inn.

"Like I said," Zach continued, "what I lack in experience, I more than make up for in enthusiasm."

"I'd need you for busing, restocking the bakery cases, dishwashing . . ." With each task Katherine rattled off, Zach nodded, the smile never wavering from his lips. "Cleaning toilets," Katherine added, and Zach laughed.

Katherine kept a straight face.

"Oh, you're serious." Zach leaned across the table. Because he was at ease with himself or eager to compare features? If Zach was her son looking for her, wouldn't he pipe up and say so? "Sorry, yeah, that's not a problem, Katherine." Same as the stranger who'd breezed through Hidden Harbor years ago, Zach pronounced her name in three distinct syllables—*Kath-ther-ine*—the sounds lingering in his mouth.

Later that same man had told her he liked having *her* lingering in his mouth.

Next booth over and behind Zach's head, one-year-old Christopher bounced on his mother's lap and gave Katherine a wide grin, his eyes gleaming with recognition. A single dimple punctuated his left cheek. Katherine smiled back, and Christopher tried to shove his entire fist into his mouth, drooling around his chapped knuckles onto his mother's shoulder.

Zach glanced over his shoulder. "Hey, big guy," he said to Christopher, and then turned back around. "What a cutie."

"That he is."

Sometimes Katherine wondered whether she'd daydreamed her pregnancy, the birth, and the man who had set the story in motion. Other times, her whole life sat on the tip of her tongue, dangerously close to release. On those rare days, she worked extra hard to keep her hands busy and her mouth shut. Over the years, she'd kept track of her son's age, imagining him a shaggy-haired boy in elementary school who favored finger paints and art class, a long-limbed runner in high school, the first in her family to earn a college degree. She had a relationship with that artistic, athletic, scholarly boy. She loved him to distraction. She would've laid down her life to save his.

Celeste came out of the kitchen, and Zach's gaze wandered across the room, his expression reminiscent of a hungry boy browsing Katherine's bakery cases and zoning in on his favorite treat. Eyes big, mouth slack, hands opening and closing. *This one. This one now.*

This young man? Katherine didn't know him from Adam.

Celeste, on the other hand, Katherine could read like a memorized recipe. She didn't need ESP to intuit whatever had happened in New York; Celeste didn't need any romantic complications. One look at Celeste's face told Katherine she was one stressor away from a full relapse.

Over at the counter, Celeste dropped muffins into a waxed bag and rang up Mrs. Jenkins. Although the woman was barely sixty, Mrs. Jenkins wore a full-length trench coat, rain or shine, and came in twice a week for half a dozen muffins—two corn, two lemon poppy seed, and two blueberry. The door jingled, Mrs. Jenkins vacating the shop. Her clear bonnet-covered gray pin curls bounced from sight.

If the day ever came when Katherine felt inclined to cut her hair and strap on a plastic bonnet, she'd give Celeste the combination to her safe, permission to make use of the .22, bring her out back, and put her out of her misery.

Celeste sent her gaze across the shop and then came over with a blueberry muffin centered on a plate, like a crown on a cushion. "Try it, you'll like it."

And, Katherine imagined, if she were to ask Celeste today, she'd shoot first, ask questions later.

"Did you tell Mrs. Jenkins you altered the recipe?"

"And give her a heart attack?" Celeste asked, her tone ripe with annoyance. "Of course not."

Celeste's voice lowered and sweetened. "One bite?"

"Not now. Later, when I'm hungry," Katherine said, even though she was pretty much always hungry. She was an emotional eater. If sales were up, she was inclined to celebrate with a slice of devil's food cake or an extra helping of apple pie. She'd polish off the leftover cannoli filling with a spoon and a grin. Way to toot her own horn, ring her bell, and tighten her waistband. A bad day? What was better to salve sadness than a good old chewy, gooey chocolate chip cookie dunked in a glass of iced milk? Some impulses were better off ignored.

Like Celeste's insistence on changing up recipes, ringing Katherine's bell, and pushing her buttons.

"Zach liked the muffin. Didn't you, Zach?" Celeste directed her question at Zach, but the little display was for Katherine alone.

Zach didn't seem to notice. Instead, he bit at his lower lip and beamed at Celeste, a guy equivalent of batting his eyelashes. A guy used to impressing girls with a wink and a nod. "Best I've ever had."

Celeste had grown up with three older brothers who taught her how to shoot the hell out of a bull's-eye, land a punch, and hold her own against obvious come-ons. In short, she didn't impress easily.

"Damn straight," Celeste told Katherine, and set the plate atop Zach's job application. Then Celeste headed off across the café. The wiggle in her walk was meant for Katherine's eyes but held Zach's attention until Celeste's behind, along with the rest of her, slipped into the kitchen.

Katherine set the muffin to the side and returned her finger to Zach's myriad list of odd jobs. "Well, looks like you've worked everywhere *except* bakeries."

"I've, uh, eaten my share of my mother's cookies. Does that count?"

"Baked cookies alongside your mo-om growing up, did you?" The word *mom* lengthened and split in two equal halves and then caught in her throat.

Zach flashed a grin, but then the sides of his smile sagged. "Sure. Me and my annoying little brothers fought over the mixing bowl. Typical kid stuff."

Little brothers.

More than Katherine and Barry could've given her son. Three rounds of IVF had taught her how to pockmark her stomach with four shots a day of ovary-stimulating drugs, how to lie still and wait for anesthesia to hum through her veins so that a trans-vaginal ultrasound could guide a needle through the back of the vaginal walls and aspirate her follicles. All the healthy eggs fertilized in the test tubes and then withered in her body. Three rounds of IVF had tapped out her ovaries, ruined her marriage, and trampled her ability to hope.

The thing about hope? Remnants grew.

If Zach had brothers, she'd done right by him. She'd done right by letting him go.

Next booth over, baby Christopher laid his head on his mother's shoulder. The two other toddlers, Sam and Jones, sat on their mothers' laps and busied themselves with their sippy cups, throwing their heads back to get the last drops. Mere weeks past picking up the boys' first birthday cakes, their mothers nibbled the edges of their lemon bars, each of them gunning for baby number two.

Common knowledge claimed having kids close in age guaranteed similarly close sibling relationships, the makings of a real family. Other people deserved such a blessing.

Other people shied away from dares.

In middle school, Zach had taken the bait of a bully and eaten a mishmash of cafeteria mystery meat, spice cake, and something icky that went crunch, just for the bragging rights. High school kids were marginally more creative, and he'd lifted the answers for his tenth-grade calculus final, even though he'd never needed to cheat for high marks. Math inherently made sense. And college? He'd dared kids to dare him. *Dare me to lock the RA in a bathroom stall, Silly String the chancellor's office, "haunt" the dorm on Halloween as the Ghost of Christmas Past.* The chains and moaning had lent a nice old-fashioned touch.

Zach wasn't a coward. So why was he acting like one? Holding his tongue when he'd waited a decade to be heard?

"You're from Arlington, Mass. How did you end up here in Hidden Harbor, Maine?" Katherine asked.

"My parents kicked me out of the house."

"Oh?" Katherine's left hand fluttered to her neck, as though she were taking her pulse.

"Kidding! They strongly suggested I get my act together and take it on the road."

Nearly six years ago, on Zach's eighteenth birthday, his parents had offered to give him nonidentifying information for his birth mother. But despite their support, he'd never taken the bait and grown up.

Until three weeks ago, when they'd forced his hand.

Zach squelched the urge to press his fingers to the pulse hammering his throat. He'd come home from an all-nighter to find his camp trunk and two suitcases by the front door, his mother's handwritten note slipped under the plastic of the luggage tag: *Find her.*

Inside the suitcase, he'd found the nonidentifying information for his birth mother. Clue number one for his Casco Bay scavenger hunt. Nothing about his biological father.

Somehow, that had made it worse.

Katherine took a breath and leaned back. A smile played at the corners of her mouth. "You're hardly a child. They must've had their reasons. Kids, adult kids, aren't supposed to live at home forever. I've been on my own since I was nineteen."

Zach shrugged, suddenly sheepish. Some people took longer figuring out what they wanted to do with their lives. Some people came home from five years of college and a double major without a single degree, looked up old high school buddies for a round of bar golfing, and tried to relive their childhoods.

Who was he kidding? He'd never gone bar golfing in high school. "Your degrees are in criminal justice and psychology," Katherine said. "Why do you want to work in my bakery?"

Zach shook his head. "I *attended* UMass Lowell. Never finished either degree."

"Why not?" she asked, curious, withholding judgment.

Polar opposite of his father's words when Zach had dropped out of school and materialized on his parents' doorstep: "What the hell is wrong with you, Zach?"

"I guess you could say I like to keep my options open."

"Really?"

"Yeah, sure. Figure this is a good time in my life to see more of the U.S. Who knows? Maybe I'd like to become a baker. How can I know until I try it, right? I'm a hands-on kind of guy. Sitting in a classroom doesn't do it for me. I mean, how did *you* know you wanted to own a bakery?" God, he sounded like a loser. A shiftless, homeless dude who wandered the streets. Was that the way the Fitzgeralds saw him?

Was that the way he saw himself?

"Strangely enough," Katherine said, "that's kind of how I ended up here myself."

Two men entered the shop. Guys looked like they were in their thirties, wearing cookie-cutter suits, their shoulders hunched from desk work. While Celeste counted out change, the taller of the two guys bit into his blueberry muffin, and his shoulders notched down. "You're the best," the customer at the register told Celeste, and his buddy nodded, crumbs slipping from his grin.

Probably the only joy in their day. They probably chewed slowly to delay getting to an office, where they crunched numbers in five-by-five cubicles inside square gray buildings. A box within a box would suffocate Zach.

He'd rather dangle over Clarendon Street or sweat it out in a bakery kitchen.

"So . . . Katherine . . . you were on a road trip, traveling around the country, when you ended up in Hidden Harbor?"

Katherine closed her eyes and shook her head. When she raised her gaze to him, she somehow managed to look both happy and sad. "I was a wanderer."

Chills prickled up the back of Zach's head and across his

shoulders. "All who wander are not lost," he said, the same phrase he'd offered his mother in response to her complaint about his aimlessness.

"I was," Katherine said.

"You are," Zach's mother had said, her eyes shiny with tears.

Katherine's eyes were dry. "Oh, sure, I had a plan. Hit every state in New England, and then continue across the country. Free as a bird, until I took a job working here. I was going to stay a few months, one season in each locale."

"So why'd you stay?"

"I fell in love."

Zach imagined Katherine decades ago, the fine lines around her eyes erased, her hair down around her shoulders. He imagined a guy, his biological father, walking into the bakery and falling to his knees.

"When?" Zach asked. "When did you fall in love?"

Katherine inhaled and held her breath. For a second, her brow knit and her chin dimpled, and Zach thought she might apologize. He could practically see the words *I'm sorry* forming on her tongue. Then her features smoothed, unreadable. "Twenty-five years ago," she said.

Perfect timing.

The conversations in the shop jumbled and blurred to a hum. Zach's head spun with the sudden shift and the impossible sensation of movement. "What was his name?"

"Who?" Katherine's hand went to her cheek. "Oh! You thought. Ah, no. There was no man. I fell in love with this place. Hidden Harbor. Maine. Lamontagne's." She shook her head. "Only the bakery was called Hazel May's, back in the day."

Katherine's words and actions didn't jibe, the sort of tells you looked for in a criminal investigation. She held her hand to her cheek, the way Zach's mother touched her face after his father swooped in for a kiss. Every single night after work.

How could a couple feel that way about each other after

decades of marriage? Every secret revealed? Nothing left to learn?

How could Katherine feel that way about a place where she worked?

"You found what you were looking for?" Zach said. "Working here?" Had Katherine chosen a bakery over a boy? A place over a person?

Her heart was big enough to wrap around the entire state of Maine but too small to fit an infant?

Too small to love him.

He'd seen the way Katherine responded to Celeste, the girl trying to please the woman, the woman's quick rebuff. He'd noticed how Celeste's expression hinged on Katherine's approval. He'd appreciated the girl's attitude, sarcasm as defense.

All these years Zach had thought the fault lay inside of him. That his birth mother had taken one look at him and deemed him unworthy of devotion. Or worse, that she'd decided way before he was born that he wasn't going to be worth the trouble. Maybe Katherine, if she was his birth mother, hadn't wanted to keep a kid she'd made with Mr. No Name.

Maybe his birth mother hadn't written down his father's name because there had been too many fucking candidates.

Literally.

Katherine's chin tightened, and she glanced around the café. Her eyes watered and she took in the pastry-filled glass cases, the carafes lining the coffee station, the tables full of early morning customers. Then her gaze returned to Zach, but she didn't look him in the eye. She nodded in his general direction. "Work is security, another kind of freedom. I found what I was looking for, and more."

Before today, Zach hadn't considered that maybe, just maybe, the fault lay not in him but in his birth parents. What if 50 percent of his DNA came from she who couldn't be bothered? What if the other half was a gift from what's his name? What if

Zach was a 100 percent loser? Genetics might fail you, but math, good old math, inherently made sense.

A wail issued from behind Zach's head, as high-pitched and insistent as any fire station's alarm. Katherine homed in on the cute, screaming toddler in the next booth.

The toddlers sitting across from the screamer focused on their buddy with their tiny brows furrowed, as though deciding whether to jump in and sing a round.

The mother of the crying baby turned and mouthed, *Teething,* to Katherine, and Katherine's eyes flashed on the word. "Hang on," Katherine told the mom. "I'll be right back," Katherine told Zach, and she race-walked past the bakery cases and into the kitchen. Her emergency stride, long and purposeful, made Zach think of his mother and all those mad dashes from their driveway and into the house for Band-Aids and bacitracin. It was a miracle Zach had any skin left on his knees.

Seconds later, Katherine returned with a white bakery bag in hand. She reached into the bag and pulled out some kind of hard-looking cookie. "Would Christopher like a banana oat teething biscuit?" Katherine asked Christopher's mother.

"He'd love one." Christopher's mother took the biscuit from Katherine and handed it to her son. Without missing a beat, the baby clamped down on the edge of the biscuit, whimpered, and quieted. Leftover tears trickled from his big blue eyes and down either shiny cheek. Zach imagined soreness leaving the boy's gums, relief taking its place.

Katherine Lamontagne, the baby whisperer. Who knew?

Christopher's mother kissed the top of her son's ear. "Thank you, Katherine! You're an angel to bake homemade teething biscuits. You don't have to—"

"That's what I'm here for." Katherine waved away the praise, but her smile, the way she tilted her chin down, said she was taking it all in. Moments ago, Katherine had claimed she'd found what she was looking for at the bakery and more. Was this what she'd meant?

"Would Jones and Sam—?" Katherine asked.

"Yes, please," the other two mothers sang out. One of the babies banged his plastic cup against the table. The other little guy opened and closed a sticky-looking hand in Katherine's direction.

Katherine gave the cookies to the moms and then slid back into the booth across from Zach. Her voice came out breathy, the way Zach's mother sounded when she was doling out praise. "Now, where were we?"

Zach offered Katherine the truest statement he'd uttered all morning. "Beats me," he said. "I haven't got a clue."

CHAPTER 3

For Celeste, junior year in high school had been a series of firsts. Her first boyfriend, Justin, had led to first sex, first breakup, and the first time she'd suffered the assault of vicious gossip. Another first? Letting her best friend, Abby Stone, take care of her. Abby, who rarely swore, had been the first to tell Celeste it was okay to haul off and tell Ed—aka Celeste's eating disorder—to shut the fuck up.

Shared DNA wasn't the only way to measure family.

When Celeste's brother Lincoln had brought her out back of their whitewashed Cape and encouraged her to point his .22 downrange and balance a photo of Justin's face in the middle of the sight, Abby had shown Celeste how to dodge harsh words and barbed looks. When Celeste had wanted to run away, Lincoln had provided her with a suitcase, a road map, and a how-to lesson on breaking into empty motel rooms for free stays. Abby had taught her how to settle down, take life in stride, and stay in Hidden Harbor. When Lincoln had teased her about her first baking frenzy and then her refusal to taste test her own baked goods, Abby had reminded Celeste how to nurture herself.

To this day, Celeste didn't fully understand how one of her greatest pleasures—food—had become her greatest fear.

From outside Briar Rose, Abby's bayside bed-and-breakfast, three in the afternoon could've been mistaken for three in the morning. Cars with license plates from Maine to Maryland crowded the darkened parking lot. Since Celeste's return to Hidden Harbor, the low-lying skies had progressed from partly cloudy to in your face and ready to burst. Celeste's inhalation rattled in her chest.

At least she'd gotten her job back.

Clearly, Katherine had missed the extra set of experienced hands. That didn't explain why Celeste's boss, usually wary of strangers, had turned around and on the spot hired Zach Fitzgerald. The guy was seriously cute, no doubt about that. Probably too cute for his own good, judging by the way he'd first attempted to flirt with Celeste and then succeeded in charming Katherine.

Katherine didn't hire strangers without bakery experience and she didn't charm easily. No doubt about that either. Six years ago, when Katherine was looking to hire, only Celeste's daily hounding and a two-week nonpaid trial run—Celeste's suggestion—had beaten out half a dozen other high school students who were hungry for work.

Three pumpkins climbed the steps to the New Englander's porch. Small, medium, and large, with the smallest gourd on the top step. Shiny orange bows fastened cornstalks to either post. Red and gold mums overflowed from a half whiskey barrel and completed the façade of domestic bliss.

Abby was a wiz at staging.

No one could've guessed the innkeeper and owner was a twenty-two-year-old single mom. No one could've imagined that Abby had lived through first a pregnancy at eighteen and then having her douche bag boyfriend freak out and take off. No one could've been prouder of her than Celeste for surviving.

Survive first and then figure out how to live. That philosophy had bound Celeste and Abby together since Mrs. Nelson's first-grade class, where, at recess, they'd caught balls, climbed jungle gyms, and run from the advances of one-sided little-boy crushes.

Celeste was thrilled her best friend's business was thriving. Really she was. But that didn't keep Celeste from wanting Abby all to herself. Celeste would've liked nothing better than to kick out Abby's guests and tell them not to come back until either the storm blew over or Celeste figured out what had happened back in New York.

She hoisted her duffel onto her shoulder and dragged herself up the steps. The new slate sign next to the front door boosted her resolve: *Enter as strangers, leave as friends.* That sounded like her Abby.

Sunshine to Celeste's snark and cynicism, Abby shared Celeste's worries, lightened her load. Abby meant popcorn and hot cocoa. The warmth of hand-knit winterberry throws around Celeste's shoulders. The comfort of home. With Abby, Celeste could tell all or tell nothing. No pressure. Just the comfort of being understood.

Sure enough, once Celeste was inside the entryway, the warmth hit her full on. The aromas of wood fire and apples filled the air. And something else. Cinnamon sticks simmering in a pot on the stove. That trick Celeste had taught Abby when they were twelve and Saturday nights meant sleepovers at either Celeste's parents' loud boy-filled house or Abby's mother's quiet only-child girly seaside cottage. Celeste's lips twitched into a grin.

Abby, cinnamon sticks, Celeste.

Celeste shook her head. If she wasn't careful, she was going to start blubbering in the middle of the bed-and-breakfast and lose the last shreds of her dignity and control.

Celeste peeked into the den, where a dark-haired mother nursed a pink-swaddled infant and a toddler played quietly on the floor amidst piles of sherbet-colored wooden blocks. Inside the dining room, a few chocolate chip cookies remained for an afternoon snack, and empty sugar packets littered the tea service tray. Two thirtyish-looking women bent over a puzzle. The cinnamon aroma peaked in the kitchen, where Celeste, sure enough, found sticks simmering on the back burner, but no Abby.

Celeste slipped back into the entryway and jingled Abby's engraved *Ring for service* dinner bell. Then, heart thrumming at her throat, she faced the closed pocket door leading to Abby's private quarters. Like magic, footsteps sounded on the other side of the door. Celeste counted backward.

Ten, nine, eight—

The door slid open, casters rattling in the metal track, and Abby appeared. Her blond curls were loose around her shoulders, the way she'd worn her hair in high school.

Abby's expression went from business-ready to happy-to-see-you to what-the-hell. "Celeste!"

Just hearing Abby speak her name lifted the edge off Celeste's troubles, and she allowed herself a full breath. "Got my old job back at Lamontagne's. Think I could maybe sleep on your couch till I find a place?"

"Of course." Abby shook her head. "What are you doing back?" she asked, her tone a mixture of rejoicing and confusion. "What's going on? What happened?"

Heat masked Celeste's face, as if she were standing over a pot of water and boiling bagels. Her temples tingled. "I—I'm not sure."

Abby lifted Celeste's duffel from her shoulder. She ushered Celeste into her apartment and slid the pocket door from the wall.

Raffi's "This Little Light of Mine" filtered through Luke's bedroom door. Celeste might've enjoyed the selection if Charlie hadn't given Luke the CD on one of his few and far between school vacation visits. No sooner would little Luke warm up to his away daddy than Charlie would go away again. Luke's toys cluttered the living room. A miniature wooden tool bench in one corner and a toy kitchen beneath the window reflected Abby's ability to play both mother and father for her son. Bright multicolored Lego towers lined the coffee table and spilled onto the equally bright and multicolored braided wool rug. "I missed you and Luke."

Abby dropped Celeste's bag on the couch. "And we missed you."

"Sorry I haven't phoned much."

"You've been busy," Abby said, making excuses for the inexcusable. *Much* meant Celeste hadn't phoned since August. "Luke and I have been busy, too."

Celeste nodded. Of course, running a B&B and raising a son on your own would be a lot for anyone to handle, even Abby. Even with her mother Lily Beth's help. As far as Celeste was concerned, Lily Beth was a goddess and a godsend. She'd let Abby and Luke live with her until Luke turned three. Then she'd helped Abby figure out her next move. If the roles had been reversed and Celeste had gotten pregnant, her parents would've still taken off. Three rowdy sons and one daughter, who was a little unwell, had maxed out her mother's ability to care. "I should've moved in with you to help you take care of Luke." The hell with guys. Except for little Luke, who needed them? What had they ever done for Celeste?

Abby barked a laugh. "Instead of following your dream and becoming an even better kick-ass baker?" Abby looked at Celeste sideways and then up and down. "Have you lost weight?" Abby said, but she might as well have asked, *Have you lost your mind?*

"Holding steady," Celeste said, an assertion Abby might've bought if Celeste's voice hadn't wavered.

Abby clasped Celeste's shoulders, leaned forward, and pressed her lips to the center of her forehead. Celeste closed her eyes, inhaled cinnamon and another scent at the tip of her tongue. Something green and fresh and masculine. Another memory just out of her reach. "Ninety-nine," Abby said. "You're running a low-grade fever. Sit. I'll go get you Tylenol."

"No!" Celeste said, louder than she'd intended. "I'm not sick. I'm just so, so *tired*." Saying the word exhausted her, drained away the smidgen of energy that she'd summoned to drive from Lamontagne's to Briar Rose. She wanted to sleep, hide inside a blanket, turn off the lights and her jumbled thoughts, and forget that no matter how hard she tried, she couldn't remember having sex with Matt.

According to Matt, Celeste had been more than memorable.

Celeste's stomach convulsed with unshed tears, and she clamped a hand over her mouth to stifle them.

Abby took Celeste's hand from her mouth. "Tell me. I'm listening," Abby said, as if Celeste were the most important person in the world. As if all the lies that had been told about her in high school, years later, hadn't come true.

Brittle leaves clung to the branches and rustled in the sea breeze. Celeste zoned to the sound of the waves and her eyelids fluttered. For a split second, she forgot who she was.

As if she'd ever known.

"Celeste." Abby peered into her face. "What happened?"

Celeste focused on Abby. Her anchor. Her port in the storm. Her best friend forever. "I did something really stupid."

"It's okay. You don't have to be perfect. Nobody's perfect," Abby said, a throwback from when Abby had misunderstood Celeste's less than ideal coping mechanism.

Thing was, to Celeste, Abby was perfect.

"C'mon. What did you do? Burn a cake?"

"Nobody burns cakes."

Abby pantomimed rolling her eyes to the ceiling. "Excuse me. Uh, did you murder someone?"

Celeste cracked a smile. More like murdered her reputation. "I went to a party with someone Monday night."

"With a date?"

"No, just a guy from school." Celeste almost added, *just a friend,* because that's what Matt had been. Whenever she tried to summon what she'd lost, she resurrected benign memories. She'd helped Matt convert recipes from measurements to weights, and he'd given her tips on photographing her finished products. Angling a croissant so the curves caught the light. Before and after photos—from raw materials to plated pastry—to document your work and detail the process. The all-important backdrop cleanup and arranging the money shot.

Matt the Rat. A decent photographer, a so-so baker, and a false friend.

Celeste wiped her eyes with either hand. Time to get real. "I—"

Luke's bedroom door burst open, releasing a louder Raffi, now singing "The More We Get Together." A small but speedy Spider-Man dashed across the room and jumped into Celeste's arms. "Hey, buddy! I didn't know it was Halloween."

"It's not!"

"Then why are you wearing a costume?"

"I'm not wearing a costume! I *am* Spider-Man!" Luke beat his fists against his chest, then nestled his nose into Celeste's neck.

A sharp tickle sensation hunched Celeste's shoulder, and she giggled. Luke nestled again, and Celeste rewarded him with a second twitch.

"Luke, stop," Abby said.

Luke lifted his head, growled, and went back in for a tickle.

"Luke," Abby repeated, and unlatched him from Celeste's neck.

Luke clamped on to Abby's hip and laid his head on her

shoulder. "He's such a flirt." Abby sniffed Luke's head and dropped a kiss into his curls, as if to prove she'd succumbed to said flirting.

"Like son, like father," Celeste said.

Abby's face did a grin and a cringe, the expression that meant she had something—or someone—to hide. And *someone* usually meant—

"Oh, hey, Celeste." Charlie Connors, aka Luke's father, aka the douche bag, walked into the living room, wearing worn jeans, threadbare socks, and looking way too comfortable for a scheduled kid visit at his ex-girlfriend's place.

Polo. The fresh, green, masculine scent Celeste had been unable to identify. Charlie's cologne was all over Luke, all over Abby's living room, and likely all over Abby.

Nailing the lid on Celeste's connection, Charlie kissed Abby on the cheek and took Luke from her arms.

As far as Celeste had heard, neither Hidden Harbor nor hell had frozen over. That could only mean her best friend had lost both her mind and her memory. How many times was she going to give in to her Charlie obsession? How many times was she going to sign up for more disappointment? How many times was she going to let Charlie hurt her? "Oh, holy hell."

Luke bounced in Charlie's arms, all smiles. "You said a bad word!" Luke said.

"Sorry," Celeste told Luke, although the apology was meant for Abby.

"You can put your eyeballs back in your head, Celeste," Charlie told Celeste.

"You can return to the rock you cr—"

Abby shot Celeste a look, jutted her head toward Luke.

Luke laughed. He held Charlie's face between his hands and gazed into the eyes that had turned girls into goofballs in high school and probably in college. Despite what Charlie had claimed when he and Abby were going out, he could've controlled the girls chasing after him, if he'd wanted to. "Silly Daddy," Luke said. "Celeste's eyeballs didn't fall out."

Charlie's loafers peeked out from under the couch skirt, as though he'd kicked them off as soon as he'd come through the door. An open Sam Adams sat on the coffee table, even though Abby would never crack a beer until Luke was in bed for the night. And, for all his faults, Charlie would never drink and drive. That could only mean he wasn't leaving anytime soon.

All the evidence had been right in front of Celeste's face, if she'd cared to take off her blinders and notice.

"Aren't you going back to school?" Celeste asked.

Charlie shot her a triumphant grin. "Yup. First bell's at seven-twenty."

"He graduated UMaine in May," Abby said, "and he got a job teaching freshman biology at Hidden Harbor High."

That made sense, in a weird way, since Charlie was about as mature as the average high school freshman. No offense to high school freshmen. "Tell me he doesn't live here," Celeste told Abby.

Abby smirked and then smoothed her features for deadpan delivery. "He doesn't live here."

"I mean, it's one thing to screw—"

Luke's big blue eyes blinked at Celeste. Abby's identical blue eyes widened at Celeste. "Luke, honey, do me a favor and go back to your room with Daddy."

"I don't want to go. I want to play with Celeste. She's pretty and she smells like frosting!"

"You'll have plenty of chances to play with Celeste. She's going to stay with us for a while."

Abby ignored Charlie's eyes popping out of his head.

For once, Celeste agreed with the douche bag.

If Celeste woke up on the couch every morning to find

Charlie sauntering out of Abby's bedroom and scratching his crotch, she'd be able to hold neither the contents of her stomach nor her tongue.

That wouldn't be a problem, if it weren't for one beautiful little boy who looked an awful lot like the daddy he adored.

"Put your eyes back in your head, Charlie. I'm not staying," Celeste said.

"Yes, you are," Abby said.

"No, I'm not."

"Yes, you are."

"Leave her alone, Abby," Charlie said. "You heard Celeste. She doesn't want to stay here."

Abby and Celeste glared at Charlie.

"What?" Charlie looked from Celeste to Abby, his facial expression the equivalent of throwing his arms up in defeat.

Only Abby cracked a smile. She brushed Charlie's hair from his eyes and touched Luke's face. "Can you take Luke—?"

"Spider-Man!" Luke said.

"Right. Take Spider-Man," she said—and Luke nodded—"to his room for a few minutes. I need to talk to Celeste alone."

"Sure, babe," Charlie told Abby. "Good to see you, Celeste," he said to Celeste, but she was sure he was thinking, *Good riddance.*

"Be good to them," Celeste said. She hoped he heard, *Don't you dare hurt them again.*

"Always," Charlie said, his voice lowered and serious. Celeste could've sworn she saw Good Time Charlie tear up. Then he snapped up his Sam Adams from the coffee table and took Luke to his room. The door clicked shut, muffling Raffi.

"He's changed," Abby said.

"Because he says so?" Celeste lifted her duffel bag from the couch to her shoulder.

"What do I have to say to make you stay?" Abby asked, her voice as full of resolve as when she'd said those words to Charlie a little over four years ago, and just as sad.

It proved Celeste's point. Staying here would only succeed in bringing Abby down.

"I gotta go," Celeste said, pretty much Charlie's response from years ago. Even though she heard it secondhand, Celeste would never forget the last conversation Abby and Charlie had before he left her the first time. Celeste didn't care to hear his second-time leaving firsthand.

In high school, Abby had never listened to Celeste's advice about Charlie. Oh, sure, Abby would nod and smile and agree to the Charlie facts. Then, one look from Charlie, and she was gone.

"Wait!" Abby said. "Let me make some phone calls for you. I'll see if another B&B has an opening. Something."

"Not really in my budget. Don't worry about me. I'll figure it out. I always do."

"*We'll* figure it out," Abby said, reminiscent of Celeste's words to Abby. The first time, when the sight of two bright pink lines had knocked Abby down. The second time, when Charlie's leaving for college had dragged her under. "Please. Let me help. Stay."

Abby had two boys to take care of. She didn't need to worry about Celeste again. She didn't need to stress over cutting up Luke's food, counting Charlie's empties, *and* hovering over Celeste's meals.

No way in hell Celeste was going back to those days.

Celeste pulled Abby into a bear hug. Celeste's heart beat hard and fast, the opposite of the slowed heart rate that earmarked starvation. This time, sleep, not food, was what Celeste's body craved.

"Miss you," Celeste said.

"I'm right here."

"You're miles away, in Charlie Land." Celeste slid open the pocket door.

The young mother from the den stood in the entryway, baby on her shoulder, toddler at her feet, Abby's *Ring for service* bell in her hand. The woman flashed Abby a smile. "Great timing! I was wondering whether—"

"Excuse me," Celeste whispered, her voice a thread of sound. Abby's hand on Celeste's arm, a last attempt to get her to stay. Celeste slipped from Abby, skirted past the mom and kids to the front door. One last backward glance at Abby's face, torn between Celeste and the rest of the world. Celeste gave Abby a nod and a smile. Then she was gone.

Celeste wasn't a gypsy. Yet, two months ago, she'd given up her apartment in Phippsburg, sold most of her possessions, driven to New York, and acted the part. She didn't recognize her own life, so in an inside-out, backward, this sucks big-time way, renting a furnished apartment in Hidden Harbor made perfect sense.

A black pleather couch and chair flanked a table made of metal and glass, all the better to peer through the center and view the tribal rug's black-and-burgundy geometric patterns that reminded her of her dentist's office. The side table held a cordless phone, one of those jobbies that never worked properly, with a humongous answering machine. And in the bedroom there was a black captain's bed, too short for her average frame, as though whoever had furnished the apartment couldn't decide whether the rental demographic was men defending their masculinity or Munchkins.

The prints covering the walls were all metal-framed, modern, and abstract. Not a seaside watercolor in the mix, as though she weren't in Hidden Harbor, as though she weren't anywhere specific at all.

The worst part? She'd signed a one-year rental agreement.

She wanted to go home. But that place didn't even exist anymore.

She unpacked her groceries in the tiny kitchen, her hands weak from exhaustion. Lined the crisper with McIntosh apples and clementines, stocked the top shelf with nonfat Yoplait yogurts, a head of romaine lettuce, and a bottle of balsamic vinegar. Before hitting the grocery aisles, she'd driven through the McDonald's drive-through, parked Old Yeller, downed a plain burger, and called it dinner. All she could manage today. Tomorrow, she'd head back to Shaw's for a full order, stick-to-your-ribs sauces, pastas, and meats. Maybe even a pint of Ben & Jerry's for a housewarming. Then she'd sit on the couch, eat the entire pint herself, and watch cellulite ripple her thighs.

She'd skip the Ben & Jerry's.

Yogurt was almost as good, right?

Celeste took a strawberry yogurt to the couch, licked the lid, and dialed her parents' Florida phone number, her parents' home phone.

She'd never get used to thinking of her second-generation, too young to retire, Hidden Harbor townie parents living on the ninth hole of a Boca Raton golf course. When she was growing up, her parents hadn't even played golf, unless you counted Bernie's Miniature Golf, the seaside attraction with the odd combination of a prehistoric green dinosaur rearing up on its hind legs, a Dutch windmill, and the ubiquitous water traps. But the week after Celeste—the last bird in the nest—graduated from high school, her parents had made their big announcement. They were selling the house and flying south to the old folks' state, supposedly past their usefulness once Celeste had managed to keep her chin up and her weight on.

Now her childhood home was as good as a junkyard, a neighborhood eyesore no amount of signatures on petitions or town meetings had succeeded in eradicating. Cars, rusted and rotting, lined the driveway where she and Abby had chalked the blacktop for hopscotch, jumped double Dutch with the neighborhood kids, and traded misinformation about boys.

Growing up in a house full of brothers had taught Celeste that boys were immature, silly, and goofy, prone to mess and insecurity. In short, they were human. So why had she expected unrelated boys to be anything special? Why had she expected unrelated boys to act as though she was special?

Her mother's latest chipper message kicked into gear. "You've reached Davey and Delilah." *Davey? Really?* "We're busy playing golf, swimming laps, and sipping tequila. Leave a message and we'll get back to you after we're off the course and dried out."

"Hi, guys," Celeste said. "I'm back in Hidden Harbor. Just thought you'd want to know. . . ."

Had her parents even realized she'd gone to New York? She'd told them she was going to culinary school—of course she'd told them—but had they even remembered? Her brothers and their families were scattered across the country; each of the once-self-described black T-shirted high school slackers had aced college, married a girl with long hair and a tiny waist, and then promptly convinced that tiny-waisted girl to push out a kid or two. Celeste's mother sent cards on the appropriate birthdays, Christmas, and Easter. According to Celeste's brothers, their parents occasionally visited, breezing into town on a Thursday, leaving on a Sunday, and preferring to stay at a hotel rather than "bother" a daughter-in-law.

In the last four years, Celeste's parents had returned to Hidden Harbor and "bothered" her exactly twice.

Didn't they miss Hidden Harbor? Didn't they miss her?

The cold pleather cushion stuck to her jeans. The chill slid to the small of her back, reminding her how fast the seasons changed in Maine. Today's cloudy, early fall sundown was giving her a taste of winter, the Earth spinning and cooling. No one had ever accused Hidden Harbor of moving fast, but Celeste could see it now, the world barreling forward, while her life was destined to move one step forward, two steps back. Thanks to first Katherine and then Matt, circumstances beyond Celeste's control.

Even Abby was moving forward, sort of, by getting back with Charlie. Maybe Charlie had changed. Anything was possible, right? Maybe Celeste was more than a little jealous of Charlie, because Abby forgave him again and again, whether he deserved it or not. That's what Celeste liked best about Abby, her ability to ignore faults and see the best in people. After all, Abby saw the best in Celeste.

Celeste snatched up the receiver and dialed Abby's number.

"Briar Rose B&B," Charlie said, and Celeste's grin deflated.

"Hello?" Charlie said. "Anybody there?"

The left side of Celeste's upper lip rose in a sneer. Unlike Abby, Celeste couldn't assume the best in Charlie. She needed proof.

"Who is it?" Luke's voice in the background, little-boy shrill but carrying a hint of huskiness. "Can I talk on the phone?"

"Anybody there?" Charlie repeated. And then to Luke, "Nobody's there, buddy, no one—" The connection cut out.

At all.

Celeste rubbed her hands together, but the cold remained. She went into the kitchen, spooned the yogurt down the drain, and ran the disposal. She leaned against the counter, and the machine vibrated through her back, a rumble against a low ache. She was impossibly tired, the sound almost soothing in its repetition. Her eyes drifted shut, and her head jerked up fast and hard. No sleeping until she showered. Steam off the last couple of days, and then—yes!—oblivion.

She let the shower run and undressed before the bathroom sink. First kicking off her bakery clogs and pulling her long-sleeved white T-shirt up over her head. Next came the chignon Katherine had fashioned. Each pin released a reciprocal sigh. Celeste rubbed the soreness from her scalp. Hair around her shoulders, she unhooked her bra, but the removal offered no relief. Her breasts ached, as though she were expecting her period. Which she was not. She unzipped her jeans, pushed them over her hips, and the fabric scraped against her thigh, shooting a pain all the way to her throat. Upon closer inspection, a wide, sensitive swatch of black-and-blue stood out against the pink flesh of her inner thigh. Not the first time sex had left her bruised.

The first time she and Justin had had sex was a disappointment. It had hurt when he'd entered her, and wasn't the tearing supposed to have catapulted her into an orgasm? She was just about ready to give up on the whole stupid sex thing. But on the third or fourth try, something clicked, she got off, and she knew she'd discovered her favorite sport of all time. Missionary style was fine by Justin, but why should they stop at one position when there were endless possibilities and contortions? Bottom, top, sideways. Hands, lips, tongue. The only thing as good as getting pleasure was giving it.

Sometimes she liked it a little bit rough, a little bit intense. Sometimes Justin called her bossy. At some point, she told Justin she found it funny that she was more into sex than he was. Then he'd called her a sex-crazed slut.

Then everything had gone to hell.

At least with Justin she remembered doing everything he claimed she'd done. But she'd only done those things with him.

Celeste slipped a hand beneath the shower spray. The water had heated, warming her hand but causing the rest of her body to shake. She took off her underwear and held it up to the medicine cabinet light. A tiny drop of dried blood stained the crotch, as though she'd been recently deflowered. And when she stood under the showerhead, the spray stung between her legs. She gritted her teeth, forced herself to endure the pain. Even when her chest convulsed, she squeezed her eyes shut and told herself to get over herself. She told herself to deal with it. Because she'd acted like a sex-crazed slut.

Because she'd remembered who she was.

Chapter 4

By quarter of five, Celeste had progressed from the worry she wouldn't be able to fall asleep to the certainty nothing could prevent another fall.

Energy jittered beneath her skin. She needed to sleep, she had to sleep. She was sick with the need for sleep. But she had the weird feeling that she also needed to stay wide awake, stand vigil over her sleeping self, and guard the door.

She'd locked the door. She'd checked the lock twice. She'd had thoughts like this before and learned to ignore them.

She tucked her blankets beneath her chin and hugged the straw-yellow, love-worn relics, buried her nose in the fluff. She'd slept with the blankets since she was two years old, the year she'd upgraded from crib to big-girl bed. One blanket comforted, two kept her warm. Tonight, she needed both. Lights out, shades drawn against the last hour of daylight, the walls of the unfamiliar bedroom seemed to throb with a pulse. But, of course, it was only her heart beating in her ears, her thoughts keeping her from sleep.

Her wrong thoughts.

Above her, the gray ceiling twirled, sleep deprivation masquerading as a hangover. For a few moments she drifted up there and spun in the murky light. Then her covers took on weight, as though a downed tree trunk were pinning her limbs.

Celeste.

A male voice breathed her name in her ear. A light flashed from her peripheral vision. And then came the knocking. Hard and sharp and insistent and reverberating in her throat.

Rap, rap, rap.

Her eyes snapped open to the nearly empty room, the blank walls, a kind of reverse nightmare. The digital clock on the dresser read 5:03 p.m.

"Shit," Celeste said, all too aware she'd made the same proclamation half an hour ago, the last time she'd awoken with a start, her own personal *Groundhog Day*. When would she get it—life—right?

The rapping, she knew, wasn't even real, just an overtired hallucination. Hypnagogia. Lincoln, the brother closest in age to Celeste and with all the answers, had explained it to her. Another life lesson from the year of hell. Yet the sound tricked her every freaking time.

Would she never learn?

Rap, rap, rap.

"What the—?" Celeste sat up, eyes wide. Her gaze shifted to the side. She was reasonably sure she was awake, so—

Rap, rap, rap.

She zipped up her hoodie till the slide nicked the skin at the base of her neck, and walked to the front door, stepping through the living room as though the furniture might reach out and take her out at the ankles. She angled her left eye to the peephole.

Nothing out there but the front step and the curve of a wrought-iron railing leading to three more concrete steps just like it.

Rap, rap, rap.

This time, she could tell the knock echoed from the rental office next door.

Was one of the tenants locked out from their place? Hurt? In need of assistance? When her brother Lincoln had been a volunteer firefighter, he'd responded to countless kitchen fires. The most popular culprit was usually a grilled cheese sandwich laid bare across the oven racks and a careless home cook who'd opened the oven door, feeding oxygen to the flames. People were their own worst enemies.

Did she smell smoke?

Celeste cracked open the door, slowly, slowly. But the stupid door creaked, igniting a heated tingle in her throat.

The guy standing on the rental office's artificial turf welcome mat, with his flannel shirt rattling in the wind, said exactly what Celeste was thinking. "No way!"

Zach Fitzgerald—Lamontagne's most recent, most curious employee—somehow managed to look both self-assured and sheepish, reminding Celeste of a stray cat she'd long ago found haunting her family's doorstop. To her family's credit, no one, not even her father—whose eyes swelled shut at the mention of *cat*—complained when they ran out of cream for their morning coffee or tuna for their brown-bag lunches.

After Zach's attempts to flirt with her that seemed more habit than heartfelt, he'd settled down. Celeste and Katherine had spent the rest of the morning and better part of the afternoon training Zach. Katherine showing Zach where to find the baker's yeast, Zach piping up to ask Celeste where Katherine kept the toilet cleaner, and Celeste making sure Zach didn't mistake one for the other.

Unlike the first time Celeste had laid eyes on Zach, she grinned, as though returning a guy's smile was her default reaction. Another one of her really bad habits. Or maybe she was relieved the knocking sound had come from someone real.

She wrapped her arms around her waist, but the wind slipped like cold hands beneath her sweatshirt and T-shirt and across her belly. "Looking for anything special?"

"That depends." Zach clambered down the rental office steps and bounded up the steps to her front door, his stray-cat look having morphed into a lost pup. Easily encouraged by a cheerful tone, too close, and with too much energy. "How much does a special apartment go for around here?"

"Five hundred a month. Unfurnished."

"That's not too bad."

"That doesn't include utilities."

"Oh." His lips twisted to the side, considering. "Hmm."

"You have to fork over first month, last month, and a security deposit. And sign a year lease."

"Geesh! What about your firstborn kid?"

"That would be illegal."

"Good point." He gazed across the parking lot. "Looks like it's another night in Matilda. Know a campground around here I can park her?"

Celeste followed Zach's gaze across the lot. An old lunch bag–brown four-door Volvo sedan was parked right next to Old Yeller. Celeste half-expected to see a woman stepping from Zach's vehicle. *Matilda* sounded like a long-legged skinny blonde who could eat anything she wanted without gaining an ounce.

Even Celeste knew that sort of person didn't exist.

"You named your car Matilda?"

"You got a problem with that?"

"Yeah, I've got a problem. She looks more like an Agnes to me. How old is she?"

"My girl's an '86. Bought her from the sweetest little old lady you'd ever want to know. Matilda's dependable and, believe it or not, good on gas, so think before you start trash-talking my girl."

Celeste waited for Zach to crack a grin. He didn't.

She made sure her door was unlocked and stepped outside. The wind carried the aroma of damp leaves and a hint of a far-off wood fire, the smell she'd mistaken for a kitchen fire fiasco. The doormat's plastic grass spiked beneath her bare insteps. "You got your car when her first owner was done with her," Celeste said. "No one expected anything of her anymore, right? So you give her the name Agnes. Old-fashioned but nothing showy. Then, when she surpasses expectations, everyone's surprised." Celeste made jazz hands around her head, widened her eyes, made her mouth into a lowercase *o*.

She was joking, sort of, but the silly face made her think of Katherine. Celeste had hoped to return to Hidden Harbor with a degree from Culinary America and enough experience to convince Katherine to sell. Celeste had never really wanted to open a bakery in New York. That threat, promise, whatever you wanted to call it, had been posturing. A test to see whether Katherine really knew Celeste at all.

Katherine had failed.

Zach folded his arms and squinted at Celeste. "First off, who's *everyone?*" he asked. "Second, who cares what hypothetical people think?"

Sadly, Celeste did give half a shit about what *real* people thought of her. And she was totally embarrassed about the shit she gave.

But of course Zach was only talking about his car, nothing deeper.

"I named my car after the movie to please myself," Zach said. "*Matilda* suits me just fine."

"Wait a minute. Matilda from the movie?" A girl born to crappy parents turns out to have magical powers. A car deemed unsuitable turns out to run well enough to convey Zach to Hidden Harbor. "I can get onboard with that. Now, when I got Old Yeller—"

"You named your car Old Yeller?"

"Yeah. What's wrong with that?"

"You know that story doesn't end well, right? You know the dog—car—"

"See? You've only just met him, and he's already surpassed your expectations."

"*Ha,*" Zach said, more an exhalation than a word, air rushing out of him in surprise.

Expression neutral, Celeste made a second show of jazz hands.

As though taking her point to heart, Zach sat down on the cement step below Celeste. "And yet I still need an inexpensive place to park Matilda for the night."

"Holiday Inn in Bath?" Celeste asked.

"I hate hotels."

"Yeah, me too." Celeste sat down on the step beside Zach, making sure to leave a space between them. A space large enough to fit an average-sized guy. A space large enough to fit Matt the Rat. She tucked the hems of her sweatpants beneath her toes, rubbed them to encourage circulation. "Just for the night?"

Zach shrugged. "Until I find an apartment without a year lease."

"I don't mean to pry—"

"Exactly what you say if you're about to—"

"I know Katherine's probably not paying you much and all. But, well, consider your training an investment in your future."

"My future cleaning toilets?"

"Your future running a bakery. Or any business, really. You've got to understand how all the parts of the machine work before you can, you know, see it as a whole." Celeste made a broad, sweeping motion, as if she were gathering ingredients and hugging them to her chest.

And with that, Celeste had resurrected Katherine's phrasing from a long-ago tutorial. The day Katherine had graduated Celeste to inventory and ordering, Celeste had walked from the shop with her head held high, a bounce, an actual bounce, in her step. The only managerial duty Katherine didn't share with Celeste was closing the shop and taking end-of-day profits to the bank. After she had been working at Lamontagne's for a year, Katherine had given Celeste a key to the shop. But the combination to the safe, Katherine shared with no one.

"Katherine told me you've worked for her for the past six years."

"Yup, with the exception of two months at culinary school in New York." Celeste's stomach dropped, a lesser cousin to the falling sensation of hypnagogia. She shook her head. "I've been nowhere else."

"So why are you still working for Katherine?"

The events of the last two days rushed through Celeste's chest and backed up in her throat.

"I mean you can bake," Zach said. "You obviously know what you're doing in the kitchen. And I saw how you and Katherine butt heads. . . ."

Celeste had gone to Culinary America to get more varied experience, not just with baking but also with bakery management. She needed to see the world outside of Hidden Harbor. Wasn't that what Katherine had told her months ago? "I'm doing this for your own good," she'd said, as though Katherine were her mother, and she the baby bird reluctant to leave the nest.

Yet here she was, nesting once again in Hidden Harbor.

"I didn't finish my degree at Culinary America. I barely started. I wanted to, but then stuff happened," she said, hating the defeated tone of her voice. She wasn't a quitter. And yet she'd quit.

Zach slid his hand a few inches along the concrete toward

Celeste, and then he pulled it back, as though his instinct were to touch her hand in solidarity, rub her back in sympathy.

Early in their friendship, Matt had done that, the lightly placed touch, but without the retreat. Never a retreat. God freaking forbid he should retreat.

She'd seen Matt scorch the top of a crème brûlée and then, rather than start over, peel off the leathered skin and marry two ramekins. He'd undercooked German chocolate cake and tried passing the raw batter off as filling. Concealed a sunken in the middle vanilla cake beneath two extra bowls of buttercream. Instead of owing up to and learning from his mistakes, he covered them up, a master of the effed-up follow-through.

The cement step numbed her flesh, but not enough. Hardly enough. She still felt raw, roughed. Her heartbeat pulsed like a ragged thing between her legs, evidence of the mistake she couldn't ignore. She shifted a couple of inches farther from Zach.

She hadn't signed up for Matt's bullshit bragging. Whatever had happened between them should've remained private.

"I didn't finish my degrees, either. Stuff has a way of happening," Zach said, his voice world-weary. Then, "Who am I kidding? I didn't finish because I didn't see the point."

Celeste turned her gaze from Zach to the parking lot. Zach's car, Matilda, looked as forlorn as her owner, in need of a good night's sleep.

Or maybe Celeste was projecting.

"So, Celeste," Zach said. "Is there a campground around here?"

"Hermit Island's down the road. Too bad it closed Labor Day."

"Story of my life. A day late and a dollar short." Zach got up and brushed off the back of his jeans. "Well, it's been real, Celeste Barnes. I'd better find a place for me and Matilda."

If Zach managed to find a bed-and-breakfast vacancy in Phippsburg, he'd need to turn out his pockets before turning in for the night. Unless he happened upon an apartment in Hidden Harbor or Phippsburg where the building manager kept long hours, Zach would end up driving all the way to Bath and staying at the dreaded Holiday Inn.

Briar Rose, Hidden Harbor's only bed-and-breakfast, was both full for the night and too expensive. But if Zach ended up there, if he ended up at Abby's door with no place to stay, she'd let him park in her lot. Why wouldn't she? She let strangers stay in her house all the time. Difference was, Abby called them guests. With the possible exception of Celeste, Abby never turned anyone away.

Okay, whatever. Leaving Briar Rose had been Celeste's doing, and Abby was trusting to a fault. But would it kill Celeste to act a little more like Abby? Nothing crazy. Celeste wasn't about to open her apartment door for Zach, but would it kill her to show him one small kindness? Would it kill her to make his life a little bit easier?

"Zach? You and Matilda can car camp in the visitor's spot. I mean, you know, just until you find a place."

"The visitor's spot that says: *No overnight parking*?"

"Oh, please. Who's going to know? If anyone asks, I'll say you're one of my brothers. I've got, like, a couple dozen of them."

"If you're sure . . ." Zach said, leaving room for her to reconsider and say no.

As of this week, she was sure of nothing.

"One thing?" Celeste said. "You have to let Katherine know if you're not keeping the job. It's a pain in the butt for her to find decent help. And kids around here are always looking for work. It's not fair to lead her on or take a needed job. So if you're not staying more than a week—if you're not going to appreciate—"

"Oh, I'm staying," Zach said. "I mean, at least for now. It's gonna take me a few months, at least, to learn all the tricks of the bakery trade, so I can compete against your blueberry muffins and Katherine's lemon bars. Right?"

Zach's tone lifted at the corners, trying to inject humor into his voice, weighed with exhaustion. Or maybe Celeste was projecting again. But she got the feeling he was telling the truth, that he'd stick around because he wanted something from Katherine.

Celeste got the feeling that something had nothing to do with baked goods.

All day Celeste had noticed Zach and Katherine sneaking peeks at each other. When Zach bused the café, loading plates and napkins into a basin, Katherine's gaze followed him across the room. Her face pulled tight in concentration, as though she were—reading glasses perched on the end of her nose—studying one of Celeste's recipes and reviewing it for flaws. And Zach? Every time he checked out Katherine, he fixed the front of his hair. More than that, his posture shifted, his gaze lowered, and he looked like a rejected puppy.

A puppy with a crush on Katherine?

Zach offered his hand to Celeste.

A thank-you handshake for letting him dock Matilda in the visitor's spot overnight or a promise to not take advantage of Katherine's goodwill?

As if anyone could get the better of Katherine Lamontagne. Six days a week her ex-husband came in for a cup of coffee, every day hoping for more, the original rejected puppy. How could Katherine fail to soften under Barry's puppy dog eyes? According to Katherine, Barry had done nothing wrong. He'd done everything right. Then why had she divorced him? Why wouldn't she take him back? Why wouldn't she answer any of Celeste's questions?

The woman was like a rock, like that loaf of Irish soda bread Celeste had baked without the benefit of soda. Once.

When it came to baking, she never made the same mistake twice.

"I'm good," Celeste said, pretending she thought Zach's hand was meant as an assist, and she stood unaided.

Zach returned his hand to his side, and her throat tightened. The feeling of wanting to cry pulsed faintly against her sinuses.

She'd mistaken Matt's friendship for brotherly love. She wouldn't make that mistake twice, either.

"Good night," Celeste said. "See you in the morning, Zach." Inside her mouth, his name buzzed with energy, fresh and new, like Zach himself. Novelty had always intrigued her. Yet another instinct she ought to ignore.

Zach was just a guy, a stranger passing through Hidden Harbor on the way to the rest of his life. But something about him seemed familiar, too. Something she couldn't get a handle on. Like a dream that, upon waking, slipped through your fingers. Like a screwdriver-drunk memory that melted with the first rays of the sun.

Zach climbed into Matilda and pulled the door shut behind him with an echoing thud.

Celeste shivered in the doorway and ducked into her apartment. A stranger's apartment, really. She felt like an intruder, as though she'd broken into someone else's home, leased someone else's life. She could understand why Zach would prefer spending one more night in his dependable old friend Matilda to checking into a cold and impersonal hotel. Fumes from the pleather couch and chair burned Celeste's nose, coated her mouth with bitterness.

She cracked open a window, inhaled through the screen. Decaying leaves smelled like the pumpkin pie her mother always left in the oven until the edges browned to deep sienna and the kitchen's smoke detector emitted a warning call. The ozone of overcast skies reminded Celeste of Katherine's lemon bars, sweet hidden within a tart cream paste. And, drawn from farther off, ocean spray was the sweetest reward of all. The aroma, spicy as a glazed cinnamon bun, and bitter as espresso, reminded her of family.

Lincoln lived in Gloucester, Massachusetts; Grant ended up in Spring Lake, along the Jersey Shore; Jeff had recently closed on a house in Topsail Beach, North Carolina. And, of course, her parents resided in Boca. Her parents and brothers had scattered—the older the family member, the farther his or her distance from Celeste—but somehow they'd all still ended up touching the shores of the Atlantic. As though they'd left Hidden Harbor to search for a facsimile of home.

Why hadn't they just stayed?

Celeste nestled beneath two layers of blankets with only her nose exposed to the cold night air. She rolled, pulling the blankets tighter around her, and tucked the tip beneath her, as though the covers were dough and she the frangipane in an almond croissant. The rich, buttery almond paste with a hint of vanilla was good enough to eat alone. Her stomach growled, speaking of deep, dark hunger.

Stop thinking about food.

The suggestion only heightened her hunger. In lieu of counting sheep, she listed ingredients, imagined them floating before her eyes. Vanilla extract she could swig, let the alcohol burn going down. The butter she'd cut into cubes and see how long it took for them to melt on the indented center of her tongue. Sugar she'd scoop from a bin, dip her tongue into the curve of a measuring cup.

Celeste's eyes lost focus. Her eyelids drifted shut. She floated in the abyss of—

An engine revving.

Was she asleep or awake?

She tried wiggling her fingers—forefinger, middle, ring, pinkie—the way Lincoln had taught her.

Her eyes popped open. Across the room, the clock read 11:21. "Shit." She waited for the car to drive away, for the sound to recede. Instead, the low rumble remained constant, the noise niggling at her rib cage.

Celeste wrapped her blankets around herself and dragged them through the living room. She squinted out the window. Cold night air whistled in through the screen, sending a chill through her torso. Beneath the parking lot light, Matilda idled.

Celeste wasn't the only person awake. Or cold, for that matter. An early fall night in Maine plus windchill could rattle even dependable Matilda. Could rattle an inlander from Massachusetts, far away from home.

She made sure the door to her apartment was unlocked, slid her feet into her bakery clogs, held her blankets around her, and trotted across the lot. Mist wet her cheeks, the first droplets of rain hitting the air. The temperature had dropped about fifteen degrees since she'd last stepped from the door. Below fifty, she'd wager. You could die from exposure in weather like this. A topsy-turvy wind howled between Old Yeller and Matilda, forcing the downed leaves between them to fall up. Matilda's parking lights glowed. The old girl rumbled, her undersides pinging from the change of temperature.

Celeste peered through the window into the backseat. Zach curled toward the seat back. His sleeping bag reached to his armpits. His head angled hard to the left. He looked like a cold, uncomfortable giant. Ill-suited for this seaside town with its winters that arrived while your beach towel still hung on the clothesline.

Celeste knocked on the window.

Zach scrambled to sitting, his arms flailing up like the flurry of leaves. A flicker of rage transformed his features, his eyes wide and ready to defend the homestead. Celeste's insides reverberated, pinging louder than the undersides of Zach's car. And then recognition softened his eyes, and his lips settled into a confused little grin.

Zach stepped from the car. She took a step back. Was she insane? It wasn't like her to go to a strange man's bed in the middle of the night. So what had possessed her to startle a man dozing in his car?

"What's wrong? You okay? You need something?" Zach's hair stood on end, a bed head without the benefit of a bed.

Celeste stifled the urge to smooth his hair, to lecture him on his choice of socks. Cotton made your feet sweat like crazy. Sweating made you freeze. Zach was a danger to himself. The pounding in Celeste's chest softened, receded.

"You shouldn't fall asleep while you're running the engine," Celeste said.

Zach bounced from foot to foot in his cotton socks. "You scared the crap out of me to deliver a public-service announcement?"

"You're running the engine because you're cold?"

"Yeah." Zach tucked his hands beneath his armpits, piss-poor defense against the windswept mist and the temperature drop.

Celeste peeled the top blanket from around her shoulders and scrunched it into a ball.

"I can't take your blanket."

"You going to run Matil—your car—out in the parking lot every hour on the half hour to stay warm?"

"May-be," he said, the word drawn out singsong and teasing.

Celeste tossed the blanket ball at Zach. Then she held the sides of the remaining blanket around her and ran back across the lot.

"I don't need—" Zach called after her, but the wind snuffed out the tail end of his denial.

Celeste turned to see Zach gathering the blanket in his arms and hugging it to his chest. "Thanks, buddy!" Zach said, but she'd have none of that buddy crap.

Her blanket delivery was nothing personal, just a desperate attempt to get some sleep. She didn't need a buddy, and she didn't need to find a frozen Zachsicle in her visitor's spot come daybreak. "Shut off your damn engine! Some people need to get up for work in a few hours!"

No verbal response from across the parking lot.

Zach climbed into the front seat of Matilda, slammed the car door behind him, and killed the engine.

All the response Celeste needed.

Inside the apartment, she locked the door, jumped into bed, and pulled the single blanket up over her head. She peeked through the blanket's weave, imagined Zach beneath her blanket's identical twin. She imagined his nose losing its likely chill, his toes defrosting, a wave of warmth crashing down his body. She pictured Zach's body relaxing into the seat cushion, his mind losing its grip on the world, his troubles—whatever they were—floating away.

Celeste's mother's oft-spoken phrase played between her ears. She needed a male friend *like she needed another hole in her head.*

The first time her mother had said it, Celeste had been fifteen and had come home with her ears double pierced. And then, eager to further shock, she'd lifted her shirt and floated the notion of a belly button piercing, until her mother had sunk the idea.

Celeste, you need a belly button ring like you need another hole in your head.

The following week Celeste had begged a ride from her brother Lincoln's friend Justin to a house deep in the woods of Phippsburg, where a woman told your fortune and pierced your belly button for twenty bucks, a package deal. At sixteen,

Celeste had let her belly button piercing close, given up on the fortune-teller's prediction she'd fall in love with a guy from far away, and told her family she was in love with Justin.

Celeste, you need a boyfriend like you need another hole in your head.

Even Lincoln had seconded her mother on that one. Celeste should've taken that as a sign. Lincoln wasn't warning her about guys in general; he'd been trying to warn her specifically away from Justin. Only she'd been too bullheaded to take the hint.

Nope, a guy friend was exactly what she didn't need. Zach was polite. He worked hard. Like Celeste, he named his cars. And he knew how to snuggle a blanket.

Beyond that, as Katherine was fond of saying, Celeste didn't really know him from Adam.

Chapter 5

Ever since Katherine was small, she welcomed the rain.

Not drizzle or mist—precipitation that couldn't seem to make up its damn mind and get serious. But torrents that hammered the roof like an imperative, flooded the front yard, and seemed to wash away your sins. Pounding rain that kept her father from driving his rust-riddled pickup down the rutted road to the liquor store. On those rare days, weekday or weekend, she'd awaken to the clatter of spatula against griddle, whisk against bowl, her mother getting busy in the kitchen. The aromas of coffee, bacon, and eggs would slip like a cartoon waft beneath Katherine's bedroom door and tweak her nose. And then, the best part, complete and utter radio silence. Her father, soothed by the rain, for once kept his damn mouth shut.

At five-thirty in the morning, Katherine left Celeste in the kitchen and stood by the front window of Lamontagne's, brushing flour from her apron and enjoying a rare moment of pre-opening peace. Silence echoed through the chilled glass, as though the world were taking a deep inhalation. Then the charcoal skies reached maximum capacity and exhaled.

Rain jackhammered the roadway, painting Ocean Boulevard slick and black as a whale beneath the streetlights. A car *shooshed* through the town center and plowed through the mother of all roadside puddles, splashing the window where Katherine stood. Katherine touched her fingertips to her chest but held her ground. She half-expected to see an ark parked alongside the town green and a man with a shepherd's hook ushering animals two by two into its protective cavern.

In reality, Katherine was waiting for Zach.

The pounding rain boxed her ears, keeping time with her overactive pulse. Her tired body's attempt to outpace the autumn chill that crept around the weather stripping. She'd slept a few winks last night. Flickers of dreams darted in and out of her awareness but nothing more substantial. Mostly, she'd toggled between worrying about Zach and fretting over Celeste.

Was Zach warm and dry and somewhere safe? Had he found a place to stay for the night? She'd given Zach a few suggestions, including Ledgewood, where Celeste had ended up renting, but low-rent apartments were few and far between in this neck of the woods. And with a job description that included wielding a toilet brush, Katherine couldn't exactly pay him top dollar without arousing—or confirming—his suspicions about her.

Her strong suspicions she couldn't confirm, either.

She wondered how long he'd remain at Lamontagne's if she didn't fess up and give him what he seemed to be looking for. She agonized over him leaving. She knew if Zach left, that would be it. Life sometimes gave you second chances, but third chances were as unlikely as a pregnancy had been after she and Barry had decided to halt the fertility treatments and go it alone. The decision to do nothing was a decision nonetheless.

Along those lines, last night Katherine had worried about whether Celeste might've skipped dinner. As soon as Celeste walked through the door this morning, Katherine had reminded her about the importance of eating breakfast.

Katherine didn't pretend to understand Celeste's eating

disorder. When Katherine was hungry, she ate. When she was full, she stopped . . . usually. But Katherine had been married to a shrink long enough to understand the way thoughts—insidious thoughts—could grow inside you. These wrong opinions, Barry had told her, festered and became your truth. The story you told yourself. She understood how these damning thoughts might have originated in your childhood. How even the smallest of acts—from the way you took your time washing a Pyrex dish, turned the pages of your dog-eared copy of *That Was Then, This Is Now,* even peeled open a bag of Lay's potato chips—could inspire a barrage of insults, questions with no right answers.

But a whole impenetrable universe wedged between understanding and soul-deep believing.

Most likely the negative thoughts were wrong, but what if they weren't?

A rap sounded through the rain racket and turned her toward the door. A face peered through the glass.

Katherine stared at the face. The face stared back. Katherine's brain scrambled to unite the features with a name. Then the puzzle pieces clicked.

"Oh, my gosh!" Katherine fumbled with the lock and opened the door.

Look what the rain dragged in, Katherine thought but wouldn't dare utter.

Mrs. Jenkins stepped into the café, wearing her usual beige trench coat but, on this day of days, sans the telling plastic bonnet. Courtesy of the rain, her gray hair hung straight to her shoulders, not a pin curl in sight. Soaked through, her hair appeared more brunette than gray. Even her face looked different. The snap of cold water tightened the pores and pinked cheeks, a trick Katherine's older sister had taught her.

Dare Katherine even think it? Mrs. Jenkins looked younger.

Celeste came out of the kitchen and refilled her coffee

cup. Then she did a double take. Bemusement washed across her features before she hid her smile behind her coffee cup, her wide gaze peeking above the lid.

"Good morning, Mrs. Jenkins," Katherine said. "What can I help you with today? Can I—may I take your coat?" Katherine didn't usually take customers' coats, but the woman was dripping on the floor, standing in one place, making a puddle. Katherine had the urge to grab a hand towel from the back room and dry the woman's hair, squeeze out the sodden ends.

"There is something you can help me with." Mrs. Jenkins strode toward the bakery cases, as though she usually visited the shop half an hour before Lamontagne's opened for business. As though today weren't even Thursday.

Mrs. Jenkins groomed her shih tzu, Annabella, on Sunday after church, delivered Meals on Wheels on Mondays, visited her widowed sister, Mrs. Something or Other, in Bath on Thursdays. She picked up her muffin order on Wednesdays and Fridays. Never on a Thursday.

Celeste scooted behind the counter and set her coffee beside the register.

In the last twenty years, Mrs. Jenkins had deviated from neither her schedule nor her muffin order.

Mrs. Jenkins turned to Katherine. "Those blueberry muffins I purchased yesterday—"

Merde.

The woman's eyes went half-mast, her hand stroked the length of her sleeve, her shoulders rose, her head canted to the side, and her lips curled into a sleepy grin reminiscent of Meg Ryan in *When Harry Met Sally*. The famous faked orgasm deli scene.

Only Mrs. Jenkins looked as though she were about to hit a high note for real.

Then she righted her head, opened her eyes, and straightened her shoulders. "Luscious," she said, and her eyes blinked twice, as though she was as surprised by her word choice as Katherine.

"I—I'm so pleased," Katherine said.

Celeste slid a white bakery box out from under the counter, assuming the sale, the way Katherine had taught her. To the untrained eye, Celeste's expression didn't change. But Katherine read *I told you so* in the way she straightened her spine, lifted her chin, and sniffed the air.

"Whatever did you put in those muffins?" Mrs. Jenkins asked Katherine.

"Oh, I've no idea," Katherine said. "They're Celeste's recipe."

"Celeste?"

"It's a secret." Celeste swiped a sheet of bakery tissue. "Your usual order, Mrs. Jenkins? Two blueberry, two corn, and two lemon poppy seed?"

Mrs. Jenkins shook her head. "Actually, if you don't mind, I'd like something different. How about"—she bit her lip, narrowed her gaze—"four blueberry muffins, one corn, and one lemon poppy seed?"

"Four blueberry muffins it is." Celeste scooped muffins into the box. Then she lifted the lid to close—

"Wait." Mrs. Jenkins bit her bottom lip. She leaned over the muffins and inhaled deeply, audibly.

When Mrs. Jenkins stepped back, Celeste tied up the box and set the muffins in Mrs. Jenkins's outstretched hands. Her gaze slid from Celeste to the bakery box, as though she'd woken from a sultry dream to find herself in a room full of strangers. "Well, you two have a nice day." She swung her head. Water droplets flung from the ends of her hair and splattered the bakery case.

The door jingled, and Zach stepped into the café, as wet as Mrs. Jenkins but none too pleased about it. He held the door for Mrs. Jenkins. "Why, thank you." Then—if Katherine could trust her eyes—she could've sworn she saw her most conservative customer check out the back of Zach's jeans before exiting Lamontagne's.

Merde.

"Morning, Kath-ther-ine," Zach said, using the same three-syllable pronunciation as yesterday. "Celeste," he said, pausing on his way into the kitchen. Nothing unusual about the way he pronounced her name. If anything, the word tumbled from his lips, either an afterthought or trying to resemble one. But it was the way he held her gaze a second too long, the way he pressed his lips into a quarter grin, the way Celeste mirrored his expression. Infused with meaning.

Katherine had been around long enough to recognize the day after a hookup's wordless lingo. And, heaven help her, but if she wasn't mistaken, she'd both given and received that same laden look from Adam.

The skin beneath Celeste's eyes glowed faintly mauve. Not as raw looking as yesterday, but she still moved slower than usual, and she was working on her third cup of coffee.

Zach dashed into the kitchen. The door to the employee bathroom closed with a telling whine, and water ran through the pipes.

"Sleep okay last night at your new place?" Katherine asked.

"Decent," Celeste said. Zach came out of the kitchen with his shirtsleeves rolled to his elbows, tying an apron around his waist and somehow looking fresher than when he'd entered. "What's up first, boss?" he asked Katherine.

Again that look between Celeste and Zach, thick as the bread aroma filling Katherine's lungs and just as evocative of shared warmth. Celeste picked something from Zach's collar, held up a bit of yellow fluff. "Don't let this drop into the pastry. We'd have to charge extra."

Zach grinned, snatched the lint from Celeste's fingers, and tucked the fluff into the pocket of his jeans. "Your blanket was warmer than it looked."

Celeste's blanket?

Katherine knew none of the rumors from years ago about Celeste were true. She'd seen firsthand the price Celeste had paid, in pounds, at the hands of her high school boyfriend's false claims she was promiscuous. In the past four years, Celeste had dated. Of course she'd dated, but on that subject Celeste rivaled Katherine's ability to keep her mouth shut.

The oven timer dinged three steady beeps. "Rye, sourdough, and baguettes," Katherine said. "Ready to rack and roll?"

"Yes, ma'am." Zach touched two fingers to his forehead and ducked back into the kitchen. Half a dozen racks of bread would keep Zach busy for a while. Had he kept Celeste busy last night?

"I suggested Ledgewood to Zach. Did you happen to see him there after work?"

"He was there," Celeste said, too offhand to be meaningless. "So . . . Mrs. Jenkins . . ."—Celeste perfectly replicated the tilt of the woman's head, her muffin happy dance—"seems to have enjoyed my blueberry muffins. She kind of scared me. For a second there, I thought she was going to launch into a striptease. I mean, what do you suppose she's wearing beneath that trench coat? Maybe she's a stripper over at The Gentleman's Club? A throwback to the olden days, heavy on the tease, light on the strip? Can you imagine?"

"I'd rather not." Katherine barked out the laugh she'd been holding back since the original Mrs. Jenkins performance.

Celeste only grinned. "What did you think of the muffins?"

"Oh, Celeste, I apologize." After Katherine had offered the job to Zach, she'd suggested he have something to eat, if he was hungry and while he had the chance. That something had ended up being the muffin intended for Katherine. "I haven't tried one yet."

"It doesn't matter."

"Of course it matters."

"Apparently, not to you."

How could Katherine argue with such an assertion? She could tell Celeste she mattered to her, that she was more important than a recipe, good or bad. Katherine could offer the truth of having been distracted yesterday by Celeste's surprise return and hiring Zach. She could admit that Celeste's recipes were often good, sometimes amazing. At the most, she could admit defeat and tell Celeste she'd been right to change up a recipe, Katherine's mentor Hazel May's recipe. The recipe that had served the town since before Celeste was born.

Whatever Katherine said would be wrong.

If you're so smart, why are you still living here?

All these years later, Katherine could still hear her father's words. The tone scraped across her nerves and sucked the spit from her throat.

In the end, it hadn't mattered that she'd shielded her mother from the worst of her father's drunken tirades. That she'd given half of her salary to her father. That despite the saying about sticks and stone and words not hurting you, she knew differently. The sharp point of a carefully selected insult sliced beneath your skin and stripped you bare.

The best defense? Keeping your damn mouth shut.

Katherine had long ago given up wondering what had been going on in her father's head, but with Celeste she came closer to understanding. Words were cheap. Celeste wanted proof.

Katherine swiped a blueberry muffin from the bakery case and, before Celeste could say another word, Katherine took a bite. Then, like a sommelier, she focused on the notes of flavor—sweet butter and tart blueberries and a surprising, enlivening zest of lemon. The texture was at once richly satisfying yet light enough to gobble. No wonder Zach had eaten two. No wonder Mrs. Jenkins had adapted. No wonder Celeste had taken offense.

Celeste stared at Katherine, her face impassive. Too impassive. Celeste's need for approval was louder than words.

Katherine set the remaining muffin on the counter. She unfolded the orange stool and stepped onto its lower rung, raising herself to the blackboard. She erased *Blueberry Muffins* and wrote *Celeste's Wild Blues* in her tidiest print. Then she stepped down and brushed the chalk dust from her hands. "Better?"

"It's a start." Once again, Celeste attempted to conceal her grin behind her coffee cup, but her smiling eyes gave her away.

Katherine made fast work of the rest of the blueberry muffin. She arched her back until her spine gave way with a satisfying crack. "They're wonderful."

"I know."

"Eaten one today?" Katherine asked, a veiled reminder about her earlier breakfast lecture.

"Later, when I'm hungry," Celeste said, letting Katherine know her reminder hadn't been all that veiled.

An odd vibrating sound came from the kitchen—the thread of a tune Zach was humming that Katherine couldn't identify.

Celeste held a cupped hand to her ear. Her gaze slid toward the kitchen, her brow creased.

"'Slide'! Goo Goo Dolls!" Celeste called into the kitchen.

"Yes!" Zach appeared in the doorway, holding a loaf of sourdough between food prep gloves. "You got that from *hmm, hmm?* Nobody has ever been able to guess a tune I was humming. You a fan?"

Celeste held up the two fingers—pinkie and pointer, thumb holding down middle and ring. "Rock on, baby."

Zach laughed, tossed up his own two-horn salute, and ducked back into the kitchen. The humming resumed.

Celeste licked her bottom lip, her gaze trained on the spot Zach had vacated.

"He seems like a nice guy," Katherine said, her words conjuring Adam and their instant, easy camaraderie. He'd seemed like a nice guy, too. "Hey, pretty girl," he'd said by way of introduction. "What time do you get off work?"

If he'd been entirely honest, he should've asked, *What time do you want to get off?*

Within an hour she'd followed him back to his hotel room, where they'd smoked a joint. Heads fuzzy, they'd made love to "Free Bird," slow and sultry giving way to fast and frenzied.

Love, she supposed, had been too strong of a word. Weeks later, she'd changed her thoughts on that front. Back then she'd loved everyone. But loving everyone was a lot like loving no one at all.

"Did you and Zach spend time together last night?"

"What do you mean, *spend time?*"

Who Celeste dated, spent time with, made love to, was none of Katherine's business. But the memory of Celeste's full-blown illness—that Katherine couldn't forget. "I mean, you've just gotten back from school," Katherine said. "It's a big adjustment, coming back to work here, and you don't do well with . . ."

"Transitions," Celeste filled in.

"Yes. Sort of. No."

"What in the world are you trying to say?"

Katherine glanced into the kitchen, where Zach slid loaves of bread into the rolling rack and hummed a wordless tune.

"With you and Zach working together, and you said he moved into Ledgewood—"

"I didn't say that."

"I couldn't help but notice you struggling with food yesterday."

"Yesterday, I'd just quit school. Yesterday, I'd just driven all night on five hours of sleep."

You'd think after ten years married to a shrink, Katherine would be better at framing her questions. "My point, exactly. So this is probably not the best time for you to start something—"

"Wait, what? What exactly do you think I've started?"

Katherine tossed a glance back toward the kitchen. Clearly, Celeste had gone through something in New York, something that had spooked her all the way back to Hidden Harbor. But in Katherine's experience, sex didn't shield you from loss. Sometimes sex—specifically sex with a stranger—only added to your long life list of regrets.

"Zach?" Celeste whispered. "Me and Zach? You think I've started something with Zach? Wh-why would you—? H-how could you—?" Celeste stammered, not with embarrassment but with rage. Katherine could feel Celeste's anger spiking hot in her own throat.

"Okay, clearly I've misunderstood," Katherine said.

"I don't get it. Am I wearing some kind of sign that says *whore?*"

"That's an ugly word, Celeste. I'd never say that."

"No? You thought it, though. What kind of woman sleeps with a guy she's just met?"

A good woman, a woman who enjoyed sex. A woman who, with all her heart, believed the adage "make love, not war."

"Zach mentioned a blanket—"

Celeste threw a look into the kitchen. "And you assumed— I didn't sleep with Zach, if that's what you're implying. And I didn't screw him either."

Another awful word. A screw was something that held you

down and pierced your flesh. To screw someone implied coercion, treachery, manipulation.

Celeste's glare seemed to say, *Screw you.*

Katherine touched Celeste's arm and watched her eyes turn liquid. Then the muscles around her mouth tightened, shades of the resolve she'd shown Katherine months ago, and moments before storming from the bakery. All righteous anger. All *I'll show you.* Celeste shook off Katherine's touch and went into the kitchen.

The humming stopped.

"'Iris'?" Celeste asked.

"Two for two," Zach said. "Two for two."

On a rain-soaked night, right before Katherine had left home for good, she'd gone out to The Watering Hole, a local joint that served pizza so greasy you had to sop up the oil with a handful of napkins, and watered-down melon balls for cheap. She'd needed to get out, to shake off the constant negative vibe that clung to the household. She'd needed to get laid. Two hours later, she'd tiptoed through the darkened house, dragging a lanky guy by the hand. Wallace or Warren, some *W* name. Three drinks had worked their magic to blind her to the negativity humming from the walls, and her father sleeping on the sofa.

Until Katherine's bedroom door creaked open behind her, right when she was sitting on top of the *W* guy. W grabbed her hips, halting her movement. Her father's sneer heated her bare back before she turned and saw the expression plastered across his scruffy face.

"Sorry, man," W said, as if he'd offended her father by bedding his daughter.

Her father lit a cigarette and leaned against the doorjamb. "Don't stop on my account," he said. "She's just a whore. Make sure you get your money's worth. Man."

She wasn't a whore. She hadn't even let W pay for her drinks.

Instead of taking it, instead of cowering, she'd retaliated. She'd felt bold, not ashamed, caught in the act of asserting her power. "Don't listen to him," Katherine had countered. "He's just a lazy welfare drunk who wouldn't be able to pay the rent without my help."

She held her father's gaze for either ten seconds or ten years. Either way, she shook, as though she were trying to withstand the pull of a black hole. The pull of the empty place where her father's soul should've been.

Her father took a long drag and then blew smoke out of the side of his mouth. "You're gonna be sorry you said that," he said without an ounce of venom. And then, soundlessly, he'd closed her bedroom door.

Katherine should've kept her damn mouth shut.

CHAPTER 6

Love is a kind of sick obsession.

Katherine understood this, as if the words had been written on her heart and on her soul, like the spiritual directive on the scroll of a Jewish mezuzah.

When Barry walked into Lamontagne's, time stood still for Katherine. The facts of her life—everything that had come to pass before she'd met her ex-husband and everything that had happened since—held no meaning. Same as the first time she'd met him, before they'd even had their first conversation, every cell in her mind and body aligned with Barry's frequency, and a twitchy, achy sensation climbed her neck.

But of course, same as always, when Barry walked through the door, only Katherine was standing still. And her life was racing forward, those she loved moving away from her. Celeste had boomeranged back, but for how long? And Zach? Well, his fate had yet to be realized. She and Zach were engaged in a game of chicken, neither of them ready to spill the beans and speak. Eventually, Barry would give up on her and leave, too.

Barry sipped his coffee and laid a dollar bill on the counter. The scent of rain-stirred downed leaves and earth emanated from Barry's hair and clothing and greeted Katherine, but he didn't say hello.

"Good morning to you, too."

"Sorry," Barry said. "The rain."

Katherine nodded. She slipped Barry's dollar into her apron pocket. Rain meant Barry had taken his rarely used Volkswagen Golf out of the garage and left his street bike hanging from the hooks. No bike meant no exercise before work. And no exercise made him, well, about as grouchy as a normal person before his first shot of caffeine.

"Made it just the way you like it," Katherine said, "nice and strong."

"Just the way I like coffee is in bed."

"Barry . . ." Katherine said, more of a sigh than a word, because she couldn't stand seeing him like this. His blatant need pulled, physically pulled, as though a hand were tearing at her solar plexus. The worst part? Knowing she'd done this to him. Inside her apron, she fisted Barry's dollar till its sharp edges stabbed the flesh of her palm.

"Just the way I like coffee is on a tray in bed between me and my wife."

"A lot has happened between us."

"The way I like coffee is with my wife in bed and—"

Celeste popped up behind Katherine. "With a blueberry muffin?"

"Sure, why not?" Barry said.

Celeste swiped a bakery tissue.

"You don't eat first thing in the morning," Katherine said, remembering their first night together and the pursuant morning she'd awoken starving. He'd made her a three-egg omelet and then watched her eat every bite.

"You don't know everything about me."

"Oh, really, now? Since when?"

Barry took a sip of his coffee, giving Katherine time to wonder what he could possibly have to hide from her. His expression gave away nothing. She didn't like it, didn't like the idea that he had a private self, that his thoughts might be as incongruous with his actions as hers.

Before they'd married, they'd stay up until the small hours of the morning talking about everything from their childhoods to world politics, from her passion for baking to his insatiable curiosity for the human psyche. When the conversations waned, Barry would roll over to pretend to try to catch a few winks before work. Katherine, needing to get up for work herself, would drop a kiss behind his ear and press her breasts between his shoulder blades.

Barry's natural inclination was to move fast, to hurry, as if sex were something about which to be ashamed. She'd shown him how to take it slow, to savor every stage of arousal. Katherine knew he'd been with other women since their divorce. She couldn't expect Barry to be celibate. But the thought of him sharing his *mind* with another woman? That unraveled a loop of Katherine's resolve and made her want to press her breasts between his shoulder blades.

"Your favorite color is aqua," she said. "You consider yourself a Reform Jew, more as a cultural thing than a religion, and you're open to the possibility of life after death. You're a registered Independent because you don't trust either party. You think Freud was at best a chauvinist, at worst misogynistic. You're overly fond of Jung."

"First date banter."

In lieu of dropping her jaw, Katherine jostled her head.

Barry mimicked Katherine's head jostle to a T, and his hand reached up to pretend to fix his hair a nanosecond before her hand followed that oft-traveled path.

"Your Bubbe Sarah lived with you and your parents in her dotage. When you woke up in the middle of the night, she warmed milk in a white enamel pot on the gas stove to help you get back to sleep. You led her to believe you had trouble sleeping, but you'd actually set your alarm for four a.m. so you could spend time alone with her and listen to her stories about growing up in Russia. Bubbe Sarah's eyes were aqua, like yours, supposedly." Katherine angled Barry a look. *What do you think of that?*

Celeste held up a blueberry muffin. "For here or to go?"

"For here," Barry told Celeste. "But I don't need a plate."

And then, for Katherine's benefit, "I tell everyone about Bubbe Sarah."

Celeste handed the muffin to Barry. "Is she the one who made the mundel bread?"

"The one and only," Barry told Celeste. But his eyes challenged Katherine.

Celeste mouthed, *Sorry,* but then she intentionally raised a shoulder and batted her eyes. Another version of thumbing her nose at Katherine.

Barry bit into Celeste's blueberry muffin and inhaled into his chest. "Mmm, this is good," he said, his voice all muffin muffled. "Better than Katherine's."

Celeste rewarded Barry with a tight-lipped proud smile.

"That's why I put them on the menu," Katherine said, catching Celeste's eye before Celeste bounced back into the kitchen. Clearly, Barry was trying to sidetrack Katherine's train of thought. She wasn't that easy. "You believe in life after death because the morning after Bubbe Sarah died, you woke up at four a.m., like always. And when you went to pour yourself a glass of milk, it had warmed in the container."

Barry's head jostled, and he took another bite of the muffin to cover.

Katherine offered her own proud smile.

Barry chewed the muffin, giving himself time, Katherine was sure, to finagle a way to insert doubt into her recollection. "Yeah. Thing was," Barry said, "when the power goes out, the fridge stops working. Instant warm milk. *Woo, woo.*" He fluttered a hand in the air to illustrate his sound effect.

Katherine nodded, as if she agreed with him. "Did I mention you're really embarrassed about believing in ghosts? Not quite sure why . . . but I do know why you're an Independent."

"Because you divorced me?" Barry said, a clever comeback that seemed to catch Barry off guard, judging by the way he feigned a sudden fascination with folding the muffin liner.

"Because your mother's a Democrat, your father a Republican. And although they've enjoyed fifty-five years of wedded bliss—"

"Fifty-six."

Right, she'd mailed a card on the first of the month. "When you were growing up, the only thing they argued about was politics. At the dinner table, they skirted religion and politics. But every night, they sat down to the evening news, channel four, 'Proud as a Peacock,' and they argued."

Barry frowned at the muffin paper, gave it a final fold, and tossed the tiny square into the trash. "They didn't really argue."

"Not directly. Not with each other. But they each disagreed strongly with journalists on the news who held the precise views of their spouse."

"Parallel argument."

"So you decided, subconsciously of course, that you couldn't be a Democrat or a Republican."

"Why?"

"To guarantee you wouldn't argue with your spouse!" Katherine said, guessing correctly and debunking Barry's strategy. The thrill of the former did little to offset the regret of the latter.

"Did you just psychoanalyze me?"

"I don't know. Did I?"

Barry nodded—slow and steady—and grinned as if he'd no idea about the debunking.

"Teach me how to do that with Celeste," Katherine said,

her voice husky and urgent. Katherine's bold-faced need warmed her cheeks. She hadn't realized how much Celeste's welfare meant to her until the request for assistance hung in the air between her and Barry like a question mark. Would Barry take the hook or leave her swinging?

"You want the secret handshake?"

The Suzy Q construction guys burst through the door, and the jingle bell clanged behind them. The sound of rain amplified and then softened. The shorter, stockier of the two men held a folded newspaper over his head, which he now unfolded and gave a resolute shake. His taller buddy stomped his boots on the mat inside the door.

Barry stepped aside from the counter and gave Katherine a nod and a grin before making a show of strolling alongside the display case.

"Working in the rain today?" Katherine asked her customers.

"Hoping it'll pass. Seems to be letting up." The shorter man directed his gaze toward the front window, where the rain flowed like a waterfall from the awning.

"Mr. Optimistic," the taller man said.

"Don't knock it till you've tried it." The man frowned at his friend but was too cheerful to appear genuinely annoyed. He slapped his dollar on the countertop before Katherine.

Katherine handed the dollar back to Mr. Optimistic. "Coffee's on the house this morning, due to the rain and all."

Mr. Optimistic gave Katherine a smile that crinkled the skin around his eyes, making him look to be in his late thirties, maybe even early forties. Younger than her but not too young. "You just made my day," he said, and his tone lightened. Was it also tinged with special meaning?

"I'm Katherine," she said, and offered her hand to Mr. Optimistic.

"Daniel," he said, holding her gaze for an extra beat. The

color of his eyes was a cross between brown and gold, a match for his short, dark-blond hair.

Barry finished browsing her pastries and came back to the counter, dragging his hand across the display case and glaring at Katherine's and Daniel's clasped hands. Beneath Barry's fingertips, the glass squealed.

Katherine let go of Daniel's hand first.

"Jeff," the other man said, and gave Katherine's hand a cursory squeeze.

Daniel and Jeff chose the table closest to the bakery case. Daniel chose the chair that faced Katherine.

Barry leaned across the checkout counter. He didn't look like his usual laid-back self. He inhaled deeply to catch his breath, as though he'd just lifted weights or was preparing to do so.

She was the weight beneath which he was straining.

"Barry—" She wanted to apologize, but for what? For hurting him? For divorcing him so she wouldn't hurt him? For continuing to hurt him?

She should tell him to stop coming into the bakery. She should, but she wouldn't. She wasn't that strong.

Barry kept his voice low. "You want the secret handshake? You want to know how to figure out Celeste? You want her to tell you why she came back?"

"You know I do," Katherine whispered, and a shiver ran up the back of her head.

"Just be there for her. Ask open-ended but specific questions. Like, uh, what classes at school were her favorites and why? Ask her to name the friends she made. What did she like about those friends? What didn't she like?"

"Right. Okay."

"When she answers your questions, if she answers your questions, you ask more. Help her to delve deeper beneath the surface of events. She doesn't want to talk about why she came back?" Barry said, and Katherine nodded. "Don't ask her again, not unless she's getting really close to telling you."

A lock of Katherine's hair swung across her vision, and she peered around it.

The pace of Barry's speech slowed, as though each word had genuine heft. "There's always a why beneath the why, even if you don't find out what's troubling her, even if she doesn't know."

Even if she doesn't know.

"How long—how long should this deep inquiry take?"

Barry chuckled. "It might take forever. It might take longer than the two of you have together. It's like that saying about leading a horse to water. Sometimes, despite your best efforts, despite being an overeducated, politically Independent, Bubbe Sarah–loving shrink, you still can't get your best patient to come clean."

And sometimes, despite your best efforts, your wife wouldn't give you a good enough reason why she wanted a divorce. You could lead a horse to water . . . Yup, Katherine was the horse.

"You try everything," Barry said, "even reread your textbook on Jung therapy, but then at some point she goes quiet. She gets that look of wanting to say something, but knowing that she shouldn't. Then she really and truly decides not to say anything. And then, finally, she just looks sad."

"Then what happens?"

"Oh, then she initiates sex, to either avoid the subject or numb out. So, you know, it's not all bad."

"Just to be clear. We're talking about me, about us, now, right? Please tell me we're talking about us, not Celeste."

"Absolutely." Barry's gaze widened, and he raised his voice. "Who'd want to talk about Celeste?"

"Just to be clear," Celeste said. "Behind you." She passed by

Katherine, guiding the bread-laden speed cart and Zach. The speed cart rattled and rolled out to the café, trailing bread scent. The humidity captured every sweet, savory nuance.

"You didn't hire the fifteen-year-old kid," Barry said.

"I was never going to hire the kid."

Katherine's help-wanted notice in the *Hidden Harbor Gazette* had brought out a few women looking for nine-to-five jobs, a gentleman asking whether he could greet customers at the door, and a boy with dirty hands, who—even if he washed his hands—wasn't available during school hours. During a moment of weakness, after the kid had brought Katherine homemade croissants and when the look on his face had reminded her of Celeste, she'd considered hiring him for cleanup duties. But then she'd told him she needed more hours, and he'd stomped out the door, really reminding her of Celeste.

Barry stared after Zach, and his eyes narrowed. "Do we know him?" Barry asked, using the plural pronoun Katherine thought they'd abandoned.

"No, not really. He's new in town," Katherine said, but Barry's face remained turned toward Zach, his expression intent.

Celeste passed loaves of sourdough from the trays to Zach, and Zach arranged them on the shelves. The two of them were orchestrated as though they'd been working together for years. Their voices thrummed the air, like background music, too low to hear the words. Then Celeste laughed, and the notes tumbled Katherine's gut. Glad, because Zach was making Celeste happy, but worried, too. If food was the way to a woman's heart, humor was the fastest route to steer her into bed.

Nurse Terry flew into the bakery with a roar of rain and wind. She pushed the door shut behind her, lowering the storm's volume, and slid the hood of her rain jacket from her head. Katherine readied the nurse's daily order—a plain croissant and a carton of OJ from the mini-fridge behind the counter. Katherine gave the OJ a shake before dropping it into the bakery bag. Fast-food drive-by restaurants had nothing on Lamontagne's.

Terry laid her money on the counter, hugged her order to her chest, and looked Katherine in the eye. "You take such good care of me," Terry said.

"Morning to you, too, Terry," Katherine said. "Stay dry out there!"

Barry thrust his chin toward Zach and Celeste. "So, the young guy, your new hire, what's his bakery experience?"

Katherine quelled the urge to roll her eyes. "I don't need someone with bakery experience. I need someone who'll work hard, someone who's ready and willing to learn. Someone who can get here before six."

Barry positioned his hands as if he were holding a clipboard. Then he drew a checkmark in the air. "No bakery experience," he told the clipboard. And then, to Katherine, "Patient avoiding the question." He drew a second checkmark.

"Don't shrink me."

A third. "And prickly."

She'd give him prickly.

Katherine's pulse sped up, responding to her directive. She took a shallow breath and inhaled the mellowness of freshly baked bread, but the aroma didn't reach her mood. She stared Barry down and inhaled from her toes. Breathing in his rain-scented clothing made her want to bury her nose in his neck and inhale his skin.

Barry's gaze wandered back to Zach. This time, Zach looked up from his task. Celeste straightened and stretched her back, reminiscent of Katherine.

Katherine was sure Celeste would be horrified to have unintentionally picked up one of her quirks.

"Does the young guy—?"

"Zach." Now that she knew his name, she couldn't allow him to go nameless. A few hours after he'd been born, a nurse had come into Katherine's room with the paperwork. To her surprise, she was asked if she wanted to give her son a name. Even though there was no way she'd ever know whether the adoptive parents would keep the name, not naming her son would've seemed like an insult.

Katherine liked the name Zach. She wished she could tell Zach's parents that she approved of their choice.

As if they'd ever approve of her.

"Does *Zach* have any restaurant or food service experience?"

"Nope."

"Any relatives who live in the area? Friends or family we know personally?"

Katherine's pulsed tripped over its own feet. "Not that I'm aware of."

Barry dropped the clipboard act. "Peculiar response."

"Only one I've got." Katherine slipped behind the showcases and examined her stock.

Barry fisted his hands and set them atop the bakery case. He flicked his gaze to Zach. "I know why you hired Zach."

Doubtful, she thought, but her pulse chose to believe otherwise.

"He looks a little bit like you," Barry said. "And we tend to trust people who look familiar."

"I don't see it." Katherine kept her gaze on a row of black-and-white cookies, and her face warmed.

"He's a good-looking young guy."

"Barry!" Katherine said, and Daniel, the guy who wasn't too young for her, glanced up from his newspaper.

As if Barry had raised his voice, he now lowered it. Another shrink trick? "What I meant was, he's in good shape."

"What do you think of me?" She wasn't one of those over-forty ladies who wore skintight clothes to cinch her expanding waistline, flocked to doctors to tighten her sagging skin, and went after men young enough to be their sons in a desperate attempt to shore up their sagging egos. She didn't have a sagging ego. And the rest of her she was too busy to notice.

Barry steepled his hands atop the bakery case. "He's staying through closing, after Celeste leaves for the day. Am I right?"

"So?"

"You want to know what I think of you?"

"Don't Jung me," she said, referring to the method of echoing the patient's concerns.

"I know you're human," Barry said.

Katherine held out her palms, shook her head.

"I know you've been anxious . . ." Barry said. "Nervous in the bakery alone."

Katherine gave a quick, sharp laugh. Barry thought she'd hired Zach as a bouncer for the bakery. She almost wished she could explain to Barry how hilarious that was. Almost.

"I'm not anxious. Why should I be anxious?" Katherine said, although her gaze wandered across the room to the yellow booth cushion that was lighter than the rest. The inability to match the original shade served as a reminder, cruel in its subtlety. A quick glance, and the yellows appeared to match. No customer could tell the difference. No one had noticed Katherine had covered up evidence of a crime, the violation. That itself felt like a violation.

Celeste headed across the café toward the coffee station.

Barry made big, sweeping motions with both hands, ushering her over. "Celeste will settle our disagreement."

Celeste mouthed, *Of course,* crossed her heart, and headed their way.

Katherine widened her eyes in a way she hoped Barry

would notice, but Celeste would ignore. Katherine turned her head from side to side, every so slo—

"Has Katherine seemed out of sorts to you," Barry asked, "a teensy bit anxious?"

"Why would she be anxious?" Celeste asked.

Nooo.

"Because of the break-in?"

"What break-in?"

Belatedly, Barry registered Katherine's wordless plea and clamped his mouth shut.

"What the hell?" Celeste said, and then looked to Katherine, as though she'd spoken her name. "There was no break-in. If there was a break-in, Katherine would've called me."

"Even if I had your phone number, which I did not, I wouldn't have called you. What possible purpose would calling you have served? What could you have done, other than worry? You were hours away."

"I'm here now," Celeste said, somehow managing to look like both a three-year-old dropped off at nursery school for the first time and a fierce, capable young woman. "So tell me."

Katherine slid her gaze to the ceiling and shook her head. She waved her hand through the air. "There was an incident, minor damage—"

Celeste looked to Barry for confirmation. *Medium,* Barry mouthed.

"Black graffiti on the walls and a booth. Childlike, really. Like a tantrum. A disorganized tantrum."

Celeste's eyes narrowed and then widened. "The booth by the bread shelves? The one farthest from the door?"

"That would be the one. But like I said, nothing to worry about. I took care of it. I took care of everything."

Celeste tapped a bakery clog against her shin.

"What are you doing?"

"Kicking myself for not asking you about the booth. I

thought it looked different. I noticed the red trim. But then I didn't trust my own memory. Maybe you'd always had one booth with red trim instead of green."

Damn. Red? Green? The two colors appeared muted and often similar to Katherine. She shouldn't have trusted her own eyes.

"And then I forgot about it," Celeste said.

"Then you remembered," Barry said.

"Always listen to your gut," Katherine said. "Otherwise, your gut stops talking to you."

"Or I could've waited for the owner of the bakery I've worked at since I was sixteen years old to tell me about the robbery herself. No, wait, your gut told you not to call me."

Katherine pressed a forefinger to the center of her lips. Her customers didn't need a serving of gossip along with their morning coffee. "There was a burglary, not a robbery," she said, her voice lowered to a three-foot range. "A robbery means a break-in, while the home or business owner is on-site. I wasn't on-site."

Zach continued to transfer loaves of sourdough onto the bread shelves, his head bent into his task. The grouchy construction worker, Jeff, sipped his coffee, indifferent. His cheerful compatriot, Daniel, alternated from pretending to read the paper to glancing across the room.

Katherine doubted anyone could hear her and Barry's conversation, but vibes were contagious. Talking about anxiety made her anxious. Was it any wonder she'd never gone to a shrink?

Barry glanced at Daniel. Then he reached a hand up to Katherine's face and slid a lock of hair back into her cowlick. "My work here is done."

She'd never *paid* for a shrink.

"Your work as a troublemaker? Your work stirring and muddying calm waters?"

"Sometimes you need to stir the waters to see what rises to the surface," Barry said. "A wise woman once told me that."

"A shrink friend?" Katherine asked.

"You." Barry held Katherine's gaze until the rest of her saying surfaced.

Otherwise the surface is deceptively smooth, and all you can see is a reflection of your own image.

"See you tomorrow," Barry said, and went out to the storm. The door jingled in his wake. The sound of the rain pounding the pavement amplified and softened. He passed by the window and through a circle of light, as though an early sunup had pierced through the storm. He looked younger, maybe a dozen years younger, the age he'd been when they'd first married and before everything had complicated and caved.

But of course the trompe l'oeil was nothing more than the predawn streetlight's illumination and wishful thinking.

"What if you'd interrupted the burglar?" Celeste whispered, her concern a mirror of Katherine's when she'd found the bakery trashed and she'd worried for Celeste.

But, of course, Celeste had been at school, miles away, safe and sound. "Then I suppose he, or she, would've become a robber."

At first, the police had assumed the intruder had hoped to find money in the till, or a safe that was easy to pick. But the open and empty cash register drawer had remained untouched, and no prints had wreathed the safe's numbered wheel, save for Katherine's.

Unable to take anything of value, a burglar would've, at the least, left with a keepsake. Something, anything, to prove he'd been there, if only to himself.

The intruder had broken into Lamontagne's to vandalize, to let Katherine know he'd traipsed through her sacred space. He'd left her evidence, made a statement, given her proof of his powers. Nothing was removed from the bakery except for Katherine's peace of mind.

"Have the police figured out who broke in? Who'd do such a thing? It's not like you have any enemies," Celeste said, having come around to another of Katherine's misguided assumptions. "It must've been a stranger, someone from another town?" Celeste said, but her statement sounded like a question.

"Actually, the police think it must've been someone who knows me, due to the damage."

Celeste shook her head. Her hand covered her mouth. "I should never have left. What if someone had hurt you?"

"No one's going to hurt me. If someone broke into the bakery again, I'd handle it myself."

Celeste grinned. "What would you do? Challenge them to a bake-off?"

Katherine gave Celeste a good, long stare. What in the world did Celeste see when she looked at her? A divorced, childless, middle-aged woman whose world began and ended at the door to her eponymous bakery? Katherine could take care of herself; she'd never had a choice. "Come in the kitchen with me for a minute."

"Zach—"

"Will be perfectly fine." Zach, Katherine was certain, could handle himself. "He'll find us if he needs us."

Inside the kitchen's stockroom, Katherine turned on the light—a pendant with a single bulb—and shut the door behind them. The dimness of the space and the need for secrecy brought to mind a tiny bathroom and the sharp smell of fear. "I have a gun," Katherine told Celeste.

Celeste laughed, as if Katherine had delivered the punch line to a joke.

"It's a Smith & Wesson .22," Katherine said. "Loaded and locked in the safe."

"I don't believe you." Celeste stared at Katherine, stone-faced, as though waiting for Katherine to change her story. Then Celeste broke into a crazy-eyed grin. "You're serious," she said, and gave her head a quick shake. "It's in the locked safe? Locked?" Celeste flapped her arms. Flour motes scattered and glimmered around them. "What good is a loaded gun in a locked safe?" Celeste emitted a combination between a growl and a snort.

Katherine folded her arms, hoping the stance would shore up her dubious argument. "It's for self-defense. I don't want to really shoot anyone. I just want to scare them."

"Okay. For the sake of argument, let's say you walk in on someone—a burglar or a robber—"

"A vandal."

"A skateboard punk rocker—whatever—and you ask them to wait for you to unlock your combination safe. And then you whip out your loaded gun and point it. But not at them, just in their general direction to scare them off because you really don't want to shoot anyone."

Katherine took a slow, steady breath. "Change your tone if you want me to hear you. Otherwise this conversation is over."

Gone was Celeste's indignity over Katherine's assumption about her and Zach, or at least set aside. And in its place? Frustration.

Long ago, a cracked bathroom mirror had reflected the same expression on Katherine's face: the pleading eyes, the determined set to her jaw. Celeste wrapped her arms around her stomach, as sick with frustration as Katherine had once been, trying to talk her mother into leaving her father. Trying to talk sense into she who refused to defend her boundaries.

Two gentle taps echoed through the stockroom door, and Katherine startled. "A customer's asking about Celeste's Wild Blues," Zach said, his voice even-keeled and upbeat.

"I'll be right out," Celeste called through the door, mimicking Zach's tone.

She and Katherine held their breath until Zach gave the door a single tap. "See you out there," he said.

"I'll teach you how to shoot," Celeste whispered, "so you don't shoot yourself in the foot." She nodded, but Katherine refused to play along.

"Go chat up your muffins. I'll be out in a minute."

"At least give me the combination to the safe," Celeste said.

For a second, Katherine thought Celeste had said *to be safe.* That combination Katherine did not have.

"Go," Katherine said, more gently, she hoped, more the way she meant the word. But words were so inexact, so open to misunderstandings.

Celeste opened her mouth, as if to protest. Then she slipped from the stockroom on a sigh, leaving Katherine alone with her memories of another room, a closed door, and two women who could not agree.

On the day of the last big talk, Katherine and her mother had huddled in their tiny bathroom, the only room with a door that locked. Back then Katherine had never heard of verbal abuse, but she'd nonetheless tried to explain it to her mother. Living things deformed when exposed to ugly words and blossomed beneath expressions of love, gratitude, and hope. Katherine had reminded her mother of the peach tree in the yard that ten years prior, when they'd first rented the cottage, had yielded healthy fruit but now sat shriveled and rotting. Surely her mother would make the connection. All life responded in kind. In this house, nothing beautiful could survive.

Instead, Katherine's mother kept bringing up the number of years she and Katherine's father had been married—twenty-five—and the two daughters they'd brought into the world. Katherine couldn't argue against the math. But none of it added up to a reason, a logical reason, why her mother would stay with her father.

Then Katherine's father knocked on the door, making Katherine and her mother jump and squeeze hands. "What the hell you girls doing in there?" her father asked. "Painting your stupid fingernails? You'd better be scrubbing that filthy toilet, you goddamn lazy, good-for-nothing . . ."

Leave, Katherine had mouthed, her eyes widened in a way she hoped her mother would translate into, *Leave him.*

And then, seeming to understand, her mother had done the strangest thing. She'd hugged Katherine to her chest, tight enough to steal her breath. The sharp angle of her mother's collarbone dug into Katherine's chest, and her mother's pulse thrummed through Katherine's body, as if they shared one heart. Her mother pressed her lips to Katherine's ear and offered an explanation for why she stayed with her father that trumped all good reason. "Because," Katherine's mother had told her, "I love him."

Love was a kind of sick obsession.

Chapter 7

Zach was a little obsessed.

He awoke with the seat belt buckle digging into his hip and his shoulder folded in a warped way no healthy shoulder ought to fold. His head tucked into his sleeping bag, the sharp smell of his own body odor burning his nose hairs. His sweaty toes didn't seem connected at the ends of his cold feet.

He poked his head from the darkness of the sleeping bag. The eyeball-aching assault of the parking lot light reminded him of the way a cop's flashlight beam had caught him with his pants down. Twice. The first time he'd been parked at Lookout Point after the prom and a cop shone a flashlight through his back window just as he and his girlfriend were getting to the good part. Thirty more seconds he'd wanted to request, but he'd thought better of turning his embarrassment into a full-out stand-up comedy routine. The second time he'd been at the receiving end of a cop's high-beam flashlight and a falsely cheery *Good morning!* was the last time Zach had had sex. A few hours before he'd stumbled home to the suitcase on the porch and his mother's *find her* note.

He was here to find his birth mother, to ask Katherine the question he'd yet to dare: *Are you my mother?*—reminiscent of the children's book his adoptive mother used to read to him and his not-adopted brothers. A million times he'd turned over the words in his head. A million times they'd sounded dumb as dirt. A million times he'd clamped his mouth shut and taken mental notes on Katherine's life, as though that would tell him how to broach the subject. Stacking bread, busing tables, and "marrying" the pastries gave Zach a front-row seat to Katherine and her customers—the way she simultaneously held them close and yet kept her distance. Katherine and Celeste weren't related—as Zach's father liked to say, thank God for small miracles—but they acted like mother and daughter.

Zach was here to reunite with his birth mother. And yet Celeste awoke his curiosity, among other things. Beneath the sleeping bag, not everything was cold.

He inhaled the blanket she'd loaned him. Sugar cookies, vanilla frosting, and something else. Nutmeg? Cinn—"Good morning, sunshine." Celeste peered through the side window. Some kind of bakery kerchief thing corralled her hair.

On Sunday, the one day of the week Lamontagne's was closed for business, Zach, Katherine, and Celeste were all working the Hidden Harbor Harvest Festival. Katherine and Celeste would stop by Lamontagne's to bake and organize, and he'd drop in an hour later to help them ferry baked goods to a booth on the town green. He'd asked Celeste to wake him up when she was heading out. He'd totally forgotten he'd asked her because he was busy thinking about her and—Slowly, he slid his hand from his boxers. The elastic waistband slapped his stomach. Inside the sleeping bag, he broke into a sweat. His pulse thrummed his armpits, making them itch.

"Can you roll down the window?" Celeste asked.

"Sure." Zach sat up and held the sleeping bag around him. He shivered in the chill air.

Celeste passed him a hot, steaming mug.

"Thank you!" He held his face over the coffee and inhaled

deeply. Heat radiated into his hands. "Oh, man, you must've read my mind," Zach said, his way of thanking God she couldn't.

She crinkled her nose, which looked really cute, until she waved her hand in front of her face. "Hate to tell you, Zach. But you kind of stink."

"Hate to tell you, Celeste, but I know." Zach slurped the coffee. "Mmm mmm good."

Celeste leaned a hand against the window frame. "Where have you been showering?"

Zach sputtered on the coffee. He coughed into his fist to clear his throat. "Lamontagne's." His voice came out as a high-pitched squeak around the coffee.

Instead of backing away from his stench, Celeste leaned in closer and lowered her voice. "There's no shower at the bakery."

Zach pretended to splash water beneath either armpit.

"You've been sponge bathing in the washroom?" she said, her voice doing its own high-rise climb.

When Zach nodded, Celeste broke into a wide grin. She slapped the roof of the car, the way a good old boy might slap his knee. "If Katherine knew she'd have a bird! No wonder you've been spending so much time in there. *Phew!* I thought you had some kind of gastrointestinal issue."

Smooth, Zach, real smooth.

Zach shrugged and took another sip of coffee.

Celeste shook her head and turned, as if to leave. Instead, she leaned against Matilda, giving him a nice view of her olive-green hoodie. By the time she turned back around, he'd drained the coffee. He didn't have a gastrointestinal issue, but his bladder was in serious need of a bathroom.

Celeste worked a key from her key ring.

Zach's heart tumbled in his chest. He broke into a grin and then purposely tamped down his automatic horndog enthusiasm.

The first time he'd laid eyes on Celeste, he'd imagined this moment, the pretty girl inviting him into her apartment. Hell, he'd imagined—in detail—her welcoming him into her bed. But, now, he wanted to go back to Wednesday and punch the Wednesday Zach in the eye. Obsession or not, woody in the sweltering sleeping bag or not. He didn't want to one-night or one-week stand this girl.

This thing he wanted . . . had no name.

Key between thumb and forefinger, she slipped her hand through the open window and then snatched it back, her fingers seeming to twitch on the retreat. She held the key against her chest. Was she shaking?

"I'm going to give you my key," she said. "You can use my apartment to shower. But there are rules."

"I'm all about the rules."

"No snooping at any of my stuff. No opening the medicine cabinet. No peeking in my drawers. Actually, no going into my bedroom at all. You go in, you shower, you get out and lock the door behind you. You got it?"

"I get in, I go straight to the shower, I get out and lock the door behind me. I keep my hands out of your drawers."

"Zach!" Celeste said, but at least she was laughing.

"Sorry," he said, "you stepped into that one. Yup, I get it."

This time, when Celeste handed him the key, when she let him take it from her hand, he paid better attention.

She *was* shaking.

This thing with no name, this new thing he felt, made him want to find out why she was shaking and hold her till she stilled.

Zach rubbed the key between his thumb and forefinger, as though it were his St. Anthony coin. He hadn't been sure how long he could keep living out of his car without a shower, but he couldn't commit to any sort of lease, any sort of guarantee he'd stay. Celeste's offer gave him time to wait and watch and stake out his life. Katherine's life. Celeste's life. "This is really nice of you."

"Yeah, it is. But don't let it get around."

"That you're nice?"

"And that you're showering at my apartment. I wouldn't want anyone getting the wrong idea."

"You and Katherine are the only people I know in the entire state of Maine. Who would I tell?"

"I'm serious. Especially don't tell Katherine. Either promise not to tell or you go back to your sponge baths."

"I won't tell anyone you're nice."

"Pro—"

"Or that you're letting me use your shower," Zach said.

Celeste didn't want anyone to think they were sleeping together. Specifically because they'd just met? Or in general, because who she slept with wasn't anyone's business? He wasn't into kissing and telling, the weekends in the dorm guys' bonding game of you tell me who you screwed, I'll tell you what the girl with the overbite and kitten posters looks like naked.

He wouldn't want a girl talking about him that way.

He'd never bought into the idea if a guy slept with a lot of girls, he was a stud, but if a girl had a track record, she was a slut.

He considered himself neither a stud nor a slut. He considered himself a guy who enjoyed sex. Didn't everybody?

Something to consider.

"See you in an hour," Celeste said. "Get ready to meet the rest of Hidden Harbor, all two thousand of them, and their dogs." Celeste got into Old Yeller and keyed the engine.

Zach thought of the Lamontagne regulars. The high school kids who dropped in after school to hang out. The girls who hugged each other, giggled loudly, and swung their hair, pretending not to notice the boys. The boys who talked sports and pretended, less convincingly, not to notice the girls. The moms with rug rats. The construction worker who seemed interested in Katherine and pretended not to notice the older guy, the reluctant cycler Zach had noticed on day one of his Lamontagne's stakeout. Wasn't he Katherine's boyfriend?

What if she'd had the same boyfriend for twenty-five years?

Zach's throat muscles spasmed. The coffee backed up into his nose. Zach swiped his nose with the back of his hand and set the coffee mug on the floor. He stumbled from the car, holding his sleeping bag around his waist, and banged on Old Yeller's passenger window.

Celeste rolled down the window. Even though he must've looked like an escapee from a funny farm sack race, she didn't even crack a grin. "The shower control works counterclockwise."

If he had any sense, he would've played along and asked her about the bathroom light, the fan, and whether he'd find the sink's cold water on the right or on the left. If he had any sense, he would've worried about sounding like a lunatic. "What's with the reluctant cycler?"

"The what?" she asked through a giggle.

Zach scrubbed a hand across his coffee-sputtered face. "The gray-haired guy who comes in to see Katherine every morning."

A wary smile tugged the corners of Celeste's lips.

Ah, hell. Too late to backtrack. He was all-in. "Is he her boyfriend?" Zach's voice, apparently having great comic timing and an intense desire to mortify him, rose two octaves.

Celeste shot him a flashlight-beam grin.

"Husband?" Zach tried.

"Ex," Celeste said.

Did he know?

Celeste really and truly slapped her knee. "Oh, my, my," she cooed.

"What? 'Oh, my, my'?"

"Oh, my, my. You have a crush on Katherine."

"Oh, no. *God,* no!"

"Nothing to be embarrassed about. It's happened before. Younger men fall for her all the time. Toddlers, some preschoolers . . ."

"That's not even funny."

"Gotta go, Zach. I'm off to hang out with your girlfriend. And that, sir, is hilarious." Celeste repositioned herself behind the wheel. "Don't worry, your secret's safe with me, baby cakes," she said before backing Old Yeller from the space and leaving Zach standing in the middle of the parking lot.

What the hell was he doing here, in the middle of this morning that looked like night, in the middle of this strange town, in another place where he didn't belong?

The wind moved through his sleeping bag, as though it were nothing, the reason he told himself he was shivering. Circulation returned to his toes, shooting daggers through his feet and nailing them to the pavement. The girl he was crushing on thought he had a crush on the woman who might be his birth mother. What was he supposed to do with that?

He was both stuck and fucked.

Zach threw back his head and yelled at the moon, "Now what!" The deaf and dumb moon stared down at him, hanging like a cardboard prop in the morning sky. His secret was safe with Celeste.

That was the funniest thing he'd ever heard.

Let the Hidden Harbor Harvest Festival begin!

Wasn't that similar to a line about a wild rumpus from the children's book *Where the Wild Things Are*? The story about a boy in a wolf suit who gets sent to bed without dinner had once been Celeste's favorite bedtime story. She'd curled in her mother's lap and slipped her fingers beneath her mother's blouse to stroke her stomach as though it were a satin ribbon. Then Celeste ran away to a foreign land and let loose the beast within her. But no matter how far she'd sailed away from home, she'd always ended where she began. In her own room and with a full belly, safe and sound.

Late morning sun blazed across the town green and highlighted the stacks of pumpkins deposited in the early hours by farmers hoping to line their pockets with both townie and tourist coin. Shops that peddled hospitality—Lamontagne's included—made the most money in the summer months, between Memorial Day and Labor Day. But lay out enough high-sugar, high-fat foods and orange gourds and offer up a blue-sky day, and townies and tourists alike returned for a last blowout, get up, and party down.

The Hidden Harbor Harvest Festival—Triple H, as the locals called it—had opened for business an hour ago. But, either slow to get the message or waiting for the last of the fair weather, fluffy clouds to drift offshore, festivalgoers were just now trickling onto the lawn, chasing the sun.

If Celeste had stayed in New York, today would've been like any other day. Maybe she would've remembered the festival, held on the same weekend each year. She might've even thought of Katherine, standing straight and tall like a security guard before their booth. But, strangely, Celeste found herself here in the midst of the organized chaos, missing the Triple H. No, *mourning* the Triple H. Her stomach ached around the thought, as though someone had sucker punched her in the gut. As though she were a pumpkin, and someone had sliced around her stem with a serrated knife and scraped her free of flesh and seeds. As if she were here, but not here, trapped in Triple H purgatory.

As if something was terribly, terribly wrong with her.

Zach bumped her shoulder. "You okay?" he asked.

When she swallowed, the tears in her sinuses made a moist sound. "I'm awesome." Celeste blinked at him.

Zach's lips pressed into one of those sympathetic smiles that simultaneously turned up at the corners while the top lip bowed upside down. One of those *I see your sadness, you who refuses to acknowledge your sadness.*

"I'm awesome, Zach. Really," she said, and turned her attention to the sugar cookies. Trays of blank-faced pumpkins, bats, and witch hats covered the better part of the children's table, awaiting frosting and decorations. She slid the colored sugars to the front of the table and then set them back in a line. She straightened the handwritten table tent signs she'd made for the colored frosting. Frightful blue, raging red, outrageous orange, and midnight black. She proactively told her eating disorder—the annoying, lingering, and much-maligned Ed—to ignore the throat-curdling smells of fried dough, French fries, and sausage.

When she'd awoken Zach, she'd been fine. Really and truly fit as a fiddle, as her dad used to say. Whatever that meant. Now she was on the verge of bending at the waist and howling.

At some point every day since she'd come back home, a feeling would pass through her, like a random bout of seasickness. She'd get a hint of knowing that reminded her of a game they'd played in culinary school. First you'd slip a blindfold over your eyes, and then your classmates would hold spices for you to identify beneath your nose. Without fail, you'd miss a scent, knowing but not knowing the smell. Then you'd rip the blindfold from your eyes, revealing your foolishness, the spice obvious now that you'd seen it in the light.

Behind her, Zach hummed, the buzzing directed at her. She deciphered the tune right away but wanted to draw out the game. "Whistle it," she said.

Without missing a beat, Zach puckered up and held his hands behind his back, making himself look like a kitschy flea market Hummel figurine. In a good way.

"Sing it," she said, the request coming too late. A traitorous sunshiny smile had knocked out her creeping crud feeling, giving her away. Too bad. She'd really wanted to hear him sing.

"You know the song," Zach said.

" 'Don't Worry, Be Happy' ?"

"Yeah, that's it. Don't worry, be happy." Zach tilted his head, and the head tilt shook out another kind of smile. Sympathetic, sure. But this time more happy than sad.

Maybe it was the breeze from their neighbor's cotton candy. Maybe she smelled a mixture of buttered popcorn and kettle corn from the cart across the brick path. Maybe what she smelled was something way simpler and way more obvious. She crinkled her nose.

Zach's gaze shifted sideways. "Hey! I showered."

"Did you use my almond body wash?"

"I got in, I showered, I got out. I followed the rules. Besides, you didn't say I couldn't."

A twinge of that earlier creeping crud feeling reappeared. How could she have answered a question he hadn't even asked? As though she were having an argument with Ed, she talked back at the irrational fear. *Get a grip, Celeste, he was kidding.*

Zach held up his hands. "Okay, okay. Here's what happened. I didn't realize I'd forgotten my soap and shampoo—"

"My shampoo, too!"

"I was soaking wet. And it was, like, either I get out and dry off and run back out to Matilda or . . ."

Celeste folded her arms, tapped her foot. Pretending to be pissed actually made her feel better. She imagined Zach soaking wet, holding a towel around his waist, and running barefoot across the parking lot. She imagined him using her shampoo and body wash and wondered whether he hummed in the shower or maybe even sang.

She held up a finger. "Answer one question for me and you're off the hook."

"Anything."

"You didn't . . . use my puff. Did you?" she croaked out in a fake stricken voice.

"Do I look like a guy who would use a puff?"

"Body wash works better with a puff."

"I didn't use the puff."

"No?" Celeste asked. And then a hint of vanilla pudding scent tweaked her nose. "Bend down," Celeste whispered.

"What?" Zach crouched, answering the question he supposedly hadn't heard. A chunk of hair fell before his eyes, shining in the sun that had sneaked beneath the booth's awning.

Celeste lowered her eyelids and inhaled a stronger vanilla pudding–like scent. Her hand rose, hovering near his head. She straightened and lowered her hand to her side, certain now about what she'd discovered. "You used my Flex conditioner," she told him, the second thought that came to mind. The first thought? She wanted to bury her fingers in his hair, the way she, when Katherine wasn't looking, hand mixed dough without using sensation-filtering food prep gloves.

Lying dormant since Monday, Celeste's below-surface and ever-present hum sprang to life, like a guy's hidden erection.

Jerk Justin had once asked her why she was always so horny. That hadn't been fair. A below-surface hum wasn't the same as being ready to go. She was only ready to go for certain guys. She could imagine being ready to go for Zach. In an alternate universe where Matt the Rat didn't exist.

Great. She'd spent so much time with Katherine, her woo-woo voice was making cameo appearances in Celeste's mind.

Zach straightened until he was looking her in the eye. "Guilty," he said. "You don't tell anyone, I won't tell anyone. Deal?"

"Deal," she said, and then her stupid hand went and touched Zach's hair anyway, the way a dieter snuck a bite of pumpkin pie, when she really wanted a whole slice. With extra whipped cream.

Zach raised his hand to his hair, retracing the path her traitorous fingers had followed. "I generally let the cowlick thingy do whatever it wants. Live and let live. You know?"

"Live and let live," Celeste said. From the corner of Celeste's eye, she spotted her first customers, a trio who'd surely test her ability to do so.

Abby, Charlie, and Luke stopped to chat with Katherine. But when the word *cookies* broke through the tangle of voices, Luke dragged Abby up to the cookie bar, leaving Charlie behind.

Good call.

"Who's this?" Celeste said. "Spiderman without his suit?"

Too late, Celeste registered Abby's cringe. "Spiderman's wearing his invisible suit today. We're saving his other suit for Halloween, so it doesn't get dirty."

"Gotcha."

Luke's big blue eyes peered over the edge of the sugar cookie decorating table. He reached up and dipped a finger into the blue frosting. Abby swooped in and stopped the finger before he popped it into his mouth. "Use a spoon, please."

"How about a stool?" Zach said, coming around the table to place one between Abby and Luke.

Abby hoisted Luke onto the stool. "Thank you!" she said, and threw a questioning look Celeste's way.

Zach answered for himself. "I'm Zach, Lamontagne's newest hire."

"Abby, Celeste's oldest friend."

Luke raised his hand. "Hey! How do I do this thing?"

"Manners, Luke."

"Hey! How do I please do this thing?"

Zach bent down to Luke's level. "First you choose a cookie—"

"Bat! 'Cause bats are cool."

"Then you put stuff on it. Frosting, sprinkles, these silver balls. Whatever you want."

Luke spooned a glob of blue frosting onto his bat. "I like frosting 'cause it smells like Celeste."

"No way, really?"

The tip of Luke's tongue peeked from the corner of his mouth, as though he were preparing to create a culinary masterpiece. With one hand, then the other, he pressed the blue frosting into the bat's wings. "It's true. Smell my hands." Luke held up two equally blue palms, and Zach bent to take a sniff.

"Yeah, maybe a little. But it's not good manners to go sniffing girls."

Luke opened his mouth as though he wanted to swallow the cookie whole and took a bite. Blue smudged the tip of his nose and lined his mouth. He chewed, and his gaze slid from side to side, like a clock pendulum. "Is he a good guy or a bad guy?" Luke asked Celeste.

"I don't know," Celeste said. "Too soon to tell. I'll let you know when I figure it all out."

Luke licked his lips and then went in for a second wide-mouthed bite.

Abby placed a hand on the arm of Celeste's sweater. "Come talk to me," Abby said to Celeste. The seriousness of Abby's tone, so Abby-like, and the dash of pleading, not usually like Abby at all, told Celeste the subject of the requested talk was Charlie.

"I'm working," Celeste said, even though at the moment her only customer was Luke and he seemed to be doing just fine.

Abby scrunched her face and held up a finger, as if she were scolding Celeste. "One lousy minute," Abby said.

"Go ahead," Zach said. "I used to do kids' birthday parties. I can handle the cookie table. No problem."

Abby jammed her hands into her pockets. Her gaze wandered over to where Charlie stood talking with Katherine.

Shame on Celeste for pushing Abby further than her three-year-old, Luke, could. Celeste wished she had a neuralyzer from the movie *Men in Black,* so she could wipe out her own memory and forget everything Charlie had ever done wrong to Abby and Luke. Celeste wished she had another device to make her remember what had happened with Matt the Rat.

"Okay, let's go talk," Celeste said, her heart like a wild thing, caged, and Abby gave her the slightest hint of a smile.

That wouldn't last long.

Celeste loved Abby, but she refused to pretend she was happy about Abby getting back with Charlie. She wasn't going to lie.

Because the thing about telling a lie, even a lie that saved someone else's feelings? You had to first make yourself believe the delusion. You had to buy into the fantasy. You had to forget everything you knew. And what the hell? Sooner or later, everyone, Abby included, needed to face the truth.

CHAPTER 8

Two roads diverged in a yellow wood . . .

Robert Frost's "The Road Not Taken" echoed through Katherine's head, simultaneously bringing her back to her seventh-grade English class, where she'd sat amidst a roiling sea of fidgeting kids and bulging backpacks, light-headed and nauseous from hunger, and anchoring her in the present, where she stood before her bakery's booth of pies and cookies and she never went hungry.

"I don't understand women . . ." Charlie Connors told her.

Abby Stone's off-again on-again boyfriend and the father of her three-year-old son, Luke, let his statement dangle, as though hoping Katherine would both represent and explain her gender.

Katherine followed Charlie's gaze to the side of Lamontagne's booth, where Abby and Celeste were embracing, after having looked anything but pleased with each other. You might be able to school your face into a desired expression, but body language never lied. Abby had jabbed her finger at Celeste, Celeste had folded into herself, and Katherine and Charlie had watched some kind of sisterly drama unfold. The subject of which was most likely Charlie.

Celeste had supported Abby through all of her Charlie

breakups. Unlike Charlie, Celeste had been present for the birth of their son. On that frigid day, a late winter storm had blanketed Hidden Harbor, one of the few times Katherine had closed Lamontagne's due to weather. The next day, Celeste had staggered into work, as devastated by lack of sleep as by worry for her best friend.

If Katherine knew Celeste, she'd right now be waiting and worrying Charlie would, once again, take Abby out at the knees.

Past behavior was the best predictor of future outcomes, and all that jazz.

Yet the second Charlie graduated from college and returned to live and work in Hidden Harbor, Abby had taken him back. The same town gossips who'd four years ago frothed at the mouth at the delicious news about "sweet as pie" Abby's pregnancy and then declared, "Like mother, like daughter," had risen up and cheered.

For the child's benefit? Or for Abby's? Did Abby still believe the fallacy that a single mom's love was second best, even after having herself been raised by a loving, capable single mother?

From Katherine's experience, being raised by married parents guaranteed nothing.

When no general explanation regarding women was forthcoming from Katherine, Charlie continued, "I don't even know why Abby's ticked at Celeste. She asks me whether she should stop by her booth or ignore her. Then she goes and does whatever she wants to do anyway. Why'd she bother asking?"

Here Katherine had some expertise. "She didn't want you to tell her what to do. She only wanted you to listen, so she could figure it out for herself." Katherine's masculine ex-husband, the very man who'd returned a button-down he claimed appeared more pink than red, made his living listening like a woman. Dear lord, had Katherine only now figured this out?

"Huh," Charlie said. "That's weird. Why didn't Abby talk to herself, then?"

Katherine considered her audience. Charlie might look like an adult—he taught at the high school, he took responsibility for his son, he played the part. But inside, most men and women in their early twenties were still children, finding their way.

"Because she didn't want the Briar Rose guests to think their innkeeper was a crazy person," Katherine said. "That's generally bad for business."

"Ah, good point," Charlie said.

A woman in a French-blue fleece, who could've passed for either Mrs. Jenkins's daughter or a youthful doppelgänger, passed before the popcorn booth and slipped into the crowd.

"Hey, I thought you said you weren't hiring just for weekends!"

Katherine startled and turned to find Blake, the kid she was never going to hire, staring in the direction of her newest hire. Blake's slender hands were clean, but he wore the same attitude that had put her off from hiring him months ago: the proverbial chip on his shoulder. He expected to be treated badly. In Katherine's experience, you always got what you expected.

Katherine shook her head and breathed through the boy's negative vibrations. "First of all, you may call me Katherine. You may not call me *hey.* Second of all, I didn't hire anyone just for weekends."

Beneath her glare—she was trying not to glare—the boy's eyes watered.

The boy was rude and spoke out of place, but she had the urge to hug and console him. The impulse thrummed like a hollow ache in her belly. "Blake," she said, "come have a piece of pie with me."

"I don't have any money," he said, his tone an accusation.

She inhaled deeply, intending to calm herself. Instead, the stench of cigarette smoke caught in her throat, dank and distinct. Secondary smoke from Blake's parents or personal use? "On the house."

"I don't need your charity, *Katherine.* I need a job."

Blake turned his skinny self around and stomped across the green.

"Blake, wait!"

"You didn't hear it from me," Charlie said, "but he's having a rough time of it at home."

The back of Blake's black hooded sweatshirt slipped between the popcorn cart and the bandstand and disappeared.

From the time Katherine was ten, she'd needed a job, too, for so many reasons. To prove herself capable. To have worth that her father couldn't disparage. To get out of the house and away from the loud, damaging chip on her father's shoulder. The chip that worked tirelessly to prove her incapable, worthless, and damaged.

Two roads diverged in a yellow wood . . .

"Is Blake in one of your classes?"

"No, but I wish he were." Charlie shrugged. "Maybe I could help him," he said, debunking Katherine's assumption about men in their early twenties in general and Charlie in particular.

Over at the cookie table, Luke licked his palms. When Zach handed Abby a stack of napkins, Luke slid from the stool and ran toward his father. And some women in their early twenties, like Abby, had been born old. Abby was just like her mother.

The summer after Katherine had given up her son, a long-legged sixteen-year-old blonde had come to Hidden Harbor for a job at Hermit Island, gotten pregnant, and stayed. Abby's mother, Lily Beth, was one of the most self-reliant women Katherine knew.

And yet here Abby was, back with the man who'd caused her so much grief.

How was Lily Beth taking the news? How did you keep your children safe from heartbreak? How could you stand back and watch them fail?

Could Katherine have gone it alone, been that self-sufficient single mom, and shown herself the way? She'd been pondering that question since the day she'd given up her son. And over the years, whenever Lily Beth had come into Lamontagne's with Abby, Katherine had silently offered up a heartfelt *huzzah!* Then she'd spent the rest of the day restless, contemplating the nature of fate versus self-determination and whipping up key lime pies so tart they'd stung her eyes.

Now Abby and Luke drew tears to Katherine's eyes. What was wrong with Katherine? She'd made her choice and so had Abby. *Huzzah!*

Charlie bent down and Luke scrambled up onto Charlie's shoulders.

Abby waved a wad of napkins in the air, even though Charlie's fisherman sweater had taken the brunt of the frosting mess. Luke's blue handprints climbed the pale knit, from Charlie's midsection to his shoulders.

Luke held on to Charlie's ears. "Whoa, buddy," Charlie said. "Mom wants us over there. Steer me back to the right."

"I want to play in the corn maze!"

"After you get cleaned up." Charlie faked to the left, pretending to wander in the direction of Luke's steering, before heading over to Abby.

"This car doesn't drive right. I want to play in the corn maze!"

Charlie bent down and set Luke in front of Abby and Celeste.

"Gotcha!" Celeste scooped Luke up and deposited him on her hip.

Abby nabbed Luke's hands and swiped off the remaining frosting. Luke hugged Celeste around the neck and rested his head on her shoulder.

"Aw, sweet boy," Celeste said.

Luke raised his head and turned to Zach. "I didn't really sniff her. I only smelled her on accident."

Zach gave Luke a thumbs-up. "Good job," Zach said, as if he understood what Luke was talking about. "Manners are hard to remember," he added, and Luke nodded, his little face serious.

Zach and Luke seeming to connect. Celeste holding Luke on her hip. Zach and Celeste sharing an unmistakable, as-yet undefined connection. The sight made Katherine feel light-headed and uneasy and lost in time.

"He wants to go to the corn maze," Charlie told Abby.

"First we're visiting Gran's booth, then we go to the corn maze. *Remember?*"

"I never played in a corn maze," Luke told Zach.

"Yeah? Me neither. Looks like fun, though."

"It does look like fun. Someday I should go, too," Katherine said.

"You're kidding." Celeste looked from Zach to Katherine. "My brothers used to take me every year and try to lose me in there."

"Oh, very nice." Katherine grinned, but a tremor ran through her lips, electric with the notion of getting left behind.

"They couldn't get rid of me that easily. They would've gotten in wicked trouble. Besides, I have a great sense of direction. And taste." Celeste nibbled Luke's cheek. "Yum, yum, yum." Luke giggled, and she passed him to Abby.

"You can walk," Abby told him. She set him on the grass and took his hand. "Call me," Abby told Celeste. "Okay?"

Celeste nodded and drew a cross over her heart.

"Pinkie swear!" Luke said.

Abby dropped Luke's hand and held up a pinkie before Celeste. "You heard him."

"Fine!" Celeste clasped Abby's pinkie in hers and set her face in a campy sneer.

"Ow!" Abby said. "You can let go now."

Celeste held up her hands. "Have it your way."

Charlie and Abby took Luke by either hand. Luke bent his legs and swung between them, yanking Abby sideways. "And we're off!" Abby looked to the sky and shook her head. "See you later."

"Bye, Luke," Katherine said. "Take care," she told Abby and Charlie, sending up a silent wish that they'd make it this time. That Abby would get the perfect little family unit she so richly deserved. "Tell your mom I said hello."

"Will do," Abby said, and they headed into the thickening crowd.

"I cannot believe you two have never walked a corn maze." Celeste lowered her head and raised her gaze to Zach. An impish grin tweaked her lips. She gestured from Katherine to Zach. "You guys should, you know, go together."

Quick as a wink, Zach mirrored Celeste's impish grin.

If Katherine didn't know better, she would've thought Celeste was trying to set them up on a date. Payback for Katherine intimating Celeste had started something with Zach?

Every Harvest Festival, Katherine had driven by the Johnson Farm maze, noting the SUVs and minivans parked alongside the road, the families unloading picnic baskets and strollers, retrievers on leashes. She'd wondered whether her son was with another family at another corn maze in another state. She'd wondered whether he was helping his folks unload brown-bag lunches and water bottles. In recent years, she'd even wondered whether the boy she'd given away was unloading an SUV and a family of his own.

Her sinuses swelled. Her jaw ached. Her heart kicked hard and fast, the way her son had once moved inside her. "Sure, why not, later, after we shut down?" Katherine asked. "If Celeste doesn't mind starting cleanup without us."

"Not a problem," Celeste said.

"You up for it, Zach?" Beneath the weight of trying to be light, Katherine's voice cracked.

"Why not?" Zach said, his voice sounding equally strained. Or was Katherine projecting, a mother imagining similarities between herself and her son?

She wasn't Zach's mother.

Zach turned his attention to a preschool boy headed their way, dragging his mother by the hand. On their heels, a woman pushed a double stroller. An infant in a blue bunting occupied the backseat, snoozing beneath the awning. The front seat was vacant, but a dad with a soft-looking middle took up the rear and carried a boy on his shoulders.

Customers converged on the pie side of the booth, and Celeste and Katherine moved into their practiced roles: Celeste taking the money and the orders and Katherine scooping vanilla ice cream onto slices of apple pie, dropping dollops of cinnamon-nutmeg whipped cream onto the pumpkin. Their first ever cookie decorating table was a hit, due to Zach's extra set of hands and his ease with the little ones. In between customers, every time Katherine looked at Zach, she caught him either looking her way, his expression narrow and impossible to decipher, or checking out Celeste's bottom with a look Katherine reserved for a steaming-hot pain au chocolat. No deciphering necessary.

In between customers, Zach and Katherine sampled pie. Apple for Katherine and pumpkin for Zach. But Celeste, the keeper of the impish grin and obvious digs? All morning and into the afternoon, she didn't eat a damn thing.

In between customers, Katherine caught Celeste staring off into middle space, wearing a hungry expression Katherine hadn't seen since the days when Celeste had starved herself, as though trying to make her exterior reflect what was eating her away inside.

No denying it, at least not to herself. Katherine had found her biological son, the child she had not raised. But her favorite girl, who didn't share Katherine's DNA but had nevertheless grown inside her heart? That child was at the center of a maze, left behind, and lost.

Children were everywhere.

In the parking lot skirting Johnson Farm. Running in circles around their harried parents. Sitting atop stacked bales of hay leading to the Johnson Farm corn maze and kicking their feet. Requesting juice and treats. *Pick me up, put me down.*

To the left of the maze, pumpkins sat in tidy orange rows, awaiting selection. On the right, the corn maze opened up to a grassy plain that slid out to the ocean.

Katherine focused on her breathing, attempting to calm the self-conscious voice in her head that chanted *my son* in the direction of Zach.

Curtis Johnson, the owner of the farm stand, wore his characteristic straw hat, uncharacteristic rainbow-colored suspenders, and organized the chaos into two jagged lines.

Katherine dug in her purse for her wallet. "My treat," she said, "since I asked you." Her words echoed back to her and sounded very much like first date lingo, as though Celeste's snarky voice had embedded in Katherine's gray matter. What had Celeste said? *You two should go together*? Why was it that the last thing you wanted to say was often the first thing that spurted from your mouth?

Zach shook his head and took his wallet from his back pocket. "I've got this," he said, and strolled up to Curtis Johnson.

When Zach slipped into the back of the line beside Katherine, Curtis held a finger to his lips. "I've got a riddle for you today," he said, and waited for the crowd to quiet. "A maze turns and twists. It leads you by the nose and pushes you into corners. It twirls you in circles. It leads you astray. Your exit may be close to where you begin . . . or far away. But no matter where you exit, you always end up . . . Where?"

Kids stared at Curtis with their mouths open. Their parents offered Curtis patient grins.

Curtis made eye contact with his rapt audience. "The answer's at the end of the maze, if you get there."

"Never heard that riddle before," Zach said. "And I used to ace the Jumbles in the Sunday paper."

"Jumbles?"

"It's a type of kid riddle?"

Katherine shook her head. "Sorry."

"Fitzgerald family tradition. Every Sunday, I got the Jumbles and my father and mother did the crossword puzzle together. Ryan got the funnies and Donovan liked the game where you had to figure out what was wrong with the picture."

Katherine shook her head again. The underside of her neck warmed with the same shame she'd experienced as a kid whenever someone normal asked her to explain her life.

"You know the two pictures that look almost identical. But there are always subtle differences between them? Like moose antlers hanging off a picture frame or a cat on someone's head or, you know, a tie shoe in one frame and a slip-on in another."

"Lamontagne family tradition. We didn't get the newspaper," Katherine said. On TV shows like *The Brady Bunch,* the king of the castle donned reading glasses and read the newspaper. Then he'd peered over those same glasses to dole out worldly advice to his offspring. Katherine's father had peered over the King of Beers to dole out personalized insults.

Curtis Johnson slipped his thumbs beneath his suspenders, playing up the farmer role. According to town gossip, back in high school he'd aspired to acting fame—the Hollywood Hills had beckoned him. But after a short stint in commercials and fifteen minutes of fame playing diarrhea in a Pepto-Bismol commercial, he'd returned to Hidden Harbor, his family's farm, and his suspender-tweaking birthright. "You kids ready to get lost?" he asked.

"Yeah!" a few kids called out, their voices thin and unsure.

Curtis, ever the showman, held a hand to his ear. "I can't hear you!"

Slightly louder calls went up from the crowd.

Curtis shook his head. "That's the best you can do?"

Zach raised a fist in the air, his face alight with mischief. "Woo-hoo! Let's do it!" No wonder Abby's three-year-old had taken an instant liking to Zach.

Curtis stared at Zach. "Now, that's more like it. Everybody in!" Curtis clapped his hands, once for each kid who entered the maze. "Go! Go! Go! Go! Go!" Parents scrambled to keep up with their kids. When Zach and Katherine passed by Curtis, he merely touched his fingers to the tip of his hat and winked. "Have a nice day, ma'am," he told Katherine. "Son," he said to Zach.

"You too, Curtis. I mean, Farmer Johnson," Katherine said, and she led Zach into the maze.

Corn rose up on either side of them. The nine-foot-high stalk walls stood about ten feet apart, impossible to see beyond but allowing plenty of space for walking side by side. Families with little ones ran ahead. Muffled, disembodied voices sounded from within the maze. Katherine squinted through the bright sun and raised a hand to her forehead as a shield. "Corn mazes weren't part of your family tradition?"

Zach pressed a forefinger to his closed fist, ticking off a list. "Pie-eating contests and bouncy houses at the Arlington Town Day. But, uh, not in that order. Tried that once, lived to regret it."

"Sounds like you have a fun family, Zach." Katherine waited for Zach to nod his agreement.

Instead, he ran his hand along the corn, making it rustle beneath his fingers, like playing cards click-clacking against bike spokes. "Singing contests."

"You sing?" Katherine said. The notion instantly and somewhat ridiculously lit Katherine up inside, as if singing were part of her genetic makeup.

"No," Zach said. "I can't sing for—" He chuckled. "I don't sing. But my parents and brothers are naturals," he said, overly emphasizing the word *naturals.*

"But not you?" Katherine asked.

"Guess I didn't get the singing DNA." Zach stared at Katherine, as though daring her to say otherwise. As though daring her to reveal herself.

Zach was good, but she was better, having spent years avoiding her ex-husband's probing questions, his gaze that lingered long after their conversations had concluded. If Katherine didn't know better, she might've concluded that Zach and Barry shared common DNA.

In the house where Katherine had grown up, she and her biological sister, Lexi, didn't share eye color, hair color, or talents. All they'd shared was a common miserable experience. Each of them had handled the crap they were dealt differently. At sixteen years old, Lexi, the wild one, had climbed out the window of the bedroom they'd shared and run away, leaving Katherine to stay and carry on her legacy.

"Any other notable Fitzgerald family traditions?" Katherine asked.

"We used to make our own costumes for Halloween," Zach said.

"Very cool."

"My little brothers dressed up as firefighters and cowboys. I made myself a silver costume with an aluminum hat."

Zach glanced at Katherine, as though pausing for her to decipher his clue. She shrugged. "So the voices couldn't get into your head?"

"Ha! Good one, but no. Because, from the time I was small I'd always felt like an alien in my family. I never felt like I belonged. . . ." Zach's voice trailed off. An opening for Katherine to offer an explanation?

"I never felt like I belonged, either," Katherine said. "I think that's a common theme, growing up. No matter what kind of a household raises you. Good or bad."

Ever since Katherine was five and her father told her kindergarten teacher she was an accident, she'd fantasized that she was adopted. That her real family shared pleasant dinner conversation every night and that they always had homemade cupcakes for dessert. That her house smelled like cinnamon toast and melted butter, instead of cigarettes and stale beer. And in this make-believe house, the father never made the mother choose between him and their children. The children always came first.

The maze forked right and left. Katherine jutted out her arm to pause Zach, the way her mother used to hold out her arm whenever she stopped short while driving. As if her slender arm could've kept Katherine from crashing through a windshield. As though her mother had cared to keep Katherine safe.

"What do you think? Right or left?" Katherine peered

down both turns, but neither offered a clue. Both appeared equally worn with equal potential.

Zach flopped his arms across each other and crossed his legs at the ankles, like the scarecrow from *The Wizard of Oz*.

"Left it is!" Katherine said.

"What about you?"

"What about me?" Katherine's midsection tightened, and her shoulders rose on a breath.

"What were your family traditions?"

Katherine chuckled. "I don't know if this is a tradition. But there is one quirk my father handed down to me, more of a nuisance than anything. I can't tell the difference between some reds and greens. And others look muted. I once scared my driver's ed instructor when I described the traffic light colors—"

Zach made a sound, a cross between a laugh and a sigh. "Orange on the top, yellow in the middle, olive green on the bottom."

"How'd you guess?"

"I'm slightly color-blind myself," Zach said, emphasizing the word *blind*.

"What a coincidence?" she said, but even to her ear, the statement sounded like a question. Would Zach notice that, too? What were the chances she'd given birth to a color-blind son? She didn't know the answer to that question. But from the look on Zach's face—his eyes wide and edged with annoyance and his head tilted—he did.

Too late to change her answer?

"Negativity," Katherine blurted out. "That was our family tradition."

"Negativity?" Zach asked, as if he'd never heard the term.

Katherine searched her memory for a pleasant tradition. Instead, dark memories scrolled by, reoccurring events having burned themselves into her brain like afterimages. Cautionary tales that might lead Zach to appreciate the family who raised him right, a family who hadn't burdened him with dark memories and darker doubts. Katherine's father had severed blood ties. Yet, back when Katherine was expecting, family ties had nevertheless tugged, threatening to pull her down. Without a doubt, she'd known she couldn't hand down that legacy to her son. She'd known he was better off without her. And then, days later, she thought she'd made a terrible mistake.

Now, having met Zach and hearing about his adoptive family, she knew differently.

"My father was a mean drunk," Katherine said. "Almost as mean as when he was sober. I truly believe he enjoyed berating people, especially those related to him. I suppose you could say he had a calling. I liked to bake, he liked to try to make his family feel terrible about themselves. I never cared that we were poor. I just wanted my father to be nice to me. All through elementary school, everything I did was an attempt to get him to come around."

Scrubbing a spotless bathroom, so he'd stop calling her lazy. Pulling all-nighters to study word problems, so he'd stop calling her stupid. Keeping herself from speaking out against him, so he wouldn't send her to bed without dinner.

"Did it work?"

"No. I found other ways to survive."

By the time she'd hit her teens, she'd mastered algebra, learned to wipe down the bathroom after each shower, realized she could tell her father where to go and what to do when he got there. He couldn't stay awake and guard the refrigerator forever.

Even sauced, her father's brain was sharp, but hers was sharper. Usually.

Katherine stopped short, hitting a cornstalk dead end. "Did

I say left? I meant right. Definitely right," Katherine said. "I've got a strong feeling about this."

Zach pretended to spin a steering wheel and turned on his heel. "And then you left home, fell in love with Hidden Harbor and Lamontagne's. Only it was called Hazel May's, back in the day," Zach said, parroting back her words to him, as if he'd memorized their first conversation and was combing it for hidden meaning.

"That's right. I mean, yes, and also left," Katherine said, turning onto the path they'd previously rejected.

Zach jammed his right hand in his pocket and gave her a tight-lipped grin. The kind that told Katherine he was encouraging himself, that everything up to this point had been small talk. She got a quivery feeling deep in her belly, that knowing before you knew. The clear-cut understanding that a big, important question was coming her way and she wasn't going to like it.

"But you did fall in love with a guy eventually." Zach's hand moved from his pocket and found the comfort of the cornstalks. He struck every third stalk, scenting the air with dusty earth.

"I told you—"

"You were married. You have an ex-husband." Zach spoke slowly, quietly, deliberately, the way you'd remind a dementia sufferer of all they'd lost. He touched a hand to his head, and it automatically gravitated to the cowlick, the lock of hair she often caught him worrying. "The gray-haired guy?" Zach said.

"Barry, of course," she said. "How did you know?"

"Celeste told me. Did you meet him right after you moved here?" Zach asked, his tone airy, not with lightness but the inability to draw a full breath. His bright eyes flashed on hers. Gone was Zach's easy smile. He pulled his expression tight and emotionless as a scarecrow, while awaiting her answer to the question behind the question. The question he hadn't dared to ask.

The understanding caught in her throat, and she took a steadying breath around it. Zach wanted to know whether Barry—the dear, sweet man she currently loved—was his biological father. She wished. She wished awfully hard. But as her mother used to say, *If I had a penny for every wish . . .*

Katherine met Zach's gaze. When she spoke, her lips trembled and the words splintered, as though they too were skittering along the wall of cornstalks, stirring up dust. "No. I didn't meet Barry until about nine years later. If I'd been younger, I don't think it would've worked out for us."

Another fork in the maze rose up before them. Without slowing, Zach chose the right-hand path. Following an innate sense of direction or youthful impulse? Only time would tell.

"You're divorced now, though," Zach told her.

Katherine laughed, her blunder bordering on ridiculous. "True enough," she said, and the path through the cornstalks widened. Children's voices grew louder, more boisterous, but they still couldn't see anyone. She and Zach were either catching up to families and nearing a way out or spinning in circles.

Yes, she was divorced—an ugly, hurtful word. She'd filled out the forms. She could've had a sheriff deliver the news, but she thought Barry deserved better. So she'd put on a black dress and served the papers to Barry in a basket of mundel bread. She'd weathered the first and only time he'd responded to her baking with the inquiry *What the fuck?* A judge had answered Barry's inquiry two months later by granting her a divorce.

But in her heart, she was still married to Barry.

"I guess you could say that years ago Barry and I had good timing and then we didn't." At thirty-two, she'd grown up and grown tired of casual affairs. And along came Barry, the perfect combination of sexy, fun, and responsible. He weighed every decision, always aiming to do the right thing. He answered his patients' calls in the middle of the night. The word *no* simply wasn't in his vocabulary. He made her want to be a better person.

"I've never had good timing with, you know, relationships." Zach gave a small chuckle. "At least not yet." He slipped his hand back into his pocket. Looking for the comfort of change?

Zach seemed like a sweet, bright young man, his heart in the right place. But he also seemed untethered as she'd once been, adrift in the world, subject to whimsy. Even if that whimsy told him to try for a relationship with Celeste and then sail out of town.

Not good timing for Celeste.

"Celeste has been like a daughter to me." The admission stole Katherine's wind and slowed her pace. If she told Celeste, she'd probably make light of Katherine's claim, giving her reason to doubt her heart. All the more reason not to tell her.

"Yeah, I really like her," Zach said. "She's wicked funny."

And sexy. Zach wasn't saying so, not in words, but Katherine had seen the way he looked at Celeste. Worse, Katherine had noticed the way Celeste responded to Zach.

Not what her girl needed at the moment.

"She's sassy," Katherine said.

"Yeah. You could say that." Without hesitating, Zach chose a left-hand turn in the maze. He raised his hand to his hair. To shade his eyes from the sun or from Katherine?

"Don't know if you've noticed, but she's awfully generous, too."

"Yup, I've noticed."

"Celeste isn't as tough as she seems," Katherine said. "And despite her sense of humor, she's a pretty serious customer. Too serious sometimes. People and relationships matter to her. She's had a lot of changes in her life recently. And dealing with change has never been her strength. Do you get my drift?"

"Not really," Zach said.

She didn't want to hurt Zach. But if he wasn't good for Celeste, then she wasn't right for him either. "Unless you have something serious in mind, now's not a good time for you to start a relationship with her."

Zach stopped short, but there was neither a cornstalk dead end nor a fork in their pathway, just a wall of words Katherine had erected. Physically, Zach didn't look anything like Celeste, but his expression bore an uncanny resemblance to Celeste's when Katherine had cautioned Celeste against starting a relationship during this stressful time in her life. Outrage, hurt, and outright confusion.

Zach hunched and slid his hands down his thighs, as though he'd a runner's cramp. When he stretched to standing, the pique was gone, save for a slight flare to his nostrils and a slighter tinge of irony to his grin. "How do you know?" he asked.

"Now I'm not getting your drift."

"How do you know whether you have something serious in mind without getting to know a girl first? I mean, isn't that what relationships are about? Getting to know people?"

"I suppose so," Katherine said.

Zach firmed his grin, nodded, and continued walking, as though something had been decided.

Every man she'd ever dated, every lover she'd taken to bed, she'd wanted to get to know intellectually. Including Adam, the lover from twenty-five years ago who'd set her on fire sexually and then skipped town. For all Katherine knew, Zach's biological father had been looking for a possible relationship, too. Just not with her.

A hairpin curve turned Katherine and Zach out to a freshly

mowed field, picnic tables, and the ocean beyond. Sudden as a nine-foot-high cornstalk dead end.

Katherine squinted through the late day sun. Tacked flat against a wooden beam, a piece of yellowing paper asked and answered Farmer Johnson's cryptic riddle.

A maze turns and twists. It leads you by the nose, and pushes you into corners. It twirls you in circles. It leads you astray. Your exit may be close to where you begin . . . or far away. But no matter where you emerge, you always end up . . . DISORIENTED.

CHAPTER 9

Was Zach the only person electric with fury?

Five-thirty at night, the Hidden Harbor Harvest Festival was like a video on rewind, a whir of noise and motion, reversing the morning's start-up activities. When the sun lowered, vendors packed up their goods, took down their easy-ups. Everyone hustled at a frantic pace, ready to rock and roll and hit the road hard.

Zach's need to flee was as great as the day his parents had told him he was adopted, the urge buzzing like a second Zach beneath his skin.

Ten years ago, his parents had put his brothers to bed and then sat him down on the squishy couch in the den. His mother on his right and his father on his left. His mother told him a story, to which he only paid partial attention. Something about his mother having a hard time getting pregnant and how she and Zach's father had really wanted to make a family together. Icky, gross, grown-up talk that had had nothing to do with Zach.

Hand dangling between his knees, legs jiggling, he waited for a break in the conversation, for his mother to draw a breath so he could ask about a soccer camp. He had the paperwork folded in the back pocket of his jeans, the one-hundred-dollar fee circled in pen and pressing through the denim like a stone. More money than he'd saved from his allowance, so he planned on offering to do chores. Not only the chores he was supposed to do and usually forgot but—

"Zach, are you even listening?" his father said. "Did you hear what your mother said?"

"Uh, you guys wanted to start a family?" Zach asked.

An hour later, he'd run away.

Now Celeste waved her two fingers in front of Zach's face. "Anybody home? How many fingers am I holding up?"

"Peace, man," he said, but he couldn't connect to the words. He was really going to miss Celeste, but what could a guy do? He didn't stay where he wasn't wanted, and Katherine didn't want him. Or, at the least, she didn't think he was good enough for Celeste. Not good enough for Katherine decades ago meant not good enough for Celeste today. Because this wasn't a good time for Celeste to start a relationship. A twist on the classic excuse "it's not you, it's me."

He got it.

Katherine needn't have gone into the elaborate explanation of her effed-up family, her drunk daddy, and how she'd been on her own since she was way younger than Zach. Obviously, she'd proven her ability to kick the shit out of her past and carve out a decent life.

Unlike Zach, Katherine's biological son.

Color-blind women gave birth to color-blind sons 100 percent of the time. Genetics never lied. And yet Katherine still refused to admit their X-chromosome connection.

"Peace, man, to you too?" Celeste said, making the statement sound like a question. "Help me take down the easy-up?"

"Yeah, sure, of course." Zach met Celeste's gaze. Her eyes were prettier than he'd realized. How had he missed that? Was he that shallow? That focused on her body?

Zach dashed to the canopy leg across from Celeste and bent to unlatch the stake. He'd really wanted to get to know Celeste better. To find out what she liked to do in her spare time. To hang out with her in her spare time. He wanted to hear about her family. All two dozen brothers. He wanted to ask her about her friend Abby who'd stopped by with the cool little kid. Zach really liked kids.

Crazy, but he wondered what Celeste looked like first thing in the morning and when she was falling asleep at night. Did she wrap a fuzzy yellow blanket around her or did she tuck it between her knees? Some of each? And what did she do with all that hair?

Yeah, he was shallow.

Katherine came across the green, having deposited the last of the leftover pastries in her Outback for conveying back to Lamontagne's. She brushed off her hands, clapping them, one against the other. Her apron she must've left in her car, too. But she wasn't dirty. She'd slung pie and ice cream, wiped every ounce of blue frosting from the kids' tablecloth without getting as much as a smudge on her clothing. Zach's apron was frosting splattered, like those tie-dyes he liked to make in summer camp. Dust and dirt from the maze caked the toes of his sneakers. But Katherine remained fresh and clean, untouched, as though some kind of force field surrounded her. Made him want to pick up a pumpkin pie and shove it in her face, following the legacy of the Three Stooges and banana cream pies.

Until Zach turned ten and got a hold of the *TV Guide,* he'd actually thought the New Year's Day Three Stooges marathon was in honor of his birthday. At eleven, he'd still believed in Santa Claus, the Easter Bunny, and a St. Patrick's Day leprechaun that hopped across your kitchen counters, leaving behind olive-green footprints and gold coins.

Give the kid a star for his ability to suspend disbelief.

Zach bent to a second post, let out a grunt, and gave the stake a mighty yank. The anchor let go, knocking him on his ass and taking a plug of grass and soil with it. A really big plug.

Katherine squatted down beside Zach, like one of those golfers you see on TV. Cool and collected, looking for the straightest line to putt the ball into the hole. "Everything okay?" she asked.

He considered telling her no, everything was not all right. In fact, everything pretty much sucked. He was a big, fat idiot for coming to Hidden Harbor and thinking she'd be glad to see him. And she was an even bigger, fatter idiot for not welcoming him. He considered admitting that, yeah, he knew he was a little immature, but what the hell? She owed him an explanation for why she gave him up—something only she could tell him—and why Carol and Everett Fitzgerald had waited so long to let him in on the joke, something Katherine would have no way of knowing.

But there was no way he was going to tell her how he felt. What was the point? What was the effing point?

Freshman year in high school, a drama coach had taught Zach how to substitute somebody from his life for a so-called fellow actor. So he looked Katherine in her brown eyes and replaced them with Celeste's goldish showstoppers.

"Beautiful," Zach told Katherine.

Katherine tilted her face and squinted at him sideways. Again, a golfer looking for her straight-line shot. "Good." She stood and brushed nonexistent dirt from her jeans.

He'd finish the booth takedown and meet Katherine and Celeste back at Lamontagne's. He'd carry in the table and chairs and leave Celeste's loaner blanket in the stockroom. Then he'd fire up Matilda, rock and roll, and hit the road hard.

Zach picked up the grass plug and replanted it back in its hole. A bare indentation rimmed the repair. He scooped displaced soil and pressed it down beneath his hands. Moist crumbs of soil clung to his fingertips. Within a day or two, grass would grow and fill the circle. To anyone who didn't know about Zach's little fit and repair, the lawn would appear seamless.

If you asked Zach to recite the capitals of all the U.S. states in alphabetical order, he could get as far as Raleigh, North Carolina, before doubting his memory. He remembered all the countries in Europe, but the spelling always messed him up. He'd stare at *Azerbaijan* and the word would start to look weird, causing him to transpose the *i* and the *j* and then switch them back again. But the moment when his parents told him he was adopted? When his father had made him pay attention and his mother had said the actual word? He remembered every detail, as if it had just happened. As if, in fact, it was happening now.

He remembered the way his dad's lips were chapped, the bottom lip dryer than the top. He remembered how the light from the reading lamp reflected off his mother's bad perm, making her hair look gray instead of blond, and the way she did that sour lemon thing with her mouth. He'd never forget the way one word, *adopted,* stripped away his entire identity.

The bell above Lamontagne's jingled. In front of Zach, Katherine carried a box of extra pies into her shop, and the lowering sun reflected off her dark hair. The air went from late day autumn chill and smelling like a campfire to the rich aroma of pastries, and the temperature rose at least fifteen degrees. Zach carried the foldaway table sideways, the edge jammed beneath his armpit. Celeste slammed Katherine's car door. When he glanced back at her, she gave him the same encouraging thumbs-up he'd offered her friend's kid and took up the rear. Zach hoped years from now he'd remember this, too.

Katherine flipped on the overheads and dropped the pies.

Broken sugar dispensers and spilled sugar piled beside the door, as if someone had stood in one place and systematically emptied and smashed every last dispenser. Half a dozen lids stood in a row on the nearest four-top. The tidiness alongside the mess made Zach think, strangely, of an apology. Of the way he'd, years ago, made his bed, hospital corners and all, before running away.

Celeste came up behind Zach, a paper bag in her arms. "What's with the slow-up?" she said.

Zach propped the foldaway table against the building. "Stay outside," he said, pretty much an invitation for Celeste to leave the paper bag on the sidewalk and plow right past him.

"Not again!" Celeste said.

"Again?" Zach asked. "This has happened before?"

Katherine glared at the mess. Zach bet if there had been an intact sugar dispenser, Katherine would've smashed it on the floor with the rest. "No," she said, but she wasn't responding to his question, she was yelling at the mess. "No, no, no."

"Get out of here," Zach said. "Go see if another shop is open and call the police." His voice sounded tight, his mouth filled with cotton. Whoever had broken in was most likely long gone, a Harvest Festival reveler gone bad. No big deal, right? But Katherine's anger seemed to vibrate the air around her, electric, different from her usual cool force field. And Zach could feel it—the energy of her anger, as if she'd transmitted her anger directly to him and he was absorbing the shock.

"The police? Really? That's your solution? That's what I did last time." Katherine opened her hands and mimed pushing motions toward the mess. Then she met his gaze and shook her head. "I'm sorry, Zach. I know you mean well. But this is my bakery. I'm not going anywhere."

Zach thought of the regulars who came into Lamontagne's—every last one of them as devoted to Katherine as to her pastries. That devotion flowed both ways. The shop was more than a job to Katherine. This was her home. And she was defending it.

"Damn straight," Celeste said, agreeing with Katherine. And then she looked as though she wanted to spit on the floor. "Douche bag," Celeste said.

Under normal circumstances, Zach bet Katherine would've had a few non–cuss words to say about Celeste's word choice. Instead, she gave Celeste a nod, flexed her fingers, as though she were readying for a boxing match, and headed across the shop.

"Hey, wait!" Zach grabbed Katherine's arm. "I'll check out the kitchen." Most likely the vandal had gone, but what if he hadn't? "Don't go in."

"She's not going to listen to you," Celeste said, hustling to keep up with Katherine and Zach. Zach's criminal justice classes had taught him that for every shop owner who'd caught a burglar in the act, fought back, and ended up on the front page of the *Boston Globe* kneeling on the perp's neck, there were two tales of average Joes or Josephines that had ended badly.

Those articles ended up in the obits.

A thud sounded through the closed stockroom door. Zach yanked the door open.

A skinny boy, wearing a black hoodie and jeans with the orange tip of a Marlboro box peeking from his back pocket, clung to the wall of shelves. His hand reached for the top-shelf flour-filled mason jars. Another jar lay on the floor beneath him, unbroken, beside the rolling ladder.

"Hey!" Zach yelled. "Get the hell down from there!"

The boy looked Zach in the eye. Surprise and numbness passed over his face, and the kid settled on a smirk. "Make me," he said, and knocked another mason jar to the floor.

Zach took the offer as a dare and went for it.

From behind him, Celeste yelled, "Zach!"—which made sense. And Katherine called out something that sounded like, *Bake!*

Zach launched himself at the boy.

The overhead bulb reflected off the whites of the boy's eyes. The boy cringed, and a tiny bead of blood welled at the center of his bottom lip.

Zach landed on a shelf, grabbed the boy by the hood, and lost his balance. They fell backward. The weight of the kid on top of Zach, the two of them flying through the air, Katherine and Celeste both calling Zach's name. Zach's lower back smacked the top of the ladder with a *whomp.* The boy bounced from his arms.

The voice in Zach's head told him not to use his hand to break the fall. And then he heard a snap.

"Don't move!" Katherine said, assessing the situation. Or trying to assess the situation, as it were. Zach and Blake lay on the floor of her stockroom with their bodies twisted in unnatural angles reminiscent of the white chalk outlines of cop shows. If they'd injured their spines, moving would make a bad situation worse.

The sound of Zach hitting the ladder thrummed through her brain like an aftershock.

Blake sat up, his face pale. "I didn't mean to!"

Mean to what? Break into her bakery today? Weeks ago? Cause injury to her son?

Her son.

Zach lay on his side, facing away from her. His legs bent, as if he were running away in his sleep.

"Are you all right? Are you all right? Are you okay?" Celeste headed for Zach, a shaking hand outstretched to him.

Katherine pointed at Blake. "Blake! You stay right there," she said, and she went to Zach's side.

"You know him?" Celeste asked.

"Blake and I are acquainted."

A sound came from Zach, a muffled chuckle. "*Blake.* That makes more sense."

"Really?" Katherine asked. "This makes sense? Perhaps you can enlighten me, then." A mirror chuckle threaded through her voice, but her mouth trembled, downturned. Her legs moved beneath her, gel filled and unfamiliar.

"Ah, shit," Zach said.

"What was that?" Katherine asked, and she exchanged a hopeful grin with Celeste. How badly could Zach be hurt if he was cursing?

Zach pushed himself to sitting with his left hand. He cradled his right hand and groaned, answering Katherine's unspoken question.

From the looks of him, his back had survived the fall, free of injury. He sat tall. He wagged his head from side to side, as though testing out its movement. He sucked a breath in through his teeth. From the looks of him, his wrist hadn't fared as well. Zach's hand bent back at an unhealthy angle, deformed and broken looking.

The backs of Katherine's knees ached.

Celeste placed a hand on Zach's shoulder, her face a study in sympathy. "You okay, Zach?"

Zach smiled up at Celeste. "I'm excellent."

"I hate to tell you, Zach," Celeste said. "But I think you broke your wrist."

"I hate to tell you, Celeste, but it's definitely broken. I heard the snap." Zach released his injured right wrist, notched his left wrist upward, and clicked his tongue. "Been here before. You never forget the sound of a breaking bone. Nineteen eighty-nine, soccer camp, central defender, left wrist."

"Nineteen ninety," Celeste said. "High school soccer tryouts, goalie, right leg."

Nineteen seventy-two, Lamontagne homestead, Katherine's

relationship with her mother. Nineteen seventy-six, Brunswick Hospital, Katherine's bond with her newborn son. Both incidents had left Katherine broken.

But a broken daughter was still someone's daughter, a broken mother still ready and willing to nurture.

"Blake, hand me an ice pack from the chest freezer behind you," Katherine said.

The freezer emitted a frosty breath. Blake held up a six-inch bendable blue pack. "This one okay?" he asked, his voice full of yearning, his eyes glossy with unshed tears.

"You little shit," Celeste said to Blake, and he blinked a tear.

"Celeste, baby," Katherine said, "hand me a tea cloth. One of the longer ones."

Celeste met her gaze. Her mouth fell open, but no words released.

"Now, let's see. It's been a while since I've done this," Katherine said. It had been a while since Katherine had reviewed the first aid instructions. She'd read and reread the American Red Cross manual, twice, with interest, and decades ago. She kept the thick manual under the sink in the employee washroom, a marker to show her when her stock of paper towels was running low.

"You're going to have to let go of your hand for a moment," Katherine told Zach. "Just a moment," she said. The word *baby* she thought but did not say.

"No problem, boss." Zach raised his left hand in the air, as though taking an oath.

Celeste kept her hand on Zach's shoulder.

Katherine wrapped the cloth over Zach's left shoulder, her mind wandering to the Brunswick Hospital maternity ward and the softness of the blanket she'd used to swaddle her son. She'd insisted on one nursing and one swaddling, as if those two acts added up to a lifetime of full stomachs and security.

When Katherine slipped the cloth beneath Zach's right arm, he coughed.

"Sorry," Katherine said.

"I'm good," Zach said. "Tickle in my throat."

Katherine brought Zach's arm to a ninety-degree angle across his chest, and he grimaced. "Hang in there." She handed the other end of the cloth over Zach's right shoulder and into Celeste's hands. Then Katherine slipped the ice pack into the well. "All right, let's snug you up," she said, but Celeste was one step ahead, tying the ends of the dishcloth, her face as serious as when she measured and weighed ingredients. Focused on making everything perfect.

As if such a state existed.

Zach coughed a second time, and Katherine patted his left shoulder. "Can you stand?"

"E-yeah. I didn't break my leg."

Katherine stood, then Celeste, then Zach, a wave unbroken.

"Good as new," Zach said.

"You will be," Katherine said, "after a little trip to Brunswick Hospital."

"What about me?" Blake asked.

Katherine stared at the boy. "Are you hurt?"

"Uh, not really."

"Good," Katherine said. "Celeste, can you drive Zach to the hospital?"

"Of course." Celeste gave her head a quick shake. "What about you?"

"I'll meet you there. Luckily, Zach's injury isn't that serious. Meaning, you're going to have a bit of a wait in the emergency room. Plenty of time for me to take care of the Blake situation."

Blake's gaze slid from Katherine's face to Zach's arm and back to Katherine. "Are you going to call the police?"

For the first time in decades, Katherine had the urge to roll her eyes to the ceiling. "No, Blake, I'm not going to call the police. But you might wish I had when I'm done with you. First you're going to clean up this mess to my specifications. Then I'm going to figure out how you're going to pay me back for all the pain and suffering."

"I'm sorry!" Blake said. "I didn't do anything! It's his own fault. He grabbed me off the shelf. If he hadn't—"

"You little shit," Celeste said.

White noise whirred in Katherine's ears. The sound of twisted logic tying a knot in her gut. Some things never changed.

Katherine rounded on Blake. "Not Zach's pain and suffering. *Mine.*" She held her hands out, flexed them, took a step back. Took a breath. "I'll meet you in Brunswick," she told Zach and Celeste, and forced a smile. "Drive safely."

Katherine brushed the flop of dark hair from in front of Zach's eyes.

Zach met her gaze. "Thanks, Katherine," he said, not drawing out the pronunciation, like Adam. Zach spoke her name with his own unique voice.

"Be careful going over bumps," Katherine said, thinking of her harried drive to Brunswick Hospital and the way her contractions had refused to synch with frost heaves and impatient motorists.

"I'll take good care of him," Celeste said.

"I know you will."

"Sorry about the accident," Blake said.

Accident? More like the on purpose. This time, Katherine did indulge in an eye roll.

Zach grinned. "In the famous words of Moe to Shemp, 'It's okay, kid. Accidents happen.' "

Celeste laughed and pantomimed swinging a bat or an ax or something. Katherine had no clue. She'd never cared for the Three Stooges, never understood the humor of violence.

★ ★ ★

Katherine restrained herself from going after Blake. Going after Blake and cleaning up after him.

Instead, she forced herself to watch while he attempted to follow her instructions. Thus far, he'd swept and mopped the café twice, because the first pass had left the grit of sugar underfoot and glass winking from the corners. Perspiration dotted his brow.

She'd needed the time to calm down, to talk sense to the voices in her head that replayed the way she'd felt the first time she'd found her shop burgled, the sense of violation and paranoia that had echoed from the incident, waves that affected her to this day. Finding her shop broken into a second time had only confirmed her fears, her adrenal glands primed and ready for overdrive, stoking her original trauma.

And all because of a boy, a scrawny teenager with ill manners, dirty nails, and a warped sense of retaliation. It was like finding out the boogeyman was a sham, a bug you could squash with the tip of your shoe. It was like discovering Oz, the all-powerful wizard, was nothing but an ordinary man who'd lost his way. The overarching lesson from the universe reminded Katherine of her father.

Boy, would Barry ever have a field day with that one. Katherine, the baby of her family, had a daddy complex. Or did she have a complex daddy?

His bark is worse than his bite, Katherine's mother used to say. Short-term, this had proven true. Long-term? Not so much.

Outside the café, the streetlamps began to light, sundown coming earlier and earlier. The way the seasons worked never failed to surprise Katherine, changing faster every year, as much a delight as a fright. And a reminder that she wasn't getting any younger.

The phone hung on the wall behind the register, a black

retro reproduction you had to dial by hand or pencil. She could call Barry—seven little numbers, seven spins of the dial. She could tell him about Blake and the break-in—the break-ins—and ask Barry to handle this clearly damaged child, way out of her comfort zone.

Barry never said no.

She indulged in the fantasy—Barry dashing through the door, the bell jingling in his wake. The two of them embracing, the solid comfort of his body against hers. He'd sit down with Blake and draw out his sweetness. He'd draw out her sweetness.

Or she could, for once, be fair to Barry, leave him alone, and attempt to channel his shrink wisdom.

Her stomach grumbled. Her head ached, a vice-like pressure against her temples. Her last meal, if you wanted to call it a meal, had been a serving of pie and ice cream. So much for her so-called diet. Might as well shoot it to hell.

She checked her watch. Ten minutes before seven. She had just enough time for a quick bite, a quicker chat, and a race to the hospital.

The image of Zach's angled wrist flashed across her internal vision, and a pain spiked her wrist. She wrapped her hand around the ache, and the pain subsided.

"Blake," Katherine said, and the boy startled from his thoughts. What they might be, Katherine hadn't a clue. "That's enough for today. What's your poison? Apple or pumpkin?"

"Apple," Blake said.

"Me too." She cut two generous servings and sat down in the booth Blake had previously damaged. If the booth choice threw him off, all the better.

Blake waited for her to dig in before he took his first bite. Then he attacked the pie, bending his head to the plate, as if he were starving. Was he?

Katherine chewed slowly. "You did a nice job cleaning up the mess you created."

Blake glanced up at her, sidelong and wary, and then went back to the pie.

"How do you suppose we deal with your incidents?"

Here Blake paused, his fork hovering over the plate.

Barry probably wouldn't have used the word *incidents.* Too circumspect and vague. She'd get to the point. "How are you going to pay me back for the property damage?"

Blake glanced right and left, as though searching for an answer.

"Okay, well. Let's get specific." Would Barry say *specific?* "Your previous break-in tantrum cost me . . ." She slid a pencil from her back pocket, swiped a napkin from the holder, and scratched out *$250.* She held up the napkin like a flash card.

"No."

"Oh, yes. I've checked and rechecked the figures." Plus, she'd paid the bills. "The sugar dispensers you're so awfully fond of smashing run a dollar thirty-nine apiece. Beginning of the month, you demolished eight of them. . . ."

Blake's mouth went slack, and he glanced to the ceiling. "Eleven dollars and twelve cents."

"Yes. Impressive," she said.

The left side of Blake's lips twitched upward, as though he was unsure whether she was generously praising his math skills or sarcastically lauding his destruction.

To the boy's credit, he didn't attempt to deny the earlier break-in. "The paint to cover your graffiti cost fifteen dollars a gallon," Katherine said. "I needed two gallons, due to the pale color. And let's not forget your crowning achievement—"

Blake lowered his fork. The tines tapped against the plate, a wordless plea. His eyes widened, huge, like an infant's. Like the child that he was. The frightened child.

Why? She thought she was being straightforward. Was something in her tone or expression scaring him?

Good lord, what if she wasn't channeling Barry? What if she was channeling her father?

She hiccupped, bitter apple liquid refluxed, and she covered her mouth. She swallowed, and her eyes watered.

Blake's expression remained unchanged, hinged and waiting for her to unhinge him. Fifteen years old and he reeked of cigarettes, shame, and fear.

From the time Katherine had been in preschool, her mother had doused her with Jean Naté after bath splash, futile against a house that stank. Yet Katherine had always been taken with scents and aromas. Their ability to conjure emotion. Their ability to cover up or attempt to conceal.

"Here's my proposal," Katherine said. "You'll work for me until you pay off your debt. Stop by tomorrow after school and we'll figure it all out."

"Okay."

"Okay. . . . Well, then," she said, and gave the tabletop a pat. "I should get going to the hospital. I'll drop you off at your house on the way."

"Thanks," Blake said, and he attempted a smile.

"One more thing," she said, careful to lighten her tone so her words wouldn't weigh too heavily upon him. "I need to talk to your parents. They should know what happened here today, and our arrangement." Katherine nodded, stood, and took her plate.

Blake gazed up at her and simultaneously sank in his seat. "I'd rather go to jail."

Katherine sat back down. "Why is that?"

Blake's mouth worked around words unspoken. He shook his head. "You wouldn't understand."

"Try me."

Barry would ask open-ended questions, gently drawing out the patient's answer, an extended analysis that could take years. Katherine didn't have that kind of time. She had, by her estimate, about ten minutes before she needed to hightail it to Brunswick Hospital, Celeste, and Zach.

Katherine's chest pounded with the desire to conceal. "Until I was twelve, my family ate dinner together every night," she said. "Sounds nice, right?"

Blake shrugged. "I guess."

"It wasn't nice at all. My father made me and my sister tell him our favorite thing that had happened to us that day," she said, and the muscles in her back clutched, as though she were still trying to defend her irrational happiness.

"So?"

"Then he'd very patiently tell us why we were mistaken. If I got a good grade on a paper, he'd say the teacher was messing with my head, teaching the class wrong. Or, if the teacher was a man, he'd suggest the teacher wanted something inappropriate from me."

"Sounds weird."

"Yeah, weird." Katherine's shoulders rose on a breath. "When I complained about my father's smoking, he dared me to smoke a cigarette with him." She shook her head. "Sorry. That was a lie. *Dare* isn't the right word. He wouldn't let me leave the house until I'd smoked it to the filter."

"Then he let you go?"

"Yes and no. I was too sick to get off the bathroom floor." Katherine had laid her face on the floor, the cold tile numbing her cheek and temple, and focused on a stain clouding the underside of the sink. The more she focused, the more the shape shifted, morphing from a bunny to a bat, a winged angel to a horned devil.

She'd been a year younger than Blake.

"That doesn't make sense," Blake said. "You didn't like him smoking, so he made you smoke?"

"I don't know. Maybe he wanted to get me hooked, so I'd shut up complaining and join him. Hard to say what's going on in someone else's mind, right?"

"When I first told my father I wanted to get a job to help out, he thought it was a great idea," Blake said. "For about half a second. Then he told me I was too stupid to get a job. He was all—" Blake went into character. He actually appeared bigger, meaner. His chest puffed out, his teeth bared, and he came out of his seat. He deepened his voice. " 'What a joke! Who in their right mind would hire a loser like you? Who the hell do you think you are? *Who the hell do you think you are?*' "

Blake made a sound, part chuckle, part *oomph* of surprise. He sat back down. He laid a shaking hand on the table, stared down at it as though it weren't connected to him, as though it were an embarrassment he wished he'd left behind.

Katherine placed her hand over Blake's and looked the child in the eye. Her ears clicked with the congestion of wanting to cry. "We'll keep our arrangement just between us then," she said. "Our little secret."

CHAPTER 10

The ghost of Katherine's past followed her from the end of Blake's wooded driveway on Route 216 to the gates of Brunswick Hospital.

Nearly twenty-four years ago, she'd awoken at three-fifteen, same as every workday, and waddled to the bathroom. Stepped carefully over the tub and into the bliss of warm water. Then the first pain had stabbed, and she'd bled. Orange droplets splashed the white ceramic, making the labor, the delivery, and her plan suddenly, horribly real.

Hazel May had offered to meet her at the hospital when it was "time." She'd volunteered to sit by her side and hold her hand. Even more amazing, Katherine's mentor had suggested she close the bakery for the day and take a hit on her livelihood. They'd discussed this day months ago. They'd made a plan. They'd both agreed. But when that first contraction had gripped, Katherine had chosen to go it alone.

When you knowingly, willingly planned to do the worst thing you'd ever done to someone you loved, did you really want a witness?

Cotton pad between her legs, she'd tossed an overnight bag in the backseat of her car and hit the road running. She'd sped all the way to Brunswick with the white of her headlights burning through the dark winter morning, contractions cresting ten minutes apart, as if by exceeding the speed limit, she could outrun her pain.

Now Katherine parked in the visitors' lot and ran through the gray streetlight shadows to the ER entrance. She'd sent Celeste and Zach ahead of her, so certain that taking the time to "deal with" Blake had been not only the right choice but the only choice.

Her own twisted logic tied her stomach in knots. In trying to do the right thing, had she given both Celeste and Zach the short end of her decision?

She could've waited to supervise the bakery cleanup. The whole Blake conversation, as enlightening to the boy's family situation as it had been, could've taken place at a later date. Hadn't she warned Zach that Celeste wasn't as tough as she seemed? Hadn't she worried about Zach? And yet Katherine had sent both of them away, as if she didn't even know her own mind.

Katherine pushed through the revolving door and blinked against the brightness, the switch from night road to parking lot to artificial daylight. Equally artificial warmth replaced the crisp chill of fall. And the air's equally crisp smell gave way to pine cleaner and stale cafeteria odors.

Three floors above, Katherine had given birth, her mind flooded with thoughts of her body's betrayal. Why was her labor progressing so quickly, the contractions coming one on top of the other, no time to catch her breath or reconsider her decision? Three pushes, and Zach had emerged, sweet and smiling, with barely a whimper.

He'd barely whimpered when he'd broken his wrist. Yet that must've hurt like hell.

In the ER waiting room, an old woman slept with her mouth open and her head on a middle-aged man's shoulder. A young couple huddled with preschool children—a boy for her and a girl for him—on their knees. Celeste sat between two empty seats, twisting her kerchief in her lap. Her hair spilled before her eyes.

"How many times do I need to tell you to keep your hair off your face?" Katherine asked.

Celeste looked up. "Everyone's a comedian."

"I've been accused of worse," Katherine said. "Where's the patient?"

"X-ray." Celeste folded the kerchief, fit it over her hair, and held out the ends for tying. "Could you?"

"Of course." Katherine sat sideways on the plastic seat beside Celeste.

"My mom used to do my hair, when I was little," Celeste said.

"Mine too," Katherine said, conjuring an image of her mother's slender fingers, the tickle of her breath on Katherine's cheek, the warmth of her love. "I used to ask for two braids. They always came out uneven and crooked, but I never complained." Katherine took the twisted ends of the cloth and quelled the urge to kiss the top of Celeste's head, the way her mother had kissed hers. Celeste's fingers trembled. From worry or malnutrition?

Katherine fit the cloth ends beneath Celeste's hair, making sure none of the baby hairs caught in the fabric. She fastened the ends and straightened the kerchief. "I'm really hungry," Katherine said, although her stomach was pleasantly full with pie. "I'm going to go search for a snack. Can I get you something to eat?"

Celeste's figure wasn't overly slender; she didn't have that body type. But with her hair held back, her eyes looked huge, too big for her face, like those poor starving children you saw in ads for humanitarian aid. Her gaze slipped to the arm of the chair between them and then came back to Katherine. "Can't. I'm too hungry," she whispered.

"Too hungry to eat?" Katherine asked, her voice a hush.

Celeste nodded, quick as a blink. "I'm queasy. If I eat something, I could, you know . . ." She swallowed and arched her hand from her belly to her mouth.

Throw up.

When Katherine had been pregnant, she was hungry all the time—ferociously and legitimately. She'd been, after all, eating for two. But sometimes, like Celeste, she'd work long hours, thinking she'd eat on her break, a nonspecific time that followed the needs of the bakery rather than her body. Then she'd end up in trouble. On her knees, porcelain trouble.

"I know what you need." Katherine stood and brushed off her jeans—from what, she'd no idea. "Sit tight. I'll be right back."

Katherine followed the signs partway to the cafeteria and ducked into an enclave of vending machines. She scanned the selections. Plain Lay's potato chips and cans of Canada Dry ginger ale. *Yes, perfect.* She fed the machines and hurried back to the waiting room, sneakers slapping the floor.

Katherine held the chips and soda before Celeste. "Starch, sugar, and salt. Plus bubbles. What do you think? Did I do good or what?"

Celeste eyed the food but made no move to take the items from Katherine's hands.

Katherine sat down and peeled open the chips. She popped one in her mouth and then angled the open bag toward Celeste. "Yum, yum."

Celeste took an audible breath, and her hand went to her mouth. "So much fat and sugar," she said. Her voice was lower than a whisper, more like an escaped thought.

"Which you need to live. Am I right?" Katherine dropped the bag on Celeste's lap.

Celeste placed a chip on her tongue. She sucked on it before chewing and swallowing. She took another chip, repeated the process. "I think the salt helps."

Katherine popped the soda's tab, sparking a fizzle. Mini ginger bubbles danced in the air. "Here you go."

Celeste took a small sip, licked her bottom lip, nodded. "I'm okay," she told Katherine. "I'm not sick. I just waited too long to eat."

Exactly the kind of stunt Celeste had pulled years ago, with the same excuse. Until she'd decided she wanted help.

"You made yourself sick," Katherine said, "because you waited too long to give your body what it needed."

"Isn't that what I said?"

For the second time that day, Katherine raised her gaze to the ceiling.

The door beside the registration desk opened. A plump chestnut-haired nurse, who looked as if she was a few years older than Katherine, brought Zach into the waiting room. Zach's arm was in a cast and a sling—a real sling made of navy medical-looking fabric, rather than a bleached white tea cloth. His flannel shirt was gone, likely cut from his body. Instead, he wore only the gray T-shirt she'd spotted beneath the flannel earlier. The nurse caught Katherine's gaze, broke into a grin, and waved a handful of papers in greeting, as though she recognized her.

Celeste shot out of her seat ahead of Katherine.

"What a nice family you have," the nurse told Zach.

"We're friends," Celeste said, to Katherine's relief.

"Oh, I thought—" Again the nurse caught Katherine's gaze. At close range, Katherine schooled her features into a neutral mask. This time, the nurse frowned. "Never mind."

"How's Blake doing?" Zach asked. "Did he clean up his mess? You sure he wasn't hurt?"

"Blake and the bakery are fine," Katherine said, feeling a

swell of irrational pride. She'd created Zach, but his sense of compassion and empathy was not of her doing. "How are you?"

"Good as new." Zach nodded at the cast. "Like you said, I will be, eventually. Right, Lois?" he asked the nurse.

"Zach has a distal radius fracture," Nurse Lois said. "Clean break, luckily, no fragments. But because of the angle, the doctor had to perform a nonsurgical reduction."

"You boiled him?" Celeste asked, referring to the culinary meaning of *reduction.*

Katherine grinned.

"Reduction is when the two pieces of a broken bone are realigned so they can grow back together." Nurse Lois brought her hands together to demonstrate proximity fusing the broken parts. "All the doctor had to do was move them back into place."

"Yeah, that wasn't my favorite part," Zach said. "Ow."

Lois patted Zach's good arm. "I've made him a follow-up appointment with the doc to make sure he's healing nicely."

"Can't wait," Zach said.

"Does he need anything for the pain?" Katherine asked.

"I'm fine, Katherine," Zach said. His exaggerated patience reminded her of the way a son might speak to his mother. His tone spoke of a long-term relationship and familiarity. All wishful thinking. In reality, Zach was one of those types who acted as though he knew you slightly better than he did.

Or was Katherine, once again, assuming Zach was like Adam—a ghost from her past she'd barely known?

"Acetaminophen and ibuprofen." Nurse Lois slipped her stack of papers into Zach's left hand. "Care instructions and appointment card."

"I've heard using your nondominant hand makes you smarter," Zach said. "Forces your brain to grow new neural connections."

Lois set a hand on her hip and shook her head. She gave

Zach a grin and looked as though she wanted to muss his hair. "I have a feeling your friends will want to spoil you. See you at your follow-up, hon," she said, and ducked back through the door to the examining rooms.

Back in the years-ago maternity ward, a pediatric nurse had made a fuss over Zach, too. The nurse had lifted him from his bassinet and kissed the top of his head before laying him in Katherine's outstretched arms. Immediately he'd turned his head to Katherine, rooting for what he needed. Her chest had swelled, a tidal wave of milk and love bursting for release. "This one takes the cake," the nurse had said, as if she were proud of him, too. "He most certainly does," Katherine had answered.

An hour later, she'd signed the adoption papers, legally breaking her own heart.

"Let's get you home," Katherine told Zach. "You got an apartment at Ledgewood, right?"

"Not exactly," Zach said.

"What exactly, then?"

"I'm staying across from Celeste's at Chez Matilda."

"Who?" Katherine asked, and Zach stepped into the automatic revolving door.

"He's been sleeping in his car," Celeste said, and followed behind him.

What?

How had Katherine missed this factoid? What else had skirted her arguably limited vision? Was she that hyper-focused on keeping her little secret about Zach that she'd risked his well-being?

Katherine stared at the revolving door, her actions spinning and churning through her mind. Hindsight wasn't twenty-twenty. Hindsight was seeing your reflection in glass, ugly and distorted. Hindsight was wondering how you could move forward when you couldn't go back.

She'd been here before, this exact spot, after she'd left the maternity ward, willing herself to walk through the hospital's revolving door. She'd faced her reflection while patients brushed by her. An elderly man and his nurse. Two middle-aged women, navigating their way on crutches. A fair-haired woman she recognized from the maternity ward, followed by her whistling husband, carrying their newborn in his blue car seat. The revolving door had spun; the winter cold had blown through her wool coat. Before her eyes, the sun had set—the parking lot dimming and darkening and lightening beneath streetlights. Only then had she mustered the nerve to walk through the revolving door and into a soul-sucking emptiness.

To the right of the cylinder that was spinning with memories, an ordinary door caught Katherine's eye. Had it been there years ago? She pushed through the door and race-walked through the lights and shadows, scanning the lot for Celeste's car. The night chill sneaked like a cold hand beneath the cotton of her sweater. The smoky autumn air hinted at the sharp, white scent of snow, as if her mind couldn't tell the difference between the present and the past. Late October or early January? The last glimpse of a newborn baby boy in a bassinet wheeling from her hospital bed and the door closing behind him or an adult Zach climbing into Celeste's yellow Cabriolet.

"Zach!" Katherine said, in a hurry to get the words out now that she'd decided. "You can stay with me," she said, her voice high and giddy. In the space of a breath, she imagined helping Zach care for his injury by slipping a sofa pillow beneath his arm at night, leaving towels for his morning shower in her bathroom, resetting the coffeemaker so Zach could enjoy a fresh cup after she'd left for the day.

"Thanks for the offer," he said. "But Celeste beat you to it."

Celeste raised her chin a notch, no doubt remembering their last conversation about Zach, and Katherine's dire warnings.

"Oh," Katherine said, and swallowed down a tremor.

"That's great!" she told Zach, willing the claim to inspire the feeling.

"I would've said yes if you'd asked me first," Zach said, his tone soothing and conciliatory. The tilt of his head hinted at regret.

Ridiculous, but Katherine wondered whether a newborn Zach would've similarly agreed to be her son had she not first decided to give him away.

Celeste helped Zach fasten his seat belt.

Thank you for taking care of my son.

"So, see you tomorrow," Celeste said, and she went around to the driver's side.

Katherine bent to Zach, the desire to hug him swelling inside her. "Guess I should've acted faster." She patted his shoulder, as though she were Nurse Lois, a middle-aged woman, charmed by a young man she barely knew. Then she shut the car door and stepped out of the way. Through the window, Zach met her gaze and gave her a left-handed thumbs-up. The car fired to life. Celeste backed from the space and slowly pulled from the hospital parking lot. Katherine stared after them into the darkness.

A soul-sucking emptiness pressed at the back of her throat, teasing her gag reflex.

Katherine should've *decided* faster. She still didn't think Celeste and Zach were a good idea—Zach with his wandering ways and his broken wrist, and Celeste with her broken spirit. But what did Katherine know, really? What did she know of love?

All she'd ever done was chase love away.

Running away was Zach's way of dealing with conflict, his modus operandi, his signature move. At twenty-three, he was a little old for his first-ever kick-ass epiphany, yet there it was.

And he resented the shit out of it.

Maybe it was the shock from his injury wearing off. At first, his wrist hadn't hurt, at least not in the way a broken-bone virgin might imagine a broken bone. But now, after a round of x-rays, when Nurse Lois had "adjusted" his hand's position, and after the realignment or reduction or whatever the heck the sadomasochistic doctor had done "for his own good," his nerve endings had fired to life.

Good morning!

Celeste slowed and glided toward a stop sign, its white lettering glowing before Old Yeller's headlights. Then Old Yeller clipped a frost heave or a speed bump or some other sort of torture device, and Zach's wrist cussed like a—like Celeste.

A noise echoed in the car, a combo of an exhalation and a grunt.

"You okay?" Celeste asked.

Zach considered telling Celeste he'd burped. Instead, he got real. "Got any ibuprofen or acetaminophen at your place?"

"Yeah."

"Think I might need a few of each."

"That's cool." Celeste yanked off her kerchief thing, tossed it into the backseat, and eased onto the road. Her face glowed, pale and pretty, like something ripe. Like something he wanted to hold in his hands. And, at the same time, like something too precious to touch. Too delicate.

Maybe Celeste had caused the epiphany. He knew she expected him to leave. She knew he knew it. Why should he live up, or down, to her expectations? Unless that was the right thing to do for everyone, including Katherine.

Maybe Katherine had caused Zach's epiphany.

Right when Zach had been sure she'd wanted him to up and leave, she'd up and invited him to stay. Not just in Hidden Harbor but with her.

But he could still leave Hidden Harbor. He could even tell himself breaking his wrist had been a sign, some kind of karmic crap letting him know it was okay to down a handful of pills, get in Matilda, and drive back to Massachusetts.

Decades of living in a town where you couldn't go a block without tripping over a health food store or a yoga studio or a granola factory must've infected his DNA.

He could tell his mother he'd found her—his birth mother. He wiggled his fingers, shooting sparks of pain through his hand, up his wrist, and to his elbow. He could drive one-handed, saving his right hand for emergency purposes only. He could choose to see the fracture as a mere complication to his plan. A test to see how badly he wanted to follow through with his intention to run.

Or he could choose to see the fracture as a stop sign, a warning to slow down, look both ways, and, for once, follow through with his original plan.

He could choose.

A muscle twinge tightened the right side of his neck. He shifted in his seat and turned his head until his gaze fell on the rear view.

"You sure you're okay to drive Matilda back to my place?" Celeste asked. "We could figure something out tomorrow."

"Nah, let's get it done."

"Cool," Celeste said. "Because we're almost home. I mean, back at Lamontagne's."

"Sweet." Home, Zach reminded himself, was wherever you hung your hat, your hoodie, or your fluffy yellow blanket. Celeste had offered him a spot on her couch, not a starring role in her life. But the word hung in the air, evoking a Cape with a shingle roof, a white picket fence, and a freshly tarred driveway. An SUV and—now he knew he was losing his mind—a couple of rug rats of his own.

He'd never before imagined himself as someone's dad.

Celeste pulled up to Lamontagne's and into the space beside Matilda. She killed the engine. "And we're back."

He'd never met anyone like Celeste before.

"Yup." Zach went for the seat buckle.

"Wait." Celeste took hold of the shoulder strap. "Okay, go ahead." When he depressed the button, Celeste leaned over him and guided the shoulder strap around his arm.

"Thanks," he told her hair.

"You're welcome," she said, her voice sweet and hushed and inches from him.

Zach wanted to brush her hair from her eyes, to search for hidden meaning, as though she were a Jumbles riddle he needed to decode. He'd never before wanted to get inside a girl this badly. A chuckle jostled his belly and tugged the corners of his lips.

He meant he'd never before wanted to get inside a girl's *mind* this badly.

Celeste helped him into Matilda, guiding the seat belt around him and tucking him in behind the wheel. Ten minutes later, they parked Matilda and Old Yeller at Ledgewood, and Celeste reversed the seat belt process.

Zach got his duffel bag and Celeste's blanket from Matilda.

"Want me to carry the blanket?" Celeste asked.

He tossed the blanket over his shoulder, lowered his nose. "I'm fine, Celeste."

"Did you sniff my blanket?"

"Uh, maybe."

"Ew," she said. "You're a sick man."

Then she led the sick man to her apartment door, turned the key, and opened the door.

"I've been meaning to ask you about this furniture," Zach said.

"You don't like it?" Celeste paused with her pocketbook in the crook of her arm. She tilted her head, widened her eyes, and gave him a half smile. Was she joking or truly peeved?

If this furniture was her style, then she was someone other than who he thought she was. The notion unsettled him, a milder version of the way he'd felt after his parents' big this-isn't-your-life reveal. "I thought—imagined—it doesn't really look like you."

Celeste laughed and tossed her pocketbook on the floor. "I'm not a five-foot-tall testosterone monkey."

"A what?"

"A short, brawny dude. The furniture came with the apartment."

"Thought so." Celeste was one of the coolest girls he'd ever met, but masculine she was not.

"Make yourself comfortable. I'll go get you some drugs," she said, and she went into the bathroom.

Zach peeked around the corner and then unzipped his jeans. He tugged them down with his left hand, unzipped his duffel, and grabbed his sweats from the top. Now what? The water ran in the bathroom. His heart raced, like some sicko about to be caught with his pants down.

He tossed the sweatpants on the floor, stepped into the legs, and pulled them up, one at a time. When the bathroom door clicked open, Zach arranged himself on the couch, his hand sticking to the black vinyl. He set his feet atop the glass coffee table. He crossed his legs at the ankles.

Celeste wore gray sweatpants and a shapeless gray hoodie. She'd braided her hair—a shiny, loose rope flopped over one shoulder. So that's what she did with her hair at night.

She set a Dixie cup of water and the pills he'd requested on the table. "Look at you, following my directions and making yourself comfortable. You *can* listen."

Zach lifted the chalky tablets to his lips. "Don't let it get around," he said, and tossed down the pills in one gulp.

"Wow."

"That's not how you do it?"

"Nope, but that's okay. We're all different. Do you want something to eat?"

"Beer?" Zach asked.

"Probably not a good idea. Plus, I don't have any. Eggs?"

"If you're making some for yourself."

"Eggs it is."

Zach took his feet off the coffee table and started to get up.

"I'm good. You stay right where you are." Celeste eyed the loaner blanket Zach had tossed on the end of the couch. She pulled the blanket over his lap, slipped the TV remote into his left hand, and left the room.

A guy could get used to this treatment, except for the whole pain issue.

Zach turned on the TV. A World War II documentary. *Flip.* A romantic comedy. He could tell because the girl was a cheerful blonde and the setting was New York City. *Flip. Cops.*

Zach had gotten caught up in the show when Celeste came into the room. "I hope you like your eggs dry because—"

Zach switched off the TV.

Celeste held two plates of scrambled eggs and a wary smile. She notched her head to the side. "What were you watching?"

Zach's heart pounded in his mouth, and his cheeks heated. "Nothin'."

"Nothin' looked a lot like something, and that something looked exactly like *Cops.*" Celeste set a plate of eggs on Zach's lap.

The plate heated Zach's thighs. The aroma of eggs and butter watered his mouth. "Surely you can't be serious."

Celeste sat down, balanced her ankle on her knee and a plate on her lap. Celeste's hands, Zach had noticed a lot. Feminine, but with short, bare nails. Her toenails were a whole different species. Blue and glittery. They looked like candy. Like something he should put in his mouth. Like something that might taste like a raspberry Pixy stick.

"I am serious," Celeste said, "and don't call me Shirley."

Zach raised his gaze. "*Airplane,*" he said. Celeste didn't seem overly eager to dig into her eggs, so he got started. He picked up the fork with his left hand and scooped a heaping forkful of eggs. Slowly, he raised the eggs to his mouth. The girl was covered up from neck to ankle, and her toes got him going?

Man whore.

"That is correct," Celeste said. "And yet it still doesn't explain your fascination with trash TV."

Zach chewed.

Celeste nibbled her eggs.

Zach swallowed. "*Cops* isn't trash TV."

"Aha! So you admit it. You were watching *Cops*. I recognized the wifebeater T-shirt and the chick with the meth addict skin."

Zach shrugged, and a buzz ran through him. The kind of buzz that tingled whenever he tried to explain himself to his parents. "All I saw was a scared woman and a guy in uniform trying to help."

Celeste's fork hovered over her eggs. "Wow. Now I feel like an ass."

"You're not an ass." Now he felt even more like an ass. He wasn't one of those people—he or she of strong opinions who needed to shove his or her strong opinions down the throat of anyone within shouting distance. "I've just, I don't know . . ."

"What?" Celeste asked.

"Did you ever go to an underage party the cops busted up, and then everyone's all trash-talking the police?"

"I'm twenty-two," Celeste said. "I'm hardly underage."

"I mean years ago," Zach said.

Celeste worked her way clockwise around her plate. "Sure. How do you think my brothers taught me how to drink without getting drunk?"

"I never trash-talked the police. Maybe because my parents taught me to respect them? I always kind of saw them as superheroes, zooming in to save the good citizens."

"Of Gotham City?"

Zach shrugged.

"That explains why you tried to leap a tall bakery shelf in a single bound."

Again he shrugged, even though he didn't consider himself a shrugging sort of guy. But Celeste brought out the little-boy shyness in him. Were they flirting? Just friends? Friends who flirted?

"What did you say you went to school for?"

"Criminal justice and psych, but I wasn't heading to any police academy. I wasn't going for a job in law enforcement." He'd figured out junior year in high school that color blindness disqualified him from police work. Research had given him that bit of bad news, but no plan B that interested him.

His body's betrayal energized his right hand, trapped in the cast. When he curled his fingers into a fist, an ache thrummed all the way to his shoulder, and he sank deeper into the couch. "What were you doing it for?"

Of this Zach was certain. "Law school. My father's a public defender," Zach said, by way of explanation.

Celeste frowned. "Isn't that similar to what the police do? Defend the public?"

"The police get to interact with the public and solve crimes. A public defender mostly interacts with papers and a desk. My father loves it. I'd go crazy."

"Don't fence you in, right? You need to be free to roam and feel the breeze in your hair. Wash high-rise windows and ski double black diamond slopes."

During one of their first conversations, he'd rattled off his list of odd jobs, full of pride and wanting to impress a pretty girl. He felt like going back to the Wednesday Zach and giving him a kick in the pants. He'd sounded like a teenager. Exactly what his mother had told him right before she'd kicked him out the door.

Shown him the door and strongly suggested he exit.

"I don't *need* to roam," Zach said, although he wasn't sure that was true, either. Wasn't that part of his MO, too? He ran and he roamed. The two went together like peanut butter and jelly.

"So you're not like your father," Celeste said. "No big deal."

Actually, it kind of was a big deal.

After Zach's parents had dropped the adoption bomb on him, they'd attempted cleanup, swearing they loved him as much as his brothers, stopping by his room every night before bed to see whether he had any questions. Letting him know their bedroom door was always open if he needed them, day or night.

But Zach hadn't believed their claims and he'd never shared his questions. Why had they waited so long to tell him the truth? Why had they eventually told? One question would've led to another and another, a maze he hadn't been willing to navigate. The easiest decision had been to do nothing, sit tight, and keep his mouth shut.

Zach's parents had called his behavior giving them the silent treatment. Zach had called it survival.

His broken wrist throbbed, tiny blood vessels growing in his fracture. He thought of the examining room conversation he'd had with Nurse Lois. He remembered the way her voice had sounded reassuring and yet matter-of-fact when she'd explained how a broken bone healed itself.

Celeste pushed her food around her plate. Her left leg jiggled. Her right food bounced. Her candy-blue toes shimmered and blurred. And just like at night, when he was alone in the back of Matilda, the air shifted and he heard the ocean. The crash of surf, the tug of undercurrent.

Tonight, Zach was pretty sure the ambient sound was happening between his ears. "Celeste?"

"Yeah?"

"I was adopted."

Celeste's leg stopped jiggling; her candy toes stilled. "That's cool."

"That's why I'm not like my dad. You know, because I was adopted."

"Really?"

"Uh-huh. So, yeah," Zach said, attempting and failing to pull off a casual tone. "My parents didn't tell me till I was thirteen. It kind of"—as in really—"effed me up. That's why I've been traveling around. To, you know, figure stuff out." Even to Zach, his reasoning sounded shaky, a close cousin to the excuse he'd given Katherine about seeing more of the U.S. and trying his hand at vocations. Only this time he was admitting to a different sort of search. One where he was looking for himself, as though different parts of him were scattered across the country.

Years of living in Arlington had seeped into his psyche. Soon he'd be sitting in lotus, chanting, *Om,* and actually thinking before he reacted, like a good Buddhist.

His mother's bad perm hadn't been her only questionable phase.

"What sort of stuff are you trying to figure out?" Celeste asked.

Zach hadn't expected a question. He'd expected Celeste to take his statement at face value. He'd expected her to react like every other girl he'd warned away from him. He cleared his throat. "Could I have a glass of water, please?"

"Sure." Celeste dashed from the room, the water ran in the kitchen, and Zach chased the last bite of egg around his plate.

Celeste returned and handed him a glass of ice water, but she wouldn't drop her stare. "Here you go."

"Thanks." *Ah*. The cold opened his throat.

Celeste plopped down on the cushion beside him. "What sort of stuff?"

Zach coughed and set down the glass. "Hmm. Nothing major. Just, you know, what we were talking about. Where I want to work?"

"You don't need to travel all over to figure that out," Celeste said.

"True."

"So in what way are you fucked up?" Celeste asked.

Zach grinned, even though Celeste hadn't meant the translation from *effed* to *fucked* as a joke. He'd told other girls he was effed up and they'd smiled and nodded, never bothering to call him out or ask him to explain himself. Celeste had surprised him with her brutally honest question. She deserved a brutally honest answer.

Problem was, he'd never bothered to fully answer that question for himself. His unrest was more of a feeling. A sick, empty hunger he'd never been able to fill. "When my folks told me I was adopted, they took away my family history," he said.

"Like where your grandparents were born?" Celeste asked.

Zach glanced to the ceiling, looking up to hold down that feeling he got whenever he heard "The Star-Spangled Banner." The urge to run and hide and defend shaky boundaries. He met her gaze. "Like for thirteen years I thought I knew who I was, and then all of a sudden I didn't. Like everything I thought about myself was a lie. Like I didn't know who I was anymore. I still don't. That kind of fucked up."

"I don't believe you."

Zach laughed, loud enough that she should've inched away from him.

Instead, Celeste leaned closer. "You found a punk climbing around Katherine's stockroom—"

"He's just a kid," Zach said.

"—and your first instinct was to dash in front of Katherine and rip the kid off the shelf."

"Maybe I should've trusted a second instinct."

"And the first thing you wanted to know, after you got out of the hospital, was whether the punk was okay."

"He's just a kid," Zach repeated.

Celeste nodded. "You know exactly who you are."

"Who am I?" For a second Zach imagined Celeste held the answer and that the answer was like his St. Anthony pocket token, something solid she could press into the palm of his hand.

"You're Zachary Fitzgerald, defender of bakery owners and skinny-assed punks." The first time Celeste had caught his eye, he'd felt like she was shaking him down to see where his character settled. Tonight, he only wished his character lived up to her opinion.

"He's just—"

Celeste brushed his hair from his eyes. But when he lifted his head, instead of taking her hand away, like he expected, she held steady. "Zach?"

"Yeah?"

"Shut up," Celeste said. Then she angled her head and pressed her lips against his until he smiled and shifted in his seat.

"You can listen," she whispered against his lips.

"Mmm," he said, and he went back for more. She smelled a little like buttercream frosting. She tasted a lot like a sweet and tangy cherry. His fractured wrist throbbed dully inside the cast. Inside his sweats, he was grateful for the extra room.

He raised a hand to her cheek. She was smiling, so he ran his good hand up the loose fabric of her sweatshirt arm and to the back of her bare neck. When she sighed into his mouth, he leaned in and pulled her face closer.

Sparklers flared beneath his lids. Crazy, happy thoughts fired, too fast for him to hold them back. He wanted to stay here forever. In this apartment. On this fugly couch. Kissing the only girl who'd ever dared to kiss him first. The only girl who'd dared him to tell the truth.

He wanted to stay with Celeste.

She made a sound, a half whimper, a maybe moan. Her breathing changed, shortening instead of deepening. Bursts of air, as though she were suffocating—*What the*—

Zach pulled away first.

CHAPTER 11

Celeste thought she was going to die.

She gasped. The sound—raspy and raw—made her lungs seize harder, ramping up her adrenaline, like a blender shifting from *shred* to *liquefy.*

For a second, Zach mirrored her likely expression. His eyes big, as though someone had jumped him from the ceiling. Then his expression went all mellow, like some kind of woo-woo Zen master. "Breathe, Celeste."

"I . . . am . . . breathing."

What's wrong with me?

No big surprise, the thought made the situation worse.

"Breathe deeper." Zach's hand hovered above her shoulder, as though he meant to comfort her, and then he set it back by his side. "A deep breath into your belly, not your chest and shoulders." Zach demonstrated with an exaggerated inhalation. "Out through your mouth," he said on an exhalation.

"Breathing lesson?" she croaked.

"Shut up, Celeste."

Celeste looked Zach in the eye. When he nodded and grinned, her chin trembled and the corners of her eyes watered. "Zach," she said, and his name sounded like a plea for help.

Zach pressed a finger to his lips. "In."

She inhaled into her belly.

"And out."

After three more breaths, the band around her chest loosened, the fire in her lungs subsided.

You're okay, Zach mouthed. And she repeated the process.

What the hell is wrong with me?

Knowing the statement wasn't helpful didn't stop her from repeating it.

Celeste focused her attention on Zach's eyes, the sharp blue of his irises. His prominent forehead, thick, dark eyebrows. His mouth, with the slight indent in the bottom lip. Moments ago, that mouth had been gently kissing her senseless. Now that same mouth was attempting to coax her back to her senses.

The sound of Zach's voice, warm and reassuring, soothed her lungs. Her breathing relaxed.

"Excuse me for a sec? I need a glass of water." Celeste stole into the kitchen, her adrenaline's blender speed lowered to a steady, humming *mince.* She ran the water, contemplated hiding in there all night. She could use a few dish towels as a pillow. Zach could stay up all night and watch *Cops* uninterrupted. They could pretend they hadn't kissed. They could pretend she hadn't freaked out on him.

Zach came around the corner.

They couldn't pretend.

She avoided his gaze and took a glass down from the sink, ran the water. Her reflection in the faucet handle stared back at her, her head small and misshapen as a deflated balloon. "Hey, injured person, you're supposed to be resting."

"You're supposed to be getting a glass of water." He reached around her, took the empty glass from her hand, held it under the water, and handed it back to her. "You okay?"

"Your breathing lesson took," Celeste said. "Otherwise?" She took a sip, wiped her mouth with the back of her trembling hand. "That's never happened to me before. Honestly? I have no clue what's wrong with me." The white lie banded her chest. Wasn't a white lie something you told for someone else's own good? She couldn't imagine Zach would want to hear about another guy she'd recently more than kissed. She *could* imagine where the panic came from and why kissing Zach had inspired the freak show.

"You had a panic attack," Zach said. "Nothing to be embarrassed about."

Easy for him to say.

Zach nodded. "First time I saw someone having a panic attack, I was giving a private ski lesson. This ten-year-old boy was so certain he was ready to try a black diamond, until we got to the top and he took a good look down."

"Then you gave him a breathing lesson."

"That I did. By the end of the day, he was racing me down that same slope."

Superhero.

Zach gave her a scrunched smile and a nod. "How about I go sleep in my car for the night?"

"No! That would make everything worse."

"Not a big deal. Matilda's very comfortable. And I'm kind of sticking to your couch anyway. I don't mind—"

"Hell, no. Get your ass back on that sticky couch."

"My ass will be fine. I shouldn't have kissed you."

"Excuse me? *I* kissed *you*."

"I shouldn't have kissed you back."

"Because you have a crush on Katherine?"

Zach laughed. The strangled, frustrated sound filled Celeste's tiny hole of a kitchen, but his gaze zoomed in on hers. "Because," he said, "I have a crush on you." And then the flirty, seemingly self-assured guy in her tiny hole of a kitchen blushed and left the room.

She'd told Zach she was clueless.

To her relief, she found him back in the appropriate position—resting on her sticky couch, with his feet up on her glass coffee table, crossed at the ankles. "You can listen."

Zach raised his brows. "Yup."

He'd trusted her with his truest, realest, stripped-down self. He'd trusted her. Could she trust him? "That stuff you told me about being adopted? All the stuff about how you don't know who you are? Thank you for sharing that with me. Thank you for sharing the specifics of your fucked-up-ness."

Zach laughed. Not a frustrated sound this time, but one with the joy of being found. That eased her adrenaline down the rest of the way. "What can I say?" Zach asked. "You bring the specifics out of me. You'd make a good detective."

Celeste sat her butt down on the sticky couch and her sweaty glass of water on the coffee table. Her body thrummed with aftershock exhaustion. If she closed her eyes, she'd fall asleep sitting up. She pulled her fuzzy yellow blanket across both their laps and wound Zach's left arm around her shoulder. She checked his face. He was smiling, slightly shy and hugely psyched. She snuggled into him and focused on the red-and-black abstract painting on the far wall, held the picture of Zach's smiling face in her mind's eye.

"Remember how you asked me specifically why I quit culinary school?"

"Sure."

"And I answered, nonspecifically, that stuff happened."

"Kind of."

"Specifically," Celeste said, "stuff happened with a guy."

"A boyfriend?" Zach asked.

"No. A guy friend. A classmate. I wasn't interested in dating anyone while I was in school. But even if I had been looking for a boyfriend"—or a hookup—"I wouldn't have been interested in him." Celeste took a loud breath, and the abstract painting blurred. The red and black blended into each other. "We were at a party, and I guess I had too much to drink."

"You guess?"

"I had a couple of screwdrivers." Celeste remembered the taste. More sour orange than bitter vodka. She'd barely tasted the vodka. The first glass had been filled to the lip with ice—clinking and melting. She'd complained that the drink was too watered down. She'd needed a release valve. She'd wanted a good buzz.

She hadn't wanted sex.

"Two drinks isn't a lot," Zach said.

She remembered kissing Matt, his face suddenly close to hers. She still couldn't remember why she'd kissed him. Then, out of nowhere, her mind released the specifics.

Matt had driven her back from Drake's, with the radio off, and he'd parked his Corvette behind the dorms. Her ears hummed with the quiet, her head buzzy and disconnected. "I betcha," Matt had said, "if I turn on the radio, Billy Joel will be singing 'Honesty.' "

"Right," she'd said. "Whatever, Matt." The clock on the dashboard had read 1:34, the numbers fuzzing and swimming before her eyes. She'd turned to Matt, and he seemed to swivel, as though his car were a merry-go-round and Matt was taking her for a spin.

"I bet it will. In fact"—he rubbed his hands together—"I'm willing to make it interesting."

"Five bucks?" she'd asked.

"A kiss," he'd said.

She'd laughed, but he'd held a steady smile. He hadn't backed down. "Go for it," she'd said, and he'd turned on the radio, blasting "Honesty" through the car, a warning she hadn't recognized.

Of course, he'd set her up. Matt never wagered unless the outcome was a sure thing.

Zach squeezed her shoulder.

"Anyway," Celeste said. "We were drinking—"

"You and the guy friend who wasn't your boyfriend?" Zach asked.

"Yeah, me and Matt." Saying his name made her heart kick into gear and her throat narrow. She took a slow breath into her belly, inhaling the fragrance of her shampoo from Zach's hair, the cottony smell of Zach's T-shirt, and the scent of Zach himself. "I must've had too much to drink because, the next thing I knew, I woke up in Matt's bed."

Zach's breathing changed—one of those shoulder breathing jobbies he'd cautioned her against.

"Still with me?" she asked.

"Right here."

"Seems Matt didn't share my memory issue. He had no trouble bragging about his little conquest to his buddies. He had no trouble with specifics." She remembered the way Matt had described her birthmark—more identifying than dental records. The fact that he'd detailed the birthmark meant they'd messed around a lot and with the lights on.

How could she have forgotten something so personal?

Another shoulder breath from Zach. She shivered, as though she were still in Matt's bed, naked and disoriented. As if she were still in the hallway outside the Barnstead Hall practice kitchen. As if Matt's words were still stripping her bare. The red-and-black painting's abstract brushstrokes swirled like a lava lamp and settled into a face. Matt's face.

"What an asshole," Zach said.

"Guys have been assholes to me before. The boy I loved in high school," Celeste said, although she hadn't intended to expand the specifics to include Justin. "After we broke up, he trashed my reputation pretty badly. It was, like, his favorite hobby. And he was good at it. That's why I think I freaked out. This kind of shit is cumulative. It makes you wonder about half the human race."

"It made you wonder about me," Zach said.

Celeste searched her mind, comparing Justin to Matt and coming up with a few similarities. Both of them were overconfident about their abilities; both refused to rectify whatever they'd done wrong. And, of course, both of them had trashed her and simultaneously bolstered their reputations.

Neither of them resembled Zach.

She turned to Zach. Sweet, sexy, defender of bakery owners and skinny-assed punks. Defender of Celeste.

"When I overheard Matt, it made me wonder about me. What had I done wrong? We were friends. Why did he turn on me? Was I that bad a judge of character?"

Zach gave her braid a tug—something Abby would do—to pull her out of the doldrums. He aimed a sympathetic smile her way.

"Justin and I were friends before we went out. He used to be good friends with one of my brothers—"

"One of your two dozen brothers."

'That's right." She grinned; she couldn't help herself. Did Zach remember everything she said to him?

"The boy you loved in high school," Zach said.

"The only guy," she blurted out, the tone hushed, as though the words were a revelation. She'd been in lust a few times since with guys she'd never considered long-term options. She'd even been in intense like.

But not love. Not couldn't-live-without-him, spark-plug-to-the-internal-organs love.

That kind of intensity would mean she had too much to lose.

"I guess you could say I'm kind of effed up, too," Celeste said.

Zach slipped his arm from around her shoulder and angled sideways on the couch so she had to look at him. "You said you only had a couple of drinks, right?" Zach asked.

"Screwdrivers."

"And you never get drunk because your two dozen brothers taught you how to drink."

"Maybe I was exaggerating. I mean, seriously, everyone gets faced sooner or later. There's a first time for everything." At least she thought everyone got faced. Somewhere between waking up in Matt's dorm room and climbing the stairs in Barnstead Hall, she'd even imagined that Matt had gotten faced, too. She'd thought he was as regretful, as horrified, as she'd been. Why else would he have sat by his bed, waiting for her to wake up?

"Celeste . . ." Zach worried the ends of her braid the way she'd seen him nervously brushing his own flop of hair from his eyes.

"What? What is it?"

"The story's not gelling for me. It doesn't make sense."

"Sounds pretty simple to me. I got drunk, I blacked out, I woke up next to a giant sphincter muscle. End of story."

"Have you ever blacked out before?"

"I didn't have anything to eat, Zach, even though I know that's a big no-no. I was saving my calories. I basically drank my dinner. I can admit when something's my fault. Okay? I got myself drunk. I trusted the wrong guy."

"And you don't remember anything, in between drinking and waking up?"

She thought about telling Zach she'd kissed Matt. That tonight she'd remembered a bit more about the game that had inspired the kiss. But how could she admit she'd kissed Matt on a bet? How could she admit to playing with someone's affection without leading Zach to wonder whether she was playing with his?

She covered her mouth, shook her head. When she met Zach's gaze, her eyes moistened.

And Zach totally misread her. He moved her hand away from her mouth and held it in his. "For one of my criminal justice classes, the professor took a true crime story and sliced it up. Every student got part of the story pie, with a slice or two missing. The assignment wasn't to figure out who did it necessarily. Although, yeah, you got extra points for that. The goal was to figure out which logical pieces were missing."

Zach gave her hand a squeeze that was meant to be reassuring. Instead, the gesture pumped adrenaline into her heart. "Hate to tell you, Celeste, but there are logical pieces missing from your story. I think—in my most humble opinion—you should play detective and dig deeper. Was there anyone who saw you drinking before the blackout? You should talk to them. You know, kick ass, take numbers, and figure out the missing pieces of the pie."

"I hate to tell you, Zach, but in my humble opinion, I believe the saying is 'shoot first, ask questions later.' Neither of which will get me any answers. Plus, I'm not going back there. Ever."

Zach notched his head toward the telephone on the side table, that curious invention that supposedly worked both ways. But she'd yet to hear back from her parents. All week, their answering machines had played a wicked game of phone tag until Celeste had lost track and given up. And every time she'd phoned one of her brothers, she got a sister-in-law on the line and a rundown of which niece or nephew had lost a tooth, learned to skateboard, or earned an A on a vocabulary pop quiz. Celeste adored her sisters-in-law, but they kept her one degree of separation from her brothers. The guys who'd seen her at her worst and loved her the best.

"There's this girl Natalie I could call," Celeste said.

"A friend of yours?" Zach asked.

Celeste grinned. Such a direct question shone light on crap she'd yet to fully consider. "Culinary school is a weird place. Everyone acts all buddy-buddy friendly. 'You help me, I'll help you.' But underneath the spin, it's a big competition for most people." Why, then, had she thought her friendship with Matt had been different? That somehow their relationship had been special and unique? That the two of them were like low tide at Popham Beach, where you could walk the exposed sandbar to Fox Island and not get marooned?

The shithead had marooned her.

"Are you like most people?" Zach asked. "Competitive?"

"No," she said, the word knee-jerk and awkward. First day of class, the dean of students had delivered a speech and urged each student to compete with him- or herself, to strive for his or her personal best. But then the grades for every Monday quiz posted on Tuesday outside the practice kitchen for the other student chefs to see, the high-minded lesson buried beneath the lowbrow subliminal truth. Success was relative.

And Matt was neither her brother nor her friend.

"Anyway, I don't know whether I had any real friends at school. But I could probably call Natalie."

Zach stroked the back of Celeste's hand with his thumb, as though she were a worry stone, a touchstone, something solid to hold on to.

She met his gaze, and the memory of their kiss—before everything had gone to panicky hell—passed between them.

Zach wasn't Matt, but he wasn't just a friend, either. The kiss and Zach's crush confession had shot that notion to hell.

"I really think you should call this girl who's not a real

friend." Zach nodded, the gesture meant to encourage Celeste's reflexive head wagging.

Celeste wasn't that easy. "I don't know. Maybe I will."

"Good girl," Zach said, as though he were trying to insert an inspirational quote into her brain, a voice of reason to rise up and do battle with the naysayers. The part of her that agreed with the way Justin had portrayed her as a sex-crazed slut and the way Matt had lent his voice to second the motion.

"We could call this girl together."

"There's only one phone."

"You could call, and I could hold your hand—"

"Seriously?"

"I could hang nearby for moral support."

Interesting choice of words.

She touched his cheek and rubbed his nighttime scruff. "You're a good guy, Zach Fitzgerald."

"You're changing the subject."

"Yes, I am."

When Celeste had nearly polished off her first drink of the night, Matt had gone to the kitchen to get her another. Celeste and Natalie had wandered into the line for the bathroom. Inside the bathroom, the buzz had hit Celeste like a rogue wave. Everything had slowed down, as though she were swimming underwater. She'd stared at her mirror reflections—the girl behind other people's fingerprints, smudges, and splatters. She'd leaned closer, trailed her fingers across her prominent cheekbones, and wondered at the transformation.

When had she stopped looking like a girl and started looking like a woman? When would her insides match what the world saw? When would she stop feeling like a fraud?

Celeste slipped her hand from Zach and gulped down the rest of her water. The cold numbed her throat and iced her belly.

When she'd stepped from the bathroom at Drake's party,

Matt had been waiting. His expression, come to think of it, was a close cousin to the look he'd sported when she'd awoken in his bed.

And Natalie had been right by Matt's side, hanging out, fussing with her short, spiked blonde hair, and letting the girl next in the line for the bathroom pass before her. "Don't you have to go?" Celeste had asked.

"Just keepin' you company, sistah," Natalie had said. Then she'd taken Celeste's empty drink from her hand and switched it out with the fresh drink Matt had been holding for her, a boozy relay race.

Celeste flipped on the TV. Middle of *Cops.* Different episode, same overall feeling of squalor and despair.

A big-ass grin spread across Zach's face.

Distraction successful.

Half-asleep with her eyes open, Celeste nestled into Zach's side. She retrieved his hand. She set her heels on the coffee table and notched up the sound on his show. A man in blue was once again speaking in hushed tones to a sickly, skinny woman.

"Are you sure?" the man in blue asked. "We can write him up, give you some time to think about this."

The camera zoomed in on the "him" in question. From the back of a police cruiser, hands cuffed behind his back, a bull of a man leaned forward and directed his crazy-ass message through the closed window at the skinny woman.

The skinny woman shivered, but she held her ground. Her man had gotten to her first. "Yeah. I'm sure," she told the officer. "Let him go. He's calmed down. He won't cause no trouble."

Another case of double negatives betraying the truth.

Celeste might take Zach's advice and give little miss "just keepin' you company" a ring. Maybe.

Cut to the officer shaking his head at the skinny woman and unlocking the bull of a guy's cuffs. Cut to the skinny woman's face, her eyes red rimmed with spent tears, staring off at the cruiser. Cut to the big scary guy leading her into their split-level house and the cruiser driving off in the distance.

The theme song played, the oh so catchy "Whatcha gonna do when they come for you?"

The bad boy had answered that question, brilliantly. Made Celeste want to don a superhero cape and save that poor woman from ending up on a future episode.

Maybe Celeste would contact Natalie. But there was no way she'd phone within earshot of Zach. When you were digging for the details of one of the worst mistakes you'd ever made, did you really want a witness?

Hell, no, sistah. Hell, no.

Chapter 12

"Monday, Monday" played in Katherine's head, The Mamas and the Papas crooning about the lack of guarantees. She hadn't thought of the tune in years. Now it arrived uninvited, clear as the daybreak that was yet to dawn, every word enunciated, on key, and emotionally true. Come nightfall, would Celeste and Zach remain in her employ and Hidden Harbor? Would Barry still love her?

Could she keep her secret about Zach without losing everyone she loved?

Celeste set a carafe full of hazelnut coffee on the Lamontagne coffee bar alongside a sugar dispenser, the lone survivor of Blake's crusade. Katherine breathed in the coffee aroma, more delicious and pulse enlivening than the best toilet water. Earlier, Celeste had ground the beans Katherine purchased from Maine Line Roasters. Katherine's flour came from Portland via a driver Katherine had known for over a decade. Her milk and cream from Bitsy's down the road and cows Katherine had personally petted and thanked. Desperate for a family, she had scrabbled together a bakery-related tree. But at the end of the day, that wasn't enough to sustain her soul.

Her real family came down to three brittle unrelated branches: Celeste, Barry, and now Zach.

Warmth from her kitchen filled every corner of her bakery, but a chill prickled her arms. "Thank you for taking care of Zach," Katherine said. "Was he comfortable enough to sleep last night?"

"He slept on my couch," Celeste said. "If that's what you're after."

"No," Katherine said. "That's not what I meant at all." Was Katherine such a bad communicator? Or was Celeste predisposed to imagining people thought badly of her? Katherine's jaw ached with the familiar childhood sensation of knowing everything she said was wrong.

In the month following Katherine's eleventh birthday, she'd used extreme measures to deal with the problem, keeping mum in hopes that her father would follow suit. But then she'd learned that body language could incite suspicion and anger and that her father—who'd never cracked the spine of a book or forked over coin for the daily news—was an excellent reader.

"Are you okay?" Celeste asked.

Katherine swiped her cheek, and her hand came away dry. "I'm perfectly fine." Her father's voice rang through her brain: *You're not crying, baby Katherine, are you?* Her father's setup was designed to make her cry and then berate her for crying. "But Zach . . . was he in pain?" Katherine cradled her right arm with her left, the way you reflexively healed yourself. Could her healing thoughts touch Zach? *May Zach be well. May Zach be happy. May Zach be at peace.*

Celeste shot Katherine a wicked smile. "I drugged him."

Even though Katherine knew Celeste was kidding, her pulse did a double take. She knew Celeste well, unless she didn't.

"What must you think of me?" Celeste held her hand to her chest, a faux-insulted gesture, but Celeste's tone and expression told the true tale. Celeste had caught Katherine's flash of concern. "Acetaminophen and ibuprofen, just what the nurse ordered. When I left, he was sleeping like a baby." Celeste fluttered her lashes. She pressed her hands together, held her hands to her cheek, and made her lips into an O.

An image of a sleeping newborn Zach flickered before Katherine's eyes. When she pushed the thought away, Zach the man pushed back—through the door and into her bakery. "Speak of the devil, who's not sleeping!"

"Get out of here, Zach," Celeste said, but she couldn't hide her pique of delight, the smile that filled every corner of her being. "You're making a liar out of me. I just got finished telling Katherine you were sleeping like a baby on my sticky couch."

Sticky?

Zach bit his lip. He made a slicing motion with his left hand, palm-side up. "I unstuck myself for my shift. Five-forty-five, right?" He looked from Katherine to Celeste and back to Katherine. "Why are you both looking at me weird?"

"I wasn't expecting you to come in this morning," Katherine said.

"Why not?" Again Zach waved his left hand.

Katherine and Celeste nodded toward Zach's right arm.

Zach peered down his nose at the sling, as though the cast were news to him. "*Pffft,*" he said through his teeth. "No big thing. I've skied with worse."

"I thought you said you broke your arm playing soccer," Celeste said.

"You thought I meant—that was the first time I broke a bone. I broke my leg skiing in '92. Broke my collarbone in '93."

"Skiing again?" Katherine asked.

"Just messing around with my best buddies. A little living room wrestling. I won the match, so it was totally worth it."

His poor mother.

Katherine's collarbone ached. Her wrist throbbed. The backs of her knees weakened. And her hand reflexively covered her heart.

"Make sure you leave a stack of dishes in the sink at the end of your shift," Katherine told Zach.

"I might be as slow as a one-armed dishwasher," Zach said, "but I can still do my job."

"As a favor to me. Blake's coming by after school. I'm making him work to pay me back for the damage."

"Brilliant!" Zach said.

"I don't know how brilliant it is," Katherine said. "He vandalized the place as payback for not getting a job here. I'm kind of giving him what he wanted. Minus the pay, of course."

"Are you going to be nice to him?" Celeste asked.

"I'm not going to be mean. I'll treat him fairly, the way I treat all my employees."

"Just be your usual exacting self," Celeste said, another one of her backhanded compliments.

"I was going to invite you and Zach over for dinner Sunday night," Katherine said. "Now, I'm not sure I want to."

"Both of us, together?" Celeste voice went high and squeaky, and she scrutinized Katherine's gaze. When Katherine nodded, Celeste beamed, giving herself away for the second time that morning. She might not need Katherine's approval, but she wanted it.

"A celebration dinner for Lamontagne's employees." Katherine held her hands up in the push-away position. "No Blake. Employees who aren't paying me back for damages. A welcome to and welcome back to Hidden Harbor celebration."

"You know it's Halloween, right?" Zach asked.

"Know it?" Celeste said, her tone turning playful. "She's practically a witch. She doesn't even need a costume."

With the exception of Barry, no one enjoyed teasing

Katherine about her proclivity for tarot card readings more than Celeste. "If you're going to be mean, I'm taking back my invitation." Katherine was only kidding. But the threat to take back what she'd offered Celeste felt mean-spirited and—God help her—familiar.

"All right, I'll be good," Celeste said.

"Don't be too good or I might not recognize you," Katherine said.

One for Katherine, Celeste mouthed, and she pretended to mark a chalkboard.

Katherine hadn't known they were keeping score. "How does an early five o'clock dinner of roast beef and root vegetables sound? Hmm? A good hearty fall dinner before candy and trick-or-treaters?" Katherine directed her question to both Celeste and Zach, but she already knew Celeste's answer. When she was growing up, roast had been Celeste's family's Sunday dinner, a loud affair with Celeste and her brothers jockeying for the crispiest potatoes. Katherine and Celeste shared an undying affection for the humble potato. The meal was one of Celeste's favorites. Food she, Katherine hoped, couldn't resist.

"Sounds great to me," Zach said. "Should we come in costume?"

"Are you thinking of dressing up like an alien?" Katherine asked.

"Nah," he said. "Been there, done that, time to move on." Zach poured himself a cup of coffee. One-handed, he nabbed two creamers and pierced the lids with his forefinger. He tore open two packets of sugar with his teeth. He ruined the rich black coffee as far as Katherine was concerned but managed to keep most of the cream and sugar from spilling on the counter. He stirred the coffee and, aware of his audience, took a loud slurp. His eyes rolled up in his head in exaggerated delight. "Ahh! All right, then. Let's get this party started. I'm ready to rack and roll!"

Katherine watched Celeste watch Zach's toosh walk into the kitchen. The sound of a metal tray clanging to the floor echoed into the shop. "I'm okay!" Zach yelled.

"This could be interesting," Katherine said.

"If by *interesting,* you mean funny as hell," Celeste said, "then I agree."

Zach peeked into the shop. The white cotton strap of his apron looped around his neck; the smock dangled over his chest. "Uh, Celeste, can I get your help with something?"

"That didn't take long," Celeste whispered to Katherine.

In the doorway to the kitchen, Celeste secured the ties of Zach's apron. From the back, Zach looked even more like Adam than from the front. His height and his broad shoulders. The way he stood tall and never slouched.

When Zach turned back around, he lowered his gaze, and his hair fell across his forehead. Her biological son was smitten with Celeste. Her nonbiological daughter?

Katherine shook her head. Zach might stay in Hidden Harbor, giving her more time to get to know him. He might even choose to never share the true reason for his trip to Hidden Harbor with Katherine. But Katherine knew the price you paid when you hid a truth of consequence from someone you loved. How long would it take for Zach to spill the beans to Celeste? How long before Celeste blabbed said beans to Barry?

How long before Katherine's secret broke Barry's heart? How long before Barry's justifiable hatred broke her?

Taking fertility drugs had made her crazy, the mother of all PMS attacks, squared. She'd tried to keep the crazy to herself, but sometimes the crazy leaked, and she'd snapped at Barry. For the way his knife scraped his dinner plate. For taking all the bedcovers. For *giving* her all the bedcovers. Then Barry would snap back. Even a gentle reminder that he too was a parent without a child undid her.

The day she and Barry had married, she'd handed him her heart and the power to crush it.

"Morning!" A woman breezed into the shop, wearing jeans and a French-blue fleece jacket. Tousled, shoulder-length gray hair. A pleasant, familiar face. She walked up to the counter, gazed up at the menu board, and then set her bright-eyed gaze on Katherine. "I'm here for more of Celeste's Wild Blues."

The woman Katherine had seen in passing at the Hidden Harbor Harvest Festival had been neither the daughter of one of her oldest customers nor a youthful doppelgänger.

"Mrs. Jenkins!" Katherine said.

"Call me Judy," Mrs. Jenkins said.

This might take some getting used to—the first name, the unbuttoned attitude, the French-blue fleece, unzipped to reveal a womanly figure. How many years had Katherine known Mrs.—Judy? Katherine had only ever seen the outer trappings. The shapeless beige trench coat, the horrible clear bonnet. Her clothing protected her from elements real and imagined. Her clothing kept her protected from the world. What a shame her clothing kept the world from seeing her.

You could be acquainted with a woman for decades without ever getting to know her.

Katherine reached beneath the counter for a bakery box, but Judy held her focus. Her enviable hourglass figure, her hair's smooth, sultry swirl. Katherine shook open the cardboard box and bent back the cover. "How many Wild Blues?"

"A dozen."

"Anything else?"

"No, thank you."

And just like that Katherine's customer, who'd been tied to a routine for a decade, doubled her count and dropped corn and lemon poppy seed muffins from her order.

"Don't get me wrong," Judy said, mistaking Katherine's surprise for feeling insulted. "All your muffins are delicious, but the blueberry muffins are my favorite. And when you find what you really want"—Judy kissed her pinched fingers—"there's nothing better. Why settle for anything else?"

"You have a point," Katherine told Judy. And then Katherine called into the back room, "Celeste! Could you come out front for a moment, please?"

Something fell to the kitchen floor, more of a dull thud this time than a clatter. "I'm okay!" Zach said. Celeste's laughter, as sweet and tart as Maine's wild blueberries, inspired a chuckle from Zach.

The ability to poke fun at your various mishaps, especially those you'd brought on yourself? Nothing better.

Celeste emerged from the kitchen with a bounce in her step and stopped short. "Good morning?" she said to Judy, her voice sweet and singsong. The tail-end upswing, the hint of a question mark, told Katherine that Celeste had no clue whom she was greeting.

"Mrs. Judy Jenkins would like a dozen of your Wild Blues," Katherine told Celeste.

"That's right," Mrs. Judy Jenkins said.

Celeste tilted her face. Katherine could almost see the realization cross Celeste's features: *Mrs. . . . Judy . . . Oh my God.* When Celeste glanced at Katherine, she read: *No freaking way!*

Then Celeste schooled her features into the professionally acceptable *pleased to see you.* "Mrs. Jenkins—"

"Judy," Judy said.

"Judy." Celeste nodded and patted one of her own French braids. "I love what you've done with your hair."

Celeste pinched bakery tissue, slid open the back of the bakery case, gathered her wild blueberry muffins.

Judy giggled like a girl, shrugged a shoulder, and touched a finger to her hair. "All I did was set it free."

"Beautiful." Celeste tied up her Wild Blues and handed them over to Judy.

Judy angled her face over the box and took a deep breath. "You ladies have a wonderful day!"

Katherine's regular Nurse Terry bustled into the bakery. Katherine nabbed and shook Terry's OJ and dropped it into her bag, prefilled with a warm croissant and a cheerful orange-striped straw. Terry set her money on the counter, blew Katherine a kiss, and flew out the door.

With Zach working in the back at half speed, now would be a good time for Barry to walk through the door. She was anxious to tell him she'd apprehended the big, bad burglar. She was anxious to ask Barry's advice about Blake. She was equally anxious for Barry not to scrutinize Zach too closely. Thus far, Barry had only seen Zach from across the room. And maybe, just maybe, the fates were conspiring to keep Zach and Barry apart. Katherine smiled in Barry anticipation and the door jingled open. Daniel the construction guy met her look of Barry anticipation with Katherine anticipation and then took the look up a notch.

Seemed the fates had something else in store for her today.

Katherine came out from behind the bakery case, craned her neck, and gazed around Daniel for his coworker. "Where's your friend?"

"You mean tall, dark, and grouchy?"

Katherine pressed her lips together, made a gesture, zipping her lips. "You said it, not me."

"I'm flying solo this morning."

"No wingman?" she asked, the term slipping out, as though she were swiveling on the stool of a singles bar instead of leaning against her bakery counter. She couldn't say she disliked the way Daniel's eyes widened in surprise and the corners of his grin hitched, taking it all in.

"I've never needed a wingman." Daniel held her gaze, confident, but he cracked his knuckles—one hand and then the other—giving away his nerves and drawing her attention to his ring finger. A pale band of skin stood out against his tan hand. A recent jewelry removal or a lingering tan line? "Ah, heck, I'll just say it."

"Go right ahead."

"The—the gray-haired guy that comes in every morning," Daniel said, giving her whiplash from déjà vu. Less than twenty-four hours ago, Zach had started an inquiry about his paternity with the same stammering statement. She was sure that wasn't where Daniel was headed. "Are you and him—?" Daniel gestured from Katherine to himself and back to Katherine again.

"Stirring the air between us?" Katherine asked.

Daniel laughed. The sound, deeper than she'd imagined, kicked up her pulse. "Are you involved?"

Katherine would've preferred a different word choice, one that didn't require skirting the truth. She and Barry were involved, intimately and continually, but only in their minds. "The gray-haired man and I got a divorce two years ago. We're just friends."

"Are you sure?"

This time, Katherine laughed. "I signed the papers," she said, aware she wasn't answering the question Daniel had asked.

The door jingled and the friend who still occupied her thoughts walked into the café, looking trim, fit, and good enough to eat. Instead of jeans and a fleece, he wore pressed khakis and a striped button-down. She could still see the relief of his bike-honed thigh muscles, the shape of his gym-rat biceps. But, as always, Barry's gaze was her undoing.

He caught her eye, her expression, and—she was sure—the way she was leaning against her counter, arms crossed to hold up her breasts. She uncrossed her arms. She crossed them lower.

"Morning!" Barry called to Katherine, with a heavy undertone of *honey, I'm home.*

Katherine moved her arms up an inch. She needed to talk to Barry, if only to let him know about the break-ins and Blake. She needed to finish dragging out an ask-out from her suddenly shy and oh so sweet construction worker friend. She needed to stop the insanity.

She wasn't Barry's property; she'd never been his property. And she was no longer Barry's wife.

She was Barry's ex-wife, a term neither of them had used before in the company of the other. As though dancing around the term made it any less true.

Barry stood behind Daniel and cleared his throat, a gesture she thought was overtly jealous and therefore below him, until he cleared his throat a second time.

She smiled, conciliatory, and Barry gave her a triumphant grin. "Barry, this is my friend Daniel . . ." *Oh, crap.*

"Anaghnostopoulos," Daniel provided. "That's okay," he told Katherine. "My mother can't even pronounce it." He angled a wink at Katherine.

"Daniel, my ex-husband, Barry Horowitz."

Barry shook his head and widened his eyes at the sound of the term. Then he pulled it together and shook Daniel's hand.

"I thought I heard your voice."

Celeste came up behind Katherine, stealthy as a thief, and then loud as a . . . as a Celeste. Actually, this was perfect.

Katherine pointed at Celeste. "You, help Barry with his order. I'm guessing you need a blueberry muffin. Am I right?"

"She always could read my mind," Barry told Daniel, all while keeping his appreciative gaze on her.

Oh, for heaven's sake. She pointed at Barry. "I need to talk to you." Her pointer swayed in Daniel's direction. "But I need to help Daniel with something first. Can you hang around for a few minutes?"

"That would be my pleasure. I need to talk to you, too."

Laying it on rather thick, don't you think?

From the smug look on his face, she'd guess that Barry could read her mind.

Before she could get to a four-top, Daniel stepped in and pulled a chair out for her. *Laying it on rather thick, don't you think?*

Barry both smiled and glared in their direction.

Katherine leaned across the table. "So, Daniel Anaghnostopoulos," she said, and the man with the surname she'd pronounced without a hitch gifted her with a belly laugh. She touched his left hand, kept her gaze on his eyes. "How old is your tan line?"

"My what?" he asked.

"The white band from your wedding ring."

Daniel flexed his fingers, as though they were cramped. "*Ha*. Women always pick up on that."

"Yes, we do."

Daniel momentarily dropped his grin and his gaze. Then both lifted to Katherine. "My wife and I have been separated about four months."

Daniel could've said, *I've* been separated, but he hadn't. In Katherine's experience, that told her everything she needed to know.

"Have you asked anyone out since your separation? Gone out on any dates?"

Daniel held a steady smile and shook his head.

"Filed for divorce yet?"

Daniel blew out a breath. "It's complicated," he said. "We have a business together—"

Daniel wasn't just a construction worker bee. He was, like her, the worker boss.

"We've been together forever," he said, answering both the question she'd asked and, perhaps, one he hadn't much considered. Did he really want a divorce?

Daniel seemed like a nice guy. Katherine could imagine spending an evening with him, filled with easy conversation. She could imagine taking him back to her apartment and getting an up close and personal tour of his construction-ready body. She could imagine the evening leading to a whole truckload of regret. For Daniel.

Right after she'd delivered the divorce papers and mundel bread to Barry, she'd parked behind his house and sat in her car for half an hour. She was either going to walk back in, take off her clothes, and make herself at home. Or she was going to drive to the nearest bar, bring a guy back to her newly rented apartment, and make sure she'd never be able to go back on her decision.

The bar's name was Murphy's Law.

"Are you planning on asking me out on a date?" Katherine asked.

"That's the general idea."

"That's very flattering," she said.

Daniel's mouth fell open. "Oh, come on." He sat up taller and shook his head. "Don't say no."

"It's just—"

Daniel held his hands in prayer position. He leaned across the table close enough for her to get a good look at his golden-brown, earnest eyes. Close enough for her to imagine him walking into her apartment, taking off his clothes, and making himself at home.

"Come on, Katherine. Come on."

Without glancing at Barry, she knew he was looking her way. The awareness of his gaze was as keen as the sensation of the chair beneath her bottom, the floor underneath her feet, her heart pounding in her chest and questioning every decision.

Katherine wrapped her hands around Daniel's. "Do you still love her?"

Daniel went silent and his gaze skittered to the side. "I don't know."

"My advice to you? See if you can work it out."

"I don't think—"

"At least figure out if there's a reason to try. Then, if and when you file for a divorce, ask me out for real." Katherine slipped her hands from Daniel's and sat up straight. "I might even say yes."

"You sure?" Daniel asked.

"I'm sure."

Daniel hung his head sideways, playing at regret. But the way he sat back in his seat, spreading out his weight, evidenced a whole truckload of relief.

"Can I get you a cup of coffee?" she asked.

"Why not?"

The speed roller rattled from the kitchen. Celeste pulled the front of the cart and Zach pushed with his left hand.

"You need some help with that?" Barry asked.

"We're good!" Zach said, using a plural pronoun.

Katherine mouthed, *Give me a minute,* to Barry. She grabbed a blueberry muffin for Daniel before swinging by the coffee bar. She set brew and pastry before him.

"Thank you, Katherine." Daniel gazed up at her. Gone was the playfulness, the flirtatiousness that shielded him from uncertainty. Stripped of falsehood, they were two adults, trying to navigate an uncertain world.

"The muffins," Katherine said, her own shyness leaving her tender at the center. "They're quite good."

"I wasn't thanking you for the muffin."

"I know," she said, and gave him a pat on the shoulder.

Across the room, Zach and Celeste refilled the bread shelves, moving sourdough loaves, baguettes, and ryes as quickly with three hands as they had with four.

Barry waited at the coffee station. He stirred cream into his coffee and kept his gaze on Katherine. A strange expression clouded his features—equal parts pleased and mischievous. But at least he wasn't zoning in on Zach. At least he wasn't getting closer to the truth.

"Took care of business?" Barry asked her when she arrived at the counter.

"I did, and now I've some interesting news to tell you."

"Oh?" Barry snapped a lid on his coffee.

"Do you recall the kid I was never going to hire? Blake?"

"I do," Barry said, holding the same strange look on his face.

"Turns out he was the big, bad wolf who broke into the bakery and made such a mess last month. Figured it out because he did it again. Only this time, we—Celeste, Zach, and I—caught him in the act."

Barry sipped his coffee, his demeanor inappropriately calm, even for Barry, considering the news. "How do you feel about this?"

"Stupid! After all of my worry. What a colossal waste of precious energy."

"See what happens when you keep your fears inside you and deny them?" Barry asked.

"I know! I feel foolish for having obsessed over—"

Barry's eyes flashed on *obsessed*. The mischievous grin playing on his lips broke out and danced.

"Celeste told you. How long were you going to let me go on?"

"How long did you need to go on?" Barry asked, completely serious and poking fun.

The conflicting instincts to either sock him in the shoulder or kiss him full on the mouth battled in her mind and body. She decided to take the high road and ignore her instincts. "I'm making Blake work for me to pay me back for the damages. On one hand, I think he's going to like it here. It will do him good to face consequences for his actions. My other hand thinks I'm way out of my league. He obviously has issues. Family problems . . ." Katherine thought of the look on Blake's face when she'd mentioned talking to his parents, the tangled ball of panic that drew her back to her own family's dark, twisted hovel.

"You'll do fine."

"I haven't even managed to get Celeste to talk to me. Forget about open-ended questions. Everything I say is wrong."

"Patience," Barry said.

"Are you referring to the state of being or those under your care?"

Barry tweaked her nose, something he hadn't done in years. "You'll do fine. You always do fine."

Katherine rubbed the tip of her nose.

"I need to get going." He tweaked her nose a second time before heading for the door.

Katherine went after him. "Wait! What did you need to talk to me about?"

Halfway out the door, Barry pulled himself back in. He tapped the heel of his hand to his forehead. "Nearly forgot," he said, reminding her of the time he'd—middle of a snow-covered night—raced out the door to help a patient and she'd raced after him to hand him his shoes.

One of her favorite memories.

"I'm going to be away at a conference all week. I can't believe I almost forgot to tell you. I'm coming back on Sunday. I didn't want you to worry when I didn't come in and send police out to the house."

His house. No matter how many times she'd told him, he refused to take her name off the deed.

"What, me worry?" she said, and she wasn't worried. A whole week when she could enjoy Zach without Barry's close scrutiny, his penchant for examining people up close, personal, and below the surface. "Have a great conference! See you Monday morning!"

Barry pulled himself back in the door. "Don't you mean Sunday? Sunday night dinner."

Then, without waiting for Katherine to gather her thoughts and fine-tune her comprehension, Barry gazed past Katherine to where Celeste stood, raised his hand in the air, and gave her what Katherine could only describe as a high five from across the room.

Barry stepped out into the first bright rays of dawn.

Katherine set her hands on her hips and her sights on Celeste.

Celeste's grin competed with the rising sun, and she answered Katherine's glare. "You're welcome!"

Chapter 13

For the second time today, Celeste faced her window of opportunity.

She would've liked it better this morning if Katherine had yelled at her for inviting Barry to Sunday dinner, if she'd shaken a finger and read her the riot act—something Celeste's mother threatened to do before a harsh reprimand. Instead, after Barry had left Lamontagne's, Katherine had calmly poured herself a cup of coffee, walked up to Celeste, and said, "You have no idea what you've done."

Weird, because Celeste had been quite aware of her accomplishment.

She was doing everything humanly possible to get Katherine and Barry back together. Since their divorce, they'd only seen each other on the neutral, public grounds of Lamontagne's. Time, Celeste figured, for something private and personal. The easiest part had been getting Barry onboard with the covert operation. Celeste had issued the invitation, Barry had figured out Katherine hadn't known about the issuing, and he'd provided a lock-safe way to get away with it. He'd be away all week at a conference, but he wouldn't tell Celeste where he was going. That way, even if Katherine had read the aforementioned riot act, she wouldn't have been able to get the secret information from Celeste. Besides, Celeste and Barry were collaborating for Katherine's own good.

Katherine would thank Celeste later.

Now Zach, her one-armed superhero friend, had gone to Shaw's to buy, as he called it, real food. Thus the aforementioned window of opportunity. Only, instead of collaborating with Barry, she needed to interrogate Natalie.

Or, as pseudo-detective Zach said, find out what she knew about the night in question.

Celeste picked up the cordless. She put down the receiver. She knocked on the side table three times, something she hadn't done in years. Following her brother Lincoln's advice to knock three times for good luck had at first seemed like a good idea. How else would she have earned an A on her ninth-grade prealgebra final exam? But then she'd needed to knock to ensure target practice bull's-eyes. She'd knocked so that she could sleep through the night without waking. She'd knocked to guarantee her parents drove to Bath and back without getting killed in a car accident.

She'd told Zach she was effed up, but she'd only touched on a few of the recent particulars.

She picked up the phone and dialed Natalie's number.

Natalie answered on the third ring. "What do you want?"

Celeste held her breath.

"Just messing with you. Who is it?" Natalie asked.

Goddamn, brassy, ballsy blonde bim—"Hi, Natalie. It's Celeste," she said in her most authentic cheerful tone. At least she hoped she sounded authentic. "Remember me?"

Celeste imagined Natalie leaning a hip against her dorm room's counter and slouching. She imagined her gathering the phone's curlicue cord and twisting it around her long, thin arm.

Celeste thought she heard Natalie chuckle, but she couldn't be sure. "How could I forget you after only one week?" Natalie asked. "How the hell have you been, sistah?" Natalie said, even though the term *sistah* had never sounded sincere coming from Natalie's lips. Was anything?

Six months ago, Natalie had legally changed her name from Cynthia, chopped off and bleached her dishwater-brown bangs and bob, and dropped out of a small community college somewhere in New Jersey, where, rumor had it, she'd studied accounting and lived in her parents' basement.

Of course, the particulars had come from Matt, so who the hell knew what to believe?

A distant relative of the panic attack from last night laid claim to Celeste's windpipe. She conjured an image of Zach's face. She focused on breathing into her belly. "I've been decent."

Natalie issued a laugh-snort. "No one's going to believe you called. Everyone's, like, wondering where you went, why you left, whether you—"

"Seriously?" Celeste asked. Or maybe she yelled. But only so she could hear herself above the ear-clogging roar of blood.

"Wh-what's that supposed to mean?" Natalie asked, an about-face from party on to pissed off.

"I know what Matt did," Celeste said.

Celeste hadn't overheard Natalie's voice coming from the practice kitchen. But what were the chances Natalie hadn't heard everything five minutes later, if not from Matt, then from the other guys?

"What are you talking about?" Natalie asked.

"I heard him." Celeste knocked once on the table, not for good luck this time but for emphasis. She only wished Matt were here so she could emphasize her point on his face. "I came to class early to check on my grade," Celeste said, tacking on a lame excuse. Unlike Natalie, Celeste had never rushed to check her Tuesday morning grades. Without trying too hard, she'd always gotten A's. She'd wanted to talk to Matt about what had happened in his dorm room. She'd worried it had ruined their friendship. Their friendship! Celeste walked to the window, gazed out at the empty visitor's spot, wished Zach were here holding her hand. "I *heard* Matt talking to Drake and a few of the guys. I *heard* him talking about me. I *heard* him bragging about—"

"Okay, okay. You heard him. I get it. What do you want from me?"

Celeste took a deep breath and smiled. She swallowed to lubricate her dry throat. How much to tell? How much to leave out? How much to trust Natalie?

"I kind of got faced at Drake's. . . ."

Natalie laugh-snorted again. "You sure did, sistah. You—"

"I never get faced."

"And yet," Natalie said, biting off her words, "you did."

"You didn't drink any of the punch, right?"

"No way I was going near any of that Drake juice. I'm not stupid."

"Me, you, and Matt," Celeste said, hating the sound of his name. Note to self: Rename that thing she stepped on by the door to wipe her feet. On second thought, the name was perfect. "We were all drinking screwdrivers. Did Matt seem like he was getting drunk off them? Were you? Because it seemed like—"

"That's what you're worried about? The fact you can't hold your alcohol?"

"Yes. No. Sort of."

"Sistah, you have bigger things to worry about."

"Whatever." Celeste forced lightness into her voice, tried imagining she was a different person, someone who cared nothing about slings and arrows. She tried imagining that nothing could pierce her skin. "I heard Matt bragging," Celeste said. "What could be bigger than that?"

"Matt took pictures and he's passing them around."

"What?" Celeste asked, her voice hushed and disconnected, as though it were coming from across the room.

"Photographs?"

Images of raspberry tarts, blueberry buckle, and almond scones played across her vision, pastries Matt had photographed in class. Pastries she'd helped him bake. The receiver trembled against her cheek. Her gaze drifted to the ceiling and traced the seams of the room, as though she were looking for a way out.

She imagined glossy four-by-six photos of pastries. She envisioned Matt laying them on the stainless steel counter of the practice kitchen the way he dealt poker cards.

"Um, what?"

"Pho-to-graphs of you," Natalie said, her voice louder, as though Celeste were hard of hearing, rather than slow to comprehend. "Nak-ed pho-to-graphs. A whole goddamn photo shoot."

Don't you worry. I'll give you proof.

Matt's overheard words played in Celeste's head. And then words she hadn't previously remembered popped up. *Go back to sleep,* Matt had said, after she'd blinked awake to the harsh light of a flash. *I have to do this.*

Have to do what? Humiliate her?

Celeste's temples pulsed. Heat prickled her skin—arms, legs, torso. She paced across the room, came to a wall, turned back around. She remembered her head cocked at an uncomfortable angle but being too tired to move. She remembered floating in a murky abyss, as though she were trapped in half-awake, half-asleep hypnagogia.

"Yeah, so, kind of sucks to be you," Natalie said. "But don't shoot the messenger."

"Shoot who?"

"The messenger!" Natalie said.

"Um, what?"

When Natalie laughed, Celeste took the receiver from her ear and set it on the hook. The cackle of Natalie's laugh echoed in Celeste's head.

Matt had taken nude pictures of her and he was passing them around campus.

Don't shoot the messenger.

Celeste didn't want to shoot the messenger; she wanted to shoot Matt. She'd gotten drunk and had ended up in bed with a so-called friend. So what! She hadn't given him permission to talk about having sex with her. She hadn't given him permission to take pictures of her. No matter what Matt or anyone else thought of her, no matter what anyone said, she wasn't a fucking whore.

Nausea tickled her throat, and perspiration beaded her forehead. She tugged at her turtleneck, paced the room. Her sinuses pounded, as though her face might explode.

Some of Matt's food photos were wide shots, panoramas to take in a dessert buffet. But most of them were up close and personal, stylized detail work. He'd arrange a slice of devil's food cake. He'd get down on his knees—

She's got the sweetest birthmark . . . I'll give you proof.

Celeste clamped her hands over her mouth and ran to the bathroom. She opened the toilet lid, just in case. She shook her head. *No. No, no, no.* Throwing up was the worst, most wretched—

Oh, shit.

Her throat refluxed, and she swallowed. With shaking hands, she bent over the sink and splashed her face with water. In the mirror, her lashes stuck together. When she was little, every night after her bath, her mother would tell her that she had eyes like a cartoon character. Lukewarm bubble baths had seemed to last for hours, until the water went cold and the bubbles faded to milky suds. Then her mother would wrap her in her hooded towel—a pink bunny with long, floppy ears. No matter how worn-thin the terry cloth, she'd always felt warm.

Celeste pressed a palm against the glass, trying to get back to that girl. She banged on the glass three times. Her cartoon character eyes stared back at her.

I can't be here.

Celeste went into the bedroom and changed in the semi-darkness, the shades pulled down from this morning. She came out of the bedroom wearing last night's hoodie and sweats, slid her feet into her bakery clogs, grabbed her pocketbook, and ran out the door. She fumbled twice with the keys before starting up Old Yeller.

Zach pulled into the spot beside her. A bunch of brown grocery bags filled Matilda's backseat. Matilda's engine cut out, and Zach burst from the car. He came around to Celeste's driver's side and she rolled down the window.

"Where do you think you're going?" he asked. "I got coffee ice cream, hot fudge, and whipped cream. And, uh, those nuts you like . . ." Zach snapped his fingers next to his head. "Pecans."

Coffee sundaes were her favorite. She'd told Zach once. He was so nice to her. Her bottom lip trembled.

"Celeste?" Zach asked.

"I can't be here."

"Huh?" he said. "What's going on?"

The sound of Natalie's laughter played in Celeste's head. The bright light from Matt's flash. His voice, telling her to go back to sleep. The girl in the mirror, so far away.

"Zach—I—he—" Celeste looked into Zach's eyes, the way she had last night. She breathed into her belly. "I can't be here."

Zach bent to the window. "So, you're going somewhere . . . ?"

How to make him understand?

"That's okay. Not a problem. You can't be here. Wherever

you're going, I'm going with you. Yup, going with you!" Zach jogged around Old Yeller and slid onto the passenger seat. With his left hand, he pulled the shoulder strap across his body and hooked the belt. "Ready to roll," he said, and she backed from the space.

She wasn't a whore, she wasn't a whore, she wasn't a whore.

They rolled down Route 209, the forest on either side thick with pines. She could jump from the car, run through the trees, and live the rest of her days in the woods like a wild thing.

Instead, she dug her nails into the steering wheel and turned onto Route 216.

Zach hummed "Slide." When that didn't work, he tried "Iris" and gave up after the third stanza.

Celeste took a left onto Perkins Farm Lane, pulled into Popham Beach State Park, paid at the parking booth, and parked Old Yeller in front of Center Beach.

Last week in October meant only a few cars were in the lot. A few solitary figures walked the beach. Cold nights meant water temperatures dipped into the low fifties. No one was crazy enough to swim in the surf, unless either they'd lost a dare or they needed to numb out.

She couldn't explain that need to Zach.

Zach slumped back in the seat and rolled his head to the side. "You wanted to go to the beach?"

Celeste nodded.

"You scared the crap out of me! I thought you were ready to drive Old Yeller off a cliff, and he's a fine car, so—"

She opened the car door. The sea breeze whipped in her face. She turned her face into the wind.

Zach appeared before her. He put a hand on the side of her face. His fingers cooled her temple, a pocket of relief. "You're burning up," he said.

"That's why we're here." She left her clogs in the car and ran down the faded dune grass trail. When she glanced over her shoulder, Zach was right behind her. She ran past the white lifeguard stand and down the beach until the soft, white sand turned dark and solid beneath her feet. To her right, Fox Island loomed before Seguin and its lighthouse. The ocean extended as far as the eye could see. And not just any ocean, the Atlantic Ocean.

October cold and touching her entire crazy-ass, scattered family.

"Beauty," Zach said.

"Yeah." Celeste pulled her sweats down over her hips, unzipped her hoodie, and tossed it onto the sand. She hadn't worn the bikini in years. She'd kept it on the bottom of her bathing suit pile as a keepsake for clothes that were either too small or no longer to her taste. This suit fit both categories. Purchased when she was fifteen and outgrown by her sixteenth birthday.

The air lashed her bare stomach, raising gooseflesh and tinkling the array of tiny bells and shells dangling from both the top of her bottom and the bottom of her top.

She turned to Zach, the feeling of his gaze as real as his touch. "I know, it's too small," she said.

"You're perfect." He held her gaze until, for a second, she almost believed him.

"No." Cloud wisps trailed across the sky, like a streak of colored frosting, white on the edges, pinkie purple at the center. What were they called? Cirrus? Her nonblood sister, Abby, would know. Abby seemed so far away—

I can't be here.

Celeste made a break for the ocean.

"Hey!" Zach yelled.

The water iced her toes. Her ankles ached, her thighs protested. Then—the worst part—she pushed herself through the birthmark and bikini-zone freeze, an assault on her most sensitive area.

Pretend it doesn't hurt.

She dove beneath the waves into the hazy green, the murky, salty ice water. Seaweed bobbed beside her. The curve of the sands passed beneath her. Then the cold seized her lungs and squeezed, forcing her to surface. She gasped for air, her heart beating like a war cry.

Zach stood at the water's edge, as if he were her lifeguard. As if he was guarding her life.

He had no idea what he was getting himself into.

Celeste stood up, her body heavy, rubbery, and numb. "Come on in, the water's freezing!"

"I'll take your word for it."

She started for the shore, and pain shot through her eardrums, like ice picks coming at her from both sides. She tried pretending that the low-hanging autumn sun was midday and August. That the heat on the shore was unrelenting. That her fear of people examining her body in detail hadn't actually come true.

Zach gave her a sad smile—his chin tight, his lips downturned, probably trying not to alarm the crazy woman.

Celeste dried herself off with her sweatpants and slipped her arms into the hoodie. She held her hands over her ears. Her ears warmed, but the pain held steady. The ocean within her raged. Wasn't blood similar to ocean water? Abby would know the answer. "Hurts," Celeste said.

"Your ears?"

"Everything."

"Let's go home," he said, and he wrapped his arm around her and helped her to her car.

Zach plucked her car keys from the driver's seat where she'd left them. "You think Old Yeller would mind?"

Her teeth rattled, like the shells and sea glass of Abby's wind chimes. Her knees buckled. Her skin puckered with the fault lines of secondary tremors. She took a shallow breath and hummed.

"The Beatles!" Zach said. "'Drive My Car.'"

"Baby, you can." Celeste let Zach open the passenger side door for her.

Maybe she loved him.

Celeste's eyes watered. "T-t-tell Old Yeller he's a good old guy."

"You're a good old guy and I hope your heat works." Zach started Old Yeller. Gaze on her, he slipped his fingers into his jeans pocket and then flipped on the heat.

Celeste flipped the heat off. "Give him a few minutes. He's slow to start, but he always comes around."

"Like his owner?" Zach asked.

"I don't know, maybe."

"Does that mean you're going to tell me what's going on?" Zach asked.

She hummed "Take Me Home, Country Roads."

"You got it," Zach said, and he backed from the spot. He turned onto 209 and then, one-handed, took the narrow hairpin turn onto Wilderness Way, back through Hidden Harbor, as if he were a born and bred local.

"Katherine tell you about the road?"

"Figured it out myself."

"You took a wrong turn?" Celeste asked.

"I took a right turn, for once." Zach kept his gaze on the winding road, his left hand easy on the wheel, his right forearm leaning in for backup. Less than twenty-four hours ago, she'd been in the driver's seat, rescuing Zach and taking him home. Less than twenty-four hours since his injury and the cast. Less than twenty-four hours, and he'd adjusted to the new normal. She wished she adjusted that easily.

Back at Ledgewood, the sun hung low in the sky, its rays trailed along the parking lot, shining into Old Yeller, her eyes, and—

"Oh, shit! The ice cream! Here you were trying to do something nice for me and—"

"Don't sweat it. It's probably still solid. Let's not assume the worst," he said, sounding unlike Zach. Maybe that's how it worked with superheroes. You had to dangle them over shark-infested tanks, take them away from their comfort zone, and threaten someone they cared about before they'd mature and come out the other end sounding like Katherine's ex-husband, Barry.

Zach cared about her.

"You should've let me go alone," Celeste said. "I shouldn't have let you come."

"I would've followed you," Zach said. Then he ducked into the backseat of Matilda and came out with a brown grocery bag. "Ice cream's a little soft, but otherwise unharmed."

Celeste grabbed a grocery bag. Sirloin steaks, potatoes, and, wonder of wonders, green beans and broccoli.

"You need to get inside and get warm. I think you're in shock."

She hoisted a second bag onto her hip. "First aid training from your stint as a ski instructor?"

"Instinct."

Celeste thought of Katherine and her warnings about paying attention to your gut. Celeste's gut was unreliable at best, telling her to care about the wrong friends, love the wrong lovers.

Justin and Matt had cared more about what they imagined other people thought of them than they'd cared about her.

Celeste stumbled up the walkway steps, readjusted a bag on her hip.

"You don't need to take two at a time. Leave it there for me. I'll take care of it."

"That's okay, I've got it," she said, her voice coming out chipped from her shivering, rough with fatigue.

"Okay," Zach said, and offered her the same sad smile he'd given her when she'd come out from her ice bath. He unlocked her door and let her pass before him.

Zach wasn't just a nice guy. He was a good man.

In her bedroom, she changed into a fresh pair of sweats and a clean, white turtleneck. She unbraided her hair and towel dried it in the bathroom. The sharp pain in her ears was dissipating, diluting to a less potent version of discomfort. Her body had partially defrosted, like the ice cream left in Matilda. And with Celeste's body's softening, the focus shifted back to the phone call that had inspired the polar plunge.

Give her physical pain any day.

Out in the living room, Zach was waiting on the couch—his makeshift bed. He held out a mug of steaming tea for her. Green and decaffeinated. A preference she'd discovered on girlhood sleepovers with Abby. "How'd you know?" she asked.

"Found it above the sink."

"You're making yourself at home," she said, her voice regaining a hint of the teasing lightness that Zach inspired. She took the mug from his hands. When she sat down on the couch, he pushed his pillow aside and wrapped his—her—fuzzy yellow blanket around her shoulders.

"Your lips are still blue."

"I know." The mug of tea shook on the way to her lips.

Zach nodded and stared her down. "You gonna tell me what's going on?"

She hadn't wanted Zach to sit by her side when she'd phoned Natalie. And yet if it hadn't been for Zach, she wouldn't have made the call. She wouldn't have ever known. Matt hadn't only bragged about screwing her, he'd launched a campaign.

"I followed your advice," Celeste said. "I called Natalie."

Zach's expression—hopeful despite the odds, worried, and a little bit psyched Celeste had listened to him—weighed on her. Anything she told him wouldn't lift him up. Did she want to let him down? Would he pity her? Would he leave?

Would he leave?

"When I was half passed out . . ."

Zach nodded, and his expression went grim.

She inhaled the tea, dropped her gaze from Zach's eyes to his left hand, set against the thigh of his jeans. His nails were clean and neatly trimmed. A few hairs crossed his slightly tan forearm. His Timex ticked, ticked, ticked.

She made herself look him in the eye. She wanted to catch his unmasked expression, to see herself as he saw her. "Matt took nude photos of me—"

Zach's whole face widened, as if an open-ocean high wind had filled his sails. And then he battened those sails, a deliberate tightening. His jawline ticked, ticked, ticked.

"And he's passing them around campus," Celeste said.

Zach breathed out through his nose, like a bull. "That's horrible," he said. "I don't even know what to say. Other than, you know, wanting to kill the criminal."

Celeste grinned. "He's an asshole, sure. I don't think that makes him a criminal, though."

"Did you tell him it was okay for him to take pictures of you?"

"Oh my God! Of course not."

"Then the criminal asshole committed a felony, punishable by a fine of five thousand dollars and up to five years in jail." Zach sat up taller. "You could have him arrested."

The thought of Matt in jail, wearing bright orange instead of chef whites, made her want to giggle. "Seriously?"

Zach nodded. "Yeah, seriously."

The thought of going to the police and having more people look at photos of her naked body made her want to jump in Old Yeller and drive into the ocean.

"Then why do I still feel like it was my fault?"

"I don't know you well enough to answer that question."

"That's okay," Celeste said. "No one does." No freaking way was she going to the police. She took another sip of her tea, and her shoulders rose in a shiver. "So, yeah, that's the end of the big, bad mystery. Matt took photos to prove to the guys he'd slept with me. I'm mad as hell. It sucks. But there's not much I can do about it. I should put it out of my mind, right? I phoned, I asked, I found out. End of horror story."

Zach bit his lip, and his gaze shifted sideways. Again he exhaled through his nose.

"What? What is it? You think Matt sent photos of me to newspapers? You think they're going to hit the nightly news? Because I don't think I can take any more. Okay. Let it be known. I've had enough crap for one lifetime. I'm done. I. Am. Done. In fact, I'm going to bed." She jumped up, or tried to jump. Her feet didn't leave the carpet. Her body was too heavy to budge, a dull thing she needed to drag around.

"But you haven't eaten dinner," Zach said, as if that were the most horrendous torture he could imagine, as if other things weren't worse. "I was going to fry up some steaks and—"

Bile rose in her throat, and she held up a hand. She swallowed, took a slow breath.

"Are you a vegetarian or something? You don't like steaks?"

"I think it was the word *fried*. You enjoy your steaks. My stomach's off—I don't think I can keep anything down."

"Make sure you hydrate." Zach stood and handed her the green tea. He took the fuzzy blanket—her fuzzy, winter-warmth blanket—off the couch and wrapped it around her shoulders.

"What if you're c-cold?" she said, and they both smiled at her unintentionally well-placed shiver.

Zach gave her shoulder a pat, held his friend's gaze. "You need to stay warm. Due to the shock and all."

"I think you're making too much out of this. I'm cold because the Atlantic is freaking freezing this time of year."

Zach gave her a placating smile. Neither of them mentioned the reason she'd set off for the ocean, her temporary inability to form words, her need to numb out and shut down.

"I'm going to close my door so I can't smell the—" Her hair ached with queasiness.

Zach nodded. "I'll run the hood fan."

"I appreciate it," she said, and she took her tea to the bedroom. She sat on the edge of the bed, and the ticker tape of her conversation with Natalie scrolled through her head. When that petered out, the most recent Matt memory played through.

She got up and locked the door. Silly, really. If Zach wanted to get into her bedroom, and her drawers, all he had to do was find a long, sharp object and poke the lock. Zach probably had a pocketknife, right? What self-respecting guy didn't own one of those? And if she didn't trust Zach, she shouldn't let him sleep on her couch.

She walked to the closed door and cocked her head. The sound of running water echoed from the kitchen. A patch of air silence and then chopping, the sound of industry. She unlocked the door and opened it a crack. Something sizzled. Zach's steak, most likely. As promised, he ran the fan. Above the low whir, Zach's humming floated through the main room and touched her like a soft kiss. "Slide" again.

Did he know the words? Yes, Zach, she did want to run away. Thank you for asking.

She left the door open and slid beneath the covers. She arranged the fuzzy blankets. Her all-seasons, standby blanket on the bottom. Her blanket reserved for cold weather, unexpected visitors, and unexpected shock went on top. Her throat still ached—that sad-sack concoction of ready-to-run panic and ready-to-hurl nausea. She breathed into her stomach. Her top blanket smelled like Zach. A little bit tart, a lot sweet, with a generous helping of boy-next-door sizzle.

Man next door.

The man cooking in her kitchen and sleeping on her couch. The man who didn't think she was a whore, despite evidence to the contrary. The man who didn't believe Matt, the voice in her head that told her she was shit.

When the voice of her eating disorder, Ed, popped into her brain to torment her, she was supposed to fight back. Tell Ed he was stupid and wrong, even when all evidence—her fat ass, her inability to eat like a normal person without gaining weight—pointed to the contrary.

Go back to sleep. I have to do this.

Now that she remembered, she couldn't get Matt's voice out of her head. She might not be shit, but she was definitely a shit magnet.

The weight of the two blankets comforted her, but the heat couldn't get through the icy layers. The bone-deep Atlantic Ocean chill she'd brought on herself. A shiver wracked her body, starting at her center and branching out, the way an earthquake originated from a fault. She sat up and drank down the rest of the green tea. She wiped her mouth with her hand.

Maybe Zach was right. Maybe she was in shock, but considering her history with guys? She wasn't one bit surprised.

Chapter 14

According to Celtic history, All Hallows' Eve was a time to take stock of the harvest and prepare for the coming winter. A day when the dead came back to life and demons haunted the world of the living. But what about the ghosts from the past that day-in, day-out replayed their story in Katherine's mind, like the endless loop of a black-and-white horror flick? What about the would've, could've, should've vampires that sucked her precious time and joy?

What about the demons from her childhood she couldn't exorcise?

The roast and root vegetables were cooking nicely, filling her apartment—the first floor of a Victorian painted lady—with literal and soul warmth. In the living room, she laid out hors d'oeuvres. Dishes of walnuts for cracking, a pyramid of clementines, crudités with a chilled buttermilk-and-dill dip. She filled a black plastic cauldron with assorted fun-sized chocolate bars and set it by the door. She set the dining room table with her seasonal china—a black transferware pattern with happy witches and pumpkins—atop black charger plates. In the center of the table, she arranged a pumpkin she'd carved with scrollwork, reminiscent of ornately decorated cakes. She lifted the jack-o'-lantern's cap, lit the tea light, and set the cap back in place. Took a moment to inhale the wax and flame and savor the glow.

Her black dress fell to her ankles, the top hugging her chest and torso, the skirt loose and swishing. A swatch of hair she'd secured with a single tortoiseshell barrette. The rest she let fall free, the way she'd worn it in her younger days when she'd hitchhiked from town to town, waited tables wherever by day, prowled bars by night. Despite the gravity of the dinner party—her growing concern over Celeste, her worry over her uninvited guest examining her latest employee—she felt energized and reckless.

A larger than usual glass of Merlot might've contributed to her contradictory state.

In her experience, a glass or two heightened awareness. Three or four numbed the senses, an out-of-body experience where you witnessed your life's traumas, the circumstances real yet seeming not quite so pressing. And five glasses of wine? She hadn't attempted that degree of debauchery in quite some time.

She was well aware of her father's alcoholic contribution to her family history.

The doorbell rang, and a satisfying chime played through her house. About an hour and a half too early for trick-or-treaters and half an hour too early for her three visitors. She peered through a sidelight to where the outside lamp cut through the early sundown and lit her doorstep.

Unless that visitor was the uninvited guest she'd been trying to track down for the better part of a week.

She opened the door and tried to set her face into a glare of annoyance but found her face unwilling to comply. "You're a hard man to track down," she said, her tone coming out all wrong, way more *glad to see you* than *mad as hell.* That made her mad as hell.

Barry wore one of her favorite outfits. A light-blue, fitted button-down brought out his eyes, and herringbone slacks hugged him in all the right places.

The trouble was she couldn't find any wrong places on his body. God knows she'd tried.

Barry carried a bouquet of yellow lilies and Gerber daisies and white roses, reminiscent of her autumnal bridal bouquet. "You going to invite me in?" he said, his voice Celeste snarky and full of assumption.

They'd married on the grounds of the Stonehouse Manor overlooking Silver Lake, the place where the Kennebec River literally wed the Atlantic. A gorgeous and utterly ridiculous affair, considering their ages, but Barry had insisted.

The day had been perfect. Something else she could use to fuel her ire.

"Versus Celeste inviting you without asking me first? Sure, why not?" Katherine's head felt light and swimmy, not from the wine but from the thought of letting him into her post-Barry home. Against the backdrop of her pale-yellow walls, his aura swirled around him. To her, the color looked gray. But she strongly suspected his aura was pink, loving and loyal.

The only other time she'd seen an aura? Thirty years ago, her father's aura had been dark brown with deception and black, to her, with righteous anger.

"I called every hotel in New England looking for you to let you know this wasn't a good idea," she said.

Barry gave her a look, a hyperbole of shock and hurt. "Really, Katherine?"

"You *know* this isn't a good idea." The heaviness of the admission hit her in the stomach, like a twenty-pound bag of flour. "There were no shrink conferences."

Barry tweaked her nose and handed her the bouquet. "Applied Psychology holds their conference same week every year, at the Marriott Marquis in Times Square. I can't—" He shook his head. "I don't believe you forgot."

Merde.

Could she have accidentally forgotten but on purpose?

"Let me put these in some water." Katherine meant for Barry to stay in the living room, so she could take a moment to compose herself. Put the flowers in water. Stick her head under the faucet. Scream.

Instead, Barry followed her into the kitchen, gazing around and craning his neck as though he were touring a museum.

She'd taken only those things she'd gone into the marriage with. Flea market and antique store prints and paintings, hand-knit curtains she'd traded for months' worth of pastries. She'd found the navy velvet sofa at an estate sale. That had inspired the purchase of the French-blue wing chair and the navy and light-blue handblown glass beads that took the place of a kitchen door. One acquisition led to another, the way one relationship invariably led to others, beads along a connected strand.

When beads loosened and fell, the rules of connection applied in reverse.

Katherine parted the beads and stepped inside. "Watch yourself."

"I'd rather watch you." Barry held her gaze until her throat ached and her sinuses filled.

"This house," he said. "It fits you."

"A slightly worn old girl in need of a paint job?"

"A beautiful woman with substance and flare," Barry said without an ounce of irony.

"You've always known how to flatter me."

"Just because it's flattery doesn't mean it's not true."

"There you go again." Katherine set the flowers beside the sink and stretched to reach the fat glass vase on the overhead shelf. Behind her, Barry made a sound, a cross between a sigh and a growl. Without turning back around, she ran the water and held her wrists beneath the cold.

Barry-shaped warmth came up behind her. "How was your date this weekend?"

"What date?" she asked, giving herself away and missing her opportunity. Why was her first inclination to tell the truth? Why couldn't she tell a straight-faced, well-meaning lie?

She wanted to ask Barry to leave. She wanted to rip off his clothes and beg him to stay. She wanted him to touch her.

She wanted him to touch her.

"Daniel," Barry said. "The short construction worker with the Greek last name you didn't know. The man who was asking you out Monday morning."

Instead of scaring Barry off, the ask-out had motivated Barry to make a move.

Katherine should've known better.

Thirteen years ago, she'd met Barry at a bar, an unlikely place for him, a likely place for her. She'd stopped in for a beer before bed, an early evening nightcap, and her low vibe had drawn the wrong element. Two guys had invaded her table for one and her personal space. She'd managed to hold them off, nursing her beer for an hour so she wouldn't have to walk back to her apartment, before Barry had walked through the door and noticed her angst. "Ready to come back home? The kids are waiting for you to tuck them in," he'd said with such certainty that the guys had fallen back. Then he'd walked her to her door and taken down her phone number. They'd been together ever since.

They weren't together.

"I turned him down."

Behind her, Barry took a breath. "Tell me why," he said, his voice husky and confident, as though he already knew her answer. As if he only awaited her confirmation. As if he could read her mind and body.

Katherine shut off the water and tried to focus on Barry's question. Her chest tingled, straining at the cotton of her bra.

She remembered an ages-ago dinner party, their kitchen with a locked door. She'd gone into the kitchen to get the tiramisu, set the teakettle on the burner, turned toward the sink. Barry had followed and locked the door behind him. He'd come up behind her. He'd lifted her skirt.

"Because . . . he . . . Daniel," she said, but she couldn't quite capture an image of the scene. In the silver faucet, her face elongated, distorted. In that ages-ago kitchen, Barry had kissed the back of her neck. He'd bent her over the sink. He'd parted her legs.

"What was that?" Barry asked now.

Katherine swallowed. "He's, um, separated but may still be in love with his wife."

"You got that out of him from a single conversation?" Barry asked. Then, without waiting for a reply, he settled behind her, his breath behind her ear. "I believe, dear heart, you might've been mistaken. Mistaken and projecting."

"Separated isn't the same thing as divorced. Divorced means the relationship is over." Katherine meant the word as a warning, a reminder of all they'd endured to get to this point of . . . what? Friendship? They'd never been only friends. Over a decade ago, he strode into that bar with a purpose, as if their relationship had been a foregone conclusion.

Of course he never would've admitted to such an ideation. No, he would've hidden his woo-woo behind logic and simple biological attraction. Or he would've told her she'd imagined their meant-to-be connection. Barry would've projected.

"Does this feel over to you?" Barry asked.

It doesn't matter.

Katherine's eyes watered. "Don't." She sucked her bottom lip into her mouth, raked the flesh between her teeth. Between her legs, she softened.

All she had to do was reach for him, a quick fix to get the temptation out of their systems.

Who was she kidding? They'd never had casual sex. From the first, they'd been committed, each touch a promise, every kiss an investment in their future.

They didn't have a future.

"It's time for us to stop playing games," Barry said.

What did he mean by that? Their daily flirting without calling it flirting? Her battle to let him go? Her equally strong and opposing desire to keep him coming back for more? Or did he know more than he was letting on? Did he know about Zach? She turned from the sink.

Barry's eyes undid her, a kick to her solar plexus and then a solid, resolute tug. "It's time for you to come home," he said, as if he too was remembering how they'd begun.

The day she moved to this apartment, she'd intended to set up each room so it looked nothing like the house she'd shared with Barry. But she'd bowed to the rules of feng shui and set her double bed diagonally across from her bedroom door. The new sofa fit perfectly beneath the living room window, the sun streaming in to fade the navy to grayish blue and soften the bright, threadbare yard sale Oriental rug till it resembled the tea-stained antique she'd left behind. Each object seemed to have volition, not unlike muscle memory, reminding her of all she'd lost.

Katherine closed her eyes, so she wouldn't see the hurt in his. "I don't have a home."

The menthol from Barry's shaving cream filled her nose, cooled her tongue. His body wasn't pressed up against hers, but she could've sworn his heart beat in her ears. In her mind's eye, she held a map of his body, detailed and topographical. His muscled thighs, his strong chest, his arms, defined. "We create our own realities," Barry said. "Whatever you believe becomes true."

She opened her eyes to Barry, a good four feet away and no

part of him touching her. Not even close. She could've sworn . . . "Something one of your shrink buddies likes to say?"

"Something Katherine Lamontagne once swore by," Barry said, and he filled her vase with water, as if their conversation had never happened.

Barry reached in the drawer to the right of the sink, found her pruning shears in the spot where they'd resided at the house he and Katherine had shared, and cut the stems of the bouquet under running water. He set the bouquet in the vase and gave her a Grinch smile, his lips curled at the edges, his eyes lit with mischief. "So, what were we just talking about? Who's joining us tonight?" he asked, as if he didn't know the way he affected her.

"Celeste," Katherine said, giving Barry her own version of the Grinch grin. "And Zach," she added, his name sending an alarm through her center. "A welcome to and back to Hidden Harbor celebration."

"The two," Barry said. "They're a couple?"

Katherine's heart gave a thud that reverberated through her body. "What makes you say that?"

"The way they stand closer than they need to," Barry said. "The way they stare at each other, memorizing the details. The way everything they say has a double meaning."

What? As far as Katherine knew, Barry had never overheard one of Celeste and Zach's conversations.

Barry took a step closer and ran his gaze down her body.

Oh, Barry wasn't talking about Celeste and Zach.

Katherine opened the oven and fiddled with the meat thermometer that didn't require fiddling.

"Are you wearing the black boots?" Barry asked.

The boots she'd worn on the evening of the dinner party, the skirt, and the locked kitchen door. She didn't have any other black boots. "They're black and they're boots. Ha, ha."

She meant to give Barry an annoyed look. Instead, her gaze wandered to his crotch.

Simple biology, right? She could ignore biology. She was stronger than biology.

"They're definitely the black boots," Barry said. "I could never forget those black boots."

"You were asking me about Celeste . . ."

"And the young guy."

Was this train of conversation any better than the last? Was any Barry conversation safe? "I can't say whether they're exactly a couple."

"Ah," Barry said, a sound, she was sure, he'd perfected during years of encouraging challenging conversations.

"I can't say that they aren't."

"I see."

Katherine took the Merlot from the cabinet. "Glass of wine?"

"Sure," he said.

She poured Barry his first glass of the evening, took down a fresh glass for herself, as though she too were indulging in her first.

"You don't approve of Celeste and Zach as a couple?" Barry asked.

Had Katherine said anything to indicate disapproval? She retraced their conversation, wondered whether a particular facial expression or stance had given away her consternation. She opened a sleeve of rice crackers and added them to the pepper jelly–covered cream cheese she'd set out to come to room temperature. She took a cracker for herself. "She's shrinking," Katherine said, and a cracker crumb lodged in her throat. She gulped the wine, managed a breath. "Literally and emotionally."

Barry leaned against the counter, sipped. "Is she having trouble eating again?"

"It would seem so," Katherine said. "I can't say what she eats off duty. But on duty? It's minimal. An apple around eight, a yogurt just past noon. Coffee every hour on the half hour."

"She's having trouble sleeping."

"That would seem to be the case. Unless . . ."

"Unless?"

An image of Celeste and Zach flashed in Katherine's mind's eye, naked and clinging to each other. The thought alarmed her. The thought pleased her, two people she cared about caring for each other. The thought made her want to cover her mind's eye. Katherine's cheeks warmed.

"Unless sleep is the last thing on Celeste's and Zach's minds." Barry waggled his eyebrow, the silly gesture he certainly didn't take seriously. "I remember those nights."

"Oh, please," Katherine said, meaning to sound put upon. Instead, she looked away, fidgeted the amethyst dangling from her left lobe, and remembered those nights. Their passion. Their soul-deep connection. The way they resented daybreak. She shook her head, picked up her wineglass. "Sleep problems or not, she's clearly troubled. She walks out to the café, stops, and stares, as if she's forgotten where she is. Until Zach goes to her and reminds her what she's supposed to be doing."

"She doesn't ask you for redirection?"

"She doesn't get the chance. Zach . . . he does his job and he keeps his eye on her."

"She hasn't said anything about New York?"

Katherine pretended to zip her lips. "Not a word. And she hasn't gotten close to sharing any deep, dark secret, so I haven't pressed."

"Ah," Barry said. "You listen to my advice when it pertains to other people."

"Other people?"

"People who aren't you." Barry picked up the vase of flowers and the plate of crackers and headed through Katherine's bead curtains. Katherine followed behind with their wineglasses, and her gaze fell to Barry's butt, the irresistible tug of biology.

Biology, she reminded herself, had pulled them apart.

The doorbell rang, and Katherine jumped, jostling the wine from her glass.

Barry set down the flowers on a side table, placed the crackers and cream cheese with the other hors d'oeuvres. He lifted a pumpkin-decorated paper napkin toward her chest. "Like some help with that?"

Katherine put the wineglasses down beside the crackers. "Don't you dare!"

"Oh, you thought . . . I was only going to help blot the stain."

"I don't need help with that." Katherine grabbed for the napkin but ended up with Barry's hand instead.

He bent to her ear. "*Tsk, tsk.* If you want me to touch you, you're going to have to ask nicely. How soon you forget." Barry handed her the napkin and ran his gaze down her body slow enough to make her squirm, letting her know he'd forgotten nothing.

Katherine pressed the napkin to her chest, and her heart beat through her hand. Zach peered through the sidelight, his hand held to his forehead like a visor, Celeste visible over his shoulder. Katherine glared sideways at Barry, ignored his smug grin, took a deep breath, and opened the door.

Celeste wore an oversized chocolate-brown sweater over snug jeans and brown combat boots. Her hair was down, save for pieces she'd swept from the sides of her face and secured in the back with a brown bow. In her hands, she carried a bouquet of yellow roses. Delicate baby's breath filled the spaces between the blooms.

Zach wore jeans, hiking boots, a blue-on-blue flannel shirt to complement his blue cast and sling, and an orange satin cape. "Celeste made me," he said, and he stepped through the door.

Barry stood tall, exuded professionalism, and jutted out his hand at Zach, as if he hadn't just been playing a wicked game with Katherine's heart . . . and other organs. "Barry Horowitz," he said. "I don't believe we've officially met."

Did Barry's gaze linger on Zach's features, his dark hair, so like hers? Did Barry glance her way, a flick of his gaze, to question why she'd never introduced him to Zach? Had Katherine's fear of revealing her secret given her secret away?

"Zach Fitzgerald. Katherine's . . ." Zach glanced her way, Katherine was sure of it. And in that moment, she almost wished he'd tell. She could almost feel the relief of letting the charade go. ". . . employee," Zach finished, and she thought she heard a trace of her father's understated anger.

Biology, or was she once again projecting her own fear?

Katherine took the flowers from Celeste's hands. "Thank you, I adore yellow roses." Yellow flowers meant friendship. Did Celeste know that?

"Cool," Celeste said. Then she glanced sideways at the living room. "I would've picked something else if I'd known they matched your walls."

"You've been here before, haven't you?" Katherine asked, but wishing didn't change reality. Her and Celeste's relationship took place within the walls of Lamontagne's. They spent more hours together than some married couples, but their time together was contained, controlled, and limited. Officially, they could tell themselves their relationship was entirely professional.

Not unlike Katherine's relationship with Barry.

"In your dreams, maybe," Celeste said, not a trace of anger. Was that a ploy to make Katherine feel guilty or Celeste being her snarky self?

Celeste looked lovely, gorgeous as ever, but something niggled at Katherine, or a combination of somethings. Celeste's big sweater, her exhaustion, confusion, and withdrawal. Even her recent limited diet.

A memory flashed of Katherine hiding in the kitchen of Hazel May's, exhausted, withdrawn, and wearing an oversized sweater to camouflage her growing belly.

Merde.

Could Celeste be pregnant?

"I should put these in water and check the roast." Katherine tried to remember whether Celeste had worn that sweater before, whether she normally preferred loose-fitting clothing. "Can I get you something to drink?" she asked Celeste and Zach, but the query was meant for Celeste. "Beer? A glass of wine?"

"Nothing for me, I'm saving myself for the roast. It smells delicious." Celeste's face twitched—a slight tic that she covered with a cough. "Besides, I'm not sure wine and beer go with Halloween candy," she added, a strange statement, even for Celeste.

"Where I come from, beer goes with everything," Zach told Celeste.

Katherine held a breath, imagining, for a moment, that Zach was referring to his biological, rather than his adoptive, family.

"Seriously. I thought the planet Krypton was a dry planet," Celeste said, explaining the reason she'd made Zach wear a cape. Secretly sweet Celeste likened Zach to Superman.

"Nah. That's just in the movie version. I'll have a beer. Need any help in the kitchen?"

Barry ran a carrot stick through Katherine's buttermilk-and-dill dip and snapped it between his teeth.

"Thank you, Zach. I was hoping Celeste could help me. . . .

But by all means, you and Barry make yourselves at home and dig in."

Barry grinned at her. Because he was unable to wink, his attempt approximated a grimace.

Katherine imagined taking Celeste aside and straight-out asking her whether she was pregnant, whether the sweater and her eating habits and her sudden return to Hidden Harbor—the only home she'd ever known—were indications that she was having a baby. Katherine also imagined this line of questioning particularly objectionable to someone who'd once—and perhaps again—wrestled with an eating disorder.

May Celeste be well. May Celeste be free from harm. May Celeste be at peace.

Katherine took a Heineken from the fridge, cracked it open, and angled a beer glass.

Celeste turned in a circle. "Cute kitchen. I love the black-and-white floor."

"The flooring was here when I moved in. The cabinets I repainted to freshen." Katherine had also smudged the kitchen and every room of the house. She'd walked through waving a burning bunch of dried sage to drive out any darkness or lingering negativity. Unfortunately, she'd yet to find a remedy to drive out her internal demons.

Katherine slid a loaf of sourdough into the oven to warm and checked on the meat thermometer. One hundred and sixty degrees. Done to medium roast perfection. She set the roasting pan on a trivet, closed the oven with her foot, stabbed a crispy potato, and waved the fork in the air. "Want a taste?"

"Oh, yeah, baby. Come to Mama," Celeste said, not what an unexpectedly expectant mother would say. Was it? Celeste blew on the nugget and popped it into her mouth. "Ooh, ah, hot." She grinned and sighed. "But oh so good."

Katherine nodded. She peeled off her black-and-white checkered oven mitts and set them on the counter. "I want to ask you a question. And I'd appreciate it if you'd give me a straightforward answer. Okay?"

Celeste chewed slowly, carefully. "Depends what the question is."

Katherine sighed, regretted telegraphing the inquiry. She gave Celeste a look she hoped conveyed seriousness, concern, and—no matter what—acceptance. "The reason you came back so suddenly to Hidden Harbor . . ."

Celeste stopped chewing.

"Did it have something, anything, to do with a man?"

Celeste's eyes watered, but she didn't look away. She sniffed, continued chewing, swallowed hard. She took a deep breath through her mouth. She blew out.

Sadness, like radio waves, emanated from Celeste. Katherine absorbed the feeling. The insides of Katherine's ears moistened, as though she might cry. "Because if there's anything I can do—"

Celeste tilted her head to the side.

"Some way I can help you—"

Celeste mouthed, *No,* and a wave of despair rolled from Katherine's stomach to her throat.

Celeste breathed in through her nose, out through her mouth, a halting, seemingly deliberate—

"Sweet child," Katherine said, a term she'd never used before with anyone, let alone Celeste, but Katherine felt it. She felt it in her soul. She'd walk through fire to save Celeste. She'd never leave her behind.

Katherine opened her hands to Celeste, a bounty, an offering. "Maybe you'd feel better if you told me."

Celeste pressed a fisted hand to her mouth, and her eyes narrowed. She blinked at Katherine.

"Sweet—"

Celeste launched herself into Katherine's arms.

Katherine had yet to experience a hot flash, but she imagined this was what it would feel like, a sudden wall of heat. Celeste hid her face in Katherine's shoulder, and Katherine gentled a hand to Celeste's head. Beneath Katherine's hand, Celeste's breathing hitched.

The sound of Zach's and Barry's voices filtered from the front of the house. Barry laughed, that *he-he-he* of delight Katherine loved to inspire. She stifled the urge to mirror Celeste's erratic breathing until Celeste's breathing mirrored hers.

Dear lord, what had happened? Had someone—a man—hurt Celeste? Had some man—

Celeste raised her head and dropped a featherlight kiss onto Katherine's cheek, two reactions she'd never seen from Celeste before in one night. She bent to Katherine's ear, as though she might tell her a secret. "I'm so sorry," Celeste said.

Katherine held her breath. She steadied her body, as though she were about to take a picture, a snapshot of this moment.

In that moment, Celeste pulled away.

Celeste's face was pale. Her eyes were dry. Her tone was adult, serious, and entirely straightforward. "I can't tell you," she said. "If I told you what I did, I'd only feel worse."

CHAPTER 15

Shame marinated you in toxins, saturated your soul, and informed all your choices. Ever since Katherine had been old enough to understand that other fathers spoke nicely to their daughters, shame had told Katherine she was unlovable.

Intellectually, she'd understood this connection for years. But she hadn't really believed the cause and effect emotionally until she'd seen the bright and beautiful Celeste unmasked to reveal the face of shame. Then Celeste had scooped root vegetables into Katherine's oversized serving bowl and mumbled something about a direct connection between potatoes and her ass, the mask snapped back into place.

Katherine carried first a warm, cloth-covered loaf of sourdough bread and butter and then the sliced roast into the dining room. "Dinner," Katherine called into the front of the house.

Barry and Zach bustled into the dining room, grinning like naughty boys and looking as though they'd shared more than crudités. "Something going on here I should know about?" Katherine asked. "Have you toilet papered my tree? Egged my house?" *Revealed my secrets?*

Katherine's gaze gravitated to Zach's clenched fist, a glossy brown wrapper peeking between his pointer and middle fingers. "Eaten all my Halloween candy?"

"Guilty, ma'am," Zach said, and he slipped the wrapper into his pocket.

"Barry?" Katherine asked.

"Nope, I don't feel guilty at all," he said, and Celeste laughed.

"Shoot," Katherine said. "I forgot Zach's beer. And Celeste's water. I'll be right back."

At the kitchen counter, Katherine snapped up the beer and water.

"Don't serve family-style," Barry said.

Katherine jostled, and beer splashed her décolleté. Droplets ran down the center of her bra. She turned slowly, careful not to spill any more beer. Any beer leaving the glass now would be destined for either Zach's stomach or Barry's face.

"You scared the cra—"

Barry tapped a finger against his lips. "Shh." He cut his gaze to the curtain and the dining area beyond. He closed the space between them. Beneath the sink's fluorescent light, his eyes shone a serious blue. "Serve everyone from the head of the table, say it's easier that way. Give Celeste a reasonable amount. More than she's been eating recently, but less than your usual offering so she doesn't feel overwhelmed."

"You have a complaint about my usual offering?"

"You tend to be . . . generous. I'm not saying that's a bad thing. I know cooking and baking is how you show love." Barry stroked her hair. A quick gesture, as though he were smoothing down a stray.

She turned toward his hand, the way you paused and angled your head in the middle of a crowd when you thought you'd heard your name.

Barry pressed a fisted hand to the counter. "If you let her serve herself, she's going to give herself less. Just give her a little bit of everything."

Katherine imagined Celeste's preferred portions—a few nontouching carrots and potatoes and a scrap of meat, rattling around first on her plate and then in her stomach. "What if she complains?"

"Even if she complains"—Barry took a balled dish towel from Katherine's counter and dried the beer from her chest—"she'll be grateful for the favor." He dropped the cloth on the counter and held aside the bead curtain.

Katherine delivered the drinks and swiped the root vegetables Zach was eyeing. "I serve from the head of the table."

Zach held his hands up. "Whatever you say, boss."

In Katherine's long-ago home, on the nights when her father passed out before dinner, her mother let her and her sister serve themselves, quickly and quietly, so as not to wake the sleeping giant on the couch. Katherine would sit on her unmade bed, back up against the wall, plate warming her lap, and flip through the glossy pages of the library's outdated *Seventeen* magazine. She'd lose herself in the fantasy of pretty faces, clear skin, and perfect bodies. The day she discovered the models were airbrushed? One of the happiest days of her life.

Celeste got up from her seat. "I don't like when people serve me."

Zach's and Barry's gazes zoomed in on Celeste.

Celeste looked from Barry to Zach to Katherine. "Sorry. That was rude," she said, and sat back down, a hint of the shame on her face Katherine had witnessed in the kitchen.

Zach put his hand on the back of Celeste's chair, a degree of separation from Celeste.

Barry was right about Celeste. He was usually right. Dang it all. Katherine's lips tingled. "No apology necessary. Eat whatever you want, leave whatever you don't." *No pressure.* Katherine glanced at Barry, looking for a sign she hadn't screwed up. Should she have even mentioned leaving food on the plate?

Should she have given Celeste an out? Should she have been that transparent?

Barry gave her half a grin and rocked in his seat.

Katherine piled vegetables on Celeste's plate, caught Celeste's unblinking gaze, and shoved a few potatoes back into the bowl. Celeste followed Katherine's serving fork as it hovered over the meat, and Katherine selected a medium-sized slice.

Barry flicked his gaze to the sourdough bread, and Katherine plucked a slice from the middle.

Then, to alleviate the empty feeling in her gut, Katherine piled love—food—onto Zach's and Barry's plates. For herself? The usual generous offering.

Kind of explained her post-divorce weight gain.

Katherine raised her glass for a toast.

"To friends, old and new!" Barry said, beating her to it.

"To friends," Katherine echoed, and she made a point of catching Barry's gaze.

Barry made a point of looking at her breasts.

They clinked glasses all around and started eating. Courtesy of Barry, the conversation meandered into the discussion of where Zach was from, his education, his plans for the future, and how well he liked Hidden Harbor.

Zach hunched over his plate, as though someone—Katherine—might swoop in and swipe it away from him. Seemingly undeterred by having to use his nondominant hand, he inhaled his meal like any other young guy. Feverishly. Quickly. Noisily. And enjoying every bite without apology.

Celeste could take a lesson from Zach.

Celeste pushed her food around on her plate. She ate slowly and deliberately. Was she selecting the tastiest-looking morsels? Trying to assume the semblance of eating?

Wasn't she hungry?

Barry chewed, and dimples popped up on either side of his mouth, sweet indentations Katherine longed to kiss. He sliced through the meat, his fork and knife held at a forty-five-degree angle, as though he sought to control the shape of every bite.

Katherine ate the last potato on her plate. Barry chewed his remaining piece of roast and washed it down with a sip of wine, the two of them finishing together. Just like when they used to have sex.

Barry glanced between their plates, waggled his brows.

Had Barry deliberately paced himself, with dinner?

"Another great dinner, honey," Barry said.

Had Barry meant to call her *honey?*

"Oh, sorry, Katherine. Force of habit," Barry told Katherine. "When we were married, I used to tell her that—'great dinner, honey'—every night after dinner." He chuckled. "Even if I made the dinner."

"That," Katherine said, "was a long time ago."

"Not so long ago. In fact, I bet . . ." Barry picked up his fork, scraped it across the empty plate.

Katherine cringed.

". . . that sound still annoys you." Barry set his fork on the plate. "People don't change."

"This coming from a shrink," Katherine said.

Barry pointed with either hand, his orchestra conductor move. "People don't *often* change."

Katherine grinned.

"Unless," Barry said, "something monumental drives them to it."

"Or they're driven to your office," Celeste said.

"Good one." Barry tried for a wink, or was that a deliberate wince? "I'd wager, Katherine still reads the tarot every night after dinner. She probably keeps a deck somewhere in the dining area or the kitchen. Correct?"

"Possibly," Katherine said.

Barry followed Katherine's traitorous gaze to the sideboard, and the drawer left slightly ajar from last night's reading. "And a deck in your bedside table?" he asked.

"Maybe."

"Yup. We're all pretty much the same inside as when we were twelve years old."

Katherine had been twelve when big sister Lexi had given Katherine her first tarot cards and shown her how to read them. The larger-than-life robed characters and the exotic scenes depicted on the twenty-two cards of the major arcana. The down-to-earth symbolism of the fifty-six minor arcana.

Whether major or minor, each card represented a chest of secrets.

Katherine and Lexi had sat on the floor between their beds, and Lexi laid out horseshoe and Celtic cross spreads. Whimsical illustrations of suns and moons, magicians and priestesses, had sympathized with Katherine's predicaments and foretold the story of her life.

"In fact," Barry said, "I'd wager, at twelve we're our best, most authentic selves."

Zach sipped his beer, and moved his mouth as if he was savoring the flavors. "Then the world steps in to throw a few punches or show you the door, and it all goes downhill from there."

Zach glanced at Katherine, and she translated *the world* to *adoptive parents.* "Sometimes the world, as in other people, has its—their—reasons for showing you the door. Sometimes the world isn't perfect and it has nothing to do with us. Sometimes parents are doing the best they can."

Parents? Barry mouthed.

"My parents are perfect," Celeste said. "My mother sent my father off to work with a brown-bag lunch every morning and had dinner on the table every night for him and the four spawns promptly at six. Dad worked for the same insurance company for thirty years. Mom raised the kids. Neither of them ever complained. I don't think they know the meaning of the word *complain*." Celeste leaned back in her seat, as though the notion of those thirty steadfast years exhausted her.

"With respect to your parents," Katherine said, "nobody is perfect." If Celeste's parents had been perfect, they might've stayed a few more years in Hidden Harbor. They might've given Celeste a few more years to grow up before abandoning her. Even college kids returned home for the long Thanksgiving weekend and an extended winter break, so they could sleep till noon and let their moms do the wash. Or so Katherine had heard. No matter your age, everyone needed someone to treat them as though they were small and precious and deserving of protection.

Katherine thought of herself as neither small nor in need of protection.

And yet every night she slept curled in a ball around her blanket or pillow or, in the middle of summer, herself. Somewhat embarrassing, and also the reason why she never let men stay the night. But nothing she could control. Whenever she'd accidentally fallen asleep on her back, a paperback splayed across her chest, nightmares would wake her, leaving her with a dark and cloying sensation of doom.

"I'll clear the table!" Celeste jumped to standing.

"Thanks, Celeste, I—"

Celeste gathered up the plates and silverware and dashed into the kitchen, but not before Katherine caught sight of Celeste's plate. She'd left half the roast, picked at her bread, and, with the exception of the beloved potatoes, forsaken the vegetables.

Katherine remembered the hollow stomachache from

being sent to bed without dinner, the stab of nausea, the trickle of sadness. Why would Celeste want to cause herself discomfort?

Katherine carried the serving platters into the kitchen. "Are you saving yourself for dessert?" Katherine asked, and her voice sounded winded, panicked. "There's a devil's food cake. I thought I'd wait a bit before serving it, but if you're hungry, I'll take it out now. Or you could indulge in the Halloween candy. I was only teasing Zach and Barry. To be honest with you, I always buy too much." Katherine cringed. "In fact, I have another two-pound bag stashed in the cabinet. You'd be doing me a huge favor if you brought some home. Why don't you—"

"Do you have a disposal?" Celeste asked.

Katherine gave her head a shake. "A what?"

"Disposal? You know, those things that grind . . ."

"Oh. No." Katherine opened the cabinet under the sink and pulled out the trash. "You can dump the scraps into the trash." By *scraps* Katherine meant Celeste's entire meal.

"Will do," Celeste said, but she didn't look Katherine in the eye. Any bread from Lamontagne's that didn't sell on the day-old shelf got donated to Annie's Daily Bread, a soup kitchen in Bath. There Annie toasted the bread and made homemade croutons for soups and salads. Celeste knew how Katherine felt about wasting food.

Barry came into the kitchen and set the bread and butter on the counter.

"Chop, chop," Barry said. "The trick-or-treaters will be here soon, and we have just enough time for that tarot reading you promised Zach."

"What are you talking about?" Katherine asked.

"Before dinner? You said you'd tell Zach's fortune?"

Katherine looked at Barry sideways. She searched her memory. Tarot, dining room, bedside table.

Barry waggled his brows.

"Are you making fun of me?" Katherine asked. "Trying to make me think I've lost my mind?"

Zach's sling plowed through the bead curtain. His orange cape tangled between the strands. "You didn't promise me anything. Don't worry about it," Zach said, but Katherine's mind stuck on *you didn't promise me anything.*

In that long-ago hospital room, before she'd said good-bye to Zach, she'd held his tiny hands. She'd kissed his tiny nose. She'd promised to love him forever.

Twelve years later, she'd offered Barry the same promise.

She honored her promises, even those she'd never made.

"I'd love to do a quick reading. What a fun idea, Zach. Thank you for asking."

"What?" Barry held a hand to his chest. "I don't get any thanks?"

Katherine held a hand to Barry's cheek, and the stinker grinned at her hand. She took back her hand. "Thank you for helping to clear the table," she said, and she slipped through the beads.

Center of the table, the light flickering through the jack-o'-lantern sent a web of shivers up the back of her hair. Sundown on All Hallows' Eve, should she risk invoking the past? Should she ask Zach to consider his present situation? What if the future disappointed him?

The last time Lexi had read Katherine's cards, she'd laid the three of swords in her future position, foretelling the pain of separation and deep sorrow.

What good was knowing about a future disaster if you couldn't prevent it?

"Shoot. I meant to put cider on the stove. I have mulling spices," Katherine said, remembering how much Barry loved the smell of cloves, how much he'd adored the way the aroma hung in the air, clung to her hair and skin.

"Save them for another night." Barry went into her sideboard drawer and took out her cards, as though he had a right to her belongings. As though the divorce papers they'd both signed meant nothing. As though he expected to return another night.

Two years ago, he'd told her she'd broken his heart. But no matter how many times she'd asked nicely, he'd refused to hate her. He'd refused to give up hope.

"She's never read my cards," Celeste told Zach. "Why do you get a reading? It's not fair! You've always been her favorite," Celeste said, making it sound as though she and Zach were Katherine's children. A joke, Katherine reminded herself. A lucky guess.

But lucky guesses were often inklings of psychic ability. The 100 percent correct interpretation of what logically you shouldn't know. Years before Katherine had left home and hit the road, she'd had a recurring dream of being the last person alive on earth. In the dream, she'd awake to an empty house, run outside and down the driveway to find the street free of cars and foot traffic. High in the trees, wind rustled the summertime leaves, and she'd walked barefoot through a dreamscape ghost town, the only sound the hollow beating of her heart.

Barry slid the tarot cards from their blue box. At the dining room table, he started to shuffle.

"Give me that." Katherine took the deck from Barry's hands and widened her eyes at him. "What's the matter with you? You know better than to touch the deck." Barry knew better than to influence the outcome of the reading. Or maybe that was his point all along?

"Horseshoe spread?" Barry asked.

The classic spread was Katherine's favorite, a story in seven cards. But the cards delved into the subject's character, his or her friends and family. Tonight, those cards could hit too close to home.

"The power of three," Katherine said. "Past, present, and future. Keeping it simple."

"Cool by me," Zach said.

Zach, Barry, and Celeste returned to the dinner chairs, as though they had assigned seating.

"Do your stuff, witchy woman," Barry said without an ounce of irony.

"Don't rush me," Katherine said. "Or you'll spoil the result."

"You know this is a game?" Barry asked. "You know deep down the cards are open for interpretation, a psychological tool for those wary of psychology?"

"You know psychology is a tool for those wary of reading the tarot?" Katherine asked.

"Yes," Barry said. "Yes, I do."

"Good answer."

Zach once again placed his hand on the back of Celeste's chair. Celeste sat with her hands folded on the tablecloth, her gaze focused on the jack-o'-lantern. Was Celeste meditating on the past? Pondering her future?

When Katherine read for herself, she took her time preparing so that she'd shield herself from other people's energies and issues. The widow lady who lived upstairs. A neighbor couple's argument. Even the high keening cry of an infant from two streets away. When you read cards for someone else? The greatest risk was mixing your energy and issues with theirs. Essentially, Katherine needed to protect the other person—Zach—from her.

In order to cleanse her energy, her hands could stand a washing. But she doubted Barry would tolerate her making another break for the kitchen. She took a few centering breaths, meant to focus her energy on the cards in her hands, but her gaze kept wandering to Zach. Katherine's feet were crossed at the ankles. She stretched out her legs, intending to ground herself, and clipped Barry's leg.

Sorry, Katherine mouthed. She shifted away from Barry and set the soles of her boots—yes, the black boots—on the floor. She took two more centering breaths. "Zach," Katherine said. "What's your question?"

Katherine kept her fingers moving, shuffling, her breathing deep, her gaze averted from Barry.

Zach grimaced. "Oh, uh, I thought you were going to tell me about my fortune, give me next month's lottery numbers."

"If I knew the lottery numbers, I'd keep them for myself." Shuffle, breathe.

"If she knew the lottery numbers," Barry said, "she'd give them away to charity."

"I don't need much."

Barry thought she was generous with her money. That, she was sure, came from having grown up with so little. With having to make do with even less. How could you fear the loss of what you'd never had?

Barry also thought she was generous with her love. Open and giving, he'd once told her, when it came to friends, neighbors, her bakery customers, even him. To a point.

Divorcing Barry had been freeing, she'd told herself. When you had nothing left to lose, you had nothing to fear.

Barry gave Katherine an encouraging grin. Zach placed his hand on Celeste's shoulder, the way he woke her when she got lost in the middle of Lamontagne's. Celeste blinked up at him.

Katherine provided the redirection. "So, this is how it works, Zach. You think of a question—one question—something you'd very much like to know about. And you focus on that one important question."

Zach slid his arm from Celeste's chair, rested his chin on his fist, and stared at Katherine.

Katherine smirked. "It's best if you say your question out loud. I can't read your mind."

"You can't?"

"Sadly, I cannot." And she heard, *Are you my mother?* The sound, she supposed, of her guilty conscience.

Why did you abandon me? popped into her head. Was she imagining Zach's question or hearing the small, buried voice of a younger Katherine?

"Ask her about your career," Celeste told Zach. "Ask Katherine what you should do for a living."

"Besides the Superman gig?" Zach stood and shook out his cape so it fell over his chair back. "I totally rock the cape."

"Don't be ridiculous," Celeste said. "I'm talking about your day job, not your secret, undercover persona. No matter what day job you choose, you get to keep the superhero gig. I mean, obviously."

Smitten, are we?

Katherine glanced at Barry, and they shared an amused look, as though they were Celeste's parents and Zach were the young man she'd brought home for their approval.

"So, what's the verdict, Zach? What's your big life question?" By *big life question* Katherine meant medium, nothing that included the word *mother.*

"Hmm." Zach scrunched his mouth to the side, cut his gaze to Celeste. "Yeah, I'm onboard with the career question."

"If you're certain, state your question plainly."

"Uh, okay. I'd like to know what job—career—I should go for. I'd like to know"—Zach shook his head, glanced sidelong at the jack-o'-lantern—"how to decide." He returned his gaze to Katherine.

Katherine tilted her head. "Okay. Zach would like to know how he can choose a career. Is that correct?"

"Something like that," Zach said, and he flashed a smile that didn't reach his eyes.

"All right."

"Do we need to join hands or something?"

"That's a séance. I don't do séances." Katherine didn't care to participate in an activity that could potentially summon the energy of low-level spirits.

She preferred summoning positive vibes from the living.

Katherine gave the cards a final shuffle and fanned them on the table before her. "Pick a card." Katherine hadn't wanted Barry to touch the cards, but she wanted to make sure the cards worked for Zach. She wanted to make sure her energy didn't hurt his ability to choose.

"O-kay." Zach tapped a card.

Katherine slid Zach's card from the fan and placed it, face-down, to the left. "Choose a second card."

Zach hesitated.

"Don't think about it," she said, and he tapped another card twice. She slid the card to the right. "Good . . . and a—"

Zach tapped a third card before the words had left her mouth. "Sure about that?" she asked, and she laid the third card to the right of the second. She took a deep breath, placed her hand on the first card. "This card represents your past. The circumstances that led to your current situation." She raised her brows. "Let's see what we have," Katherine said, and she turned over the card.

The Lovers, reversed.

Facing Katherine, the illustration depicted Adam and Eve, the world's original lovers, naked in the Garden of Eden before the knowledge of their own shame. Behind the couple, the high tops of mountains peaked before the archangel Raphael and the sun's blinding rays.

A warning note of tinnitus rang through Katherine's ears. Barry stroked his beardless chin, leaned closer to examine the card. Zach scratched his cheek. Celeste squinted, and Katherine held up the card. "Relax," she said. "It's not what you think."

"They're naked." Celeste covered her mouth. Did the broad-stroked drawing embarrass her? Katherine placed the card back on the table, reversed to face her, and Celeste's hand drifted back to the table.

"I should probably explain," Katherine said. "The cards aren't necessarily literal." Unless, of course, this one was. Unless her unwashed hands and her monkey mind had hijacked Zach's reading. Adam was Zach's biological father. Did that make her Eve? "Lovers often depict nonromantic relationships, fathers and sons, mothers and daughters." Katherine glanced out to the living room, the darkness edging the room. "Mothers and sons. Zach, in the past, have you perhaps had trouble communicating with loved ones or a loved one?"

"Oh, yeah," Zach said.

"The Lovers card often tells of a time when you had to make a choice, an important choice." Katherine had faced her pregnancy alone. Communicating with Zach's father had never been an option. Communicating with her parents? Even less likely.

"Like dropping out of college," Zach said. "Yeah, my parents weren't too thrilled about that."

"But it's what you thought best. Perhaps you didn't want to waste your time with something you weren't certain about?"

"Or their money."

"Or their money. Very thoughtful," Katherine said. "And, would you say, the greatest problem arose from your indecision? And did that indecision come from your fear of hurting someone close to you?" Katherine had never been certain of her decision. No matter how many times she'd consulted the tarot, she couldn't figure out what might've happened if she'd chanced keeping her son. That road remained unknowable.

"My father," Zach said, and he scratched his head. "You're freaking me out, man. I mean, Katherine."

In all of this, Katherine hadn't considered Zach's adoptive father.

"What else does the card say?" Zach asked.

"The reversal usually means that you'd like to have it both ways, rather than make a decision. Does that make sense?"

"Unfortunately."

Barry tapped a finger against his chin.

Celeste ran her hand up and down her water glass. She swiped the condensation across her forehead.

"You feeling all right, Celeste?" Katherine asked.

"Um, what?"

Zach bent to Celeste and spoke softly. "She wants to know if you're feeling okay."

Celeste straightened. "Oh, yeah, totally." She pulled at the neckline of her sweater. "I'm just a little warm."

If anything, Katherine kept her house on the cooler side. "Why don't we move on to the second card?" she asked, and Zach nodded.

"Behold, the present," Katherine said, and she turned over the Empress, resplendent in flowing robes and a jeweled crown and—

"What do you know?" Barry said. "Zach's a pregnant woman."

Celeste laughed, an overly enthusiastic burst of comic relief.

Katherine's cheeks warmed. "Settle down, children. Not literal," she repeated, but she wasn't convinced. "The Empress indicates your present situation is fulfilling your needs."

"Does this mean you're giving me a raise?" Zach aimed the elbow of his sling at Katherine. "It's been hard work leaving a mess for Blake at the end of my shift."

"I appreciate your effort, but no, not at this time." If the card was meant for Katherine, she might ask herself who she felt protective toward. She might answer with the name of every person in this room. She might ask herself whom she was mothering, from whom she was withholding affection, and whether she herself was in dire need of attention.

She'd have to admit that, yes, she was feeling sensual.

The Empress symbolized a woman wanting to bring either children or her passions into the world. The punishment for ignoring those passions? Your children or passions died a slow, smoldering death.

That, Katherine supposed, had happened in the past. All those children she imagined having with Barry. All those precious souls who'd rejected her body before she could reject them.

Her collarbone ached, a remnant, a memory of loss.

Barry placed a hand on her shoulder.

"What? I'm sorry . . ."

"Zach asked whether this means he has a prosperous future ahead of him in dishwashing."

"Ha, ha," Katherine said.

Zach set his left elbow on the table, fingers closed and straight.

"What the hell is that? A karate chop?" Celeste asked.

"My one-handed prayer position."

Katherine grinned. "Sadly, no. I do not see dishwashing in Zach's future, at least not professionally." She took a deep breath, as though they were speaking of matters greater than dishwashing or even career choices. "Sometimes our current situation is preparing us for a future in ways we can't yet understand."

"Well put," Barry said. "Are you sure you're not secretly a shrink?"

"That," Katherine said, "is the only thing I'm certain of . . . and now, Zachary Fitzgerald—"

"Zachary Frank Fitzgerald."

On the way to turn the card symbolizing Zach's future, Katherine's hand trembled over the past. She was back in the maternity ward, nursing her son. She was signing the papers. She was breaking her own heart. "Wh-wh-what did you just say?"

Zach laughed. "I know it's a horrible middle name, but it's not worth crying over."

Katherine had filled out the birth certificate, naming her son Frank, after her mother, Francesca. She'd assumed her son's adoptive parents had ignored the name, preferring to wipe away evidence that he'd ever been anything but theirs. She'd never imagined they'd wanted to keep a piece of her alive in their son.

"I'm not crying," Katherine said. "I'm just"—Katherine glanced at Celeste—"a little warm. Anyway, Zachary Frank." Katherine took a sip of her wine, and the alcohol heated her skin. "Let's see what your future holds," she said, and she turned over The Wheel of Fortune.

Katherine finally realized the card she'd once misinterpreted to mean she'd settle down with Zach's biological father had foretold her putting down roots for Zach himself.

"Beauty!" Zach said. "This one I can take literally, right? This one means I'm going to make tons of money."

"I can't answer that question for you. My guess would be that you're going to get to know yourself better. That events are, literally, in motion for your future career." Katherine also couldn't imagine that money drove the wheels of Zach's motivation. He didn't strike her as a man who put money above people. On Monday, Zach had volunteered an hour of his own time to help her with Blake. If she'd broken her wrist scuffling with the boy, she doubted she would've been quite as forgiving.

The chimes of her doorbell rang through the house, and Katherine stood. "Saved by the literal bell. Happy Halloween, folks."

Beneath the front door's light, a seven-year-old boy in a lobster costume waited in a cage, a piece of paper with the words *Free Me* tacked to the front. The lobster's lobsterman father, Donald, hunched in his usual oil jacket and muck boots.

"What's going on here, Jeremy?" Katherine asked the seven-year-old.

"I'm a vegetarian," he said, and poked a white pillowcase through the bars of the cage. "Trick-or-treat!"

Katherine grabbed a handful of fun-sized chocolates and tossed them into the pillowcase.

"Cool costume, dude," Zach said.

"So original," Celeste added.

"Nicely done." Barry unwrapped a milk chocolate bar and popped it into his mouth.

"What happened?" Katherine asked Donald.

"They say you should bring your kid to work with you. They say it will be good for him to see what his dad does. They say it'll improve the kid's confidence."

"Who exactly are *they?*"

"The wife."

Katherine grinned. "Can't argue with them."

Donald shook his head and helped his lobster down the walkway. A few more kids and parents made their way down the street. Flashlights bobbed in the dark. The high voices of children, the deeper sound of their parents' replies. And the smell of the season's first wood fires. She could see neither bay nor open ocean from her house, but she could hear it, its roar so much more pleasant than the drone of highway traffic. The background sound track of her childhood.

Katherine shut the door, caught Barry and Zach digging into the candy. Good. "Where'd Celeste go?"

"Ladies' room," Zach provided.

Katherine peered out the sidelight. "Do me a favor and man the door." She grabbed a box of Whoppers for herself and went back to her seat at the dining table. She popped one in her mouth, concentrated on the soft chocolate giving way to the sweet, pithy malt ball. She gazed at the jack-o'-lantern's flame-brightened scrollwork, set the soles of her boots on the floor. She scooped up the three cards from the table. Without looking down, she shuffled.

Will I keep my secret?

She was so much like Zach. She wanted to have a relationship with Zach. She wanted to keep the secret of Zach from hurting Barry. She wanted it both ways.

Will I keep my secret?

At the front of the house, Barry and Zach stood on either side of the black cauldron, munching on the Halloween candy. Zach glanced her way. He bent his head to Barry and spoke too low for Katherine to make out the words clearly.

She took a centering breath that tickled her throat. She flexed the cramps from her fingers and gave the cards a final shuffle.

Will I keep my secret?

"Cool, see you around eight," Zach told Barry, the words hushed but unmistakable.

It was ten past six. If Zach and Barry stayed until the end of the two-hour trick-or-treat block, of course they'd see each other around eight. But they wouldn't talk about it. *See you around eight* meant Zach and Barry were planning on leaving before eight. *See you around eight* meant they were planning on meeting up later tonight. *See you around eight* could mean they were planning on talking about Katherine.

Energy jittered through her hands.

Will I keep my secret?

Barry held up a candy wrapper close to his face, as though he were trying to read it without his reading glasses. He handed the wrapper to Zach.

Katherine slid a single card from the center of the deck and laid it on the table before her.

Katherine's arms and legs felt rubbery and foreign, as though she were a stranger in her own body. Her mind buzzed with a confusion of white noise. Her vision blurred around the edges of the card.

A bolt of blue lightning jagged from a cadmium-yellow cloud and struck a slender building. Bricks tumbled from the structure. A man and a woman dove headlong from a Gothic arched window. Flames rose from the folds of their sapphire-blue robes.

Out of seventy-eight cards, Katherine had pulled The Tower, the tarot's greatest symbol of crisis and upheaval.

Chapter 16

Barry Horowitz reminded Zach of his father.

Both men had this easygoing way about them. When you were talking to them, you never got the feeling they'd rather be somewhere else, your presence an inconvenience on their way to either a more interesting activity or their own thoughts. Whether Zach was talking to his father about a job or the Red Sox or the latest way he'd screwed up, Everett Fitzgerald would take off his reading glasses, rub his face, and look at Zach with fresh eyes. If his father was watching the evening news, he'd turn off the set and pat the seat cushion beside him. When Zach asked for help or redirection, his father had never turned him away.

Whether Zach always agreed with his father's suggestions was an entirely different story.

That didn't entirely explain why Zach had claimed he needed to go for a beer run, dropped Celeste at her apartment door, and sped off for a secret meeting with Barry Horowitz at his house.

Before peeling out of the parking lot, Zach had memorized the directions Barry jotted down on the back of his business card. That business card now sat in Zach's pocket where he'd first slipped it earlier, alongside a Hershey's milk chocolate wrapper and his St. Anthony pocket token. Zach drove with his left hand, stretched the fingers of his right hand from the sling, and patted above the pocket for good luck. He passed through the center of town, followed Ocean Boulevard for about two and a half miles, and slowed to watch for Barry's driveway. Under the light of the waning half-moon, a marsh took shape on his right.

He'd gone too far.

Zach pulled to the side of the road, banged a uey, and found Barry's driveway: a hairpin switchback with a simple mailbox. The names *Lamontagne* and *Horowitz* gleamed in Matilda's headlights. Zach pulled into the wooded driveway, grinning and shaking his head at no one.

The Barry and Katherine duo reminded Zach a little of his parents.

Katherine and Barry spoke their own language, a comedy routine where Barry was the joker, Katherine was the straight man, but they were both in on the joke. Zach got the distinct feeling that, despite her protests, Katherine was crushing on her ex-husband. Why else would she have invited him to dinner? And even if Barry hadn't kept Katherine's name on his mailbox, there was no hiding the obvious. Barry couldn't keep his eyes off Katherine.

That still didn't explain the secret Fitzgerald-Horowitz rendezvous.

Matilda bumped up the driveway, pitch-dark beneath the thick pine forest. Zach hummed a song that seemed to start in his center, the way you were supposed to sing, and thrummed his vocal cords. "Prince, 'I Would Die 4 U.' Nice," Zach said, naming the song and praising himself for the naming.

He liked it better when Celeste was sitting by his side, playing along, and he couldn't keep his eyes off her.

This thing with Celeste that had no name? He was getting closer to naming.

As promised, the road opened up to a shared drive. Zach veered right, and the back of a white New Englander rose from a grassy hill. He parked against the scrub, unlatched his seat belt, and slid the St. Anthony token from his pocket. For the second time since coming to town, he recited the prayer, asking for the restoration of things lost or stolen. "I would die for you," he told the darkness. He liked the sound of the words.

Zach jogged around to the front of the house and found Barry sitting on the porch in one of those metal chairs. Beyond a small front yard, Barry faced the woods and a killer view. A maze-like tidal river glowed beneath the half-moon and emptied into the night.

"Wow." Zach squinted up at the two-story house. Judging by the height and width, he estimated a good three thousand square feet and at least three bedrooms. "You live here alone?"

"Just me and my thoughts."

"You and Katherine didn't have any kids," Zach said, more of a statement than a question.

"That," Barry said, "wasn't for lack of trying." Barry's voice sounded winded, like a Boston Marathon runner who stumbled across the Copley Square finish line hours after sundown. When Barry stepped from the porch, Zach caught a glimpse of his expression, a grimace of regret. Then Barry tilted his head to the night sky.

Zach followed Barry's lead, and his stomach took a nosedive. The Milky Way stood out against the dome-shaped jet-black backdrop, a collection of every star visible with the naked eye. Zach's gaze gravitated to the Big Dipper and the seven stars that marked its path. Sure enough, just like his father had taught him, in autumn the Big Dipper hung low in the sky, its handle pointing straight at Polaris, the North Star.

Zach's father used to say that no matter where you were,

you could always find your way home. All you had to do was look up.

When Zach was thirteen and he'd run away, he'd only gotten as far as Harvard Square. There he'd met a group of like-minded kids, teenagers in search of a place to call home. After the local crowds had dwindled, the tourists and college kids tucked themselves into hotels and dorm rooms, he'd followed the ragtag bunch to the sheltered entryway of the Harvard Coop. In place of dinner, they'd passed around something in a greasy brown bag that tasted like NyQuil and inspired an instant dreamless sleep. But when he'd awoken sometime past midnight to the loud rumble of a boy snoring and the soft gurgle of a girl crying, Zach had struggled from the sleeping bag and stared up at the sky, his father's voice echoing in his head.

Tonight, away from the city glare, the light pollution, Zach was finally able to connect the stars between Polaris and the Little Dipper's outer bowl. Turned out, after years of pretending for his father's sake, Zach had only needed the clarity of a country sky to see through his father's eyes.

"Beauty," Zach said.

"So," Barry said, "about your girl, Celeste."

Zach grinned. He liked a guy who got to the point. He liked that Barry thought beauty was synonymous with Celeste. He liked that Barry had called Celeste his girl. He liked Barry.

"Am I a worrywart?" Zach asked, his mother's phrase conjuring an image of his mother. Even though she'd sent him away, was she worried about him?

He'd never considered that.

Before dinner, Zach had told Barry he was worried Celeste had some kind of eating disorder. He'd asked Barry to watch the way Celeste ate. He'd asked Barry for a secret consultation. If they were talking about Celeste behind her back but for her own good, were they still gossiping?

Zach had never considered that either.

Instead of answering Zach's question, Barry offered one of his own. "Did Celeste eat more than she usually does for dinner?"

"Maybe," Zach said, thinking back to the few times he'd seen Celeste eating dinner. "She usually hides when she's eating. She'll sneak off to the kitchen or go into her bedroom and shut the door."

"You're living together, but you take your meals separately?" Barry asked.

"We're not really living together," Zach said. "I'm sort of crashing on her couch."

Zach thought of the Harvard Square kids again. He'd asked them what they did to survive the winter, and they'd told him they couch surfed, the time-honored tradition of another kid—usually an older kid—with a room or an apartment laying out the welcome mat for homeless travelers in need.

Now Zach hoped Celeste would let him help her. He might not understand the meaning of life or even what he was supposed to do for a long-term job. But trying to unravel whatever had happened to Celeste back in New York and help her deal with the fallout? That meant everything.

"When I went into the kitchen before dinner," Barry said, "I advised Katherine to serve from the head of the table."

Zach nodded. "No wonder she practically grabbed the vegetables out of my hands."

Barry sighed, a heavy sound. "If you allow someone with anorexia to feed themselves, they'll take as little as possible. For that reason, when they're struggling, it's best for family and friends to measure the patient's food."

"Celeste isn't a patient," Zach said, his need to defend rising from his stomach to his throat. "I mean, she's not really sick."

Barry caught Zach's eye. How much did Barry know about Celeste? How much of her history? Had Barry known her back when she'd had that trouble with the boyfriend from high school?

Crazy, but for a second Zach was jealous of Barry for being a part of Celeste's life before Zach had even known she'd existed. Standing under the night sky had always given Zach the strangest feeling of being lost in time, of time being like a river that could flow in either direction.

But, of course, you could only paddle the curvy path forward.

"She's not sick," Zach repeated, but this time the statement sounded like a question.

Barry clamped a hand to Zach's left shoulder, as if sensing Zach needed grounding, as if he could read all the questions behind Zach's questions and everything he feared. "Plan special meals with her," Barry said.

"How about dessert?" Zach thought of the ice-cream sundae fixings. Every day he'd checked and found the ice cream unopened, the hot fudge sitting in the refrigerator door behind his yellow mustard. The whipped cream—how could you ignore whipped cream?—hiding behind the OJ. The pecans looked as if Celeste had opened the bag and eaten exactly three halves.

"Dinner, dessert. Doesn't really matter. I suggest you plan on eating as many meals as possible with Celeste. Make sure you plate the food for her."

Zach chuckled. "She *loves* when people serve her."

"Zach," Barry said.

A shiver ran up the back of Zach's head. Whenever his father was about to tell him something important, he'd say Zach's name, too.

"If Celeste is struggling with an eating disorder, everything about eating is stressful for her, including deciding how much food to put on her plate."

"So I'd be, like, helping her get better?"

"Exactly. And sitting down to eat with her is helpful, too. You're showing her an example of someone who's svelte and has a good appetite. I noticed how much you enjoyed Katherine's cooking."

Was there anything this guy didn't notice?

Zach's hand wandered to his belly, the muscles corralling three servings of roast and seconds on the best devil's food cake he'd ever tasted. And yet he was still hungry. He pretty much never got full. "My mother says I have a separate dessert stomach."

Barry patted Zach on the back. "Enjoy it while you're young."

"I don't get it," Zach said.

"When you get older, your metabolism slows down, and—"

Zach sighed, a sign he was getting older. "I mean, about Celeste. Why would someone try to starve themselves? Even if someone needed to lose weight, which Celeste doesn't, it would be the worst torture imaginable."

"Have you ever been stressed out?"

"Sure," Zach said. "Who hasn't?" Zach slipped his hand into his pocket, and he rubbed the token between his thumb and forefinger.

"Have you ever felt overwhelmed, like everything is out of control? You know you've done nothing wrong, yet someone or something has taken away your power?"

"Definitely."

Zach's mind glanced off the memory of his parents telling him he wasn't who he thought he was, jumped over his search for his birth mother and his relationship with Katherine, and landed on the cause of Celeste's stress.

Barry crossed his arms and turned his gaze to the tidal river. "Eating disorders are just another unhealthy way of attempting to cope with a stressor. There's so much you can't control, so you shut down and control what you can."

"I still can't imagine . . ." Zach said, and then, out of nowhere, he could.

He remembered the weeks after his parents' confession and their plea for him to come to them with questions. He remembered his mind bursting with questions. He remembered fearing those questions, and the way he needed to close his bedroom door, curl into a ball, and clamp his mouth firmly shut to keep them contained.

"You can't make me," he'd said. Beneath his cool, white sheets, his words had wrapped him in a hot, humid bubble of protection.

His parents could unlock his bedroom door, but they couldn't make him talk.

"You'll figure it out," Barry said, sounding more like Zach's father than ever. "I have faith in you."

"Thank you, sir. I appreciate your advice." Zach reached out his left hand for a shake.

Barry took Zach's hand and then clamped a second hand on top, letting Zach know he was important to him. Then Barry tugged on the back of Zach's shirt. "You know Halloween is over? You know you can put away the cape for another year, right?"

Zach laughed. Even under the light of the half-moon, the Superman cape glowed. Obvious, now that Barry had pointed it out to him. "I guess I forgot to take it off," Zach said.

In his car, Zach slid the St. Anthony token from his pocket. *Something's lost that can't be found.*

Celeste couldn't remember everything that had happened back in New York. But did she really want to know? When Zach had tried to push her on it, she'd retreated behind her bedroom door. Had she accidentally forgotten but on purpose?

What the hell did he know? He wasn't a shrink. He wasn't even a detective. He was just a guy working as a dishwasher, wandering through life, and trying to figure out how to stay in one place.

Zach untied the cape from around his neck and set it on the seat beside him. Then he refolded the cape so the yellow *S* blazed through the darkness, Superman as his copilot.

When the knock came that Katherine had been expecting, she was sitting on the velvet sofa in the living room, training her unfocused gaze on the half-dozen tea lights she'd set atop the mantel, trying to hold down her dinner and stop the forward motion of time.

She unfolded her legs from under her, got up from the sofa, and took a sip of her water. She'd switched from wine to water hours ago. And in the split second it took for her to make her way to the door, she regretted it, the desire to be stark-raving drunk burning in her like a flame. She checked the sidelight, took a deep breath, and opened the door.

Barry hadn't changed. He was still wearing the gray slacks and the shirt that brought out his Bubbe Sarah pale eyes. Only this time, his shirt was rumpled and horizontal creases marred the crisp lines of his slacks. He leaned against her door frame. His eyes looked exhausted yet quietly determined. "You going to invite me in?" Barry asked. This time, instead of sounding snarky, his tone spoke of more serious matters.

Katherine had been expecting this, too.

She nodded, stood back, and closed the door behind them.

Barry stared at her and shook his head. "Zach came to see me tonight."

"Just say it." She tried to speak up, but her voice came out as a whisper, her pulse tapping at her bottom lip like the woodpecker that woke her at 5:00 a.m. on her day off. She couldn't imagine Barry throwing a fit. But whatever Barry needed to say she deserved to hear. Even if he called her every name in the book, even if he called her names that summoned back darkness and self-hatred.

Barry's arms hung by his sides. "He's a nice young man."

"I think so, too." That was it? Was Barry going to congratulate her on having reunited with her biological son? Ignore the fact she'd lied to Barry for years? Lied to countless doctors? Caused years of baby-making frustration and ruined their marriage? Sick, but she wanted him to yell at her. She needed the final release of his hatred. She needed to stop bracing for the inevitable.

Barry issued an uncomfortable chuckle. "I have a confession. I'm feeling a wee bit guilty."

"Whatever for?"

"Zach came to talk to me about Celeste."

Katherine made a sound, air rushing out of her that she thought she'd needed to withstand Barry's tirade. A tirade that wasn't coming. She breathed around her slowing pulse, but she didn't like the way Barry was standing. Facing her but with his feet angled toward the door. "What's going on?"

"Seems you're not the only friend of Celeste's who's worried about her eating. Zach wanted to know how he might help her."

"That's wonderful." Could she be proud of Zach, even though she hadn't raised him? Could she take a tiny bit of the credit? "What did you tell him?"

"I explained about measuring her food. I strongly suggested he eat with her to show off his healthy appetite."

Katherine grinned. He'd inherited that appetite from her. "So what's the problem?"

"I consider Celeste a friend, and I feel bad keeping the meeting from her. Secrets . . . I don't like them. Never have, never will."

"You've advised friends before about their loved ones. Celeste has never been a patient of yours. It's not a breach of confidence."

"Then why do I feel so guilty?" Barry's eyes shone through the darkness. They were two friends looking out for a third, a continuation of the conversation they'd begun the day Celeste had returned to Hidden Harbor. They could fall into the same old banter. Katherine imagined the two of them continuing their back-and-forth into their dotage, like a couple celebrating their golden wedding anniversary.

Nothing needed to change.

"Are you sure you're not Catholic?" Katherine asked, falling into her role. "Catholic by reverse inoculation?" She waggled her brows, the imitation of Barry's silly gesture likely lost beneath her hair and in the candlelight.

"If only . . ." Barry said, his voice wistful, refusing to play, and stripped of hope.

"Barry," she said. "What's wrong?" Barry Horowitz was one of the most naturally happy people she'd ever known. He loved what he did for a living. He loved where he lived. He loved nature and exercising his beautiful body and everything. Until she'd undergone the first round of IVF, she'd rarely seen him frown.

He was frowning now.

"Nothing," Barry said. "Just wanted you to know about the conversation I had with Zach. Wanted you to know someone else is looking after your girl." Barry nodded, as if he were ending their conversation. "I thought you had a right to know. I owe you that much."

Déjà vu thrummed through Katherine. The sensation started as an ache in her arms, tightened her throat, weakened her legs. She had a vision of bringing Barry the basket of mundel bread and the divorce papers, a slap wrapped in sugar. She'd told him she didn't want a sheriff to deliver the bad news. She'd told him she owed him that much.

Katherine's woodpecker pulse revived. "You could've phoned."

"No filters," Barry said.

Barry wasn't a fan of telephones or anything else that made it easier to skirt, muddy, or soften the truth. He was a big proponent of looking people in the eye. He was a believer in listening for voice cues and interpreting body language.

A feeling of heaviness hit her, as though someone had removed all her blood and replaced it with a transfusion of batter. "Why couldn't you wait until tomorrow morning? Why couldn't you—" She clamped a hand over her mouth.

Barry took her hand from her mouth. He tipped up her chin. He made her look him in the eye. "I'm not stopping by the bakery tomorrow."

"You have another conference," she said. "A—a patient who needs you. You never turn anyone away. You're one of the kindest men—"

"Katherine," he said. "Stop. I'm not coming back in. Ever. I'm done." The words were the harshest she'd ever heard coming from Barry, but they were delivered flat, drained of life. He'd given up.

But she couldn't. "You'll be in later in the week. Wednesday or Thursday. That's fine!" Her voice rose above them, a shrill bird on wing. "I'll take your dollar from you, but I won't put it in the register. I never put your money in the register or deposit it in the bank. Did you know that? I put it in the safe, in its own separate envelope." She held her hands together, as if she were gathering together the stack of dollar bills. Between them, her hands formed the shape of a heart. "I keep your envelope with everything that's precious to me."

Barry drew in a breath, and he took a step back, back toward her door.

"Don't leave me," she said.

"This," Barry said, "from the woman who left me."

On the day she'd delivered the divorce news, instead of heading to a bar and a stranger's bed, she should've gone back into their house. She should've taken off her clothes, every means of concealing herself, and given herself to Barry. She should've changed her mind.

Was it ever too late to redeem yourself?

Katherine made herself hold Barry's gaze. She absorbed every bit of anger emanating from his body. She owed him that much. She owed him so much love.

Barry's chin dimpled, his anger softening to sadness. Less than a flicker, but she'd seen it. She'd seen the opening, and she stepped into the space. She threw her arms around him, fingers splayed against his shoulders. She inhaled the starch of his shirt, the warmth of his body. She listened to his breathing, the steady thump-bump of his heart beneath her ear. Then his arms unhinged from his sides and wrapped around her, solid and strong and hers, and they rocked.

A pressure started in her chest, rose through her throat, and thrummed through her closed lips. "Hmm, hmm, hmm, hmm . . ."

Barry kept his hands on her arms and pulled away from her, but his lips were smiling. "Huh?"

This wasn't the way Celeste and Zach played the game. "Let me try again. Hmm, hmm, hmm. Hmm—"

Barry pressed his lips to hers, sending a wicked shock through the center of her body. She raked her fingers along his chest, firmer than years ago, and along the biceps that could lift her onto him. She plunged her hand into his hair that needed a trim, fondled the soft curls. She tasted the tongue that spoke of positivity and healing, the kiss long and slow and taking its sweet time. Then she rested her forehead against his and hummed the song a third time. "Crowded House," she said. "'Don't Dream It's Over.'"

Her conservative shrink ex-husband lifted the back of her

skirt, grabbed her ass with both hands, and pulled her against her second-favorite part of his anatomy. Her most favorite part was his mind. He slipped his hand into her panties. His fingers followed the contours of her body, rediscovering all her soft, warm places. "Does this feel like it's over?" Barry asked, his voice as husky and sure as when he'd posed the question earlier tonight.

She pressed herself against him until he groaned. "This," she said, "feels like heaven."

"Tell me if you want me to stop."

"Just for a minute." She stripped off everything except the black boots, took Barry by the hand, and led him into her bedroom.

In the middle of the room, he worked his way down her body until her head swam, her legs trembled, and she pulled away. Barry sat down on the edge of her bed. "Ready to come back home?" he asked, the first words he'd ever spoken to her.

She took a condom from her lingerie drawer, right where she kept them beside her bedside box of tarot cards. She unbuttoned his shirt, unzipped his pants, and shoved him back onto her bed. Barry landed with a laugh, a beautiful man splayed across her midnight-blue-and-gold quilt. "God, I've missed you." His eyes blinked up at her, as though he might cry.

Katherine kissed his forehead, his cheeks, his chin. Five kisses, ten. A million kisses wouldn't have been enough.

Not half as much as I've missed you.

She unfurled the condom and climbed on top of him, jolting her body and confirming the tarot's promise of the return of lost love.

Hers to lose.

CHAPTER 17

If Celeste was going to be perfectly honest, her first love hadn't been Justin but food. Specifically, ice cream. Because years before her mother had taught her how to bake cakes and cookies and roll out pie crusts, she'd learned how to make frozen confections all by herself.

When Celeste was eight years old, her mother had taken her to the Hidden Harbor Library tag sale. There they'd walked past the gently used Barbie dolls and ragged Chinese jump ropes, the piles of oversized arcade teddy bears. The thickened half-full bottles of pink and purple sparkly nail polishes she'd picked up and then put back down. Nothing had really spoken her name until her gaze fell upon a battered electric ice-cream maker.

"Celeste," Zach said. "Tell me again why you don't want any ice cream." He was standing behind her in the apartment, no more than four feet away.

Wasn't it obvious?

She had her head buried in the refrigerator, her fat ass hanging out in the kitchen, her jeans so tight that they should probably pick out a china pattern and make an honest woman of her. She was putting away the last of the groceries. Yoplait yogurts and McIntosh apples, a loaf of low-fat, whole wheat sandwich bread and skim milk. At Shaw's, she'd considered the iceberg lettuce and then set the whitish head back on the shelf. She couldn't get it up for something so pale and tasteless.

She could always get it up for ice cream.

Celeste straightened the blueberry yogurts so they lined up with the strawberry and shut the refrigerator door. She pushed her hair away from her face and over her shoulders. "I ate a couple slices of bread and an apple on the way back." She'd really only eaten a single slice of bread. And the apple, she'd given up on after sinking her teeth into a brown spot.

"I wouldn't call that dinner," Zach said. "I'd barely call that a snack. In fact, just hearing about your snack makes me hungry."

"Again?" Celeste asked. She'd avoided Zach's dinner offer by making a run for Shaw's, leaving Zach to dine alone on roast chicken, baked potato, and green beans. From the looks of it—the dishes he'd washed and stacked and the lack of leftovers—he'd done fine without her. The lingering dinner smells made her stomach cramp around her single slice of bread and mealy bite of apple.

"I'm a growing boy." Zach slid a bottle of whipped cream from the refrigerator door, gave the bottle a shake, tilted his head back, and pointed the nozzle into his mouth. *Shhwp.* The aroma of sugar and cream spiked the air. "Want some?" he asked, and his voice came out garbled.

Yes. "No."

Zach cocked his head and offered her a frown of disbelief. "More for me," he said, and he gave himself another shot.

"Don't waste it!"

Zach swished the cream around in his mouth. "The way I see it, you're the one who's wasting it." He raised the canister a third time.

Celeste grabbed his arm. "We're saving it for sundaes!"

Zach lowered his arm and gave her an abbreviated version

of Barry's waggling eyebrows. "Now you're talking." He set the canister down and took a jar of hot fudge from the fridge. Not homemade—nothing compared to homemade hot fudge, whipped cream, and ice cream—but a solid, drool-worthy second best.

"I didn't say I wanted one now."

Zach reached beneath the sink and took out a small saucepan. "Are you trying to lose weight?"

He thought she needed to lose weight. He'd noticed the size of her ass. Everyone noticed—

"Because you totally do not need to lose weight." Zach unscrewed the hot fudge jar and spooned it into the pan. "Your body is . . ."

"Sturdy?" Celeste asked, using the term she'd heard her mother use around her twelfth birthday. Between eleven and twelve, her calorie intake had stayed pretty much the same and she'd packed on fifteen pounds.

"I was going to say svelte."

That sounded like a word Barry would use.

Zach lit the burner.

Celeste turned the dial from medium to low. If he was going to make it, he might as well make it right. "Seriously? My ass is not svelte."

Zach looked her in the eye, as if he'd previously memorized the body part under discussion. "That," he said, "I'd describe as shapely."

Right, because round was a shape.

The aroma of the heating fudge ramped up her pulse at the base of her throat, the intermittent low warning of a fat detector. "A hot fudge sundae contains, like, two thousand calories. More than most people need for their entire daily calorie intake."

Did she just say that out loud?

Shut up, eating-disorder Ed. You are a freaking kill joy.

If she ate an ice-cream sundae, her so-called shapely ass

would grow two sizes rounder. Her thighs would do that wiggle-jiggle thing when she walked. And she'd lose her waistline. She'd look—

"Why are you trying to starve yourself?" Zach stirred the hot fudge. His facial expression betrayed a mild curiosity. But she still heard the unspoken end to his sentence: *to death*.

She let out a nervous laugh. "I'm not trying to starve myself."

"Those anorexic, skinny models in magazines—I don't like them. Their faces are all . . ." Zach sucked his cheeks into his mouth till his lips puckered. He put a hand on his hip, slid an annoyed gaze to the side. Then he became Zach again, normal. Well, close enough. "You're much prettier."

Did Zach just say *anorexic?* No one, not even Abby, had dared use that word in Celeste's presence. They might've thought it, but no one had dared to say it out loud.

She loved Zach for it. She hated him for it, too.

"I'm not trying to impress you." Celeste stared at Zach until his spoon stilled in the saucepan.

"Fair enough," he said, and he turned off the heat.

"And I have no interest in trying to look like a model."

"Yeah, you don't seem like the type," he said.

"What type do I seem like?" Her voice betrayed nothing more than mild curiosity. Her voice was a liar.

Zach twisted his lips to one side and lowered his gaze. "The type that's fun to be around. The type I like to be around."

Except for when it came to watching her try to starve herself to death. Zach didn't say it, but he didn't have to.

One at a time, he got two blue bowls from the cabinet and set them on the counter. He got the pecans from the cabinet on the other side of the kitchen. He took the coffee ice cream from the freezer.

"I could eat two ice-cream sundaes," Celeste said. "I could sit my ass on the sticky couch every night and eat until my eyes rolled up in my head and the button on my jeans popped and ricocheted off the walls."

"My kind of girl."

"If I did that every night, I'd get obese. Do you like enormous women?"

"Do you like coffee ice-cream sundaes?"

Celeste's head ached, the dull throb she got when she wasn't eating enough. When she was doing really badly, the sensation made her feel vaguely superior to others—those people who couldn't control their appetites. She didn't feel superior today. She felt hungry.

"I love coffee ice-cream sundaes." A warm flush washed over her, as if she'd told Zach she loved hot sex.

She did, but she wasn't about to tell him.

"One sundae isn't going to hurt you." Zach fished around in the utensil drawer. He clamped the ice-cream carton between his cast and the refrigerator door and used his left hand to pry off the lid, revealing the smooth, beige surface.

Celeste rubbed the back of her neck and bit her lip, as though they were about to have hot sex.

"You okay?"

She was going to want more ice cream. She'd finish the sundae and then sneak into the kitchen and polish off the rest of the carton, standing over the sink.

Shut up, Ed.

Celeste nodded and took a slow breath.

Zach scooped ice cream into the bowls. "This one's yours," he said, pointing to the bowl with one scoop. He ladled hot fudge over the ice cream and squirted two reasonable towers of whipped cream. He sprinkled the pecans and added spoons. "What do you say we sit our shapely asses down on the sticky couch and eat our faces off?"

"Sounds good," Celeste said, and they carried their bowls into the living room.

Zach took his bed pillow and tossed it onto the chair. The yellow blanket he shoved to the side. Instead of flicking on the TV, he angled toward her and dug into his sundae. He grinned and rolled his eyes up in his head. He lifted his T-shirt from where it covered the button of his jeans, revealing an innie belly button and a flat stomach with a bit of dark hair. She imagined laying her head on his stomach. She imagined his stomach solid and warm beneath her cheek. She imagined moving her head lower. "What do you know?" Zach asked. "Button's still there."

Celeste could watch Zach eat all day. The way he licked his lips, sighed, and went back for more. She considered herself a kind of food voyeur.

Zach took another bite, pointed his spoon in her direction. "Don't waste it," he said.

Celeste slid her spoon in the side, made sure to take a sample of everything. A mini-sundae in one spoonful slid into her mouth. Sweet, light whipped cream. Thick, rich hot fudge. Cold, creamy coffee. And the salty crunch of pecans.

"What's the verdict?" Zach asked.

"So good!" Her eyes really and truly rolled up in her head, and a shiver ran across her shoulders and down her thighs, as if she were having an orgasm.

She wasn't about to share that thought with Zach.

Zach's grin wrapped her like a hug. "I'm glad you're enjoying yourself," he said. Without looking down, he dug into the sundae, not seeming to care whether he got equal amounts of ingredients in each bite. The spoon slid from his mouth with a smooth mound of ice cream.

Celeste took another carefully planned bite.

Zach considered his spoon, turned it over, slid it back into his mouth, and scraped the remaining ice cream off with his teeth. "Everyone in my family loves to eat. Even my mother.

Especially my mother. But then she does this annoying girl thing."

"Excuse me," Celeste said, her voice garbled, her mouth full of yum. "You're generalizing my gender!"

"Maybe I am, maybe I'm not. We'll get done eating something awesome. She'll seem like she's enjoying herself. And then she goes and mumbles about how she's going to regret what she's eaten in the morning. It's not even like she wants us to say anything to her. It's like she needs to talk to herself, to make it okay she's eaten."

Zach's mother needed to alleviate her guilt.

Zach took another bite, rubbed his belly, and put on a cartoon girly voice. "Boy, that sure was tasty. Not that I needed the extra calories."

The thing about stereotypes? Sometimes they were true.

Celeste wasn't going to share that thought with Zach either. "When I, uh, get worried about food, I'm supposed to talk to myself."

Zach stuffed his face, squinted at her sideways.

"It's called self-talk." Celeste envisioned a female shrink's office. She remembered curling up on the shrink's stereotypical couch and the nonstereotypical shrink with the dyed red hair and henna tattoos telling her to fight back. "So, a long time ago, I went to a stress management psychiatric type person, and she said when I had thoughts about food that made me nervous, I should talk back to them. I could even call the wrong thoughts Ed."

"Ed?"

"Um, yeah." Celeste's jeans pressed into her stomach, a sure sign the ice cream was going straight to her waist. Screw it. Why should Zach have all the fun? She took another bite and lowered her gaze to the sundae. "*Ed* stands for 'eating disorder.'" Celeste made her face go dead serious and she tried imitating the voice of that long-ago shrink. "'You know that's not true.

Celeste is not a big, fat pig.' " She was trying for the lightening lift of humor. Instead, her little comedy routine weighted her down.

"How's that working out?" Zach asked.

"Decent," she said. "As long as I remember to fight." She looked at Zach. "Sometimes I get tired and I need a little help."

"Like someone who says"—Zach slipped back into his cartoon girly voice—" 'Celeste is not a big, fat pig. She's a scorching hot babe. Not that she's trying to impress Zach or anything.' "

Celeste cracked up. "Sort of. I'm not sure about the female voice. You might want to stick with your own."

"Made you smile, though, didn't I? And look how great you're doing with that sundae." Zach's voice went high, naturally, the way you sounded when you were excited about another person's success.

Celeste scraped the bowl and licked the spoon, like when she was eight years old. Twelve. Fifteen. She wanted to throw her arms around Zach and bury his face in kisses. She wanted to give him more. "I know it's wrong, but I think if only I can get to such and such weight, I'll be happier. Or when I can fit back into jeans I haven't worn in years, everything will be . . . more manageable. But when I'm, you know, not doing so well and I get to a certain weight, I change the goal. I can be what you'd call superambitious, when it comes to competing against myself."

"Why not just decide to be happy now?"

"Because Ed's superambitious, too?" she asked.

Zach set his empty bowl on the coffee table and leaned closer. He smelled like coffee and cream and all kinds of yum. He smelled like Zach. "Tell Ed I said he should fuck off."

Celeste's pulse delivered a solid punch to the center of her chest, as if her heart wanted to break through and embrace Zach, too. "I'll do that," she said, and her lips trembled into a smile. "With the exception of that one stress specialist person, I've never really discussed my . . . eating thing with anyone before."

Zach gave her a good, long stare. "What about Katherine?"

Celeste made a *pfft* sound. "No way." She thought about the conversation she'd had with Katherine last night and how close she'd come to revealing her latest screwup.

At least Katherine and Barry seemed to be getting it together. First thing this morning, Barry had strolled into Lamontagne's with a huge grin on his face, looking as if he were about to vault over the bakery counter and jump Katherine. When Celeste had asked if he wanted a cup of coffee, he'd said, "No thanks," and hummed Squeeze's "Black Coffee in Bed."

Katherine had whacked Barry over the head with a baguette.

"Your best friend, Abby?" Zach asked.

Celeste shook her head. She was a terrible friend. Despite the pinkie swear promise to call, she hadn't spoken to Abby since the Hidden Harbor Harvest Festival. Celeste couldn't get herself to support the Abby-Charlie reunion.

Even for Abby, Celeste couldn't fake it.

She could sympathize with the way Barry must've felt when a court had granted Katherine their divorce. She could imagine showing up on Abby's doorstep every morning for a cup of coffee and a second chance.

She couldn't imagine that going over well with Charlie.

"Abby helped me eat, but we more like talked around the eating disorder." Celeste drew a circle in the air. "We never used the word *anorexia*." When Zach met her gaze and his mouth fell slack, Celeste swallowed and blinked at the ceiling. She took a slow, deep breath, the way Zach had taught her.

Zach sucked his lips into his mouth and shook his head. "I lied to you. I didn't go for a beer run last night."

"You didn't?"

"Nope."

"But you bought beer," Celeste said, her voice getting high and tight. Her mind flashed on the night her mother had told her she and her father were selling their house and moving to Florida. "But you love it here," Celeste had said, as if anyone needed a reminder of who, or what, they loved.

Was Zach planning on leaving Hidden Harbor, too?

Zach tried for a grin, but it looked more like an apology. "Drove to the state liquor store, after I stopped by Barry's house."

"Why were you at Barry's?"

"I wanted to talk to Barry about how I could help you with your eating thing. The anorexia," he said, getting way too comfortable with the term.

Zach had sneaked off to hold a powwow with shrink Barry to try to figure out how to get her to stop making herself sick.

Celeste kind of loved Zach for that. She kind of hated him for it, too.

"Anything else you've lied to me about? Anything you'd like to get off your chest?"

Zach crossed his ankle on his left thigh. He raised and lowered his left leg four times, thudding his heel against the rug. Zach gave his body a half rock. He scrunched up his mouth, as if he were working on another squirt of whipped cream. His gaze dropped to his sling and then came back to her eyes. "I'm somewhat color-blind."

"No way! Katherine's color-blind, too. She's the only woman—"

"I think I'm Katherine's biological son."

Celeste blinked. She tugged at her earlobe, as though to clear post-swim water. "Katherine doesn't have a son. She and Barry tried for years. They went through three rounds of IVF. She had to give herself shots, but they never took. . . ." Twenty-four years ago, Katherine and Barry hadn't even known each other. Katherine would've been new to town. She would've been Celeste's age. She could've given away a son. That son could've been Zach.

"Surely you can't be serious," Celeste said, but Zach wasn't taking the classic movie bait. And he'd never looked more serious. "Why do you think Katherine is your mother?"

Zach said something about a registry and nonidentifying information. He babbled about traveling from town to town and bakery to bakery and then chickening out on the follow-through. He told Celeste his birth date.

Celeste thought about the way Zach and Katherine stared at each other and how she'd mistaken their odd familiarity for a May-September crush. Last night, she'd even sensed that Katherine didn't want Barry and Zach getting too chummy.

Could Katherine have given away a son and not told Barry? Could giving away a son have fueled her desperation for having a baby? She'd made herself into one stressed and obsessed pincushion. Trying to conceive, unsuccessfully, had put a strain on Katherine and Barry's marriage and led to their divorce.

". . . so I'm, like, ninety-nine percent sure Katherine is my birth mother."

"Do-do-do-do. Do-do-do-do," Celeste said.

"Yeah. *Twilight Zone,* all the way."

Celeste set her bowl on the coffee table and edged closer to Zach. "Let me get this straight. You've never discussed this with Katherine? You ate your way clean across Casco Bay and managed to get Katherine to give you a job. But you're too much of a fraidy cat to ask her if she's ever given up a kid for adoption?"

Zach's hand fidgeted the cowlick that flopped across his forehead, a close cousin to the lock of hair that escaped the front of Katherine's sculpted hairdos. Zach's features were different from Katherine's. His nose was broader where Katherine's was straight and narrow. But they both had the high cheekbones, square jaw thing going for them.

"We've sort of talked around the issue." Zach drew a circle in the air. A joke, but his lips and eyes turned down.

"That's pathetic," Celeste said, trying to tease out a smile.

Zach blinked at her, but his expression didn't change. "I know."

"Does anyone else know about you and Katherine? I mean, besides you and Katherine?"

"Nope."

"Thank you for sharing your secret with me," Celeste said. "Thank you for trusting me." *Thank you for trusting me with your heart.*

Zach leaned his left shoulder against the back of the couch, as if he needed to take a nap. "You're welcome."

Celeste nodded. "Two pathetic people like us? We kind of, sort of deserve each other." She cocked her head to the side, leaned forward, and pretended to pout. "Don't you think?" She reached up and touched his hair, ran her finger along the dark, shiny wave.

Zach went still, as if he were afraid to move.

She rose up on her knees and kissed the tip of his nose. Then she dropped a kiss onto the warm pulse of his broad forehead. She ran her fingertips along his face—jawline to chin.

Zach's gaze flicked from her eyes to her lips, but he still held his ground.

Celeste sat back down. "Don't you want to kiss me?"

"I want to do a lot more than that."

Celeste laughed. "So what's the problem?"

"As I recall, the last time we kissed, it didn't go so good. I don't want to hurt you," Zach said.

She frowned at him. Melodrama much? She'd had a panic attack, nothing life shattering. Nothing she hadn't gotten over.

She stroked his bottom lip, ran her fingertip along the center indentation. "What if we try again?"

"Celeste," Zach said, his tone pleading, as though urging her toward reason. But then his gaze softened.

"Fraidy cat," she said, into his face.

Zach gave her hair a tug, like a little boy crushing. He leaned forward, met her in the middle, and took her challenge.

His lips were ice creamy and sticky, sweet and soft against hers. Her pulse pounded, but her throat didn't close. No panic clogged her airway, like a marshmallow in a straw. No pains compressed her chest as if she were going to die.

Zach stroked her hair and he pulled away. "You okay?" he asked, and she answered him with a second kiss.

Celeste rested her hand against his chest. Zach's slow and steady kiss made her head feel heavy and light at the same time. She kind of loved Zach. She wanted to kiss him. She deserved a superhero. She deserved—

Zach smacked his lips. "Still okay?"

"Yeah," she said, and a wacky ache zipped up and down both of her arms.

"Mind if we get comfy?" he asked, and he kissed the word *sure* right from her lips.

Zach leaned forward slowly, waiting for her to adjust and lean back, until she lay on the couch, with Zach on top of her.

His chest pressed against hers, his cast in the sling between them. He swung his leg over her, and his pelvis dropped down against hers. A flush of heat washed over her, the kind you get when you're about to get sick.

Celeste stroked Zach's hair. She fisted her hand around the back of his flannel shirt collar.

Relax, it's just Zach, your superhero. Your giver of sweet, soft kisses.

Ever so slightly, her superhero ground his pelvis against hers, and everything went black.

* * *

She woke up in a darkened room with a weight on top of her. A noise sounded above her, more of a growl than a man's voice. The room spun like a merry-go-round.

"What the hell is wrong with you?" Matt asked.

They were in Matt's dorm room. They were naked. His intentions loomed above her, a gross, pink, bobbing thing wrapped in a rubber.

"Stop," she said. "I don't want to do this. I want to go home." For the first time in ages, she thought of the white picket fence house she'd grown up in, and her bedroom with the ball fringe curtains. For the first time in ages, she wanted her mother.

"Ex-fucking-cuse me?" Matt's face took shape in the dark—his straight hair unleashed from its short ponytail and falling to his shoulders, and his narrow lips, but she didn't recognize him. She didn't know him at all.

"I said no!" Her voice sounded wobbly and thin. She wriggled beneath him, her reaction time delayed, her limbs slow with alcohol. "Get off me. Get the hell off me!"

Matt stared down at her, unmoving. "It's a little late for *no.* It's a little too late to change your mind."

How could she change her mind if she'd never made a decision?

Celeste's adrenaline spiked, her body understanding what was happening, how little leverage she had, half a beat before her mind registered the urgency.

"No!" Celeste's fist connected with a satisfying, bone-cracking *thwap*.

Celeste opened her eyes.

She was in her apartment, breathing hard, sitting on her couch, and fully clothed. She squinted against the light. Her scream echoed in her head.

Zach held his left hand to his face.

Celeste's mouth was cottony. Her words sounded like pieces of paper rubbing against each other. "What just happened?"

Zach moved his hand from his face. The skin beneath his left eye glowed red with a fresh, angry bruise. But Zach, her superhero Zach, was apologizing to her. "I'm so sorry. I am so sorry," he said, his voice thick and hushed. His gaze met hers, both eyes glassy. Both eyes were wet with tears, for her. He held out his hand.

Celeste shook her head and pulled back. "Oh, no."

"Let me help you," Zach said.

A current of tremors traveled from her stomach and up her chest and down both arms. Her fingers quivered. Her jaw ached, her teeth chattering as though she'd plunged into the October-chill waters of the Atlantic.

"It's going to be okay," Zach said.

"Oh, no." Celeste stood up. She had to get out of here. She had to run somewhere, anywhere. Other girls picked up strangers at bars and got into bad situations. Other girls took shortcuts home, alone, through city alleyways and got jumped by lowlife scumbags.

Zach stood up, his hand outstretched between them. He tried to give her an encouraging smile, but his lips quivered, downturned and telling the truth.

"Oh, no," Celeste said.

Other girls got raped.

CHAPTER 18

When you realized the girl you loved had left you, you searched for her in all the obvious places first. When you realized you were in love, you never let go.

At two in the morning, Zach woke up on the sticky couch, with his legs wrapped around Celeste's two yellow blankets but no Celeste. His wrist ached from holding Celeste against him while she'd trembled. His eye socket throbbed from the punch she'd landed. His head tingled from sleep deprivation.

When you realized someone had raped the girl you loved, your heart actually hurt, as if that someone had torn your heart from your body and crushed it in his hand.

Zach wanted to go after Matt and pound his face until even Matt's mother wouldn't have recognized him. Zach wanted to punish Matt for getting away with rape.

With neither a witness nor physical evidence, a rape charge came down to a pissing match of he said, she said. And even if Celeste could manage to get sexual assault charges lobbed against Matt, any defense attorney worth his or her salt would rip Celeste apart on the stand.

Probably the reason Zach's father refused to take on rape cases.

A girl who got drunk and willingly went back to a guy's room didn't stand a chance. The rape wasn't Celeste's fault. But if Zach was going to be brutally honest, he'd have to admit he was a little irked with Celeste for ending up drunk in Matt's bed. Did that make Zach a monster, too?

For the second time in two days and without the benefit of the night sky, that feeling of being lost in time came over Zach. He wished he could go back in time to the moment when Celeste had decided to follow Matt to his room. Better yet, Zach imagined going back to that party Celeste had mentioned, where he'd rip the drink from her hands and hand her life back to her, shiny and bright as a promise ring.

Zach struggled to standing and stretched out a kink in his lower back, his body's way of complaining about sleeping on his side on the squishy couch. His father had a bad back, having thrown it out once playing baseball, another time helping a colleague move filing cabinets. Could you take on someone's physical attributes by virtue of proximity? People who didn't know Zach was adopted often claimed to see a family resemblance, their minds playing tricks on them and superimposing comfort for the truth.

He plodded into the kitchen and scanned the clean counters for new smudges and crumbs. He went to the bathroom and yanked aside the flowered shower curtain, swiped the tub with his hand and found it dry. He knocked on Celeste's bedroom door and then, heart hammering, threw the door wide. He slammed on the lights and tore the top sheet from her bed.

Out in the parking lot, without Old Yeller, Matilda looked worn and tired, the old girl belatedly showing her age.

Maybe he was being a worrywart. Two o'clock was early for Celeste's shift, but maybe she'd gone in to work on a batch of biscotti or a three-tier wedding cake or to blow off some steam. He stared into middle space, finger combing his hair, and then gave himself a shake and found Katherine's number programmed into the phone.

Katherine answered on the first ring, as if she'd been waiting for his call. When she asked what was wrong, Zach took a chance and told her about the rape. She needed to know Celeste's state. Zach needed an ally. Celeste could punch his other eye out later.

Fifteen minutes later, Zach and Katherine met at the door to Lamontagne's. He'd tossed a hoodie over his flannel, but he shivered in the night air. Katherine turned the key in the door. She squinted beneath the lights. "What happened to your eye?"

Zach squinted back at her, only his squint was lopsided. "Celeste."

"Did you deserve it?"

"Not really."

Katherine's dark eyes glowed, bloodshot, as if she'd been crying for Celeste. Katherine glanced down at Zach's sling and then brought her gaze back to his shiner. She shook her head. "This town is bad for your health."

For the first time since the shiner, Zach grinned. "Tell me about it."

Inside the kitchen, the counters were squeaky clean. Blake had washed, dried, and put away every last dish, pot, pan, and mixing bowl.

A seam of light seeped from around the closed stockroom door. Katherine and Celeste's blackboard to-do list, usually propped by the door, lay on its side. Katherine opened the stockroom door. Rolling ladder, bins, shelves stacked with canned goods and mason jars, chest freezer and marble worktable. Same as the kitchen, nothing was out of place.

When Katherine went into the room, Zach intended to right the blackboard. Instead, he discovered the to-do list erased from Celeste's column and a note taking its place:

Forgot something in New York. Be back tomorrow. ☺ *C.*

Zach's left eyelid ticked. The smiley face made him want to puke.

Inside the stockroom, Katherine was on her knees before the skirted worktable, as if she'd read his mind.

Zach thought of the Arlington Unitarian church, the voices rising up in prayer, and offered up the prayer first spoken by his mother: *Find her.* Then he added a prayer of his own: *Save Celeste.*

Katherine lifted the skirt, bent her head beneath the worktable, and riffled through something Zach couldn't see. "Celeste left us a note," he told the back of Katherine's head. "She's gone to New York." Zach thought of the right hook Celeste had landed and the man she'd intended to punch.

The man Celeste meant to punish. "She's gone after him," Zach said.

"*Merde,*" Katherine said, the first time Zach had heard her speak a word of French. The cussing didn't bother him, but the inflection was hushed and understated, similar to the way Celeste had said, "Oh, no," last night, right before she'd collapsed in his arms. In the warm, closed space, Katherine's inflection shot a web of shivers up the back of Zach's head.

Zach got down on his knees beside Katherine.

A two-foot-by-two-foot metal safe sat beneath the worktable. Its combination door swung wide.

"She got into the safe," Katherine said.

"Celeste would never steal money from you," Zach said, even as his mind wondered how much money she'd have in her pocketbook and whether, in her state of mind, she could've borrowed from the till.

Katherine turned to Zach, her eyes widened, as though a

cold blast of air had shot her in the face. "She didn't steal money from me. She borrowed my loaded gun."

"Oh, shit," Zach said.

"Exactly. She's going to kill the son of a bitch." Katherine's eyes watered and she rolled her lips into her mouth, but she almost sounded glad about it. Her voice rose an octave, as though she'd announced the daily bread on special.

"Let's hope not," Zach said, but a tiny corner of his mind imagined Celeste getting away with murder. A tiny corner of his mind hoped for vengeance.

He was better than his worst thought.

Katherine threw him a look. "I know we can't let her. We'll have to call ahead, of course, let the school know—"

"What?" Zach asked. "That a girl hell-bent on revenge is coming after one of their students with a loaded gun? The school would call the police. The police would be waiting for her. . . ." Zach's mind unspooled the scenario. He imagined Celeste bursting into a classroom or—this one made him sick—Matt's dorm room. He imagined men in blue just doing their jobs and taking Celeste into custody, instead of the rapist. God bless the American justice system for believing a person was innocent unless you could prove him guilty in a court of law.

Usually that thought came around *without* a generous helping of sarcasm.

"I don't think Celeste is capable of murder," Zach said, his statement not sounding as sure as he'd intended. Who knew what another person was capable of when pushed to the brink? Right now Zach wouldn't trust himself near Matt with a loaded gun and a clear shot.

"I'm going after her," Zach said.

"*We're* going after her."

The phrase, *Surely you can't be serious,* played in his head, churning out an image of Celeste so crisp he half-expected her to appear in the doorway, wearing her starched apron and sarcastic grin.

"What? It's my gun," Katherine said. As if Zach would believe Katherine cared anything for material goods.

"You know, maybe you shouldn't have given her the combo to your safe." Zach knew he wasn't being fair, but there, he'd said it anyway. Yeah, hindsight sounded like an angry, finger-pointing thirteen-year-old boy. The one that lived inside him.

"I didn't," Katherine said. "I was wondering how she figured it out myself," she said, her expression a cross between an open question and an accusation.

Typically, people chose the most obvious combinations for their safes. Their wedding anniversary, their birthday, their spouse's birthday, or—number one on the list—the birth date of one of their children.

Zach's ears clogged, same as when Matilda crested a hill faster than his body could adjust to the altitude.

He closed the door to the safe and spun the dial to reset the lock. He turned the dial twice to the right and fit the black notch of number 1 against the white indicator. He turned the wheel twice to the left and stopped on 1 a second time. From behind him, Katherine took an audible breath. His skin warmed. His pulse pinched his eardrums.

He could stop right now, leave the lock, hit the road with Katherine, and continue to circle the issue of his identity. Inside Zach's head, Celeste called him a fraidy cat. Zach glanced over his shoulder, and Katherine nodded for him to continue. Slowly, Zach turned the wheel to the right—past 90, past 80, all the way to 76.

He turned the handle and opened the door.

Instead of his pulse doing a crazy dance, the pounding slowed and settled. He breathed into his stomach and turned to face Katherine.

Zach might be a fraidy cat, but he'd done his research. Before leaving Arlington, he'd stopped at the library. He'd researched adoptee reunion scripts. He'd read about breaking the news to the birth mother gently. He'd absorbed the importance of not acting too fast and scaring her away.

Maybe he'd taken the advice too much to heart. "I know this might come as a shock to you," he said. "But does the date January 1, 1976, mean anything to you?"

Katherine's expression didn't change. She looked numb, but tears flowed from her eyes, spilling down her cheeks. She didn't bother wiping them away. She didn't even seem to notice. "I'm so sorry, Zach. I was afraid I wouldn't make a very good mother. What I told you about my family . . . I'm still trying to figure out. I came from such a horrible place. I didn't want to hurt you. I've never wanted to hurt you. I only wanted you to be happy."

"I'm happy to hear that," Zach said, his voice suddenly formal and shy with a woman he'd known for weeks. A woman he'd grown to care for and respect.

Katherine wiped the tears from her face with the palms of her hands. "Do you want to see something?" She tucked her hair behind one ear, hunched in the safe. Something plastic looking poked from her fisted hand. Two somethings. She handed them to Zach.

Lamontagne, Katherine was printed across the longer, thicker plastic strip, a hospital ID bracelet. On a tiny ID bracelet, someone had handwritten *Baby Boy Lamontagne.* Zach laid the bracelet across his wrist.

"You wear it around your ankle." Katherine laughed and covered her mouth. "Wore it around your ankle. Hard to imagine . . ."

"Not for you."

"No," she said, "I haven't forgotten a thing. Every single

day since I gave you away—" Katherine took a shaky breath. "I've regretted it."

Zach handed the bracelets back to Katherine. "Don't."

"Don't cry or don't regret it?"

"Both, I guess."

Katherine rubbed the ID bracelets between her fingers, the way Zach worried his St. Anthony token to find his center. "Your middle name, the one you despise so?" Katherine said. "That was my doing, the name I put on your original birth certificate. I named you after my mother, Francesca. Your parents are incredibly generous to have kept that name. I imagine they're wonderful parents."

"They are," Zach said. "At the moment, sorry to say, they're not exactly thrilled with me. My dad—he hoped I'd follow in his footsteps to Harvard Law. I'm kind of a big disappointment." Zach thought of the way, ten years ago, his father had responded to his phone call and picked him up in Harvard Square. Bleary-eyed and slack-skinned, Everett Fitzgerald had looked worse for wear than Zach. But his father hadn't even yelled at him. Everett had told Zach to get in the car. Then his father had locked the car doors, hung his head, and sobbed.

That had felt so much worse than getting yelled at.

"In my limited experience with childbearing," Katherine said, "when you have a child, you might wonder what they'll choose for a career. You might even dream about it. But hope—you just hope they're happy."

"I guess," Zach said.

"Have you and your dad sat down and discussed the whole law school issue?"

"We've sort of talked around it." Zach drew a circle in the air.

"This circling thing"—Katherine drew her own circle in the air—"has a limited appeal. I strongly suggest you and your dad hash it out."

"I might just do that."

"I might hold you to it."

Katherine stared at him, and he thought she might start crying again. "We should get going."

Zach got up from the floor and then he offered his hand and helped Katherine to standing. Even though she was wearing boots with a heel, he towered over her. With her hair down, he could easily imagine her as a woman of twenty-two, alone in the world, adrift without a family to ground her. How would he have turned out if he hadn't had the Fitzgeralds? How would he have turned out if he hadn't been ridiculously loved? Why else would they have put up with his childish crap?

"Okay if I give you a hug?" Katherine asked.

"Of course," Zach said, and he hugged her first. She radiated warmth through her thin blouse. Her embrace felt strangely familiar, as if somehow he remembered being an infant in her arms.

For the third time in two days, that feeling of being adrift in time came over Zach. Only this time, he didn't fantasize about going back in time to change history. He didn't imagine himself as an adult Zach who'd walk into the young Katherine's hospital room and tell her not to make the biggest mistake of her life and give him away.

This time, if Zach could go back in time, he wouldn't change anything at all.

By the time the sun rose over the Mass Pike, Katherine had watched Zach inhale four biscotti, three lemon bars, and half a dozen sugar cookies. Then his stomach had growled, as though he were just getting started.

Katherine had polished off the remaining pastry—a plain croissant—and a small black coffee. Her left leg ached heel to hip, the sciatica by-product of standing on her feet for decades. She was seriously contemplating letting Zach drive her Outback the rest of the way to New York. Besides that, she was blushing, painfully, like a woman caught enjoying herself with a man she'd barely known.

"So what did you say his last name was?" Zach asked, referring to his biological father.

"I didn't," Katherine said. "But he told me it was Bell."

"Adam Bell," Zach said, adding his father's first and last names together and seeming to come to some conclusion. "Anything else? Where's he from?"

"I got the feeling he was from somewhere in New England. That he was in the early phases of his journey."

"Basing this feeling on anything concrete?"

Here Katherine grinned. "I consulted neither the tarot nor a crystal ball."

Zach chuckled.

"I don't know. It was so long ago. . . . His accent or lack of a discernible accent? His level of enthusiasm? You know how you're excited at the beginning of a trip, but then as the realities of the road make themselves evident, you lose steam?" Katherine flexed her left foot until the ache receded.

"But you have no clue where Adam was headed."

"Of that, I have no idea."

The sun peeked over the horizon, washing out the road. Katherine and Zach flipped down their sun visors.

"If I'd known where he was going, I promise you, I would've contacted him." Katherine's throat tightened. A question she was sensing from Zach or one she needed to answer for herself? She glanced at Zach, but his expression betrayed little. Side view, he looked nothing like her or Adam. He only looked like himself.

Himself with an eye socket that had gotten in the way of Celeste's fist.

"Not to hold him to any sort of responsibility, mind you," Katherine added. "Just because he had a right to know about you."

Zach nodded and drummed on the glove compartment with one fist.

Katherine turned on the radio to static and then turned it off.

"I bet I could find him," Zach said. "I bet I could track down Adam Bell."

The back bumper of a sedan came into view before Katherine, and she slowed. "I bet you could, if that's what you need. I bet you'd make a great detective. After all, you found me," Katherine said, thinking of Zach eating his way across the bakeries of Casco Bay in search of a baker who'd lived there twenty-four years ago. She hoped he'd one day tell the story to his children. She hoped she'd one day *know* his children.

That brought Katherine to Celeste and the reason Katherine had thus far delayed stopping for gas and giving her one-armed, squinty-eyed friend Zach the wheel. Even if they drove into Underhill, New York, on engine fumes, even though they couldn't be certain when Celeste had left or if they had a chance in hell of getting to the campus of Culinary America ahead of her, they had to try. They had to keep going.

Two hours ago, by mutual consent, they'd both agreed not to freak out about Celeste until they neared the campus. So far, they'd been mostly successful.

"I bet," Zach said, his tone playful, "I could locate your parents for you, if you're interested. Where did you say you grew up?"

"Stoughton," she said, the word sounding hushed, like a guilty confession. Like something you hid behind a closed door and a locked safe. Like something you hid away so you wouldn't frighten yourself. There was nothing wrong with the town. Anywhere she'd lived with her father would've been hell.

"Yeah, Stoughton. Have you gotten in touch with your mother since you left?"

"No, I have not."

Zach drummed again on her glove box. His way, Katherine surmised, of organizing his thoughts. "Then how do you know they don't still live there?"

"Oh. Hmm." Again Katherine blushed, reduced to a small, helpless child. Or an unloved teenager.

On the day she'd left the cottage her family rented, it was raining. The good, pounding kind of rain that worked wonders to calm her father. The good, pounding kind of rain that softened the dirt beneath the tires of his pickup. The good, pounding kind of rain that covered up a multitude of sins.

Katherine's pulse echoed in her stomach, the backbeat of guilt. She'd already told Zach so much—about her angry father, about the mother she'd tried to protect. Was a lie by omission still a big, fat lie if you altered the details to protect someone they might hurt, even if that someone was you?

As if keeping the truth to herself had ever done her any good.

Zach touched his hand to her shoulder. "Sorry, if you don't want to talk about it."

Just like that day, her life pounded in her ears, loud and echoing, as she'd torn through the house and discovered her parents' bed stripped and the kitchen cupboards bare. The driveway empty, save for mud ruts and tire tracks.

"She left me," Katherine said.

"What was that?" Zach had been drumming again. He hadn't even heard.

Katherine laughed. Sometimes she felt as though the universe was working against her and she was a cosmic, ironic punch line. Other times, like now for instance, she felt like the universe was simply urging her to speak up. Or maybe it was merely the road trip, the experience of once again finding herself speeding down a highway, unhinged from everything she called home.

"My mother and my father," Katherine said. "They left me. They left my home before I did. I was nineteen years old, and I woke up one day and they were gone. After years of trying to get my mother to leave my father. After making myself stay to watch over her, she made her decision. She chose my father over me. She chose him." Katherine shrugged, and her seat belt dug into her shoulder, a sensation she welcomed. She pressed down on the accelerator and eased into the passing lane. The image of Francesca Lamontagne made her want to aim the front end of her Subaru at the nearest November-bare tree. The thought of her mother made her grateful for the seat belt holding her together.

Her father's words played in her head: *You're going to be sorry.*

And people called Katherine the fortune-teller.

"And that, Zachary Frank, is one of two secrets I've kept close to my heart for decades."

Zach dug into the pocket of his sweatshirt. He gave her a sad smile and passed her a napkin. "I think it's, like, mostly clean."

Katherine laughed. "Keep it. I think I, like, mostly don't need it." She swiped at a renegade tear. "Mostly."

Zach patted her arm and left the napkin on her leg.

Katherine checked her rearview, made out the bleached forms that were cars, and eased into the middle lane.

Zach took a sip of coffee and drummed on the glove box. "How do you know it wasn't your mother's idea to take off on you?"

Katherine glanced at Zach. He was peering into the empty bakery bag, guileless, as if he might find a sugar cookie or lemon bar he'd previously overlooked. "That's not very nice," Katherine said.

"What if it was very nice? What if it was the nicest thing

your mother ever did for you?" Zach asked, his voice garbled. The corner of a sugar cookie peeked out from his fist.

She was certain he'd eaten all six.

"Would you have hung around?" Zach asked. "Would you have stayed as long as you did, without your mother?"

"Of course not. The plan, if you could call it a plan, was to stay until I could convince my mother to leave him. I couldn't leave her with a monster. I couldn't leave . . ." Katherine was the only thing keeping the full force of her father's tirades from her mother, a barrier island preventing storms from eroding the shoreline. Katherine wasn't blushing. There was nothing to be embarrassed about, nothing to raise shame-faced heat to her cheeks. But her underarms itched with perspiration, the sheer fabric of her blouse sticking to her body. And her chest didn't feel right, her pulse picking up speed for no good reason.

Zach waved a lemon bar in the air. He'd eaten all three. At least she'd thought he'd eaten all three. Had she seen him with the same lemon bar three times? "I bet your mother knew you wouldn't leave without her."

"That could be true."

"I bet she felt like she couldn't leave your father."

"Sure . . ."

Zach gulped his coffee. He cleared his throat. "Don't you see? Your mother didn't just leave with your father, your mother got your father away from you." Zach smacked his hand against his chest, and crumbs rained onto his lap, like a confetti celebration.

"Maybe . . ." Katherine said. What if her mother had convinced her father to leave behind the house and the bills, the overdue rent and Katherine? What if, after years of Katherine holding her mother's hand and telling her she shouldn't put up with Katherine's father's drinking and yelling, his anger looking for a reason, her mother had found her voice and spoken up, not for her benefit but for Katherine's? What if her mother had loved Katherine so much that she'd sacrificed their relationship and instead given Katherine her only chance for happiness? After all, that's what Katherine had done for Zach.

For twenty-seven years, Katherine had been focused on her father's words, the supposed harbinger of doom. *You're going to be sorry.* What if for the past twenty-seven years, she'd focused on the wrong thing?

"Something's in the road up ahead," Zach said.

The sun spiked off something metallic and black. "I see it." Katherine checked the rearview. A van was coming up fast on her left, a sedan close behind. On her right, another SUV paced her.

"Hold on." Katherine dug her nails into the steering wheel, held to her lane, and kept her foot steady on the accelerator.

Sometimes there was no getting around the one thing you were trying to avoid.

Celeste made a point of avoiding the elevator.

She'd spent the last six hours in Old Yeller. Six hours to drive through the night and across five states and then watch the sun wink between the last mottled-brown leaves clinging to the maple trees that dotted the campus of Culinary America. In the last six hours she'd made up her mind, and un–made up her mind, at least half a dozen times. Now was the time to get off her numb ass and get moving.

She gave Old Yeller a final love pat, rebraided her hair to keep it out of the way, tucked her decision in the deep pocket of her sweatshirt, and pressed the metal shape into her belly. Then she closed the glove compartment and headed through the damp air to the back entrance of Cunningham Hall. Matt's dorm. A student had wedged a cinder block between the heavy door and the frame. One less door for Celeste to deal with. One less crime for her to commit. She slipped into the building and took the first step.

The stairwell stank of industrial cleaner, with a secondary note of low-pile carpeting. She breathed through her mouth and thought instead of the tall grass that had tickled her bare legs on early morning outings with her big brother Lincoln. They'd slipped behind their mother's lilac bushes and followed the path through dense hardwoods, until it spilled out at their family's shooting range.

By the second floor, her ass was regaining feeling, the movement bringing her body back to life, exactly as she'd intended. Too early for the sounds of student life. No footsteps tapped across the carpeted hallways, no water shushing through pipes or pummeling the shower floors. Just the sound of her pulse and the weight of her decision.

She wasn't certain how this was going to end, only that it would.

She thought of Zach and Katherine opening Lamontagne's without her. She even thought of Barry, who never gave up, stopping by the bakery to get an eyeful of Katherine. But mostly, Celeste's guilt led her to Lincoln. She'd liked the way the grass smelled fresh and green in the early mornings, before the sun had dried the dew from its blades. She'd liked the stillness and the silence. Mostly, she'd liked the compliment of alone time with her favorite brother.

At fourteen, she'd tried out the CC75B, the compact Lincoln said she "couldn't shoot for shit." She'd shot marginally better with the Beretta 92 7-round. But Lincoln's .22? Celeste and that .22 had become fast friends. She hadn't even cared that Lincoln had told her a .22 was a girl gun.

Lincoln would shake his long hair from his eyes, give her the signal, and she'd line up her sights. She'd make the hay bale–backed bull's-eye sit like a red ball on top of the middle sight, take a breath, and fire halfway through the exhalation. She'd hit the mark, every single time.

Lincoln's number one rule? Never point a gun at a person you didn't want to kill.

At Matt's door, Celeste paused to catch her breath and weigh her decision. She held her hand to her pocket and thought of going back to Old Yeller and that glove box. She thought of the decision she'd made and un-made as she'd traveled the highways. No matter what roads she'd traveled, the asphalt glowed black before her headlights, and the memory of what Matt had done played on repeat.

Celeste apologized to Lincoln for using one of his lessons to commit a crime. She flexed her hands to release the tremors. She slipped her Visa card from her back pocket and into the doorjamb behind the bolt. She pulled the card toward her and turned the handle. The door opened. She stepped into Matt's dorm room, shut the door, and turned the doorknob so it wouldn't click.

In the shade-darkened room, Matt slept in the bed, curled on his side and innocent looking. The covers pulled beneath his neck, one foot poking from the end of his comforter.

Stale laundry piled on his desk chair—jeans, socks, the jacket of his chef whites. For a second, she thought she might throw up. Nausea clogged her throat, and she swallowed, too loudly for the close space. For a second she marveled that her heartbeat, loud and hard and—to her mind—filling the room, hadn't woken Matt. For a second she hesitated, hand on her pocket.

Then she stepped up to the end of Matt's bed, took a wide, even stance, slid her weapon of choice from her pocket, and hit the light.

Temporarily blinded, Matt gave a growl of surprise and scrambled to sitting. She lowered her arm slightly, letting him blink. He stared straight at her, suddenly awake and understanding the situation.

How the hell do you like it?

For the first time since last night, Celeste grinned. "Start talking, douche bag."

CHAPTER 19

Her hands jerked to the right. The impact didn't sound like a gunshot, like most people would think, but a puncture. The slow, clattering release of air reminded her of needles tumbling inside a rain stick.

"Blowout!" Zach yelled, as if Katherine hadn't known. "Don't hit the brakes!"

"I've got this." Katherine pressed down on the accelerator to compensate for the loss of momentum. The SUV that had been pacing her had fallen behind, so she veered in the direction of the skid and into the right-hand lane. Katherine straightened the steering wheel, careful not to *over*compensate, and then tapped the hazard lights. She reminded herself to breathe and eased her foot off the gas. "We're okay," Katherine told Zach, although he hadn't made a sound. "I need to wait for the car to slow down before I can pull over."

"You're doing great," Zach said.

No vehicles were behind her, the other drivers giving her a wide berth. She flicked on the directional, tightened her grip on the steering wheel, and tapped the brake. When the vehicle jerked beneath her, she let out a whimper.

"You can do it," Zach said. "Keep going."

Katherine repeated the process three more times. Each attempt yielded a little less of a jerk and a softer whimper. Then she glided into the breakdown lane, put the car in park, and cut the engine. Her skin hummed. When she unclamped her hands from the steering wheel, her fingers did a roadside jitter. She stared in stunned silence at the traffic whooshing by, the wind from the passing motorists buffeting the Outback.

Zach let out a whoop. "You kicked ass!"

Katherine gave her head a shake and laughed. They could talk about her kick-ass ways later, after they'd caught up with Celeste and brought her back home, safe and sound. "Let's change that tire."

"Uh, no. *I've* got this," Zach said, and he dashed from the car, sling and all. He opened her hatchback and pulled out the rubber trunk liner. *Hmm, hmm, hmm* pulsed through the air.

Katherine had no clue what song he was humming, but she smiled anyway.

One-handed, Zach raised the floor to get to the spare tire.

Katherine turned back around, allowed herself a deep breath, and sank into the seat.

Zach opened the passenger door, crouched, and peered into the car. He cocked his head. His brows rose, and his forehead furrowed. "Is there something you neglected to tell me? Something you might've forgotten?"

"I've told you everything—" Katherine stared at Zach, a memory hovering at the corners. They'd discussed Zach's biological father and the way her parents had left her. Then the tire had blown out, testing her skills a second—"The spare tire," Katherine said, her voice hushed with realization. "I never replaced it after the first time I had a blowout."

By mutual consent, Katherine and Zach agreed to freak out about Celeste.

Celeste refused to freak out.

When Matt's hand shot in the air and he flicked on the

overhead light, she shut off her flashlight, but she kept it pointed at Matt. If need be, she could use the heavy metal flashlight as a weapon. She'd seen the damage she could accidentally do to a guy with her fist alone, when amply motivated. She'd never had more motivation in her life.

Not that she intended to let Matt close enough to test her theory.

"How the hell did you get in here?" Matt asked.

"I ask the questions, you answer them. Got it, douche bag?"

Matt chuckled, not all haughty and derisive, as she'd expected, but normal. More like the old Matt. "I really miss that about you."

"What?"

"Your cockiness." Matt stared her down, as though daring her to flinch.

Celeste forced herself to think of a rooster, strutting around a barnyard. She knew that wasn't the image Matt had in mind.

Matt stood up—bigger and stronger than her and wearing nothing but tightie-whities. His weapon of choice was bunched beneath the cotton.

"Stay there!"

He held up his hands. This time, his laugh was derisive. "I was gonna get my pants. But, hey, if that's not what you want . . ."

Celeste grabbed Matt's jeans from the desk chair and tossed them at him.

Matt caught the jeans in one hand. "Thank you," he said, using his deeper, defensive voice. The voice he slipped from his back pocket and tried on whenever an instructor grilled him on his latest and greatest baking flub-up. Or, as Celeste liked to think of them, the 101 ways slacker Matt attempted to fake his way through culinary school. You could take the guy out of his job as a food stylist, but you couldn't take the food stylist out of a cheater.

The rasp of his zipper sent an ache down her arms. Another buried memory? Another detail of a horror story she'd yet to uncover?

Matt took a step toward her, but his hands dangled by his sides. "Ask me anything you want, baby. I've got nothing to hide."

Baby?

Matt didn't sound like Matt being an asshole, he sounded like Drake. Drake, who'd asked her out at the beginning of school and then dealt with her rejection by spending the better part of a week acting as though she were a lover he'd jilted.

Matt wasn't just a stylist and a cheater, he was a chameleon, willing to lower himself to fit in.

That explained why he'd bragged about having sex with her. That didn't explain the photos. And the thing he did to her in this room—

The floor tilted. Celeste's hands trembled, and she tightened her grip on the flashlight. She thought of Zach's breathing lesson. She thought of Zach, holding her through the night. She thought of Zach and the way he'd sounded as though he'd forgotten how to breathe.

If Matt wanted to prove he had nothing to hide, he needed to get real.

"What did you put in my drinks?" Celeste asked. "What crap did you drug me with?"

"Ah, honey, I didn't drug you."

"Stop it! Stop talking like that. I don't know who you are. I want to talk to the Matt who used to be my friend." Her voice echoed back to her, sounding shrill and panicked. She couldn't let Matt hear that. She couldn't let him get to her. She couldn't let him know she'd once believed he was a decent person.

With his longish hair and the way they'd joked around and spent time together, Matt had reminded Celeste of her brother

Lincoln. She'd taken a few sketchy details, and then her brain had filled in the rest.

Matt was nothing like her brother. Matt wasn't even a good imposter.

"Whatever." Defiance laced Matt's voice, but his expression softened. She'd taken the wind out of his bullshit sail.

"What did you do to my drinks?" Celeste asked. "I shouldn't have gotten plastered on two screwdrivers."

Matt turned his head, a slight movement, an opening.

"Come on! I know you put something in my drinks." The question had pestered her from Maine to New York. If Matt had slipped her one of those pills she'd read about in the newspapers, she might've never remembered the rape. Instead, the memory would've stayed trapped in her mind and body, along with all the other Celeste-is-crap lies she told herself.

"Did you slip me a roofie?"

"No," Matt said.

"G?"

"Don't be ridiculous."

"Special K?"

"I didn't slip pills into your screwdrivers, okay? I'd never do *that,*" he said.

Spoken like a criminal. A criminal who set his own moral code and then violated everyone else's.

"What *would* you do?" Celeste asked. "What would you put in my screwdrivers that I didn't know about?"

Matt swung his hair from his eyes, his gaze a cross between wary and angry, like a boy caught shoplifting bubble gum or a pen or some other worthless trinket. He crossed his arms. "Switched out your vodka for grain alcohol."

The obvious thing she'd missed.

No wonder she hadn't tasted the vodka. No wonder she'd gotten plastered. No wonder she'd gotten raped.

Alcohol was a date rape drug, too.

Celeste brought the flashlight up against her chest. "Why would you do that? Why would you drug me?" she asked.

"Get a grip. I didn't drug you. You were already drinking. I just switched your drinks. Big deal!"

More lies he told himself.

Celeste wanted to calmly walk up to Matt, smash him over the head with the flashlight, and watch him bleed out. *Get a grip, Matt. It's not like I* shot *you in the head!*

If she got into a shouting match with Matt, she'd never find out what really happened. On *Cops,* the officers always kept their calm. On *Cops,* they talked to the douche bags as if they were reasonable human beings. On *Cops,* the men in blue made friends with their not-friends. "Why did you bother switching my drinks?"

Matt shrugged one shoulder. His gaze went to a spot on the floor between them, and Celeste thought of their instructor, Chef Jones, reprimanding Matt in front of the entire class.

The answer's not on the floor, Matthew. It's in your head. Find it.

Celeste thought of Natalie, her not-friend Natalie, pacing her every move at Drake's party while Matt went to get her a second drink.

"Why was Natalie in on it?" Celeste asked.

"Why-why would you . . . ?" Matt asked, a lame attempt at denial. Even though his stammer betrayed him first, his flushed cheeks came in as a close second. More embarrassed about Natalie's involvement than having drugged and raped Celeste?

Celeste made herself chuckle. "It's not like I can do anything about it, right? I just want to know. What's the big deal?" she said, throwing his words back at him.

"Yeah, sure." Matt sat down on the edge of his bed and then glanced at the spot beside him, as if he thought she might join him. "You know Drake is a total dick, right?" Matt asked.

"Okay." Yet Drake hadn't been the monster who'd attacked her. Funny—as in not at all—how these things turned out.

"You know how he's always baiting us," Matt said. "You know, really looking for a place to stick in the knife." Matt gritted his teeth and made a twisting motion with his fist.

Celeste's breath stuck in her lungs, trapped, as though Matt were still pressing his mouth against hers. She flicked her gaze to the door, but Matt remained seated.

"So one day after class," Matt continued, "Drake noticed me looking at your ass, and he goes, 'I bet you can't hit that.' "

Celeste imagined Matt running after her and smacking her butt. She knew that wasn't what Drake had meant. Funny—as in not at all—how Matt had used the term *baiting*. Because he'd totally taken Drake's.

Drake had used Matt to get back at her.

"You made a bet that you could get me." Celeste thought of a faceless figure jumping out from an alleyway at night. She thought of the way something deep and dark in someone's mind could take him over, like an illness, until the friend you knew, the friend you thought you knew, ceased to exist.

Matt's smile made her take a step back. "That's right, kiddo."

Celeste made a rolling motion with the flashlight. "So, Natalie . . ."

"Was the only other person who bet against Drake," Matt said.

Other person?

"No wonder Natalie was shadowing me. She wanted to make sure your plan panned out. She wanted in on her payday." How could Natalie do this to another woman?

How could Natalie have done this to another human?

"So this was about money?" Celeste asked.

"Don't be ridiculous. This was about me sticking it to Drake."

By sticking it to her.

"Why did you take the nude photos of me?"

Matt slid his hands from his thighs to his knees and shook his head. "I had to do it," he said, and Celeste thought of the words he'd spoken when she'd blinked awake from her drugged stupor: *Go back to sleep. I have to do this.*

"But why?" she asked.

"To prove it," Matt said.

Matt had tried to prove himself real by drugging and raping her and taking posed photos after she'd passed out.

"You cheated," she said.

"So what? I still won."

No, you didn't.

The day she'd overheard Matt bragging in class, she'd thought herself a slut and a fool for letting him betray her. When she'd learned about the photos, she'd understood he'd violated her, but she'd still deep down felt like it had been her fault. But when she'd remembered that he'd raped her? Then, finally, *she'd* gotten real.

"Okay, douche bag. Now you're going to listen to me. You're going to listen to the truth."

A smile tweaked the corners of Matt's mouth. Amused? Nervous? She hoped he was scared to death.

Celeste pointed the flashlight at Matt. "First, you drugged me."

"Grain alcohol!" Matt said, as if he was frustrated with her inability to believe the bullshit lies he told himself.

"Alcohol's a drug," Celeste said.

"Jesus! You were already drinking." Matt used his deep, angry voice, like an animal blowing itself up to scare away a larger prey.

Defensive much?

Celeste took a deep breath into her belly, the way Zach had taught her. If Zach knew she were here in this room, he'd jump into Matilda and come to her rescue, no red cape required. She was glad Zach didn't know where she was.

She made sure to look Matt in the eye. "When I woke up, you raped me."

Her pulse battered between her ribs. Her skin fired with the need to run. Her eyes refused to blink.

Matt's gaze skittered to the side. When he looked back in her direction, his leg was bouncing, same as the morning she'd awoken to confusion, sunlight seeping around the blinds, and Matt sitting in the desk chair. He'd been waiting for her to wake up. Had he been worried that she wouldn't?

She needed to stop trying to figure out what douche bags were thinking.

"We were practically doing it," Matt said.

She wanted Matt to see what she saw. She wanted him to see his real self.

"I said no. I told you to stop. But you wouldn't. You shoved your disgusting—" Her breath clattered through her teeth. "No matter what you tell yourself, that's the definition of rape. I could barely breathe, and you were crushing me. You were hurting me. And all the while you were having your great, good time, like I was some piece of shit. Like I wasn't even there. Like I didn't even exist." What he did to her affected not just her body but also her soul. "You almost killed me."

Matt blinked at her. "I was just messing around, buddy."

"Exactly what a rapist would say."

Matt made a sound, a cross between an exhalation and an annoyed chuckle. He squeezed his lips together and shook his head. "I feel sorry for you, Celeste." He pointed to his ear and made the universal sign of a crazy person.

"I hope you never hurt another girl. I pray to God you never get the chance. You're a lousy baker, a terrible friend, and a rapist. *I* feel sorry for *you*." Celeste turned and took hold of the doorknob.

Matt stood up. "Celeste, wait."

For the first time this morning, his eyes looked different. Turned down with sadness rather than widened in fear. For the first time this morning, his stance looked more aw-shucks embarrassed than what-the-fuck angry. For the first time, he looked as though he might turn into the old Matt and try to apologize.

Celeste kept her hand on the doorknob. "What is it?"

"You, um. You're not going to the police, are you?"

Are you kidding me?

Was a lie still wrong if you lied for all the right reasons, even if one of those reasons was revenge?

She was a good girl, but she wasn't that good. "I'm not going to the police," she said. "I already went."

Matt's body went rigid, his expression tight and pained. For a second, she was back in that bed with Matt above her, having his great, good time. For a second, her vision clouded. For a second, she was everywhere and nowhere. Then she pulled herself together. "In fact," Celeste said, "they're on their way to arrest you right now. If I were you, I'd grab a few things and take off. If I were you, I'd run."

"Thank you for warning me."

For the first time this morning, Matt sounded sincere.

That, she figured, was as close as she'd ever get to an apology.

Celeste slipped out of Matt's room and closed the door behind her. The rush of a flushing toilet echoed from the bathroom at the end of the hall. Somewhere nearby, music filtered through a student's closed door. She race-walked down the center of the hallway. Then she yanked open the door to the stairway, pounded down the stairs, flew out the wedged-open doorway and into the freedom of the new day. Beneath achingly blue skies, old faithful Old Yeller sat steady and true.

She'd let every Celeste-is-crap lie in her head seep into

what she'd thought had happened with Matt, and then she'd let that infested mixture grow into its own big, fat lie.

She needed to stop spreading lies about herself.

Hidden inside Old Yeller's glove box, behind the folder with her insurance, registration, and service records, was Katherine's .22, the gun she could've used to blow Matt's brains out. Lincoln would've been proud she hadn't lowered herself to Matt's level. She was proud she hadn't lowered herself to Matt's level.

Instead of shooting first and asking questions later, she'd taken Zach's advice, kicked ass, and gotten answers.

Celeste held her hands up to her mouth like a megaphone and let out a whoop. The echo bounced off the redbrick buildings and roared back to her, the sound of her own strong voice. She stomped her feet and raised her arms up in triumph.

Just because she had the power didn't mean she needed, or wanted, to use it.

She felt more than a little smug about her ability to resist temptation. She felt freaking superior.

She felt like a freaking superhero.

Katherine wasn't certain how this was going to end, only that it would.

Outside of her apartment, the sun was setting, the sky pulling down the shades on another Wednesday. Any minute now, Barry would arrive at her door. Once again, she sat waiting on the sofa, the support solid beneath her legs, the velvet soft beneath her hand. Yet half of her mind was stuck on yesterday's events.

A mere thirty-five hours ago, she stood on the westbound side of the Mass Pike, with her hip thrust toward oncoming traffic and her thumb protruding, and rediscovered her decades-ago affinity for hitchhiking. Only this time, instead of twentysomething guys with long hair and oily voices pulling over to give her a lift, a forty-something woman in a silver Corolla had pulled into the breakdown lane and donated a tire. The woman—who could've been Katherine's sister, Lexi, if Lexi had also been African American—had purchased the tire the previous week, after having dreamed she'd blown out a tire on the Mass Pike. The dream, she'd told Katherine and Zach, must've been about Katherine.

Synergy? Flow? The universe paying Katherine back for years of events not lining up in her favor? At that point, Katherine would've agreed to plain old dumb luck.

Thirty-two hours ago, Katherine and Zach had arrived on the campus of Culinary America and gone straight to the dean of students to find their friend Celeste Barnes's dorm room. The dean told them Celeste had left school unexpectedly weeks ago and that they should alert him if they found her. Then, in a move that solidified Katherine's impression of Zach as a terrific detective, he admitted Celeste was his girlfriend and claimed he was afraid she'd come back to rekindle a romance with another student, a certain Matt Something. The dean, clearly flustered, admitted that a certain Matt Something had stopped by his office earlier that morning to withdraw from school.

Something had happened between Celeste and Matt. But no guns blazed. Neither a SWAT team nor the local police careened onto the campus with their sirens blaring to apprehend a woman hell-bent on revenge. After twenty minutes of debate, Zach and Katherine had decided to trust Celeste's note, promising her return, and they headed back to Maine. At three o'clock this morning, they found Celeste back at her apartment, safe and sound and munching out on a plate of toast and eggs big enough to satisfy Zach's bottomless pit. Celeste had quite a tale to tell herself.

Katherine was about to add another tale to her cache of life stories.

The overhead and table lights blazed. No candles sat on her

mantel to set or accent a mood. Neither appetizers nor dinner covered the tables to distract from the necessary conversation.

She'd secured the tarot decks in their drawers.

She wore jeans and a plain white T-shirt, and she'd pulled her hair from her face with a ponytail holder found rattling around in the bottom of her purse. Her feet were bare. She'd left the black boots in the closet.

Barry would appreciate the absence of filters.

Even sex was a distraction, a pleasant way to avoid challenging emotions. She and Barry had made love on Sunday, breaking down a physical barrier and giving them the semblance of progress but changing little.

Barry still hated secrets. She hated keeping secrets. But letting go? Who knew what the truth would ultimately unleash?

She was about to find out.

When Katherine stood to get the door, her sight grayed, like pixels of a photograph, and she remembered that she'd forgotten about lunch. For the first time in her life, she'd been too anxious to eat. She held on to the door for balance.

"What's wrong?" Barry asked.

When he'd come into the bakery this morning, she'd shared an abbreviated version of the road trip—why she and Zach had gone and how they'd eventually returned and found Celeste. Katherine had promised to tell Barry a longer version of the story tonight. She'd promised to tell him all he deserved to know. She owed him . . . so much love.

"What if nothing at all is wrong?" Katherine asked. "What if everything is finally right?"

Barry placed a hand at the small of her back. The other hand took hold of her upper arm. "Sweetheart, sit down."

Katherine's legs wavered beneath her, like timeworn, sea-weakened dock stanchions, but she refused to sit. If she sat down, she'd collapse. If she sat, she'd lose her nerve. Barry's gaze held so much love for her. If she sat, she'd never know whether his love depended on a false image of her he'd created from her lies.

Would her admission convince him he'd never really known her at all? That the woman he'd loved was nothing more than a figment of his imagination?

She'd never know unless she risked another loss.

"What if, nearly twenty-four years ago, I gave birth to a son, and gave him away for adoption?" Katherine asked.

Barry's expression flicked from concern to confusion. His hand fell away from her back. "What are you saying?" he asked. And his eyes, those loving eyes, blinked at her, as though breaking up her image might bring the meaning of her words into sharper focus.

What had she done?

She felt light, as if she were somehow floating above herself. She forced herself to stay in her body, where the fibers of the Oriental rug pricked the soles of her feet, Barry's hand squeezed her arm, and his gaze tumbled her heart. She forced herself to just say it. "Zach is my son."

Barry's jaw slackened, and his expression went blank. A professional side effect, no doubt, from years of listening to horrors and revelations while remaining sympathetic yet objective.

He released her arm and, days after Halloween, seemed to summon the energy of a low-level spirit. For the first time, Barry reminded Katherine of her father, his eyes dark with disappointment, his face contorted with anger. "How could you have kept this from me? A—a son? How could you have lied to me?"

Katherine's pulse pounded in her belly, hollow sounding as a spoon against a stainless steel mixing bowl. But even though she'd wronged Barry, even though every bit of his anger was justified, she refused to absorb it. She took a deep breath and, in return, offered him love. "I'm so sorry. I was afraid if I told you I'd given away a child, you'd question whether I deserved to be a mother."

"Uh-uh," Barry said. "Don't you dare put this on me. You're the one who thought you didn't deserve to be a mother. I never would've entertained such a thought. You're one of the most nurturing women I've ever known," he said, and her eyes watered. Barry shook his head, sighed. "Zach's father?" The tightness in Barry's jaw and the slight widening of his eyes betrayed a hint of jealousy.

Katherine forced herself to hold Barry's gaze. "No one I knew especially well," she said. When Barry didn't blink, she answered his next logical question. Barry she did know especially well. "No one I knew how to contact."

Barry nodded. "This explains so much." He sat down on the sofa, hung his head, and pinched the bridge of his nose.

Katherine sat far enough away to give him space but near enough that he could choose to reach for her. She folded her hands in her lap.

When Barry looked up, his eyes were wet. "I'm so angry at you."

"I know," she said, and a tear slid down her cheek.

"I don't think you do. In fact, I don't think you have a clue why I'm angry."

Katherine squeezed her hands together and rattled off her long list of faults. "I lied about never having a child. After years of suffering the stress and disappointment of IVF and driving each other up the wall, I insisted upon a divorce because even though I didn't have the guts to tell you about the son I'd given up for adoption, I wanted to give you a chance for a family."

Barry's chin dimpled, as though he might sob. "That's not the worst part."

"You're kidding. I missed something?"

"I know you're not as tough as you seem. I know how

much keeping that secret must've cost you. I know how much you've suffered. *I know you.*" Barry took her hand, and her hand trembled in his warmth. "The worst part," he said, "is that you didn't trust I'd love you no matter what. That's what hurts the most."

"Do you still love me?"

"I never stopped loving you." Barry gave her a tight smile and squeezed her hand. "But I'm still angry at you."

Katherine issued a laugh-cry and covered her mouth. She ran a shaky hand over his curly hair. As if forgetting their conversation, Barry held her hand to his lips. They made quite a pair. "Do you remember the question you asked me Sunday night?" she asked.

"Whether you still served coffee in bed?"

"Earlier Sunday night. The question I didn't answer."

Barry grinned, like a boy about to get everything he'd ever wanted. Like a man who deserved everything she owed him. Like a man capable of forgiveness.

"Yes," she told him. "I'm ready to come home."

Chapter 20

The end of the world came with a sound track.

Katherine spent New Year's Eve at home with her family: her ex-husband she'd remarried, Barry; her biological son, Zach; and his live-in girlfriend, Katherine's sort of daughter, Celeste. Katherine and Barry cuddled on the grayish-blue velvet sofa she'd brought home from her apartment. Celeste and Zach took the French-blue wing chair, Celeste slung across Zach's lap. Zach ran his right hand up Celeste's tights, from her ankle to the hem of her miniskirt. The fingers of Zach's left hand sneaked beneath the bottom of a sweater Katherine saw as olive colored, even though Celeste insisted it was emerald green.

Katherine grinned and shook her head. Ever since Zach had gotten his cast off three weeks ago, he seemed determined to make up for lost time by not being able to keep *both* of his hands off Celeste. Yesterday at Lamontagne's, Katherine had threatened to spray Celeste and Zach with water, as if they were cats in heat. That had only encouraged them to slip into the stockroom and shut the door behind them.

Minutes before midnight, a bottle of Freixenet sparkling wine chilled in a silver ice bucket alongside the coffee table, four crystal flutes sat at the ready, and the warm fireplace air held the aromas from their lucky New Year's Eve dinner. Black-eyed peas for humility and good fortune. Collard greens, because who doesn't need a few more greenbacks? Long noodles to encourage longevity. And a pork roast to represent the richness of happiness.

Inside the refrigerator, a ring-shaped Dutch chocolate cake awaited Zach's birthday and symbolized coming full circle.

Across the living room, ABC and the perennially young Dick Clark broadcasted from Times Square. Crowds of revelers wore winter jackets and multi-colored hats and waved twisted balloons beneath electronic news tickers and Jumbotrons. Above the throng, the glittery white New Year's ball readied for its plunge into the new millennium.

In Hidden Harbor, the weather was clear and cold, the thermometer on the porch hovering below twenty degrees, but Zach insisted they leave the farmhouse's fireside warmth and venture outside to take in the last view of 1999.

The tidal river glowed faintly beneath the waning crescent moon. Barry snuggled up behind Katherine and wrapped his arms around her. She held on to Barry's hands and hugged the moment. Zach positioned himself behind Celeste and asked that they tilt their heads to the night sky.

Zach pointed to the Big Dipper, standing erect as a shepherd's hook, and the outer stars in the celestial bowl pointing a straight line to the North Star. "My dad taught me about the constellations when I was a kid," Zach said. "And on Christmas Eve, we all went out to the yard to show Celeste how to stargaze like a Fitzgerald."

By *all,* Zach meant his adoptive parents, Everett and Carol Fitzgerald, Zach's brothers, Donovan and Ryan, and Zach himself. Last week, Zach had brought Celeste to the Arlington home where he'd grown up to meet his family, but not before he'd let Celeste and Katherine know he considered Hidden Harbor his permanent home. He wasn't going anywhere.

Katherine and Barry's calendar was open to possible travel. Then, after exploring the world beyond Hidden Harbor, Katherine wanted to explore a job in social services, starting as a volunteer for CASA, Court Appointed Special Advocates. Blake had inspired her. The simple act of giving him a job and becoming his friend had improved his behavior, his grades, and his self-confidence. She wanted to help as many at-risk kids as possible.

Katherine and Celeste had drafted a plan. Next month Katherine would sell Lamontagne's to Celeste, but Katherine would stay on till the spring to help Celeste with the transition. Celeste had already selected a new name for her bakery: Sugarcoated, a fitting nod to Celeste's snarky and newly recovered voice. Thanks to weekly visits with a shrink Barry recommended, Celeste was making amazing progress dealing with her eating disorder and coming to terms with the assault.

Katherine and Celeste had both discovered the benefits of speaking out versus holding on to secrets and sugarcoating the truth.

"If you've got something to say, speak now," Katherine said, "before we all freeze to death."

"Actually, I've got a couple of somethings to say," Zach said. "When I was little, my dad taught me, if I was away from home, I could always look up to the night sky to find the North Star and my way home." Zach sighed, a heavy sound that came out as a great white cloud. "So . . . yeah . . . after I pass next week's physical fitness and mental fitness exams, and after I get into the academy . . ."

Katherine's teeth chattered, and Barry rubbed her shoulders. "For the sake of our dwindling circulation, while we're still middle-aged," Barry said. This from the man who'd ridden his bike to work up until a week ago.

"My dad and I hashed it out," Zach said, "and Katherine was right. He's cool with me not going to law school and applying to the Maine Criminal Justice Academy instead."

"But how?" Katherine asked. "Your color blindness . . ." After she'd learned she'd passed her deficiency to Zach, she'd looked further into the ramifications. Certain careers were off-limits to those with color confusion. Law enforcement topped the list.

"Dad found out about a doc in Maryland who invented color-correcting contact lenses, and got me an appointment," Zach said. "Yes, Katherine, Celeste's sweater really is emerald green."

"I'm so proud of you!" Celeste turned in Zach's arms, and he lifted her off the ground to kiss her on the mouth.

Extrasensory perception, clairvoyance, or similarly minded women thinking the same good thought? Celeste said exactly what Katherine was thinking.

Katherine gave Zach a kiss on the cheek. Barry offered Zach his hand for a shake, but when Zach took it, Barry laughed and pulled him into a bear hug instead.

"Wait, what does this have to do with your Big Dipper speech?" Celeste asked.

"Oh, that." Zach's hand went up to where his hair usually flopped over his brow. Last week, in the middle of Maine's deep freeze, he'd inexplicably decided upon a shorter than usual haircut. Now Katherine knew why. He was trying on the outer trappings of his future role as a police officer.

Zach chuckled. "The Criminal Justice Academy is an eighteen-week residential program."

"Zach!" Celeste said.

"I get to come home on weekends. And during the week, if you miss me, all you have to do is look up to the night sky and know I'll be looking at the same bright stars." Zach's voice went from sure to shy. "You know, so we're never, like, too far apart."

"Beautifully said," Katherine said.

Celeste held Zach's face between her hands. "That's the most romantic thing I've ever heard."

Zach peeled Celeste's hands from his cheeks. "Give me a minute and you might change your mind," he said. Then he got down on one knee.

Katherine held her hand to her chest, her heartbeat accelerating through the orange yarns of her sweater. Barry wrapped himself back around her, and she squeezed his hand.

Dear God, thank you for sustaining me to this day.

"Celeste," Zach began. "My density has brought me to you."

Celeste giggled. "What in the world are you talking about?"

"That's not the right line," Zach said. "Haven't you seen *Back to the Future*?"

"No."

"Ah, heck. In that case." Zach reached into his back pocket and produced a velvet box. He flipped open the lid to reveal a ring. Under the starlight Katherine couldn't make out the jewelry's details, but there was no mistaking where this was headed.

"I'm crazy in love with you," Zach told Celeste. "Will you marry me and make me crazy for the rest of my life?"

So much for Zach winning any romance awards.

Celeste didn't seem to mind. She covered her face with her hands. Zach stood up, and Celeste peeked through her fingers.

"Is that a yes?" Zach asked.

"Yes!" Celeste yelled, her voice choked with happiness. "Yes, yes, yes!"

Zach slid the ring onto Celeste's finger, and she jumped into his arms for a kiss, hooking her legs around his waist.

"Oh, good, we can go inside now," Barry said.

"Barry!" Katherine popped him on the shoulder.

"Kidding! Congratulations, kids. And let's go inside." Barry took Katherine by the hand. "Like we didn't see that one coming," Barry said.

"One can't assume," Katherine said, even though Celeste and Zach had recently moved to an unfurnished apartment in Ledgewood and they'd spoken of saving money for a Cape with a white picket fence, a shingle roof, and a blacktop driveway.

"Why not?" Barry asked. "I always assumed you'd come back to me."

"Until you gave up," she said.

"For all of five minutes."

Zach carried Celeste up the steps to the porch and then set her down so they could fit through the kitchen door. Celeste held on to Zach with her right hand. She extended her left hand beneath the stove's hood light, revealing a square gem that looked goldish to Katherine.

"What kind of stone is that?" Katherine asked.

"It's a peridot," Zach said. "Celeste's birthstone, plus it matches her beautiful green eyes."

Now *that* was romantic.

"It's the most beautiful thing I've ever seen in my life," Celeste told Zach. Then, to Katherine, "You know what I want to do right now?"

"Call Abby?" Katherine asked.

Celeste nodded, her smile tight. "Do you think she'll be okay with this? I mean, because of her and Charlie?"

After Celeste had returned from New York a second time, she'd spent a few days with Abby, and their friendship had been going strong ever since. Abby and Charlie's on-again, off-again romance had recently experienced a downturn, and they were taking a break.

"I think Abby would be upset if you didn't call her. I know she'll be over the moon for you, because that's how I feel." Her biological son and her sort of daughter would marry, making Celeste her sort of daughter-in-law. Katherine might *plotz* from joy. She looked away before Celeste could see tears pricking the corners of her eyes.

Barry was right. Katherine was Jewish by inoculation. She was a Jewish mother.

Celeste kissed Katherine on the cheek, letting her know she'd gotten away with exactly nothing.

"Your parents?" Katherine asked Zach.

"I'll call them tomorrow," Zach said. "They already know I was planning on proposing."

Katherine nodded. Of course. As an adult, Zach didn't require his parents' approval, but he still wanted it, still craved their acceptance.

Some things never changed.

Celeste dragged Zach to the phone. Katherine took Barry by the hand and they went through the dining room to the living room's fireside warmth and the TV's New Year's Eve broadcast.

Katherine started to sit down on the sofa, and Barry lifted her onto his lap. "Too far away," he said, and Katherine nestled into his neck.

"Perfect timing," Barry said, and for a second Katherine thought he was referring to the two of them getting back together and remarried, and Celeste and Zach's engagement. Then she turned her attention to the TV and the ball lowering over Times Square toward the glittering, numerical year 2000.

Barry slid a hand beneath her sweater and rubbed her back. Of course, he'd also meant *their* perfect timing.

The broadcast zoomed in on a young man in the crowd, waving madly at the camera. From the studio above the fray,

Dick Clark told him to say hi to his mom, because she was watching him on TV.

True enough. The whole country was watching Dick Clark.

When Dick Clark told the viewers to get close to somebody they loved, Katherine held on to Barry a little tighter. She thought of Celeste and Zach in the kitchen. She couldn't hear them through the blare of the TV, but their love was as palpable as the sofa beneath her.

Were her mother and her sister, Lexi, sitting on sofas somewhere, chilling champagne and watching the ball drop into the new millennium?

Zach had decided he wasn't interested in finding his biological father, Adam Bell. But Katherine had yet to commit one way or the other to Zach's offer to search for her mother and Lexi. Did she really want to know what had become of them?

Celeste skipped into the room, pulling Zach behind her, proof that sometimes what you found was even better than what you could imagine. Zach sat down at the other end of the sofa and gathered Celeste into his lap.

Dick Clark told them to get ready, and they counted down the last seconds of the twentieth century. ". . . Five! Four! Three! Two! One! Happy New Year!"

"Wahoo!" Celeste yelled. "Best freaking New Year's Eve ever!"

Zach dug some kind of token from his pocket, kissed it, and slipped it back into his jeans. "Best birthday ever!"

The second time Katherine had spent Zach's birthday with her son.

"Happy birthday, sweet boy," Katherine said, the same thing she'd told Zach on the day he was born. Katherine hugged Zach and then covered her eyes and burst into tears. Barry gathered her in his arms and she sobbed into his shirt.

Over her head, Barry told Zach and Celeste she was *verklempt,* the Jewish word for "filled with emotion." Katherine raised her head and wiped her eyes. "I'm fine," she said, and then turned her face to the ongoing broadcast so she could catch her breath.

Barely audible behind the roar of Times Square revelers, "Auld Lang Syne" played, the sound track of New Year's Eve.

Contrary to all the Y2K doomsayers, the world did not end. And if every single computer in the country crashed, Katherine would still be overflowing with happiness.

On a decades-ago New Year's Eve, when Katherine was still young enough to think staying up late was a treat, she and Lexi had been allowed to watch the ball drop. "Auld Lang Syne" played, and Katherine's father had been the parent who'd known the song's meaning. For once, his words had been a gift, instead of a curse, that remained with Katherine to this day.

Zach slipped the champagne from the ice bucket, wiped the wet bottle with his shirt, and popped the cork. Sweet, white grape effervescence scented the air. Zach filled their champagne flutes and passed them around.

Barry raised a glass and took up the toast. "To family," Barry said, and they tapped glasses. Katherine's bottom lip trembled. She was dangerously close to losing it again. Dangerously, wonderfully *verklempt*.

Katherine thought of the way Zach and Celeste planned on staying connected when apart by gazing into the night sky's constellation of stars. She wondered whether her mother and Lexi were both watching the New Year's Eve broadcast and thinking of her.

Katherine hoped her mother and Lexi were with people they loved, safe and sound.

Right beside Katherine, Zach and Celeste snuggled, crazy in love and safe and sound. Katherine gave Barry's hand a squeeze.

Everything she'd loved and lost she'd now recovered.

Katherine raised her glass of champagne to the TV screen. "To auld lang syne," she said. And then she thanked her father for giving her one true thing and spoke the translation out loud. "To times gone by."

Acknowledgments

For my niece Rebecca Thomson. You are beautiful, inside and out. Thank you for providing the research piece for Celeste's eating disorder and helping us all come closer to understanding anorexia. Your message to be happy and accepting of what you have shines through the story.

I'm eternally grateful to my family. My husband, Bill, continues to hike simply for the where's-Bill photo ops. (That's the only reason, right?) And that photo where you're reading and wearing the Lord of the Pies apron over your swim trunks? Genius. Thanks, honey! To my children: Ben, Josh, and Leah. I've only one bird left in the nest, but the three of you are always in my heart.

Thank you to my oldest friend, Ellen Kushner, for providing adoptee expertise and helping me slip beneath Zach's skin.

Thank you to Jimmy, Kevin, and Jody Nason at Nason's Stone House Farm in West Boxford, Massachusetts, for opening up your kitchen and sharing your considerable bakery expertise. (Especially Jimmy.) Research is delicious!

Thank you to sharpshooters Jim and Nancy DeMarco for taking me out to the shooting range at the Horse Pond Fish & Game Club of Nashua and keeping me safe. I fondly recall the CC75B compact that Jim said I couldn't "shoot for shit." Thanks for the great line! (In my defense, I did a lot better with the .22.) I'd also like to thank Mike Rhodes, a stranger who showed up and lent his guns and expertise. It's amazing what you can get away with when you say you're a writer.

Sylvie Kurtz provided the recipes for Celeste's Wild Blues and Katherine's Zesty Lemon Bars. Anything else you'd like me to taste test? I'm willing, able, and grateful.

As always, I depend upon feedback from my talented critique

partners, Sylvie Kurtz and Ellen Gullo. Every chapter feels like a victory. A billion hugs and tons of dark chocolate!

To my agent, Jessica Alvarez, and the team at BookEnds. Thank you for everything I know you do, and everything I'm probably not even aware of. I'm glad we're in this together.

To my editor at Kensington Books, Peter Senftleben. You are amazing! Thank you for believing in me and my stories and making us both look good. (He gets me, he really gets me!) I'm fortunate to have you in my corner.

I'd be remiss if I didn't mention Jessica and Peter's accidental collaboration. They're responsible for the wonderful title *A Measure of Happiness.*

To Kensington cover designer Kristine Noble. When I saw the cover for the first time, I laughed with delight. You did it again! The image expresses the story's essence, reaches out to grab you, and pulls you in. I love it.

To everyone at Kensington Books—Karen Auerbach, Vida Engstrand, and countless others—for spreading the word about my books and making sure they're available to readers.

Thank you to my readers. One of my greatest joys is connecting with you.

A READING GROUP GUIDE

A MEASURE OF HAPPINESS

Lorrie Thomson

ABOUT THIS GUIDE

The following discussion questions are included to enhance your group's reading of *A Measure of Happiness.*

DISCUSSION QUESTIONS

1. How does Katherine's childhood influence her self-image and impact the decisions she makes throughout her life?

2. After waiting nearly twenty-four years to reunite, Katherine and Zach are afraid to step up and claim their identities. Why?

3. Celeste tells Zach that she once went to a "stress management psychiatric type person" who told her to talk back to her eating disorder, aka Ed. What other naysayers are stuck in her head? How does the theme of negative voices thread throughout each character's journey?

4. Katherine is overly fond of using tarot readings to guide her decisions. Why do you suppose she relies on this crutch? What finally convinces her to trust herself?

5. Katherine worried that her childhood experiences would've kept her from being a good mother to her son. But Zach, having been raised by a loving family, still has identity issues. Why? Do you think nature or nurture plays a greater role in creating character?

6. A bad high school breakup sparked Celeste's first experience with anorexia. What other issues predisposed her to this mental illness?

7. The theme of shame threads throughout the story. Discuss each character's relationship with food. Discuss each character's relationship with sex.

8. Barry never gave up on Katherine, even after she divorced him. Do you think this makes him a weak or a strong character?

9. According to Katherine, the Wednesday morning mothers' group took her advice regarding lemon bars representing the sweet and sour experience of motherhood and then promptly got pregnant within weeks of one another. Katherine calls the lemon bars a placebo treatment. But nobody tells Mrs. Jenkins that Celeste's Wild Blues will make her more youthful and happy. How, then, do you explain Mrs. Jenkins's metamorphosis?

10. What event from Zach's past mirrors Celeste's anorexia and sparks his understanding of her disorder?

11. What do you think of Celeste's road trip after her memory returns? Is her behavior extreme? Dangerous? Exactly what she needs to heal?

12. What role does Blake serve for Katherine? Who or what does Blake represent at the beginning of the novel? The middle? The end? How is Katherine and Blake's relationship ultimately healing?

13. Discuss Zach's take-away insight from the show *Cops*. What does this say about his character and the way he views identity?

14. Celeste admits to Zach that even though she knows it's wrong, she thinks if she gets to such and such weight, she'll be happier. But when she gets to a certain weight, she changes the goal. Zach says, "Why not just decide to be happy now?" When have you followed Zach's life lesson? When have you relied

upon circumstances beyond your control to dictate your happiness?

15. When it comes to the theme of identity, Matt is the ultimate cautionary tale. Why?
16. Do you think Katherine will ever search for her mother and Lexi? Why or why not?

Celeste's Wild Blues

2 cups flour
⅔ cup sugar
1 teaspoon baking powder
1 teaspoon baking soda
½ teaspoon salt
1 cup plain yogurt (not Greek-style)
Juice of 1 lemon
¼ cup butter, melted and cooled
1 egg
2 teaspoons grated lemon peel
1 teaspoon vanilla
2 cups wild Maine blueberries

Glaze
½ cup sugar
Juice of 1 lemon
1 teaspoon grated lemon peel (optional)

Preheat oven to 400 degrees Fahrenheit. Grease 12 regular-sized muffin cups or 36 minis.

In a large bowl, whisk together flour, sugar, baking powder, baking soda, and salt until blended.

In another bowl, stir together yogurt, butter, egg, lemon juice, lemon peel, and vanilla until blended.

Make a well in the dry ingredients. Add yogurt mixture. Stir until just combined. Fold in blueberries. (If you must use frozen blueberries, thaw and drain before folding in.)

Spoon batter into prepared muffin cups. Bake regular-sized muffins 20 to 25 minutes and minis 12 to 17 minutes or until cake tester comes out clean.

Remove muffin tin(s) to a wire rack. Let cool for 5 minutes.

While muffins cool, stir sugar and lemon juice together for the glaze. If you want extra lemon flavor, grate a teaspoon of lemon peel into the mixture.

Remove muffins from cups. Spoon or brush glaze over hot muffins. Let cool before serving for a crunchy sugarcoated topping.

Katherine's Zesty Lemon Bars

For the Crust
1½ cups flour
½ cup powdered sugar
¾ cup (1½ sticks) butter, softened

For the Filling
4 large eggs
1½ cups granulated sugar
½ cup fresh-squeezed lemon juice
2 tablespoons flour
2 to 3 teaspoons lemon zest

For Sprinkling
Additional powdered sugar

Crust. Preheat oven to 350 degrees Fahrenheit. Line a 13x9x2-inch baking pan with parchment paper.

With an electric mixer, blend crust ingredients on low speed until crumbly. Press crust into pan. Bake 20 minutes or until light brown.

Filling. Beat ingredients till blended and pour over warm crust.

Bake lemon bars—crust and filling combo—15 to 20 minutes, till filling is set and bars are brown around the edges. Remove from oven and cool on a wire rack. Lift parchment, place bars on a cutting board, and sprinkle with powdered sugar. Cut into rectangles or squares.

36–40 servings